OXFORD WORLD'S CLASSICS

EDITH WHARTON

The Custom of the Country

Edited with an Introduction by
STEPHEN ORGEL

OXFORD
UNIVERSITY PRESS

OXFORD
UNIVERSITY PRESS

Great Clarendon Street, Oxford OX2 6DP

Oxford University Press is a department of the University of Oxford.
It furthers the University's objective of excellence in research, scholarship,
and education by publishing worldwide in

Oxford New York

Athens Auckland Bangkok Bogotá Buenos Aires Calcutta
Cape Town Chennai Dar es Salaam Delhi Florence Hong Kong Istanbul
Karachi Kuala Lumpur Madrid Melbourne Mexico City Mumbai
Nairobi Paris São Paulo Singapore Taipei Tokyo Toronto Warsaw

with associated companies in Berlin Ibadan

Oxford is a registered trade mark of Oxford University Press
in the UK and in certain other countries

Published in the United States
by Oxford University Press Inc., New York

Introduction, Note on the Text, Select Bibliography © Stephen Orgel 1995
Chronology © Martha Banta 1994

The moral rights of the author have been asserted
Database right Oxford University Press (maker)

First published as a World's Classics paperback 1995
Reissued as an Oxford World's Classics paperback 2000
Reissued 2008

British Library Cataloguing in Publication Data

Data available

Library of Congress Cataloging in Publication Data

Wharton, Edith, 1862–1937.
The custom of the country / Edith Wharton ; edited with an
introduction by Stephen Orgel.
(Oxford world's classics)
Includes bibliographical references.
1. City and town life—New York (N.Y.)—Fiction. 2. Divorced
women—New York (N.Y.)—Fiction. 3. Upper classes—New York (N.Y.)—
Fiction. I. Orgel, Stephen. II. Title. III. Series.
[PS3545.H16C8 1994b] 813'.52—dc20 94–11774

ISBN 978-0-19-955512-3

CONTENTS

Acknowledgements   vi

Introduction   vii

Note on the Text   xxiv

Select Bibliography   xxv

A Chronology of Edith Wharton   xxvi

THE CUSTOM OF THE COUNTRY   I

Explanatory Notes   373

ACKNOWLEDGEMENTS

I am indebted for elucidation on various points to Anne Barton, Faith Evans, Timothy Hampton, John Hollander, Randall S. Nakayama, Anthony Newcomb, and John Stokes.

INTRODUCTION

Readers who are unfamiliar with the plot may wish to treat the Introduction as an Afterword.

Edith Wharton completed *The Custom of the Country* in the autumn of 1913, six months after her divorce from Edward Wharton became final; she had moved permanently to France, and had definitively taken control of her life. If the novel's principal subject, like that of so much of Wharton's fiction, is marriage, its subtext is, even more powerfully, divorce. Undine Spragg, by the novel's end, has succeeded in dissolving three unsatisfactory marriages, and experiences, on the novel's last pages, the beginnings of her dissatisfaction with a fourth. Wharton's satiric edge does not entirely conceal a note of admiration, perhaps even of envy. She grew up in a society where divorce was all but unmentionable—the society described in the account of Ralph Marvell's family, like Wharton's parents, old New York aristocrats. *The Custom of the Country* is set in the first decade of the twentieth century; the Marvells and Dagonets are the ghosts of the world Wharton was to anatomize so brilliantly in *The Age of Innocence*. They are dowdy but elaborately principled, and when Undine, at a dinner early in her engagement to Ralph, casually mentions the possibility of one of her friends divorcing, Ralph's mother responds, 'with a constrained smile', 'I believe in certain parts of the country such—unfortunate arrangements—are beginning to be tolerated. But in New York, in spite of our growing indifference, a divorced woman is still—thank heaven!—at a decided disadvantage' (p. 61). Since Undine herself is at this point already a divorced woman, her very presence at the family gathering is subversive, and would, indeed, be unthinkable if the fact were known. It is, moreover, a fact of which even we are kept ignorant; though we learn shortly after this scene that there is some dangerous secret in Undine's relation to her old acquaintance Elmer Moffatt, the fact that the secret is a divorce is not revealed until almost the end of the book.

Harriet Ray, the woman Ralph's family consider the ideal wife for him, is in every way the antithesis of Undine, 'neither vulgar nor ambitious. She regarded Washington Square as the birthplace of Society, knew by heart all the cousinships of early New York, hated motor-cars, could not make herself understood on the telephone, and was determined, if she married, never to receive a divorced woman' (p. 50). What Ralph sees in Undine is a beauty and a vitality that are unknown in Washington Square, but most of all what he sees, so delusively, is the chance of an escape from it. It is Ralph's tragedy that he is able to see beyond that perspective, and yet remains trapped within its values; indeed, the despair that leads to his death is the direct result of his inability to contend, in the most basic, practical ways, with his own divorce.

Nevertheless, Wharton herself writes from within a large double standard; like so many novelists of the upper reaches of society, she holds her characters to a code of behaviour far more rigid than any she found within her own circle, or indeed, any she observed herself. By the time the novel appeared, she was not only a divorcée, but had been engaged for several years in a love-affair with her close friend and indispensable interpreter of the expatriate life Morton Fullerton, the Paris correspondent for the *New York Times*. She was perfectly discreet, unquestionably, a person about whom no breath of scandal was ever breathed; but precisely for that reason, her own career must have served her as the best critique of her heroine's perennially frustrating attempts to balance the demands of marriage and freedom without compromising her respectability. Throughout her fiction, Wharton played out the potential disasters she herself had avoided; all her heroines lose the battles she had so decisively won.

It is easy to say that what Undine wants from Ralph is not a husband, but an entry into the world of money and society, which constitute for her, as she tells Ralph's grandfather, 'everything'. Marriage is nothing but money and position; she is appalled at the idea of having children (Wharton herself during the twenty-seven years of her marriage had none, presumably not by choice), and neglects the son she bears; she has no interest in a home as anything but a place to entertain in the right part of town; above all, Ralph constitutes no more to her than her father was, a means of supplying her pleasures. Late in the novel, Wharton sums it up succinctly: what Undine wants out of life is amusement with respectability. This is quite damning, but it is in fact hardly more egotistical than what Ralph wants from Undine. She is to be the blank page on which he will compose his ideal woman, the untrained and unaffected creature he will effortlessly mould into the world of his fantasies, his escape from the stifling world of his family and his society. Wharton clearly empathizes deeply with Ralph, but her sense of his self-centred misapprehension of Undine's true nature is clear and powerful. The most obvious fact about her, that she is extravagant and mercenary, is as unreal to him as the fact that he is not rich is to her.

The moment in the young couple's honeymoon when Ralph finally penetrates beyond the beautiful façade he himself has constructed for Undine is one of the great moments of pure revelation in Wharton's fiction, both comic and potentially— and ultimately—tragic. Ralph's Italian idyll has, it turns out, been experienced quite differently by his bride. Undine speaks to her husband for once with real passion: 'It's dirty and ugly— all the towns we've been to are disgustingly dirty. I loathe the smells and the beggars. I'm sick and tired of the stuffy rooms in the hotels. I thought it would all be so splendid—but New York's ever so much nicer! . . . All these places seem as if they were dead. It's all like some awful cemetery' (p. 96).

The sense of mutual unreality and self-delusion, however, extends far beyond the relations of the young couple. The indictment of their marriage rendered by the shadowy family friend Charles Bowen is, indeed, an indictment of the whole of American society at the beginning of the twentieth century, a society that systematically excludes its women from the most important part of its life, the world of business. 'Why haven't we taught our women to take an interest in our work? Simply because we don't take enough interest in *them*' (p. 129). And he proceeds to a cultural comparison:

Why does the European woman interest herself so much more in what the men are doing? Because she's so important to them that they make it worth her while! . . . Where does the real life of most American men lie? In some woman's drawing-room or in their offices? The answer's obvious, isn't it? The emotional centre of gravity's not the same in the two hemispheres. In the effete societies it's love, in our new one it's business. In America the real *crime passionel* is a 'big steal'—there's more excitement in wrecking railways than homes. (p. 130)

He concludes that Undine is 'a monstrously perfect result of the system: the completest proof of its triumph', adding that 'it's Ralph who's the victim' (p. 131).

This is an extraordinary moment, though it is an analysis that is never fully integrated into the novel as a whole—the new American world of capitalist enterprise is, in fact, nearly as opaque to Wharton as it is to Undine. It is a critical common-place that the Great War destroyed the world Wharton believed in, but it is clear from *The Custom of the Country* that by 1908, when she began her intermittent work on this most thoroughly satiric of her novels, that world was, for her, long dead.

Wharton writes, in fact, with an insistent sense of her alien-ation from the world she depicts. No novelist, not even James, is more aware of the craft of fiction than Wharton, and her prose is a precise index to her own place in her story. In particular, through the persistent use of inverted commas she seems almost to be writing in a foreign language; we are told of 'a languid "bell-boy"', that 'Mrs Heeny had had such "cases" before', that Mr Spragg was resolved 'to "see through" the New York adventure', that Indiana Frusk was 'the freckled daughter of the plumber "across the way"', that 'Undine's chief delight was to "dress up" in her mother's Sunday skirt and "play lady"', that Claude Popple 'murmured something "artistic" about the colour of her hair', that Undine forced 'her parents to take her "east" . . . to a Virginia "resort"', where she went 'on a "buggy-ride"', that the hotel they stayed in 'was "exclusive"', and 'the other "guests"' ignored them, that Mrs Spragg was resigned 'to the mysterious necessity of having to "entertain" a friend of Undine's', that 'Mr Spragg had "helped out" his ruined father-in-law', that 'the Spraggs had been "plain people"', that Undine was eager 'to "get even" with' those who snubbed her, even that she was to 'have the "handsomest" wedding the New York Press had ever celebrated'. Wharton's very punctuation establishes her distance from her characters, insists that this is not her language; the decorum of her style in the novel not only does not admit slang, but even undertakes to insulate itself from the natural changes of the language—the norm is the polite usage of 1880, the English of the Harriet Rays of Wharton's world. The technique is by no means unique to this novel, but it is especially noticeable here, and serves as a dramatic device even more than as a stylistic one.

Throughout the first part of the novel, the chronicle of Undine's life in New York at the turn of the century, Wharton's satiric detachment from her heroine is cool and unvarying. Undine's cultural *naïveté* is a matter for nothing but amused condescension; try as she may, she always gets things a little bit wrong. What is missing from Wharton's picture is precisely what makes Undine so attractive to every society she moves in: we are told over and over that she is beautiful, but dramatically she is singularly charmless, scheming in private, foolish, uncomprehending or indiscreet in public. And yet the culture Undine wants to acquire is the culture of Wharton's world, the best opera, the right paintings, the latest theatre. These are rendered with great precision in the novel; most of the allusions to theatrical and operatic performances are traceable in the theatre pages of the *New York Times* between 1900 and 1905— Wharton is writing about a world that was her own. Undine is faulted for not really caring for such things, only for the world to which they provide a key, but in fact, as Wharton presents that world, it constitutes little more than a continual round of dinners and theatre parties—constitutes, in fact, precisely what Undine wants from it. Her failure to appreciate Sarah Bernhardt, after all, might in another context stamp her as an intellectual: by the time the great actress was, as Shaw put it, going 'round the world pretending to kill people with hatchets and hairpins',[1] jokes about her were a mark of intellectual sophistication. Undine is no more contemptible for her bafflement at Bernhardt's fame than the young Marcel is for being underwhelmed by his first experience of 'Berma' in *Swann's*

[1] In a review of Sardou's *Gismonda* (1895), *Our Theatres in the Nineties* (London, 1932), i. 138.

Way. The joke in Proust's case, however, is allowed to be on Bernhardt.

Like her sense of the cultural scene, Wharton's New York is rendered with great precision, and its geography is an aspect of its social consciousness. The Spraggs have settled in a huge apartment hotel on Central Park West and 72nd Street—Wharton calls it the Stentorian; the hotel on the site was in fact called the Majestic, as is the magnificent art deco apartment building that replaced it and stands on the site today. It seems to its midwestern tenants both luxurious and genteel; but as Undine gradually acquires some New York sophistication, she begins to see it, and her friends in it, as pretentious and vulgar. It is also in the wrong part of town, the *nouveau riche* West Side, which had recently become gentrified with the construction of vast apartment houses like the famous Dakota, across the street from the Majestic, and the monstrously vulgar Ansonia on 73rd Street and Broadway (both of these survive; the Ansonia's vulgarity is undimmed, but the Dakota, despite its flamboyant clientele, has acquired an air of almost dowdy gentility). In keeping with the district's pretensions, Broadway above 59th Street was called The Boulevard: the name had been given it in 1869, when the street was opened through an area still basically rural, which the developers imagined transformed into a Parisian *quartier*. (By the 1920s, the area had lost its pretensions, and the street, as a continuation of Broadway, took its name.) One of the most keenly felt of Undine's disappointments in her marriage is the economic necessity of continuing to live on the West Side, in the West End Avenue house her father owns. Society lives on the East Side.

The East Side—east of Fifth Avenue, but as a social classification, east of Central Park (half of the socially impeccable Washington Square is technically on the West Side)—had been gentrified only a little earlier; old New York society had always lived downtown, in Washington Square, University Place, and lower Fifth Avenue: it is a measure of the eccentricity of Mrs Manson Mingott, the matriarch of *The Age of Innocence*, that in the 1870s she chooses to inhabit a house 'in an inaccessible wilderness near the Central Park'. But by the 1890s society, or at least moneyed society, had moved north—specifically, north of Commodore Cornelius Vanderbilt's newly constructed terminus for his New York Central Railway, Grand Central Station on 42nd Street and Fourth Avenue. In keeping with the street's new grandeur, therefore, Fourth Avenue became Park Avenue in 1888. This is the geographical world of the society Undine craves, whereas her husband's family lives downtown in the faded precincts of old New York gentry, or even worse, in the distinctly unfashionable area south of Grand Central. The ancestral geography, in fact, gives Undine her first inkling that she has made a mistake, that her adoring, charming, aristocratic husband will not enable her to move at last into the right part of town.

How does an outsider learn the rules, even the rules of geography, in so arcane a culture? Undine's guide through these mysteries, her most enduring and faithful confidante, is not a friend who has preceded her into the sacred precincts but a figure both indispensable to New York society and almost unnoticeable in it, a certain Mrs Heeny, masseuse and beautician, intimately familiar with all the fashionable houses and luxurious hotels on both sides of the park. Mrs Heeny is the ideal guide; endlessly good-natured, but also astute, observant, and a voracious reader of the society pages, she is an inexhaustible source of the gossip and trivia that constitute the working capital of this, as of any, social circle. Even more important, she is Undine's pilot through the shoals of its manners and conventions. Mrs Heeny is a representative of that largely invisible class that allows society to function, the underworld of its servants. Undine learns her social skills from the ground up.

Wharton's title is proverbial, combining the implications of the phrase 'the way of the world' with the wisdom that success lies in doing, when in Rome, as the Romans do; but it also alludes to a play by Phillip Massinger and John Fletcher set in a kingdom in which the women are literally for sale. Undine appears particularly cold-blooded in her erotic negotiations, but as success is conceived in the novel—and Wharton provides nothing in the way of moral alternatives—her heroine operates with the only capital she has. Since American customs include divorce, her capital, despite her prospective mother-in-law's horror at the idea, is considerably larger than it would be in another country. Early in the book, it is suggested that she is a version of her father, and more generally, of the business-oriented world of post-Civil War America:

Mr and Mrs Spragg were both given to such long periods of ruminating apathy that the student of inheritance might have wondered whence Undine derived her overflowing activity. The answer would have been obtained by observing her father's business life. From the moment he set foot in Wall Street Mr Spragg became another man. (p. 76)

Undine is a child of this world, one in which success requires ruthlessness and a willingness to take large risks, combined with a detailed understanding of the prospects. In such an enterprise, moral questions are all but irrelevant. Nor is Undine in fact out of place in the world of Fifth Avenue: Ralph's cousin and closest friend, Clare Van Degen, whom he himself once hoped to marry, has sold herself to a rich vulgarian quite as cold-bloodedly as Undine proposes to do—and Peter Van Degen is no less vulgar for having the right antecedents and living on Park Avenue. Even the fastidious and high-principled Ralph, faced with the necessity of making his way in the business world of his father-in-law, ignores the shady aspects of a deal he senses is corrupt.

Corruption, indeed, is endemic to the public sphere; businessmen make their money in cahoots with politicians and legislators. Undine's father initially became rich as a speculator, the embodiment of American ingenuity and independence, with a strong streak of the public benefactor. The beneficence began at home: he accepted some worthless land from his hard-pressed father-in-law in payment of a bad debt. He went on to found a new water company for his town of Apex City, some-where in the Midwest: Wharton never specifies the state, though since the Spraggs' neighbours the Frusks have named their daughter Indiana, this may imply—if they are natives of the place, or at least if the child was born there—that Apex City is in Indiana. On the other hand, when Moffatt and Undine elope, they marry in a fictitious town aptly named Opake, which is in Nebraska (p. 292). Doubtless it was a good idea to leave the state to accomplish the marriage, but Nebraska is very far from Indiana, at least six hundred miles, whereas it is just across the border from Kansas or Missouri, which suggests that Apex City is further west. The very ambiguousness of the geography underlines the essential rootlessness of Undine's antecedents, but it bespeaks even more the vagueness of the New Yorker's sense of America beyond the Hudson.

Spragg proceeded to sell his worthless land to his own water company for its reservoir at a handsome profit. This was not pure financial juggling: the water system he provided for Apex gave the town drinking-water that was clean and safe for the first time, rescuing it thenceforth from the periodic typhoid epidemics that had killed two of his own children. It also made him a millionaire, but there is no necessary contradiction between profit and good works; his success was the reward of his virtue—that, at least, is how Ralph understands the family history Undine's mother recounts as her way of entertaining him: 'out of those two disinterested impulses, by some impressive law of compensation, material prosperity had come' (p. 52). By the time Abner Spragg moves to New York, however, to try his hand with his erstwhile and future son-in-law Elmer Moffatt in the world of big money, his benevolence has been jettisoned as unmarketable, and his ingenuity is all in the service of making deals. At this, it transpires, he is only intermittently successful, though it is also suggested that his failure is in part due to the continuing necessity of supplying his daughter's inexhaustible requirements. But he does so with goodwill and total devotion, and it is consequently Undine, not he, who makes a success of New York.

Becky Sharp has often been cited as a model for Undine, but Wharton's vision includes nothing so witty, charming, genteel, and, above all, moralized—no patiently normative Amelia, no sermonizing about the anti-heroine's corrupt heart. The literary tradition out of which Wharton writes is that of the late Trollope of *The Way We Live Now* and *The Prime Minister*; Wharton's social milieu is akin to that of Balzac's *Illusions perdues* and *Splendeurs et misères des courtisanes*. Years later she was to write to Bernard Berenson, 'I've gone back to "Can You Forgive Her?" and "The Prime Minister"—& oh, how good they are! Somehow, Trollope seems to have got nearer the eternal verities than Thackeray. He's more grown-up, & belongs rather with Tolstoy and Balzac.'[2]

But Undine's story is not only that of a ruthless American fortune-hunter; it is also a story about the education of American innocence, an education that, by definition, can never be sufficient or complete—as her friend the Princess Estradina remarks late in the novel, 'I always say when people talk to me about fast Americans: you're the only innocent women left in the world' (p. 323). All Undine's successes are therefore ultimately hollow: having won her place in the society of old New York, she is astonished to learn that her husband is neither rich nor fashionable—'she had found out that she had given herself to the exclusive and the dowdy when the future belonged to the showy and the promiscuous' (p. 121); having acquired a millionaire admirer, she finds that her ruthlessness and independence are suddenly liabilities; having become the Comtesse de Chelles, her consignment to the insanely boring life of a magnificent French château comes as nothing but an unpleasant revelation; having landed, at last, the husband who is in most respects her true counterpart, and has, moreover, all the money in the world, she is suddenly aware of a whole new world of desires that is closed to her.

Much of the novel's power derives from Wharton's unwillingness to romanticize Undine, to present her as her admirers see her. Even her name, so romantic to Ralph as he begins to woo her, is relentlessly deconstructed. Initially it recalls to him Montaigne's characterization of the infinite variety of humankind, *divers et ondoyant*, various and like waves of the sea. The legendary Undine is a water-nymph, beautiful but soulless; she gains a soul by falling in love with a handsome knight and marrying him, but the transformation brings her only sorrow and proves fatal to her husband. The story became famous as retold for generations of nineteenth-century children by Friedrich de la Motte Fouqué. But neither of these, it turns out, is the Undine the Spraggs had in mind when they named their only daughter. Mrs Spragg is unabashed to reply to Ralph's

² *Letters*, ed. R. W. B. Lewis and Nancy Lewis (New York, 1988), 575.

praise of the wonderful perfection of the name, '"Why, we called her after a hair-waver father put on the market the week she was born——" and then to explain, as he remained struck and silent: "It's from *un*doolay, you know, the French for crimping . . ."' (p. 51). The sources of the essential Undine are the simple, the practical, the inventive. Their transformation into the monstrous is, as Wharton presents the matter, simply a function of the ordinary American ambition to better oneself, the same ambition that motivates most of the novel's world.

And yet, at various moments most of the novel's major figures, cynical or pathetic, successful or not, are represented as in some measure victims of the social system. Wharton's emphasis on the maintaining of respectability as the crucial element in modern society is not mere cynicism; but the problem, as the novel so superbly dramatizes it, is that respectability is never a constant. Though Undine flirts with *louche* playboys and intermittently runs with a dubious set, it is her husband's standards that appear to be out of step with social reality. Her ignorance of the rules of propriety is perfectly genuine, but the fact is that, as Undine moves along the social scale, the rules keep changing. The novel does, moreover, undeniably have a number of double standards. For example, at several points it is implied—discreetly—that Clare Van Degen wants Ralph for a lover. This is a measure of Clare's unhappiness, an index to the dissatisfactions of her marriage; nothing in it is allowed to constitute an indictment of Clare's character or humanity, and least of all of her right to be considered respectable. The discretion, that is, is not in the quality of Clare's desires, but in Wharton's treatment of them.

Charles Bowen's pessimistic analysis of American society places the condition of women firmly at its centre:

If we cared for women in the old barbarous possessive way do you suppose we'd give them up as readily as we do? The real paradox is the fact that the men who make, materially, the biggest sacrifices for their women, should do least for them ideally and romantically. And what's the result—how do the women avenge themselves? All my sympathy's with them, poor deluded dears, when I see their fallacious little attempts to trick out the leavings tossed them by the preoccupied male—the money and the motors and the clothes—and pretend to themselves and each other that *that's* what really constitutes life! . . . it's less and less of a pretense with them, I grant you; they're more and more succumbing to the force of the suggestion; but here and there I fancy there's one who still sees through the humbug, and knows that money and motors and clothes are simply the big bribe she's paid for keeping out of some man's way! (p. 130)

The determinism of this is notable, but what is most striking about it is how little range it allows women for independent action, or even for rational desires. It is an assessment that is, moreover, thoroughly borne out by the novel. No marriage in the book is happy or successful, and the notion of a truly independent woman taking control of her life, as Wharton had certainly taken control of hers, is all but inconceivable. It is not only for Undine that freedom is a function of large sums of money and an absent husband. These are the conditions of the world Wharton has created.

What rings least true in the novel is the world of big business. The vagueness of Elmer Moffatt's dealings has a thematic significance: Wharton allows us to understand no more about them than Charles Bowen says American men allow their wives to know. Wharton in this respect significantly feminizes her audience; nevertheless, the book's subtext, and the source of its basic assumptions, has to do precisely with the masculine world of business and politics—this is what has transformed America into the subject of Wharton's satire. Moffatt's success in that world, while hardly unequivocal, is presented as the only real success in the novel. His career is a parallel to Undine's, but without the ironies and dissatisfactions she endures—in the world of men, Wharton implies, it really is possible to succeed.

Moffatt is, like Abner Spragg, a self-made man out of the Midwest; but where Spragg is cautious, reserved, and laconic, Moffatt is flamboyant and a taker of great risks. He is also ruthless, though he has a real fondness for Undine, and, more strikingly, a good-natured and affectionate concern for the son she ignores. His good nature is, indeed, his saving grace, and it gives him a degree of humanity that is largely absent from Undine. In the world of New York finance, however, his success is directly related to his ruthlessness, his ignorance or disregard of the gentlemanly code that governs honourable dealing in the society Ralph Marvell belongs to. Nor, for all his fondness for Undine, is he above using the dangerous secret of his brief marriage to her as a way of advancing his fortunes: he threatens her father with the revelation that would render her marriage into New York society impossible; the price of silence is Spragg's betrayal of the trust of a former Apex friend and associate, someone who stands in the way of Moffatt's concluding a lucrative deal.

It is Moffatt's politic silence, then, that enables Undine to marry Ralph Marvell. Moffatt also provides the means for her to extricate herself from that marriage, and shows her how to use the child she does not care for to extort money from Ralph—money that, moreover, has been made in a deal engineered by Moffatt; and it is Moffatt who ultimately rescues Undine from the misery of her life as the Marquise de Chelles, to become, for the second time, Mrs Elmer Moffatt. We are allowed to understand less about the nature of his success in business than about his social and erotic negotiations, but it is clear that all his enterprises are on a grand scale, highly speculative, and involve a large degree of opportunism and a willingness to use anything and anyone to gain his ends. They also involve an unshakeable belief in himself, and a powerful resilience in the face of his occasional failures—another respect in which he resembles Undine.

Undine is keenly aware of Moffatt's crudeness, and prepared to be embarrassed by it in the context of her husband's friends; but when, at Moffatt's urging, she invites him to dinner, the evening is surprisingly successful. Ralph is especially taken with him, finding 'something epic about him—a kind of epic effrontery. . . . The man's a thundering brute, but he's full of observation and humour' (p. 160). Crude, certainly, but also charismatic and large-minded, he fascinates his decorous hosts, and in fact shines in the rarified world of the Marvells and Dagonets. This, indeed, is part of his power, his ability to manipulate the fascination of high civilization for crude power. And he gets from Ralph exactly what he wants; the social occasion is in fact a brilliant business *coup*, and Ralph, only half understanding what is involved, is entirely oblivious to the fact that he is being manipulated.

But Moffatt has another side—one that is, indeed, an essential aspect of early twentieth-century American capitalism. For all his vulgarity, he has taste, and it is only partly a paradox to say that he has all the taste that money can buy: money *can* buy taste, as it bought Andrew Carnegie's, Henry Clay Frick's, Isabella Stewart Gardner's, Henry Huntington's. Moffatt has put as much energy and intelligence into learning what the most valuable objects are as he has put into learning what the most lucrative investments will be. He reappears in Undine's life, in her magnificent, intolerable French château, as a connoisseur of tapestries and a world-class collector of art. Nor is there any suggestion that his expertise is not genuine; on the contrary, the superlative quality of his collection is an index to his shrewdness and perspicacity, and most of all to his ability, at last, to get anything he wants, to command the best. It is this sense of authority that, from the first, had fascinated Undine—he is the only man she instinctively feels she cannot control. He is also, for the same reason, the man who can free her from the disaster of her French marriage; but though his power is real, the freedom is a delusion: she becomes simply another of his possessions, though one that, unlike her other husbands, he can afford.

Undine's situation is only an extreme example of the position of women generally in Wharton's world: men act, women fill their time. But Wharton also allows us a glimpse of an alternative world. The French women of Undine's society as Comtesse and later Marquise de Chelles are as stylish and moneyed as her American friends, but their conversation reflects a different set of values, a real concern for culture and ideas— Undine is gently told, for the first time, that much of her difficulty in establishing herself in her French husband's milieu stems from the fact that though still extremely beautiful, she is a bore. As her friend the Marquise de Trézac, who has successfully made the transition from American débutante to French aristocrat, puts it,

you don't work hard enough—you don't keep up. It's not that they don't admire you—your looks, I mean; they think you beautiful; they're delighted to bring you out at their big dinners, with the Sèvres and the plate. But a woman has got to be something more than good-looking to have a chance to be intimate with them: she's got to know what's being said about things. I watched you the other night at the Duchess's, and half the time you hadn't an idea what they were talking about. (p. 339)

Undine's attempts to rectify her failures by cultivating her mind—she 'went so far as to spend a morning in the Louvre and go to one or two lectures by a fashionable philosopher'—bring only the revelation that 'everybody appeared to know about the things she thought she had discovered, and her comments clearly produced more bewilderment than interest' (p. 339). She had been equally at sea in the intellectual world of Ralph Marvell's New York, but in that context her ignorance had had no consequences. The kind of cultural seriousness Undine cannot hope to acquire extends to other sorts of seriousness as well. Raymond de Chelles declares his mother's business sense to be the equal of any man's, and in fact both he and Moffat do undertake to talk to Undine of their (and thereby of her) financial affairs; but here too she is presented as being unable to follow them. Some women, therefore, are as strong-minded and independent as men—only they are French, the product of an ancient culture with real beliefs and powerful family ties.

Despite the fact that by 1913 Edith Wharton had lived in Paris for seven years, the Paris in which she places Undine is as topographically vague and unnuanced as her New York is precise and subtle. Undine's Paris world has only two geographical poles, the ancient, aristocratic Faubourg St Germain, where the Hôtel de Chelles is located, and the new, glossy Champs-Elysées, where the Nouveau Luxe Hotel caters to rich Americans. But the city's social values are rendered with a detailed and hard-edged clarity, and here there is no Mrs Heeny to guide Undine through the complexities of her husband's world—the Marquise de Trézac can do no more than explain to Undine why she has no hope of succeeding. Her unwillingness to accommodate herself to the life of her French in-laws becomes a touchstone not simply for the ignorance and callowness of modern America, but for something much more dangerous: its destructive cynicism. De Chelles's indictment of American society goes far beyond his anger at his wife; it is sweeping and violent, and constitutes one of the greatest moments of passion in the book:

You come among us from a country we don't know, and can't imagine, a country you care for so little that before you've been a day in ours you've forgotten the very house you were born in—if it wasn't torn down before you knew it! You come among us speaking our language and not knowing what we mean; wanting the things we want, and not knowing why we want them; aping our weaknesses, exaggerating our follies, ignoring or ridiculing all we care about—you come from hotels as big as towns, and from towns as flimsy as paper, where the streets haven't had time to be named, and the buildings are demolished before they're dry, and the people are as proud of changing as we are of holding to what we have—and we're fools enough to imagine that because you copy our ways and pick up our slang you understand anything about the things that make life decent and honourable for us! (p. 341)

This is prompted by Undine's attempt to raise money by selling a family treasure, the splendid set of Boucher tapestries that Moffatt, with his expertise, recognizes as 'the best', and therefore covets. It is an act that, for de Chelles, constitutes the last straw in the marriage, and extinguishes whatever vestige of feeling he retains for Undine. What her husband sees as an inalienable part of his patrimony, something to be carefully preserved for future generations, she sees as only potential cash, and the desire to realize it (and immediately spend it) is entirely in character. But of course, Undine's character in this respect has been entirely consistent; de Chelles has been as blind to his wife's essential and obvious qualities as Ralph Marvell had been. Dramatically, indeed, it is difficult to see why de Chelles ever wanted to marry Undine in the first place; and it is to the point that his greatest passion is manifest in his disillusionment with her, not in making love to her. The family sense, which Undine cannot share, remains paramount; as the troubles in their marriage increase, it is made clear to Undine that she has no hope of retaining her husband's interest because she has not borne him a child, and that this is considered, moreover, to be somehow her fault, the ultimate failure of her duty to the family—the son she did not want by Ralph now returns as a reproach to her. Ironically, there will be no heir to inherit the patrimony Undine has been so furiously prevented from liquidating. De Chelles's energetic affection for his American stepson Paul Marvell throws into striking relief his mother's chronic neglect of him, her—America's—deficient concern not simply for family, but even for her own posterity. Paul himself feels that de Chelles is the only father he has ever had, and in one of the few genuinely touching scenes in the novel, he is left to construct his family history out of Mrs Heeny's newspaper clippings.

Even the New York of Wharton's childhood suffers by comparison with Raymond de Chelles's France. In contrast to de Chelles's sense of tradition, the convictions of old New York society, of Ralph Marvell's mother and grandfather, seem mere superstition—Ralph thinks of them as 'sign-posts warning off trespassers who have long since ceased to intrude' (p. 195). The invidious comparison, however, offers no solution to the cultural conundrum Wharton has constructed. The intellectual independence of French women does not liberate them from stifling marriages and tedious, pointless social chores, it only enables them to accept the inevitability of these arrangements. The depiction of life among the de Chelles, indeed, constitutes a powerful counter-claim to Charles Bowen's praise of French as against American marriages. The scenes of Undine as chatelaine constitute the only part of the novel where she is represented as positively justified in repining at the conditions of her marriage. They are conditions from which, once again, divorce offers a convenient escape, but it is only an escape into yet another unsatisfying marriage. The customs of Wharton's country are universal.

NOTE ON THE TEXT

The Custom of the Country was published serially in *Scribner's Magazine* beginning in January 1913, at which time Wharton had not yet written the final chapters. She completed the work only in August, and revised the text for the book version, which Scribner's published in October 1913. The present text follows this edition; several typographical errors have been silently corrected.

SELECT BIBLIOGRAPHY

The first, most essential context for *The Custom of the Country*, and the best study of Wharton's sense of American cultural insecurities at home and abroad, is her own memoir *A Backward Glance* (New York, 1934). The standard biography is R. W. B. Lewis's *Edith Wharton* (New York, 1975), a superbly researched study which includes incisive and enlightening readings of the fiction. Cynthia Griffin Wolff's *A Feast of Words* (New York, 1977) gives a detailed, if sometimes rather mechanical, psychoanalytic account of the life and work, and includes a valuable discussion of *The Custom of the Country*. Candace Waid's *Edith Wharton's Letters from the Underworld* (Chapel Hill, NC, 1991) contains an especially fine chapter on the novel; and Gloria C. Erlich's *The Sexual Education of Edith Wharton* (Berkeley, Calif., 1992) is provocative and relevant. Among individual articles, Robert Caserio's 'Edith Wharton and the Fiction of Public Commentary' (*Western Humanities Review*, 40: 3 (1986), 189–208) is unique in taking the political and capitalistic aspects of the novel seriously, and Q. D. Leavis's 'James's Heiress', reprinted in her *Collected Essays*, volume ii (Cambridge, 1987), has a wonderful couple of pages on the novel, which she declares 'unquestionably . . . Wharton's masterpiece', and suggestively compares it with *Middlemarch*. There is, finally, an ingenious and original essay on *The Custom of the Country* in relation to La Motte Fouqué's romance *Undine* by Richard H. Lawson in *Edith Wharton and German Literature* (Bonn, 1974).

A CHRONOLOGY OF
EDITH WHARTON

1862   (24 January) Edith Newbold Jones, only daughter of George
        Frederick Jones and Lucretia Rhinelander, born in New York
        City. Early years alternate between houses in Newport and
        Manhattan. Called 'Pussy' by her family and 'Lily' by friends.

1873   Writes first story and verses.

1877   Completes novella, 'Fast and Loose' (unpublished). Avid reader
        of Goethe ('Faust' her favourite), Keats, and the Elizabethan
        dramatists.

1878   *Verses*, collection of poems, privately printed. 'Comes out' at
        her society début; has many male admirers.

1879–80 First publication: three poems appear in *Atlantic Monthly* and
        New York *World*. (Ten years pass before she publishes again.)

1880   To Europe for an extended stay.

1882   Father's death in Cannes on the French Riviera; returns with
        her mother to Newport; breaks engagement with Harry
        Stevens.

1883   Brief romance with Walter Berry; meets Edward (Teddy)
        Wharton of Boston.

1885   (29 April) marries Wharton; six weeks later learns of Harry
        Stevens's death. Settles in Newport, with frequent trips abroad.

1888   Receives handsome legacy from a relative, which, when added
        to her trust fund and Teddy's allowance, provides the Whartons
        with solid financial security.

1889   Begins to suffer attacks of asthma, nausea, extreme fatigue.
        Rents house on New York's Madison Avenue. Starts writing
        lyric poetry after hiatus of ten years. Poetry published in
        Scribner's Magazine, starting her long professional relationship
        with editor Edward Burlingame.

1890   Burlingame accepts 'Mrs Manstey's View' (short story),
        Wharton's first published work of fiction.

1891   Purchases small house on Park Avenue and builds large house in
        Newport.

1897   Co-author of *The Decoration of Houses* with Ogden Codman.
        Receives first royalty cheque for $39.60.

1898   Suffers nervous collapse; placed under the care of S. Weir
        Mitchell, famous Philadelphia physician whose rest-cure works
        for her as it had not for Charlotte Perkins Gilman. Walter Berry

re-enters her life and becomes her closest friend and literary advisor.

1899   Publishes first collection of short stories, *The Greater Inclination*.

1900   Publishes novella, *The Touchstone*.

1901   *Crucial Instances*, her second short-story collection, is published. Death of her mother.

1902   Appearance of *The Valley of Decision*, her first full-length novel. With Teddy, moves into The Mount, the house she designed in Lenox, Massachusetts. Keeping a separate bedroom, her health improves; Teddy becomes frequently ill and increasingly dependent. Plans new novel entitled 'Disintegration', which does not appear until 1925 as *The Mother's Recompense*. Involved in a variety of literary activities: translations, reviews, poetry, essays on Italy, several unfinished plays.

1903   Publishes novel, *Sanctuary*; *Italian Villas and Their Gardens*. Meets Henry James. Teddy's health deteriorates.

1904   Third collection of short stories, *The Descent of Man*. Begins work on new novel, first entitled 'A Moment's Ornament', then 'The Year of the Rose', and finally *The House of Mirth*.

1905   *The House of Mirth* appears serialized in *Scribner's Magazine* between January and November. The book is published by Charles Scribner's Sons on 14 October.

1907   Publishes novel, *The Fruit of the Tree*. Starts planning *The Custom of the Country* but puts it aside. Teddy suffers major nervous collapse. After meeting Morton Fullerton, starts writing her 'love diary' in October.

1908   Begins love affair with Fullerton. Reading Nietzsche. Publishes travel book and another collection of stories.

1909   *Artemis to Actaeon and Other Verse* is published. Teddy seriously mismanages her funds.

1910   *Tales of Men and Ghosts* appears. Affair with Fullerton ends. Settles in Paris.

1911   Publishes *Ethan Frome*, the novella she claimed ended her apprenticeship.

1912   *The Reef*, her first major novel since *The Fruit of the Tree*, published by Appleton, marking the conclusion of her long relationship with Scribner's.

1913   Marriage to Teddy ends in divorce. Publishes novel, *The Custom of the Country*.

1914   Travels extensively in North Africa. Takes up permanent residence in France and becomes active in war-relief.

1915   Visits battle-areas and publishes essays, *Fighting France*.

1916   Edits *The Book of the Homeless* to raise funds for war-relief. Publishes *Xingu and Other Stories*. Begins work on novel, *The Glimpses of the Moon*.

1917   The novella, *Summer*, appears, her 'hot' pairing to her 'cold' story, *Ethan Frome*.

1918   Publishes *The Marne*; begins the never-completed novella, *The Necklace*, and *A Son at the Front*, not published until 1923. Purchases eighteenth-century house outside Paris.

1919   Publishes essays, *French Ways and their Meanings*; buys château on French Riviera.

1920   During this productive year publishes novel, *The Age of Innocence*, and essays, *In Morocco*. Writes fragment of 'Beatrice Palmato', proposed story about incest.

1921   Awarded the Pulitzer Prize for *The Age of Innocence*.

1922   Publishes novel, *The Glimpses of the Moon*.

1923   Makes final visit to the States; granted honorary degree from Yale. Appearance of *A Son at the Front*.

1924   Publishes four novellas under the title *Old New York*.

1925   *The Mother's Recompense*, first outlined in 1901, is published, as is *The Writing of Fiction*.

1926   Publishes *Here and Beyond*, collection of stories.

1928   Publishes novel, *The Children*.

1929   Publishes novel, *Hudson River Bracketed*. Almost dies of influenza.

1930   Short story collection, *Certain People*, appears.

1932   Publishes *The Gods Arrive*, sequel to *Hudson River Bracketed*.

1933   Another collection of short fiction, *Human Nature*, appears.

1934   Publishes reminiscences, *A Backward Glance*. Begins work on final novel, *The Buccaneers*, which is never finished.

1936   *The World Over*, containing some of her best-known short stories, is published.

1937   Dies on 11 August of heart failure and is buried at Versailles.

THE CUSTOM OF
THE COUNTRY

BOOK ONE

I

'UNDINE SPRAGG—how *can* you?' her mother wailed, raising a prematurely-wrinkled hand heavy with rings to defend the note which a languid 'bell-boy' had just brought in.

But her defence was as feeble as her protest, and she continued to smile on her visitor while Miss Spragg, with a turn of her quick young fingers, possessed herself of the missive and withdrew to the window to read it.

'I guess it's meant for me,' she merely threw over her shoulder at her mother.

'Did you *ever*, Mrs Heeny?' Mrs Spragg murmured with deprecating pride.

Mrs Heeny, a stout professional-looking person in a waterproof, her rusty veil thrown back, and a shabby alligator bag at her feet, followed the mother's glance with good-humoured approval.

'I never met with a lovelier form,' she agreed, answering the spirit rather than the letter of her hostess's enquiry.

Mrs Spragg and her visitor were enthroned in two heavy gilt armchairs in one of the private drawing-rooms of the Hotel Stentorian. The Spragg rooms were known as one of the Looey suites, and the drawing-room walls, above their wainscoting of highly-varnished mahogany, were hung with salmon-pink damask and adorned with oval portraits of Marie Antoinette and the Princess de Lamballe.* In the centre of the florid carpet a gilt table with a top of Mexican onyx sustained a palm in a gilt basket tied with a pink bow. But for this ornament, and a copy of 'The Hound of the Baskervilles'* which lay beside it, the room showed no traces of human use, and Mrs Spragg herself wore as complete an air of detachment as if she had been a wax figure in a show-window. Her attire was fashionable enough to justify such a post, and her pale soft-cheeked face, with puffy eye-lids and drooping mouth, suggested a partially-melted wax figure which had run to double-chin.

Mrs Heeny, in comparison, had a reassuring look of solidity and reality. The planting of her firm black bulk in its chair, and the grasp of her broad red hands on the gilt arms, bespoke an organized and self-reliant activity, accounted for by the fact that Mrs Heeny was a 'society' manicure and masseuse. Toward Mrs Spragg and her daughter she filled the double rôle of manipulator and friend; and it was in the latter capacity that, her day's task ended, she had dropped in for a moment to 'cheer up' the lonely ladies of the Stentorian.

The young girl whose 'form' had won Mrs Heeny's professional commendation suddenly shifted its lovely lines as she turned back from the window.

'Here—you can have it after all,' she said, crumpling the note and tossing it with a contemptuous gesture into her mother's lap.

'Why—isn't it from Mr Popple?' Mrs Spragg exclaimed unguardedly.

'No—it isn't. What made you think I thought it was?' snapped her daughter; but the next instant she added, with an outbreak of childish disappointment: 'It's only from Mr Marvell's sister—at least she says she's his sister.'

Mrs Spragg, with a puzzled frown, groped for her eye-glass among the jet fringes of her tightly-girded front.

Mrs Heeny's small blue eyes shot out sparks of curiosity. 'Marvell—what Marvell is that?'

The girl explained languidly: 'A little fellow—I think Mr Popple said his name was Ralph'; while her mother continued: 'Undine met them both last night at that party downstairs. And from something Mr Popple said to her about going to one of the new plays, she thought——'

'How on earth do you know what I thought?' Undine flashed back, her grey eyes darting warnings at her mother under their straight black brows.

'Why, you *said* you thought——' Mrs Spragg began reproachfully; but Mrs Heeny, heedless of their bickerings, was pursuing her own train of thought.

'What Popple? Claud Walsingham Popple—the portrait painter?'

'Yes—I suppose so. He said he'd like to paint me. Mabel Lipscomb introduced him. I don't care if I never see him again,' the girl said, bathed in angry pink.

'Do you know him, Mrs Heeny?' Mrs Spragg enquired.

'I should say I did. I manicured him for his first society portrait—a full-length of Mrs Harmon B. Driscoll.' Mrs Heeny smiled indulgently on her hearers. 'I know everybody. If they don't know *me* they ain't in it, and Claud Walsingham Popple's in it. But he ain't nearly *as* in it,' she continued judicially, 'as Ralph Marvell—the little fellow, as you call him.'

Undine Spragg, at the word, swept round on the speaker with one of the quick turns that revealed her youthful flexibility. She was always doubling and twisting on herself, and every movement she made seemed to start at the nape of her neck, just below the lifted roll of reddish-gold hair, and flow without a break through her whole slim length to the tips of her fingers and the points of her slender restless feet.

'Why, do you know the Marvells? Are *they* stylish?' she asked.

Mrs Heeny gave the discouraged gesture of a pedagogue who has vainly striven to implant the rudiments of knowledge in a rebellious mind.

'Why, Undine Spragg, I've told you all about them time and again! His mother was a Dagonet. They live with old Urban Dagonet down in Washington Square.'*

To Mrs Spragg this conveyed even less than to her daughter. ''Way down there? Why do they live with somebody else? Haven't they got the means to have a home of their own?'

Undine's perceptions were more rapid, and she fixed her eyes searchingly on Mrs Heeny.

'Do you mean to say Mr Marvell's as swell as Mr Popple?'

'*As swell?* Why, Claud Walsingham Popple ain't in the same class with him!'

The girl was upon her mother with a spring, snatching and smoothing out the crumpled note.

'Laura Fairford—is that the sister's name?'

'Mrs Henley Fairford; yes. What does she write about?'

Undine's face lit up as if a shaft of sunset had struck it through the triple-curtained windows of the Stentorian.

'She says she wants me to dine with her next Wednesday. Isn't it queer? Why does *she* want me? She's never seen me!' Her tone implied that she had long been accustomed to being 'wanted' by those who had.

Mrs Heeny laughed. '*He* saw you, didn't he?'

'Who? Ralph Marvell? Why, of course he did—Mr Popple brought him to the party here last night.'

'Well, there you are . . . When a young man in society wants to meet a girl again, he gets his sister to ask her.'

Undine stared at her incredulously. 'How queer! But they haven't all got sisters, have they? It must be fearfully poky for the ones that haven't.'

'They get their mothers—or their married friends,' said Mrs Heeny omnisciently.

'Married gentlemen?' enquired Mrs Spragg, slightly shocked, but genuinely desirous of mastering her lesson.

'Mercy, no! Married ladies.'

'But are there never any gentlemen present?' pursued Mrs Spragg, feeling that if this were the case Undine would certainly be disappointed.

'Present where? At their dinners? Of course—Mrs Fairford gives the smartest little dinners in town. There was an account of one she gave last week in this morning's *Town Talk*: I guess it's right here among my clippings.' Mrs Heeny, swooping down on her bag, drew from it a handful of newspaper cuttings, which she spread on her ample lap and proceeded to sort with a moistened forefinger. 'Here,' she said, holding one of the slips at arm's length; and throwing back her head she read, in a slow unpunctuated chant: ' "Mrs Henley Fairford gave another of her natty little dinners last Wednesday as usual it was smart small and exclusive and there was much gnashing of teeth among the left-outs as Madame Olga Loukowska gave some of her new steppe dances after dinner"—that's the French for new dance steps,' Mrs Heeny concluded, thrusting the documents back into her bag.

'Do you know Mrs Fairford too?' Undine asked eagerly; while Mrs Spragg, impressed, but anxious for facts, pursued: 'Does she reside on Fifth Avenue?'

'No, she has a little house in Thirty-eighth Street, down beyond Park Avenue.'*

The ladies' faces drooped again, and the masseuse went on promptly: 'But they're glad enough to have her in the big houses!—Why, yes, I know her,' she said, addressing herself to Undine. 'I mass'd her for a sprained ankle a couple of years ago. She's got a lovely manner, but *no* conversation. Some of my patients converse exquisitely,' Mrs Heeny added with discrimination.

Undine was brooding over the note. 'It *is* written to mother—Mrs Abner E. Spragg—I never saw anything so funny! "Will you *allow* your daughter to dine with me?" Allow! Is Mrs Fairford peculiar?'

'No—you are,' said Mrs Heeny bluntly. 'Don't you know it's the thing in the best society to pretend that girls can't do anything without their mothers' permission? You just remember that, Undine. You mustn't accept invitations from gentlemen without you say you've got to ask your mother first.'

'Mercy! But how'll mother know what to say?'

'Why, she'll say what you tell her to, of course. You'd better tell her you want to dine with Mrs Fairford,' Mrs Heeny added humorously, as she gathered her waterproof together and stooped for her bag.

'Have I got to write the note, then?' Mrs Spragg asked with rising agitation.

Mrs Heeny reflected. 'Why, no. I guess Undine can write it as if it was from you. Mrs Fairford don't know your writing.'

This was an evident relief to Mrs Spragg, and as Undine swept to her room with the note her mother sank back, murmuring plaintively: 'Oh, don't go yet, Mrs Heeny. I haven't seen a human being all day, and I can't seem to find anything to say to that French maid.'

Mrs Heeny looked at her hostess with friendly compassion. She was well aware that she was the only bright spot on Mrs Spragg's horizon. Since the Spraggs, some two years previously, had moved from Apex City to New York, they had made little progress in establishing relations with their new environment; and when, about four months earlier, Mrs Spragg's doctor had called in Mrs Heeny to minister professionally to his patient, he had done more for her spirit than for her body. Mrs Heeny had had such 'cases' before: she knew the rich helpless family, stranded in lonely splendour in a sumptuous West Side hotel, with a father compelled to seek a semblance of social life at the hotel bar, and a mother deprived of even this contact with her kind, and reduced to illness by boredom and inactivity. Poor Mrs Spragg had done her own washing in her youth, but since her rising fortunes had made this occupation unsuitable she had sunk into the relative inertia which the ladies of Apex City regarded as one of the prerogatives of affluence. At Apex, however, she had belonged to a social club, and, until they moved to the Mealey House, had been kept busy by the incessant struggle with domestic cares; whereas New York seemed to offer no field for any form of lady-like activity. She therefore took her exercise vicariously, with Mrs Heeny's help; and Mrs Heeny knew how to manipulate her imagination as well as her muscles. It was Mrs Heeny who peopled the solitude of the long ghostly days with lively anecdotes of the Van Degens, the Driscolls, the Chauncey Ellings and the other social potentates whose least doings Mrs Spragg and Undine had followed from afar in the Apex papers, and who had come to seem so much more remote since only the width of the Central Park* divided mother and daughter from their Olympian portals.

Mrs Spragg had no ambition for herself—she seemed to have transferred her whole personality to her child—but she was passionately resolved that Undine should have what she wanted, and she sometimes fancied that Mrs Heeny, who crossed those sacred thresholds so familiarly, might some day gain admission for Undine.

'Well—I'll stay a little mite longer if you want; and supposing I was to rub up your nails while we're talking? It'll be more sociable,' the masseuse suggested, lifting her bag to the table and covering its shiny onyx surface with bottles and polishers.

Mrs Spragg consentingly slipped the rings from her small mottled hands. It was soothing to feel herself in Mrs Heeny's grasp, and though she knew the attention would cost her three dollars she was secure in the sense that Abner wouldn't mind. It had been clear to Mrs Spragg, ever since their rather precipitate departure from Apex City, that Abner was resolved not to mind—resolved at any cost to 'see through' the New York adventure. It seemed likely now that the cost would be considerable. They had lived in New York for two years without any social benefit to their daughter; and it was of course for that purpose that they had come. If, at the time, there had been other and more pressing reasons, they were such as Mrs Spragg and her husband never touched on, even in the gilded privacy of their bedroom at the Stentorian; and so completely had silence closed in on the subject that to Mrs Spragg it had become non-existent: she really believed that, as Abner put it, they had left Apex because Undine was too big for the place.

She seemed as yet—poor child!—too small for New York: actually imperceptible to its heedless multitudes; and her mother trembled for the day when her invisibility should be borne in on her. Mrs Spragg did not mind the long delay for herself—she had stores of lymphatic patience. But she had noticed lately that Undine was beginning to be nervous, and there was nothing that Undine's parents dreaded so much as her being nervous. Mrs Spragg's maternal apprehensions unconsciously escaped in her next words.

'I do hope she'll quiet down now,' she murmured, feeling quieter herself as her hand sank into Mrs Heeny's roomy palm.

'Who's that? Undine?'

'Yes. She seemed so set on that Mr Popple's coming round. From the way he acted last night she thought he'd be sure to come round this morning. She's so lonesome, poor child—I can't say as I blame her.'

'Oh, he'll come round. Things don't happen as quick as that in New York,' said Mrs Heeny, driving her nail-polisher cheeringly.

Mrs Spragg sighed again. 'They don't appear to. They say New Yorkers are always in a hurry; but I can't say as they've hurried much to make our acquaintance.'

Mrs Heeny drew back to study the effect of her work. 'You wait, Mrs Spragg, you wait. If you go too fast you sometimes have to rip out the whole seam.'

'Oh, that's so—that's *so*!' Mrs Spragg exclaimed, with a tragic emphasis that made the masseuse glance up at her.

'Of course it's so. And it's more so in New York than anywhere. The wrong set's like fly-paper: once you're in it you can pull and pull, but you'll never get out of it again.'

Undine's mother heaved another and more helpless sigh. 'I wish *you'd* tell Undine that, Mrs Heeny.'

'Oh, I guess Undine's all right. A girl like her can afford to wait. And if young Marvell's really taken with her she'll have the run of the place in no time.'

This solacing thought enabled Mrs Spragg to yield herself unreservedly to Mrs Heeny's ministrations, which were prolonged for a happy confidential hour; and she had just bidden the masseuse good-bye, and was restoring the rings to her fingers, when the door opened to admit her husband.

Mr Spragg came in silently, setting his high hat down on the centre-table, and laying his overcoat across one of the gilt chairs. He was tallish, grey-bearded and somewhat stooping, with the slack figure of the sedentary man who would be stout if he were not dyspeptic; and his cautious grey eyes with pouch-like underlids had straight black brows like his daughter's. His thin hair was worn a little too long over his coat collar, and a Masonic emblem dangled from the heavy gold chain which crossed his crumpled black waistcoat.

He stood still in the middle of the room, casting a slow pioneering glance about its gilded void; then he said gently: 'Well mother?'

Mrs Spragg remained seated, but her eyes dwelt on him affectionately.

'Undine's been asked out to a dinner-party; and Mrs Heeny says it's to one of the first families. It's the sister of one of the gentlemen that Mabel Lipscomb introduced her to last night.'

There was a mild triumph in her tone, for it was owing to her insistence and Undine's that Mr Spragg had been induced to give up the house they had bought in West End Avenue, and move with his family to the Stentorian. Undine had early decided that they could not hope to get on while they 'kept house'—all the fashionable people she knew either boarded or lived in hotels. Mrs Spragg was easily induced to take the same view, but Mr Spragg had resisted, being at the moment unable either to sell his house or to let it as advantageously as he had hoped. After the move was made it seemed for a time as though he had been right, and the first social steps would be as difficult to make in a hotel as in one's own house; and Mrs Spragg was therefore eager to have him know that Undine really owed her first invitation to a meeting under the roof of the Stentorian.

'You see we were right to come here, Abner,' she added, and he absently rejoined: 'I guess you two always manage to be right.'

But his face remained unsmiling, and instead of seating himself and lighting his cigar, as he usually did before dinner, he took two or three aimless turns about the room, and then paused in front of his wife.

'What's the matter—anything wrong down town?' she asked, her eyes reflecting his anxiety.

Mrs Spragg's knowledge of what went on 'down town' was of the most elementary kind, but her husband's face was the barometer in which she had long been accustomed to read the leave to go on unrestrictedly, or the warning to pause and abstain till the coming storm should be weathered.

He shook his head. 'N—no. Nothing worse than what I can see to, if you and Undine will go steady for a while.' He paused and looked across the room at his daughter's door. 'Where is she—out?'

'I guess she's in her room, going over her dresses with that French maid. I don't know as she's got anything fit to wear to that dinner,' Mrs Spragg added in a tentative murmur.

Mr Spragg smiled at last. 'Well—I guess she *will* have,' he said prophetically.

He glanced again at his daughter's door, as if to make sure of its being shut; then, standing close before his wife, he lowered his voice to say: 'I saw Elmer Moffatt down town to-day.'

'Oh, Abner!' A wave of almost physical apprehension passed over Mrs Spragg. Her jewelled hands trembled in her black brocade lap, and the pulpy curves of her face collapsed as if it were a pricked balloon.

'Oh, Abner,' she moaned again, her eyes also on her daughter's door.

Mr Spragg's black eyebrows gathered in an angry frown, but it was evident that his anger was not against his wife.

'What's the good of Oh Abner-ing? Elmer Moffatt's nothing to us—no more'n if we never laid eyes on him.'

'No—I know it; but what's he doing here? Did you speak to him?' she faltered.

He slipped his thumbs into his waistcoat pockets. 'No—I guess Elmer and I are pretty well talked out.'

Mrs Spragg took up her moan. 'Don't you tell her you saw him, Abner.'

'I'll do as you say; but she may meet him herself.'

'Oh, I guess not—not in this new set she's going with! Don't tell her *anyhow*.'

He turned away, feeling for one of the cigars which he always carried loose in his pocket; and his wife, rising, stole after him, and laid her hand on his arm.

'He can't do anything to her, can he?'

'Do anything to her?' He swung about furiously. 'I'd like to see him touch her—that's all!'

II

UNDINE'S white and gold bedroom, with sea-green panels and old rose carpet, looked along Seventy-second Street toward the leafless tree-tops of the Central Park.

She went to the window, and drawing back its many layers of lace gazed eastward down the long brownstone perspective. Beyond the Park lay Fifth Avenue—and Fifth Avenue was where she wanted to be!

She turned back into the room, and going to her writing-table laid Mrs Fairford's note before her, and began to study it minutely. She had read in the 'Boudoir Chat' of one of the Sunday papers that the smartest women were using the new pigeon-blood note-paper with white ink; and rather against her mother's advice she had ordered a large supply, with her monogram in silver. It was a disappointment, therefore, to find that Mrs Fairford wrote on the old-fashioned white sheet, without even a monogram—simply her address and telephone number. It gave Undine rather a poor opinion of Mrs Fairford's social standing, and for a moment she thought with considerable satisfaction of answering the note on her pigeon-blood paper. Then she remembered Mrs Heeny's emphatic commendation of Mrs Fairford, and her pen wavered. What if white paper were really newer than pigeon-blood? It might be more stylish, anyhow. Well, she didn't care if Mrs Fairford didn't like red paper—*she* did! And she wasn't going to truckle to any woman who lived in a small house down beyond Park Avenue . . .

Undine was fiercely independent and yet passionately imitative. She wanted to surprise every one by her dash and originality, but she could not help modelling herself on the last person she met, and the confusion of ideals thus produced caused her much perturbation when she had to choose between two courses. She hesitated a moment longer, and then took from the drawer a plain sheet with the hotel address.

It was amusing to write the note in her mother's name—she giggled as she formed the phrase 'I shall be happy to permit my daughter to take dinner with you' ('take dinner' seemed more elegant than Mrs Fairford's 'dine')—but when she came to the signature she was met by a new difficulty. Mrs Fairford had signed herself 'Laura Fairford'—just as one schoolgirl would write to another. But could this be a proper model for Mrs Spragg? Undine could not tolerate the thought of her mother's abasing herself to a denizen of regions beyond Park Avenue, and she resolutely formed the signature: 'Sincerely, Mrs Abner E. Spragg.' Then uncertainty overcame her, and she re-wrote her note and copied Mrs Fairford's formula: 'Yours sincerely, Leota B. Spragg.' But this struck her as an odd juxtaposition of formality and freedom, and she made a third attempt: 'Yours with love, Leota B. Spragg.' This, however, seemed excessive, as the ladies had never met; and after several other experiments she finally decided on a compromise, and ended the note:

'Yours sincerely, Mrs Leota B. Spragg.' That might be conventional, Undine reflected, but it was certainly correct.

This point settled, she flung open her door, calling imperiously down the passage: 'Céleste!' and adding, as the French maid appeared: 'I want to look over all my dinner-dresses.'

Considering the extent of Miss Spragg's wardrobe her dinner-dresses were not many. She had ordered a number the year before but, vexed at her lack of use for them, had tossed them over impatiently to the maid. Since then, indeed, she and Mrs Spragg had succumbed to the abstract pleasure of buying two or three more, simply because they were too exquisite and Undine looked too lovely in them; but she had grown tired of these also—tired of seeing them hang unworn in her wardrobe, like so many derisive points of interrogation. And now, as Céleste spread them out on the bed, they seemed disgustingly common-place, and as familiar as if she had danced them to shreds. Nevertheless, she yielded to the maid's persuasions and tried them on.

The first and second did not gain by prolonged inspection: they looked old-fashioned already. 'It's something about the sleeves,' Undine grumbled as she threw them aside.

The third was certainly the prettiest; but then it was the one she had worn at the hotel dance the night before, and the impossibility of wearing it again within the week was too obvious for discussion. Yet she enjoyed looking at herself in it, for it reminded her of her sparkling passages with Claud Walsingham Popple, and her quieter but more fruitful talk with his little friend—the young man she had hardly noticed.

'You can go, Céleste—I'll take off the dress myself,' she said: and when Céleste had passed out, laden with discarded finery, Undine bolted her door, dragged the tall pier-glass forward and, rummaging in a drawer for fan and gloves, swept to a seat before the mirror with the air of a lady arriving at an evening party. Céleste, before leaving, had drawn down the blinds and turned on the electric light, and the white and gold room, with its blazing wall-brackets, formed a sufficiently brilliant background to carry out the illusion. So untempered a glare would have been destructive to all half-tones and subtleties of modelling; but Undine's beauty was as vivid, and almost as crude, as the brightness suffusing it. Her black brows, her reddish-tawny hair and the pure red and white of her complexion defied the searching decomposing radiance: she might have been some fabled creature whose home was in a beam of light.

Undine, as a child, had taken but a lukewarm interest in the diversions of her playmates. Even in the early days when she had lived with her parents in a ragged outskirt of Apex, and hung on the fence with Indiana Frusk, the freckled daughter of the plumber 'across the way,' she had cared little for dolls or skipping-ropes, and still less for the riotous games in which the loud Indiana played Atalanta* to all the boyhood of the quarter. Already Undine's chief delight was to 'dress up' in her mother's Sunday skirt and 'play lady' before the wardrobe mirror. The taste had outlasted childhood, and she still practised the same secret pantomime, gliding in, settling her skirts, swaying her fan, moving her lips in soundless talk and laughter; but lately she had shrunk from everything that reminded her of her baffled social yearnings. Now, however, she could yield without afterthought to the joy of dramatizing her beauty. Within a few days she would be enacting the scene she was now mimicking; and it amused her to see in advance just what impression she would produce on Mrs Fairford's guests.

For a while she carried on her chat with an imaginary circle of admirers, twisting this way and that, fanning, fidgeting, twitching at her draperies, as she did in real life when people were noticing her. Her incessant movements were not the result of shyness: she thought it the correct thing to be animated in society, and noise and restlessness were her only notion of vivacity. She therefore watched herself approvingly, admiring the light on her hair, the flash of teeth between her smiling lips, the pure shadows of her throat and shoulders as she passed from one attitude to another. Only one fact disturbed her: there was a hint of too much fulness in the curves of her neck and in the spring of her hips. She was tall enough to carry off a little extra weight, but excessive slimness was the fashion, and she shuddered at the thought that she might some day deviate from the perpendicular.

Presently she ceased to twist and sparkle at her image, and sinking into her chair gave herself up to retrospection. She was vexed, in looking back, to think how little notice she had taken of young Marvell, who turned out to be so much less negligible than his brilliant friend. She remembered thinking him rather shy, less accustomed to society; and though in his quiet deprecating way he had said one or two droll things he lacked Mr Popple's masterly manner, his domineering yet caressing address. When Mr Popple had fixed his black eyes on Undine, and murmured something 'artistic' about the colour of her hair, she had thrilled to the depths of her being. Even now it seemed incredible that he should not turn out to be more distinguished than young Marvell: he seemed so much more in the key of the world she read about in the Sunday papers—the dazzling auriferous world of the Van Degens, the Driscolls and their peers.

She was roused by the sound in the hall of her mother's last words to Mrs Heeny. Undine waited till their adieux were over; then, opening her door, she seized the astonished masseuse and dragged her into the room.

Mrs Heeny gazed in admiration at the luminous apparition in whose hold she found herself.

'Mercy, Undine—you do look stunning! Are you trying on your dress for Mrs Fairford's?'

'Yes—no—this is only an old thing.' The girl's eyes glittered under their black brows. 'Mrs Heeny, you've got to tell me the truth—*are* they as swell as you said?'

'Who? The Fairfords and Marvells? If they ain't swell enough for you, Undine Spragg, you'd better go right over to the court of England!'

Undine straightened herself. 'I want the best. Are they as swell as the Driscolls and Van Degens?'

Mrs Heeny sounded a scornful laugh. 'Look at here, now, you unbelieving girl! As sure as I'm standing here before you, I've seen Mrs Harmon B. Driscoll of Fifth Avenue laying in her pink velvet bed with Honiton lace sheets on it, and crying her eyes out because she couldn't get asked to one of Mrs Paul Marvell's musicals. She'd never 'a dreamt of being asked to a dinner there! Not all of her money couldn't 'a bought her that—and she knows it!'

Undine stood for a moment with bright cheeks and parted lips; then she flung her soft arms about the masseuse.

'Oh, Mrs Heeny—you're lovely to me!' she breathed, her lips on Mrs Heeny's rusty veil; while the latter, freeing herself with a good-natured laugh, said as she turned away: 'Go steady, Undine, and you'll get anywheres.'

Go steady, Undine! Yes, that was the advice she needed. Sometimes, in her dark moods, she blamed her parents for not having given it to her. She was so young . . . and they had told her so little! As she looked back she shuddered at some of her escapes. Even since they had come to New York she had been on the verge of one or two perilous adventures, and there had been a moment during their first winter when she had actually engaged herself to the handsome Austrian riding-master who accompanied her in the Park. He had carelessly shown her a card-case with a coronet, and had confided in her that he had been forced to resign from a crack cavalry regiment for fighting a duel about a Countess; and as a result of these confidences she had pledged herself to him, and bestowed on him her pink pearl ring in exchange for one of twisted silver, which he said the Countess had given him on her deathbed with the request that he should never take it off till he met a woman more beautiful than herself.

Soon afterward, luckily, Undine had run across Mabel Lipscomb, whom she had known at a middle western boarding-school as Mabel Blitch. Miss Blitch occupied a position of distinction as the only New York girl at the school, and for a time there had been sharp rivalry for her favour between Undine and Indiana Frusk, whose parents had somehow contrived—for one term—to obtain her admission to the same establishment. In spite of Indiana's unscrupulous methods, and of a certain violent way she had of capturing attention, the victory remained with Undine, whom Mabel pronounced more refined; and the discomfited Indiana, denouncing her schoolmates as a 'bunch of mushes,' had disappeared forever from the scene of her defeat.

Since then Mabel had returned to New York and married a stock-broker; and Undine's first steps in social enlightenment dated from the day when she had met Mrs Harry Lipscomb, and been again taken under her wing.

Harry Lipscomb had insisted on investigating the riding-master's record, and had found that his real name was Aaronson, and that he had left Cracow under a charge of swindling servant-girls out of their savings; in the light of which discoveries Undine noticed for the first time that his lips were too red and that his hair was pommaded. That was one of the episodes that sickened her as she looked back, and made her resolve once more to trust less to her impulses—especially in the matter of giving away rings. In the interval, however, she felt she had learned a good deal, especially since, by Mabel Lipscomb's advice, the Spraggs had moved to the Stentorian, where that lady was herself established.

There was nothing of the monopolist about Mabel, and she lost no time in making Undine free of the Stentorian group and its affiliated branches: a society addicted to 'days,' and linked together by membership in countless clubs, mundane, cultural or 'earnest.' Mabel took Undine to the days, and introduced her as a 'guest' to the club-meetings, where she was supported by the presence of many other guests—'my friend Miss Stager, of Phalanx, Georgia,' or (if the lady were literary) simply 'my friend Ora Prance Chettle of Nebraska—you know what Mrs Chettle stands for.'

Some of these reunions took place in the lofty hotels moored like a sonorously named fleet of battle-ships along the upper reaches of the West Side: the Olympian, the Incandescent, the Ormolu; while others, perhaps the more exclusive, were held in the equally lofty but more romantically styled apartment-houses: the Parthenon, the Tintern Abbey or the Lido. Undine's pref-erence was for the worldly parties, at which games were played, and she returned home laden with prizes in Dutch silver;* but she was duly impressed by the debating clubs, where ladies of local distinction addressed the company from an improvised platform, or the members argued on subjects of such imperish-able interest as: 'What is charm?' or 'The Problem-Novel'—after which pink lemonade and rainbow sandwiches* were consumed amid heated discussion of the 'ethical aspect' of the question.

It was all very novel and interesting, and at first Undine envied Mabel Lipscomb for having made herself a place in such circles; but in time she began to despise her for being content to remain there. For it did not take Undine long to learn that introduction to Mabel's 'set' had brought her no nearer to Fifth Avenue. Even in Apex, Undine's tender imagination had been nurtured on the feats and gestures of Fifth Avenue. She knew all of New York's golden aristocracy by name, and the lineaments of its most distinguished scions had been made familiar by passionate poring over the daily press. In Mabel's world she sought in vain for the originals, and only now and then caught a tantalizing glimpse of one of their familiars: as when Claud Walsingham Popple, engaged on the portrait of a lady whom the Lipscombs described as 'the wife of a Steel Magnet,' felt it his duty to attend one of his client's teas, where it became Mabel's privilege to make his acquaintance and to name to him her friend Miss Spragg.

Unsuspected social gradations were thus revealed to the attentive Undine, but she was beginning to think that her sad proficiency had been acquired in vain when her hopes were revived by the appearance of Mr Popple and his friend at the Stentorian dance. She thought she had learned enough to be safe from any risk of repeating the hideous Aaronson mistake; yet she now saw she had blundered again in distinguishing Claud Walsingham Popple while she almost snubbed his more retiring companion. It was all very puzzling, and her perplexity had been farther increased by Mrs Heeny's tale of the great Mrs Harmon B. Driscoll's despair.

Hitherto Undine had imagined that the Driscoll and Van Degen clans and their allies held undisputed suzerainty over New York society. Mabel Lipscomb thought so too, and was given to bragging of her acquaintance with a Mrs Spoff, who was merely a second cousin of Mrs Harmon B. Driscoll's. Yet here was she, Undine Spragg of Apex, about to be introduced into an inner circle to which Driscolls and Van Degens had laid siege in vain! It was enough to make her feel a little dizzy with her triumph—to work her up into that state of perilous self-confidence in which all her worst follies had been committed.

She stood up and, going close to the glass, examined the reflection of her bright eyes and glowing cheeks. This time her fears were superfluous: there were to be no more mistakes and no more follies now! She was going to know the right people at last—she was going to get what she wanted!

As she stood there, smiling at her happy image, she heard her father's voice in the room beyond, and instantly began to tear off her dress, strip the long gloves from her arms and unpin the rose in her hair. Tossing the fallen finery aside, she slipped on a dressing-gown and opened the door into the drawing-room.

Mr Spragg was standing near her mother, who sat in a drooping attitude, her head sunk on her breast, as she did when she had one of her 'turns.' He looked up abruptly as Undine entered.

'Father—has mother told you? Mrs Fairford has asked me to dine. She's Mrs Paul Marvell's daughter—Mrs Marvell was a Dagonet—and they're sweller than anybody; they *won't know* the Driscolls and Van Degens!'

Mr Spragg surveyed her with humorous fondness.

'That so? What do they want to know you for, I wonder?' he jeered.

'Can't imagine—unless they think I'll introduce *you*!' she jeered back in the same key, her arms around his stooping shoulders, her shining hair against his cheek.

'Well—and are you going to? Have you accepted?' he took up her joke as she held him pinioned; while Mrs Spragg, behind them, stirred in her seat with a little moan.

Undine threw back her head, plunging her eyes in his, and pressing so close that to his tired elderly sight her face was a mere bright blur.

'I want to awfully,' she declared, 'but I haven't got a single thing to wear.'

Mrs Spragg, at this, moaned more audibly. 'Undine, I wouldn't ask father to buy any more clothes right on top of those last bills.'

'I ain't on top of those last bills yet—I'm way down under them,' Mr Spragg interrupted, raising his hands to imprison his daughter's slender wrists.

'Oh, well—if you want me to look like a scarecrow, and not get asked again, I've got a dress that'll do *perfectly*,' Undine threatened, in a tone between banter and vexation.

Mr Spragg held her away at arm's length, a smile drawing up the loose wrinkles about his eyes.

'Well, that kind of dress might come in mighty handy on *some* occasions; so I guess you'd better hold on to it for future use, and go and select another for this Fairford dinner,' he said; and before he could finish he was in her arms again, and she was smothering his last word in little cries and kisses.

III

THOUGH she would not for the world have owned it to her parents, Undine was disappointed in the Fairford dinner.

The house, to begin with, was small and rather shabby. There was no gilding, no lavish diffusion of light: the room they sat in after dinner, with its green-shaded lamps making faint pools of brightness, and its rows of books from floor to ceiling, reminded Undine of the old circulating library at Apex, before the new marble building was put up. Then, instead of a gas-log, or a polished grate with electric bulbs behind ruby glass, there was an old-fashioned wood-fire, like pictures of 'Back to the farm for Christmas'; and when the logs fell forward Mrs Fairford or her brother had to jump up to push them in place, and the ashes scattered over the hearth untidily.

The dinner too was disappointing. Undine was too young to take note of culinary details, but she had expected to view the company through a bower of orchids and eat pretty-coloured *entrées* in ruffled papers. Instead, there was only a low centre-dish of ferns, and plain roasted and broiled meat that one could recognize—as if they'd been dyspeptics on a diet! With all the hints in the Sunday papers, she thought it dull of Mrs Fairford not to have picked up something newer; and as the evening progressed she began to suspect that it wasn't a real 'dinner party,' and that they had just asked her in to share what they had when they were alone.

But a glance about the table convinced her that Mrs Fairford could not have meant to treat her other guests so lightly. They were only eight in number, but one was no less a person than young Mrs Peter Van Degen—the one who had been a Dagonet—and the consideration which this young lady, herself one of the choicest ornaments of the Society Column, displayed toward the rest of the company, convinced Undine that they must be more important than they looked. She liked Mrs Fairford, a small incisive woman, with a big nose and good teeth revealed by frequent smiles. In her dowdy black and antiquated ornaments she was not what Undine would have called 'stylish'; but she had a droll kind way which reminded the girl of her father's manner when he was not tired or worried about money. One of the other ladies, having white hair, did not long arrest Undine's attention; and the fourth, a girl like herself, who was introduced as Miss Harriet Ray, she dismissed at a glance as plain and wearing a last year's 'model.' The men, too, were less striking than she had hoped. She had not expected much of Mr Fairford, since married men were intrinsically uninteresting, and his baldness and grey moustache seemed naturally to relegate him to the background; but she had looked for some brilliant youths of her own age—in her inmost heart she had looked for Mr Popple. He was not there, however, and of the other men one, whom they called Mr Bowen, was hopelessly elderly—she supposed he was the husband of the white-haired lady—and the other two, who seemed to be friends of young Marvell's, were both lacking in Claud Walsingham's dash.

Undine sat between Mr Bowen and young Marvell, who struck her as very 'sweet' (it was her word for friendliness), but even shyer than at the hotel dance. Yet she was not sure if he were shy, or if his quietness were only a new kind of self-possession which expressed itself negatively instead of aggressively. Small, well-knit, fair, he sat stroking his slight blond moustache and looking at her with kindly, almost tender eyes; but he left it to his sister and the others to draw her out and fit her into the pattern.

Mrs Fairford talked so well that the girl wondered why Mrs Heeny had found her lacking in conversation. But though Undine thought silent people awkward she was not easily impressed by verbal fluency. All the ladies in Apex City were more voluble than Mrs Fairford, and had a larger vocabulary: the difference was that with Mrs Fairford conversation seemed to be a concert and not a solo. She kept drawing in the others, giving each a turn, beating time for them with her smile, and somehow harmonizing and linking together what they said. She took particular pains to give Undine her due part in the performance; but the girl's expansive impulses were always balanced by odd reactions of mistrust, and to-night the latter prevailed. She meant to watch and listen without letting herself go, and she sat very straight and pink, answering promptly but briefly, with the nervous laugh that punctuated all her phrases—saying 'I don't care if I do' when her host asked her to try some grapes, and 'I wouldn't wonder' when she thought any one was trying to astonish her.

This state of lucidity enabled her to take note of all that was being said. The talk ran more on general questions, and less on people, than she was used to; but though the allusions to pictures and books escaped her, she caught and stored up every personal reference, and the pink in her cheeks deepened at a random mention of Mr Popple.

'Yes—he's doing me,' Mrs Peter Van Degen was saying, in her slightly drawling voice. 'He's doing everybody this year, you know——'

'As if that were a reason!' Undine heard Mrs Fairford breathe to Mr Bowen; who replied, at the same pitch: 'It's a Van Degen reason, isn't it?'—to which Mrs Fairford shrugged assentingly.

'That delightful Popple—he paints so exactly as he talks!' the white-haired lady took it up. 'All his portraits seem to proclaim what a gentleman he is, and how he fascinates women! They're not pictures of Mrs or Miss So-and-so, but simply of the impression Popple thinks he's made on them.'

Mrs Fairford smiled. 'I've sometimes thought,' she mused, 'that Mr Popple must be the only gentleman I know; at least he's the only man who has ever told me he was a gentleman—and Mr Popple never fails to mention it.'

Undine's ear was too well attuned to the national note of irony for her not to perceive that her companions were making sport of the painter. She winced at their banter as if it had been at her own expense, yet it gave her a dizzy sense of being at last in the very stronghold of fashion. Her attention was diverted by hearing Mrs Van Degen, under cover of the general laugh, say in a low tone to young Marvell: 'I thought you liked his things, or I wouldn't have had him paint me.'

Something in her tone made all Undine's perceptions bristle, and she strained her ears for the answer.

'I think he'll do you capitally—you must let me come and see some day soon.' Marvell's tone was always so light, so unemphasized, that she could not be sure of its being as indifferent as it sounded. She looked down at the fruit on her plate and shot a side-glance through her lashes at Mrs Peter Van Degen.

Mrs Van Degen was neither beautiful nor imposing: just a dark girlish-looking creature with plaintive eyes and a fidgety frequent laugh. But she was more elaborately dressed and jewelled than the other ladies, and her elegance and her restlessness made her seem less alien to Undine. She had turned on Marvell a gaze at once pleading and possessive; but whether betokening merely an inherited intimacy (Undine had noticed that they were all more or less cousins) or a more personal feeling, her observer was unable to decide; just as the tone of the young man's reply might have expressed the open avowal of good-fellowship or the disguise of a different sentiment. All was blurred and puzzling to the girl in this world of half-lights, half-tones, eliminations and abbreviations; and she felt a violent longing to brush away the cobwebs and assert herself as the dominant figure of the scene.

Yet in the drawing-room, with the ladies, where Mrs Fairford came and sat by her, the spirit of caution once more prevailed. She wanted to be noticed but she dreaded to be patronized, and here again her hostess's gradations of tone were confusing. Mrs Fairford made no tactless allusions to her being a newcomer in New York—there was nothing as bitter to the girl as that—but her questions as to what pictures had interested Undine at the various exhibitions of the moment, and which of the new books she had read, were almost as open to suspicion, since they had to be answered in the negative. Undine did not even know that there were any pictures to be seen, much less that 'people' went to see them; and she had read no new book but 'When The Kissing Had to Stop.'* of which Mrs Fairford seemed not to have heard. On the theatre they were equally at odds, for while Undine had seen 'Oolaloo' fourteen times, and was 'wild' about Ned Norris* in 'The Soda-Water Fountain,' she had not heard of the famous Berlin comedians who were performing Shakespeare at the German Theatre,* and knew only by name the clever American actress* who was trying to give 'repertory' plays with a good stock company. The conversation was revived for a moment by her recalling that she had seen Sarah Burnhard in a play she called 'Leg-long,' and another which she pronounced 'Fade';* but even this did not carry them far, as she had forgotten what both plays were about and had found the actress a good deal older* than she expected.

Matters were not improved by the return of the men from the smoking-room. Henley Fairford replaced his wife at Undine's side; and since it was unheard-of at Apex for a married man to force his society on a young girl, she inferred that the others didn't care to talk to her, and that her host and hostess were in league to take her off their hands. This discovery resulted in her holding her vivid head very high, and answering 'I couldn't really say,' or 'Is that so?' to all Mr Fairford's ventures; and as these were neither numerous nor striking it was a relief to both when the rising of the elderly lady gave the signal for departure.

In the hall, where young Marvell had managed to precede her, Undine found Mrs Van Degen putting on her cloak. As she gathered it about her she laid her hand on Marvell's arm.

'Ralphie, dear, you'll come to the opera with me on Friday? We'll dine together first—Peter's got a club dinner.' They exchanged what seemed a smile of intelligence, and Undine heard the young man accept. Then Mrs Van Degen turned to her.

'Good-bye, Miss Spragg. I hope you'll come——'

'—to dine with me too?' That must be what she was going to say, and Undine's heart gave a bound.

'—to see me some afternoon,' Mrs Van Degen ended, going down the steps to her motor, at the door of which a much-furred footman waited with more furs on his arm.

Undine's face burned as she turned to receive her cloak. When she had drawn it on with haughty deliberation she found Marvell at her side, in hat and overcoat, and her heart gave a higher bound. He was going to 'escort' her home, of course! This brilliant youth—she felt now that he *was* brilliant—who dined alone with married women, whom the 'Van Degen set' called 'Ralphie, dear,' had really no eyes for any one but herself; and at the thought her lost self-complacency flowed back warm through her veins.

The street was coated with ice, and she had a delicious moment descending the steps on Marvell's arm, and holding it fast while they waited for her cab to come up; but when he had helped her in he closed the door and held his hand out over the lowered window.

'Good-bye,' he said, smiling; and she could not help the break of pride in her voice, as she faltered out stupidly, from the depths of her disillusionment: 'Oh—good-bye.'

IV

'FATHER, you've got to take a box for me at the opera next Friday.'

From the tone of her voice Undine's parents knew at once that she was 'nervous.'

They had counted a great deal on the Fairford dinner as a means of tranquillization, and it was a blow to detect signs of the opposite result when, late the next morning, their daughter came dawdling into the sodden splendour of the Stentorian breakfast-room.

The symptoms of Undine's nervousness were unmistakable to Mr and Mrs Spragg. They could read the approaching storm in the darkening of her eyes from limpid grey to slate-colour, and in the way her straight black brows met above them and the red curves of her lips narrowed to a parallel line below.

Mr Spragg, having finished the last course of his heterogeneous meal, was adjusting his gold eye-glasses for a glance at the paper when Undine trailed down the sumptuous stuffy room, where coffee-fumes hung perpetually under the emblazoned ceiling and the spongy carpet might have absorbed a year's crumbs without a sweeping.

About them sat other pallid families, richly dressed, and silently eating their way through a bill-of-fare which seemed to have ransacked the globe for gastronomic incompatibilities; and in the middle of the room a knot of equally pallid waiters, engaged in languid conversation, turned their backs by common consent on the persons they were supposed to serve.

Undine, who rose too late to share the family breakfast, usually had her chocolate brought to her in bed by Céleste, after the manner described in the articles on 'A Society Woman's Day' which were appearing in *Boudoir Chat*. Her mere appearance in the restaurant therefore prepared her parents for those symptoms of excessive tension which a nearer inspection confirmed, and Mr Spragg folded his paper and hooked his glasses to his waistcoat with the air of a man who prefers to know the worst and have it over.

'An opera box!' faltered Mrs Spragg, pushing aside the bananas and cream with which she had been trying to tempt an appetite too languid for fried liver or crab mayonnaise.

'A parterre box,' Undine corrected, ignoring the exclamation, and continuing to address herself to her father. 'Friday's the stylish night, and that new tenor's going to sing again in "Cavaleeria," '* she condescended to explain.

'That so?' Mr Spragg thrust his hands into his waistcoat pockets, and began to tilt his chair till he remembered there was no wall to meet it. He regained his balance and said: 'Wouldn't a couple of good orchestra seats do you?'

'No; they wouldn't,' Undine answered with a darkening brow.

He looked at her humorously. 'You invited the whole dinner-party, I suppose?'

'No—no one.'

'Going all alone in a box?' She was disdainfully silent. 'I don't s'pose you're thinking of taking mother and me?'

This was so obviously comic that they all laughed—even Mrs Spragg—and Undine went on more mildly: 'I want to do something for Mabel Lipscomb: make some return. She's always taking me 'round, and I've never done a thing for her—not a single thing.'

This appeal to the national belief in the duty of reciprocal 'treating' could not fail of its effect, and Mrs Spragg murmured: 'She never *has*, Abner,'—but Mr Spragg's brow remained unrelenting.

'Do you know what a box costs?'

'No; but I s'pose you do,' Undine returned with unconscious flippancy.

'I do. That's the trouble. *Why* won't seats do you?'

'Mabel could buy seats for herself.'

'That's so,' interpolated Mrs Spragg—always the first to succumb to her daughter's arguments.

'Well, I guess I can't buy a box for her.'

Undine's face gloomed more deeply. She sat silent, her chocolate thickening in the cup, while one hand, almost as much beringed as her mother's, drummed on the crumpled table-cloth.

'We might as well go straight back to Apex,' she breathed at last between her teeth.

Mrs Spragg cast a frightened glance at her husband. These struggles between two resolute wills always brought on her palpitations, and she wished she had her phial of digitalis with her.

'A parterre box costs a hundred and twenty-five dollars a night,' said Mr Spragg, transferring a tooth-pick to his waistcoat pocket.

'I only want it once.'

He looked at her with a quizzical puckering of his crow's-feet. 'You only want most things once, Undine.'

It was an observation they had made in her earliest youth—Undine never wanted anything long, but she wanted it 'right off.' And until she got it the house was uninhabitable.

'I'd a good deal rather have a box for the season,' she rejoined, and he saw the opening he had given her. She had two ways of getting things out of him against his principles; the tender wheedling way, and the harsh-lipped and cold—and he did not know which he dreaded most. As a child they had admired her assertiveness, had made Apex ring with their boasts of it; but it had long since cowed Mrs Spragg, and it was beginning to frighten her husband.

'Fact is, Undie,' he said, weakening, 'I'm a little mite strapped just this month.'

Her eyes grew absent-minded, as they always did when he alluded to business. *That* was man's province; and what did men go 'down town' for but to bring back the spoils to their women? She rose abruptly, leaving her parents seated, and said, more to herself than the others: 'Think I'll go for a ride.'

'Oh, Undine!' fluttered Mrs Spragg. She always had palpitations when Undine rode, and since the Aaronson episode her fears were not confined to what the horse might do.

'Why don't you take your mother out shopping a little?' Mr Spragg suggested, conscious of the limitation of his resources.

Undine made no answer, but swept down the room, and out of the door ahead of her mother, with scorn and anger in every line of her arrogant young back. Mrs Spragg tottered meekly after her, and Mr Spragg lounged out into the marble hall to buy a cigar before taking the Subway to his office.

Undine went for a ride, not because she felt particularly disposed for the exercise, but because she wished to discipline her mother. She was almost sure she would get her opera box, but she did not see why she should have to struggle for her rights, and she was especially annoyed with Mrs Spragg for seconding her so half-heartedly. If she and her mother did not hold together in such crises she would have twice the work to do.

Undine hated 'scenes': she was essentially peace-loving, and would have preferred to live on terms of unbroken harmony with her parents. But she could not help it if they were unreasonable. Ever since she could remember there had been 'fusses' about money; yet she and her mother had always got what they wanted, apparently without lasting detriment to the family fortunes. It was therefore natural to conclude that there were ample funds to draw upon, and that Mr Spragg's occasional resistances were merely due to an imperfect understanding of what constituted the necessities of life.

When she returned from her ride Mrs Spragg received her as if she had come back from the dead. It was absurd, of course; but Undine was inured to the absurdity of parents.

'Has father telephoned?' was her first brief question.

'No, he hasn't yet.'

Undine's lips tightened, but she proceeded deliberately with the removal of her habit.

'You'd think I'd asked him to buy me the Opera House, the way he's acting over a single box,' she muttered, flinging aside her smartly-fitting coat.

Mrs Spragg received the flying garment and smoothed it out on the bed. Neither of the ladies could 'bear' to have their maid about when they were at their toilet, and Mrs Spragg had always performed these ancillary services for Undine.

'You know, Undie, father hasn't always got the money in his pocket, and the bills have been pretty heavy lately. Father was a rich man for Apex, but that's different from being rich in New York.'

She stood before her daughter, looking down on her appealingly.

Undine, who had seated herself while she detached her stock and waistcoat, raised her head with an impatient jerk. 'Why on earth did we ever leave Apex, then?' she exclaimed.

Mrs Spragg's eyes usually dropped before her daughter's inclement gaze; but on this occasion they held their own with a kind of awe-struck courage, till Undine's lids sank above her flushing cheeks.

She sprang up, tugging at the waistband of her habit, while Mrs Spragg, relapsing from temerity to meekness, hovered about her with obstructive zeal.

'If you'd only just let go of my skirt, mother—I can unhook it twice as quick myself.'

Mrs Spragg drew back, understanding that her presence was no longer wanted. But on the threshold she paused, as if over-ruled by a stronger influence, and said, with a last look at her daughter: 'You didn't meet anybody when you were out, did you, Undie?'

Undine's brows drew together: she was struggling with her long patent-leather boot.

'Meet anybody? Do you mean anybody I know? I don't *know* anybody—I never shall, if father can't afford to let me go round with people!'

The boot was off with a wrench, and she flung it violently across the old-rose carpet, while Mrs Spragg, turning away to hide a look of inexpressible relief, slipped discreetly from the room.

The day wore on. Undine had meant to go down and tell Mabel Lipscomb about the Fairford dinner, but its aftertaste was flat on her lips. What would it lead to? Nothing, as far as she could see. Ralph Marvell had not even asked when he might call; and she was ashamed to confess to Mabel that he had not driven home with her.

Suddenly she decided that she would go and see the pictures of which Mrs Fairford had spoken. Perhaps she might meet some of the people she had seen at dinner—from their talk one might have imagined that they spent their lives in picture-galleries.

The thought reanimated her, and she put on her handsomest furs, and a hat for which she had not yet dared present the bill to her father. It was the fashionable hour in Fifth Avenue, but Undine knew none of the ladies who were bowing to each other from interlocked motors. She had to content herself with the gaze of admiration which she left in her wake along the pavement; but she was used to the homage of the streets and her vanity craved a choicer fare.

When she reached the art gallery which Mrs Fairford had named she found it even more crowded than Fifth Avenue; and some of the ladies and gentlemen wedged before the pictures had the 'look' which signified social consecration. As Undine made her way among them, she was aware of attracting almost as much notice as in the street, and she flung herself into rapt attitudes before the canvases, scribbling notes in the catalogue in imitation of a tall girl in sables, while ripples of self-consciousness played up and down her watchful back.

Presently her attention was drawn to a lady in black who was examining the pictures through a tortoise-shell eye-glass adorned with diamonds and hanging from a long pearl chain.

Undine was instantly struck by the opportunities which this toy presented for graceful wrist movements and supercilious turns of the head. It seemed suddenly plebeian and promiscuous to look at the world with a naked eye, and all her floating desires were merged in the wish for a jewelled eye-glass and chain. So violent was this wish that, drawn on in the wake of the owner of the eye-glass, she found herself inadvertently bumping against a stout tight-coated young man whose impact knocked her catalogue from her hand.

As the young man picked the catalogue up and held it out to her she noticed that his bulging eyes and queer retreating face were suffused with a glow of admiration. He was so unpleasant-looking that she would have resented his homage had not his odd physiognomy called up some vaguely agreeable association of ideas. Where had she seen before this grotesque saurian head, with eye-lids as thick as lips and lips as thick as ear-lobes? It fled before her down a perspective of innumerable newspaper portraits, all, like the original before her, tightly coated, with a huge pearl transfixing a silken tie . . .

'Oh, thank you,' she murmured, all gleams and graces, while he stood hat in hand, saying sociably: 'The crowd's simply awful, isn't it?'

At the same moment the lady of the eye-glass drifted closer, and with a tap of her wand, and a careless 'Peter, look at this,' swept him to the other side of the gallery.

Undine's heart was beating excitedly, for as he turned away she had identified him. Peter Van Degen—who could he be but young Peter Van Degen, the son of the great banker, Thurber Van Degen, the husband of Ralph Marvell's cousin, the hero of 'Sunday Supplements,' the captor of Blue Ribbons at Horse-Shows, of Gold Cups at Motor Races, the owner of winning race-horses and 'crack' sloops: the supreme exponent, in short, of those crowning arts that made all life seem stale and unprofitable outside the magic ring of the Society Column?

Undine smiled as she recalled the look with which his pale protruding eyes had rested on her—it almost consoled her for his wife's indifference!

When she reached home she found that she could not remember anything about the pictures she had seen . . .

There was no message from her father, and a reaction of disgust set in. Of what good were such encounters if they were to have no sequel? She would probably never meet Peter Van Degen again—or, if she *did* run across him in the same accidental way, she knew they could not continue their conversation without being 'introduced.' What was the use of being beautiful and attracting attention if one were perpetually doomed to relapse again into the obscure mass of the Uninvited?

Her gloom was not lightened by finding Ralph Marvell's card on the drawing-room table. She thought it unflattering and almost impolite of him to call without making an appointment: it seemed to show that he did not wish to continue their acquaintance. But as she tossed the card aside her mother said: 'He was real sorry not to see you, Undine—he sat here nearly an hour.'

Undine's attention was roused. 'Sat here—all alone? Didn't you tell him I was out?'

'Yes—but he came up all the same. He asked for me.'

'Asked for *you*?'

The social order seemed to be falling in ruins at Undine's feet. A visitor who asked for a girl's mother!—she stared at Mrs Spragg with cold incredulity. 'What makes you think he did?'

'Why, they told me so. I telephoned down that you were out, and they said he'd asked for me.' Mrs Spragg let the fact speak for itself—it was too much out of the range of her experience to admit of even a hypothetical explanation.

Undine shrugged her shoulders. 'It was a mistake, of course. Why on earth did you let him come up?'

'I thought maybe he had a message for you, Undie.'

This plea struck her daughter as not without weight.

'Well, did he?' she asked, drawing out her hat-pins and tossing down her hat on the onyx table.

'Why, no—he just conversed. He was lovely to me, but I couldn't make out what he was after,' Mrs Spragg was obliged to own.

Her daughter looked at her with a kind of chill commiseration. 'You never *can*,' she murmured, turning away.

She stretched herself out moodily on one of the pink and gold sofas, and lay there brooding, an unread novel on her knee. Mrs Spragg timidly slipped a cushion under her daughter's head, and then dissembled herself behind the lace window-curtains and sat watching the lights spring out down the long street and spread their glittering net across the Park. It was one of Mrs Spragg's chief occupations to watch the nightly lighting of New York.

Undine lay silent, her hands clasped behind her head. She was plunged in one of the moods of bitter retrospection when all her past seemed like a long struggle for something she could not have, from a trip to Europe to an opera-box; and when she felt sure that, as the past had been, so the future would be. And yet, as she had often told her parents, all she sought for was improvement: she honestly wanted the best.

Her first struggle—after she had ceased to scream for candy, or sulk for a new toy—had been to get away from Apex in summer. Her summers, as she looked back on them, seemed to typify all that was dreariest and most exasperating in her life. The earliest had been spent in the yellow 'frame' cottage where she had hung on the fence, kicking her toes against the broken palings and exchanging moist chewing-gum and half-eaten apples with Indiana Frusk. Later on, she had returned from her boarding-school to the comparative gentility of summer vacations at the Mealey House, whither her parents, forsaking their squalid suburb, had moved in the first flush of their rising fortunes. The tessellated floors, the plush parlours and organ-like radiators of the Mealey House had, aside from their intrinsic elegance, the immense advantage of lifting the Spraggs high above the Frusks, and making it possible for Undine, when she met Indiana in the street or at school, to chill her advances by a careless allusion to the splendours of hotel life. But even in such a setting, and in spite of the social superiority it implied, the long months of the middle western summer, fly-blown, torrid, exhaling stale odours, soon became as insufferable as they had been in the little yellow house.

At school Undine met other girls whose parents took them to the Great Lakes for August; some even went to California, others—oh bliss ineffable!—went 'east.'

Pale and listless under the stifling boredom of the Mealey House routine, Undine secretly sucked lemons, nibbled slate-pencils and drank pints of bitter coffee to aggravate her look of ill-health; and when she learned that even Indiana Frusk was to go on a month's visit to Buffalo it needed no artificial aids to emphasize the ravages of envy. Her parents, alarmed by her appearance, were at last convinced of the necessity of change, and timidly, tentatively, they transferred themselves for a month to a staring hotel on a glaring lake.

There Undine enjoyed the satisfaction of sending ironic post-cards to Indiana, and discovering that she could more than hold her own against the youth and beauty of the other visitors. Then she made the acquaintance of a pretty woman from Richmond, whose husband, a mining engineer, had brought her west with him while he inspected the newly developed Eubaw mines; and the southern visitor's dismay, her repugnances, her recoil from the faces, the food, the amusements, the general bareness and stridency of the scene, were a terrible initiation to Undine. There was something still better beyond, then—more luxurious, more exciting, more worthy of her! She once said to herself, afterward, that it was always her fate to find out just too late about the 'something beyond.' But in this case it was not too late—and obstinately, inflexibly, she set herself to the task of forcing her parents to take her 'east' the next summer.

Yielding to the inevitable, they suffered themselves to be impelled to a Virginia 'resort,' where Undine had her first glimpse of more romantic possibilities—leafy moonlight rides and drives, picnics in mountain glades, and an atmosphere of Christmas-chromo* sentimentality that tempered her hard edges a little, and gave her glimpses of a more delicate kind of pleasure. But here again everything was spoiled by a peep through another door. Undine, after a first mustering of the other girls in the hotel, had, as usual, found herself easily first—till the arrival, from Washington, of Mr and Mrs Wincher and their daughter. Undine was much handsomer than Miss Wincher, but she saw at a glance that she did not know how to use her beauty as the other used her plainness. She was exasperated, too, by the discovery that Miss Wincher seemed not only unconscious of any possible rivalry between them, but actually unaware of her existence. Listless, long-faced, supercilious, the young lady from Washington sat apart reading novels or playing solitaire with her parents, as though the huge hotel's loud life of gossip and flirtation were invisible and inaudible to her. Undine never even succeeded in catching her eye: she always lowered it to her book when the Apex beauty trailed or rattled past her secluded corner. But one day an acquaintance of the Winchers' turned up—a lady from Boston, who had come to Virginia on a botanizing tour; and from scraps of Miss Wincher's conversation with the newcomer, Undine, straining her ears behind a column of the long veranda, obtained a new glimpse into the unimagined.

The Winchers, it appeared, found themselves at Potash Springs merely because a severe illness of Mrs Wincher's had made it impossible, at the last moment, to move her farther from Washington. They had let their house on the North Shore, and as soon as they could leave 'this dreadful hole' were going to Europe for the autumn. Miss Wincher simply didn't know how she got through the days; though no doubt it was as good as a rest-cure after the rush of the winter. Of course they would have preferred to hire a house, but the 'hole,' if one could believe it, didn't offer one; so they had simply shut themselves off as best they could from the 'hotel crew'—had her friend, Miss Wincher parenthetically asked, happened to notice the Sunday young men? They were queerer even than the 'belles' they came for—and had escaped the promiscuity of the dinner-hour by turning one of their rooms into a dining-room, and picnicking there—with the Persimmon House standards, one couldn't describe it in any other way! But luckily the awful place was doing mamma good, and now they had nearly served their term . . .

Undine turned sick as she listened. Only the evening before she had gone on a 'buggy-ride' with a young gentleman from Deposit—a dentist's assistant—and had let him kiss her, and given him the flower from her hair. She loathed the thought of him now: she loathed all the people about her, and most of all the disdainful Miss Wincher. It enraged her to think that the

Winchers classed her with the 'hotel crew'—with the 'belles' who awaited their Sunday young men. The place was forever blighted for her, and the next week she dragged her amazed but thankful parents back to Apex.

But Miss Wincher's depreciatory talk had opened ampler vistas, and the pioneer blood in Undine would not let her rest. She had heard the call of the Atlantic seaboard, and the next summer found the Spraggs at Skog Harbour, Maine. Even now Undine felt a shiver of boredom as she recalled it. That summer had been the worst of all. The bare wind-beaten inn, all shingles without and blueberry pie within, was 'exclusive,' parochial, Bostonian; and the Spraggs wore through the interminable weeks in blank unmitigated isolation. The incomprehensible part of it was that every other woman in the hotel was plain, dowdy or elderly—and most of them all three. If there had been any competition on ordinary lines Undine would have won, as Van Degen said, 'hands down.' But there wasn't—the other 'guests' simply formed a cold impenetrable group who walked, boated, played golf, and discussed Christian Science and the Subliminal, unaware of the tremulous organism drifting helplessly against their rock-bound circle.

It was on the day the Spraggs left Skog Harbour that Undine vowed to herself with set lips: 'I'll never try anything again till I try New York.' Now she had gained her point and tried New York, and so far, it seemed, with no better success. From small things to great, everything went against her. In such hours of self-searching she was ready enough to acknowledge her own mistakes, but they exasperated her less than the blunders of her parents. She was sure, for instance, that she was on what Mrs Heeny called 'the right tack' at last: yet just at the moment when her luck seemed about to turn she was to be thwarted by her father's stupid obstinacy about the opera-box . . .

She lay brooding over these things till long after Mrs Spragg had gone away to dress for dinner, and it was nearly eight o'clock when she heard her father's dragging tread in the hall.

She kept her eyes fixed on her book while he entered the room and moved about behind her, laying aside his hat and overcoat; then his steps came close and a small parcel dropped on the pages of her book.

'Oh, father!' She sprang up, all alight, the novel on the floor, her fingers twitching for the tickets. But a substantial packet emerged, like nothing she had ever seen. She looked at it, hoping, fearing—she beamed blissful interrogation on her father while his sallow smile continued to tantalize her. Then she closed on him with a rush, smothering his words against her hair.

'It's for more than one night—why, it's for every other Friday! Oh, you darling, you darling!' she exulted.

Mr Spragg, through the glittering meshes, feigned dismay. 'That so? They must have given me the wrong—!' Then, convicted by her radiant eyes as she swung round on him: 'I knew you only wanted it *once* for yourself, Undine; but I thought maybe, off nights, you'd like to send it to your friends.'

Mrs Spragg, who from her doorway had assisted with moist eyes at this closing pleasantry, came forward as Undine hurried away to dress.

'Abner—can you really manage it all right?'

He answered her with one of his awkward brief caresses. 'Don't you fret about that, Leota. I'm bound to have her go round with these people she knows. I want her to be with them all she can.'

A pause fell between them, while Mrs Spragg looked anxiously into his fagged eyes.

'You seen Elmer again?'

'No. Once was enough,' he returned, with a scowl like Undine's.

'Why—you *said* he couldn't come after her, Abner!'

'No more he can. But what if she was to get nervous and lonesome, and want to go after him?'

Mrs Spragg shuddered away from the suggestion. 'How'd he look? Just the same?' she whispered.

'No. Spruced up. That's what scared me.'

It scared her too, to the point of blanching her habitually lifeless cheek. She continued to scrutinize her husband broodingly. 'You look fairly sick, Abner. You better let me get you some of those stomach drops right off,' she proposed.

But he parried this with his unfailing humour. 'I guess I'm too sick to risk that.' He passed his hand through her arm with the conjugal gesture familiar to Apex City. 'Come along down to dinner, mother—I guess Undine won't mind if I don't rig up to-night.'

V

SHE had looked down at them, enviously, from the balcony— she had looked up at them, reverentially, from the stalls; but now at last she was on a line with them, among them, she was part of the sacred semicircle whose privilege it is, between the acts, to make the mere public forget that the curtain has fallen.

As she swept to the left-hand seat of their crimson niche, waving Mabel Lipscomb to the opposite corner with a gesture learned during her apprenticeship in the stalls, Undine felt that quickening of the faculties that comes in the high moments of life. Her consciousness seemed to take in at once the whole bright curve of the auditorium, from the unbroken lines of spectators below her to the culminating blaze of the central chandelier; and she herself was the core of that vast illumination, the sentient throbbing surface which gathered all the shafts of light into a centre.

It was almost a relief when, a moment later, the lights sank, the curtain rose, and the focus of illumination was shifted. The music, the scenery, and the movement on the stage, were like a rich mist tempering the radiance that shot on her from every side, and giving her time to subside, draw breath, adjust herself to this new clear medium which made her feel so oddly brittle and transparent.

When the curtain fell on the first act she began to be aware of a subtle change in the house. In all the boxes cross-currents of movement had set in: groups were coalescing and breaking up, fans waving and heads twinkling, black coats emerging among white shoulders, late comers dropping their furs and laces in the red penumbra of the background. Undine, for the moment unconscious of herself, swept the house with her opera-glass, searching for familiar faces. Some she knew without being able to name them—fixed figure-heads of the social prow—others she recognized from their portraits in the papers; but of the few from whom she could herself claim recognition not one was visible, and as she pursued her investigations the whole scene grew blank and featureless.

Almost all the boxes were full now, but one, just opposite, tantalized her by its continued emptiness. How queer to have an opera-box and not use it! What on earth could the people be doing—what rarer delight could they be tasting? Undine remembered that the numbers of the boxes and the names of their owners were given on the back of the programme, and after a rapid computation she turned to consult the list. Mondays and Fridays, Mrs Peter Van Degen. That was it: the box was empty because Mrs Van Degen was dining alone with Ralph Marvell! '*Peter will be at one of his club dinners.*' Undine had a sharp vision of the Van Degen dining-room—she pictured it as oak-carved and sumptuous with gilding—with a small table in the centre, and rosy lights and flowers, and Ralph Marvell, across the hot-house grapes and champagne, leaning to take a light from his hostess's cigarette. Undine had seen such scenes on the stage, she had come upon them in the glowing pages of fiction, and it seemed to her that every detail was before her now, from the glitter of jewels on Mrs Van Degen's bare shoulders to the way young Marvell stroked his slight blond moustache while he smiled and listened.

Undine blushed with anger at her own simplicity in fancying that he had been 'taken' by her—that she could ever really count among these happy self-absorbed people! They all had their friends, their ties, their delightful crowding obligations: why should they make room for an intruder in a circle so packed with the initiated?

As her imagination developed the details of the scene in the Van Degen dining-room it became clear to her that fashionable society was horribly immoral and that she could never really be happy in such a poisoned atmosphere. She remembered that an eminent divine was preaching a series of sermons against Social Corruption, and she determined to go and hear him on the following Sunday.

This train of thought was interrupted by the feeling that she was being intently observed from the neighbouring box. She turned around with a feint of speaking to Mrs Lipscomb, and met the bulging stare of Peter Van Degen. He was standing behind the lady of the eye-glass, who had replaced her tortoise-shell implement by one of closely-set brilliants, which, at a word from her companion, she critically bent on Undine.

'No—I don't remember,' she said; and the girl reddened, divining herself unidentified after this protracted scrutiny.

But there was no doubt as to young Van Degen's remembering her. She was even conscious that he was trying to provoke in her some reciprocal sign of recognition; and the attempt drove her to the haughty study of her programme.

'Why, there's Mr Popple over there!' exclaimed Mabel Lipscomb, making large signs across the house with fan and play-bill.

Undine had already become aware that Mabel, planted, blond and brimming, too near the edge of the box, was some-how out of scale and out of drawing; and the freedom of her demonstrations increased the effect of disproportion. No one else was wagging and waving in that way: a gestureless mute telegraphy seemed to pass between the other boxes. Still, Undine could not help following Mrs Lipscomb's glance, and there in fact was Claud Popple, taller and more dominant than ever, and bending easily over what she felt must be the back of a brilliant woman.

He replied by a discreet salute to Mrs Lipscomb's intemperate motions, and Undine saw the brilliant woman's opera-glass turn in their direction, and said to herself that in a moment Mr Popple would be 'round.' But the entr'acte wore on, and no one turned the handle of their door, or disturbed the peaceful somnolence of Harry Lipscomb, who, not being (as he put it) 'onto' grand opera, had abandoned the struggle and withdrawn to the seclusion of the inner box. Undine jealously watched Mr Popple's progress from box to box, from brilliant woman to brilliant woman; but just as it seemed about to carry him to their door he reappeared at his original post across the house.

'Undie, do look—there's Mr Marvell!' Mabel began again, with another conspicuous outbreak of signalling; and this time Undine flushed to the nape as Mrs Peter Van Degen appeared in the opposite box with Ralph Marvell behind her. The two seemed to be alone in the box—as they had doubtless been alone all the evening!—and Undine furtively turned to see if Mr Van Degen shared her disapproval. But Mr Van Degen had disappeared, and Undine, leaning forward, nervously touched Mabel's arm.

'What's the matter, Undine? Don't you see Mr Marvell over there? Is that his sister he's with?'

'No.—I wouldn't beckon like that,' Undine whispered between her teeth.

'Why not? Don't you want him to know you're here?'

'Yes—but the other people are not beckoning.'

Mabel looked about unabashed. 'Perhaps they've all found each other. Shall I send Harry over to tell him?' she shouted above the blare of the wind instruments.

'No!' gasped Undine as the curtain rose.

She was no longer capable of following the action on the stage. Two presences possessed her imagination: that of Ralph Marvell, small, unattainable, remote, and that of Mabel Lipscomb, near-by, immense and irrepressible.

It had become clear to Undine that Mabel Lipscomb was ridiculous. That was the reason why Popple did not come to the box. No one would care to be seen talking to her while Mabel was at her side: Mabel, monumental and moulded while the fashionable were flexible and diaphanous, Mabel strident and explicit while they were subdued and allusive. At the Stentorian she was the centre of her group—here she revealed herself as unknown and unknowing. Why, she didn't even know that Mrs Peter Van Degen was not Ralph Marvell's sister! And she had a way of trumpeting out her ignorances that jarred on Undine's subtler methods. It was precisely at this point that there dawned on Undine what was to be one of the guiding principles of her career: '*It's better to watch than to ask questions.*'

The curtain fell again, and Undine's eyes flew back to the Van Degen box. Several men were entering it together, and a moment later she saw Ralph Marvell rise from his seat and pass out. Half-unconsciously she placed herself in such a way as to have an eye on the door of the box. But its handle remained unturned, and Harry Lipscomb, leaning back on the sofa, his head against the opera cloaks, continued to breathe stertorously through his open mouth and stretched his legs a little farther across the threshold . . .

The entr'acte was nearly over when the door opened and two gentlemen stumbled over Mr Lipscomb's legs. The foremost was Claud Walsingham Popple; and above his shoulder shone the batrachian countenance of Peter Van Degen. A brief murmur from Mr Popple made his companion known to the two ladies, and Mr Van Degen promptly seated himself behind Undine, relegating the painter to Mrs Lipscomb's elbow.

'Queer go—I happened to see your friend there waving to old Popp across the house. So I bolted over and collared him: told him he'd got to introduce me before he was a minute older. I tried to find out who you were the other day at the Motor Show—no, where was it? Oh, those pictures at Goldmark's. What d'you think of 'em, by the way? You ought to be painted yourself—no, I mean it, you know—you ought to get old Popp to do you. He'd do your hair rippingly. You must let me come and talk to you about it . . . About the picture or your hair? Well, your hair if you don't mind. Where'd you say you were staying? Oh, you *live* here, do you? I say, that's first rate!'

Undine sat well forward, curving toward him a little, as she had seen the other women do, but holding back sufficiently to let it be visible to the house that she was conversing with no less a person than Mr Peter Van Degen. Mr Popple's talk was certainly more brilliant and purposeful, and she saw him cast longing glances at her from behind Mrs Lipscomb's shoulder; but she remembered how lightly he had been treated at the Fairford dinner, and she wanted—oh, how she wanted!—to have Ralph Marvell see her talking to Van Degen.

She poured out her heart to him, improvising an opinion on the pictures and an opinion on the music, falling in gaily with his suggestion of a jolly little dinner some night soon, at the Café Martin,* and strengthening her position, as she thought, by an easy allusion to her acquaintance with Mrs Van Degen. But at the word her companion's eye clouded, and a shade of constraint dimmed his enterprising smile.

'My wife—? Oh, *she* doesn't go to restaurants—she moves on too high a plane. But we'll get old Popp, and Mrs ——,

Mrs ——, what'd you say your fat friend's name was? Just a select little crowd of four—and some kind of a cheerful show afterward . . . Jove! There's the curtain, and I must skip.'

As the door closed on him Undine's cheeks burned with resentment. If Mrs Van Degen didn't go to restaurants, why had he supposed that *she* would? and to have to drag Mabel in her wake! The leaden sense of failure overcame her again. Here was the evening nearly over, and what had it led to? Looking up from the stalls, she had fancied that to sit in a box was to be in society—now she saw it might but emphasize one's exclusion. And she was burdened with the box for the rest of the season! It was really stupid of her father to have exceeded his instructions: why had he not done as she told him? . . . Undine felt helpless and tired . . . hateful memories of Apex crowded back on her. Was it going to be as dreary here as there?

She felt Lipscomb's loud whisper in her back: 'Say, you girls, I guess I'll cut this and come back for you when the show busts up.' They heard him shuffle out of the box, and Mabel settled back to undisturbed enjoyment of the stage.

When the last entr'acte began Undine stood up, resolved to stay no longer. Mabel, lost in the study of the audience, had not noticed her movement, and as she passed alone into the back of the box the door opened and Ralph Marvell came in.

Undine stood with one arm listlessly raised to detach her cloak from the wall. Her attitude showed the long slimness of her figure and the fresh curve of the throat below her bent-back head. Her face was paler and softer than usual, and the eyes she rested on Marvell's face looked deep and starry under their fixed brows.

'Oh—you're not going?' he exclaimed.

'I thought you weren't coming,' she answered simply.

'I waited till now on purpose to dodge your other visitors.'

She laughed with pleasure. 'Oh, we hadn't so many!'

Some intuition had already told her that frankness was the tone to take with him. They sat down together on the red damask sofa, against the hanging cloaks. As Undine leaned back her hair caught in the spangles of the wrap behind her, and she had to sit motionless while the young man freed the captive mesh. Then they settled themselves again, laughing a little at the incident.

A glance had made the situation clear to Mrs Lipscomb, and they saw her return to her rapt inspection of the boxes. In their mirror-hung recess the light was subdued to a rosy dimness and the hum of the audience came to them through half-drawn silken curtains. Undine noticed the delicacy and finish of her companion's features as his head detached itself against the red silk walls. The hand with which he stroked his small moustache was finely-finished too, but sinewy and not effeminate. She had always associated finish and refinement entirely with her own sex, but she began to think they might be even more agreeable in a man. Marvell's eyes were grey, like her own, with chestnut eyebrows and darker lashes; and his skin was as clear as a woman's, but pleasantly reddish, like his hands.

As he sat talking in a low tone, questioning her about the music, asking her what she had been doing since he had last seen her, she was aware that he looked at her less than usual, and she also glanced away; but when she turned her eyes suddenly they always met his gaze.

His talk remained impersonal. She was a little disappointed that he did not compliment her on her dress or her hair—Undine was accustomed to hearing a great deal about her hair, and the episode of the spangles had opened the way to a graceful allusion—but the instinct of sex told her that, under his quiet words, he was throbbing with the sense of her proximity. And his self-restraint sobered her, made her refrain from the flashing and fidgeting which were the only way she knew of taking part in the immemorial love-dance. She talked simply and frankly of herself, of her parents, of how few people they knew in New York, and of how, at times, she was almost sorry she had persuaded them to give up Apex.

'You see, they did it entirely on my account; they're awfully lonesome here; and I don't believe I shall ever learn New York ways either,' she confessed, turning on him the eyes of youth and truthfulness. 'Of course I know a few people; but they're not—not the way I expected New York people to be.' She risked what seemed an involuntary glance at Mabel. 'I've seen girls here to-night that I just *long* to know—they look so lovely and refined—but I don't suppose I ever shall. New York's not very friendly to strange girls, is it? I suppose you've got so many of your own already—and they're all so fascinating you don't care!' As she spoke she let her eyes rest on his, half-laughing, half-wistful, and then dropped her lashes while the pink stole slowly up to them.

When he left her he asked if he might hope to find her at home the next day.

The night was fine, and Marvell, having put his cousin into her motor, started to walk home to Washington Square. At the corner he was joined by Mr Popple.

'Hallo, Ralph, old man—did you run across our auburn beauty of the Stentorian? Who'd have thought old Harry Lipscomb'd have put us onto anything as good as that? Peter Van Degen was fairly taken off his feet—pulled me out of Mrs Monty Thurber's box and dragged me 'round by the collar to introduce him. Planning a dinner at Martin's already. Gad, young Peter must have what he wants *when* he wants it! I put in a word for you—told him you and I ought to be let in on the ground floor. Funny the luck some girls have about getting started. I believe this one'll take if she can manage to shake the Lipscombs. I think I'll ask to paint her; might be a good thing for the spring show. She'd show up splendidly as a *pendant* to my Mrs Van Degen—Blonde and Brunette . . . Night and Morning . . . Of course I prefer Mrs Van Degen's type—personally, I *must* have breeding—but as a mere bit of flesh and blood . . . hallo, ain't you coming into the club?'

Marvell was not coming into the club, and he drew a long breath of relief as his companion left him.

Was it possible that he had ever thought leniently of the egregious Popple? The tone of social omniscience which he had once found so comic was now as offensive to him as a coarse physical touch. And the worst of it was that Popple, with the slight exaggeration of a caricature, really expressed the ideals of the world he frequented. As he spoke of Miss Spragg, so others at any rate would think of her: almost every one in Ralph's set would agree that it was luck for a girl from Apex to be started by Peter Van Degen at a Café Martin dinner . . .

Ralph Marvell, mounting his grandfather's doorstep, looked up at the symmetrical old red house-front, with its frugal marble ornament, as he might have looked into a familiar human face.

'They're right,—after all, in some ways they're right,' he murmured, slipping his key into the door.

'They' were his mother and old Mr Urban Dagonet, both, from Ralph's earliest memories, so closely identified with the old house in Washington Square that they might have passed for its inner consciousness as it might have stood for their outward form; and the question as to which the house now seemed to affirm their intrinsic rightness was that of the social disintegration expressed by widely-different architectural physiognomies at the other end of Fifth Avenue.*

As Ralph pushed the bolts behind him, and passed into the hall, with its dark mahogany doors and the quiet 'Dutch interior' effect of its black and white marble paving, he said to himself that what Popple called society was really just like the houses it lived in: a muddle of misapplied ornament over a thin steel shell of utility. The steel shell was built up in Wall Street, the social trimmings were hastily added in Fifth Avenue; and the union between them was as monstrous and factitious, as unlike the gradual homogeneous growth which flowers into what other countries know as society, as that between the Blois gargoyles on Peter Van Degen's roof and the skeleton walls supporting them.

That was what 'they' had always said; what, at least, the Dagonet attitude, the Dagonet view of life, the very lines of the furniture in the old Dagonet house expressed.

Ralph sometimes called his mother and grandfather the Aborigines, and likened them to those vanishing denizens of the American continent doomed to rapid extinction with the advance of the invading race. He was fond of describing Washington Square as the 'Reservation,' and of prophesying that before long its inhabitants would be exhibited at ethnological shows, pathetically engaged in the exercise of their primitive industries.

Small, cautious, middle-class, had been the ideals of aboriginal New York; but it suddenly struck the young man that they were singularly coherent and respectable as contrasted with the chaos of indiscriminate appetites which made up its modern tendencies. He too had wanted to be 'modern,' had revolted, half-humorously, against the restrictions and exclusions of the old code; and it must have been by one of the ironic reversions of heredity that, at this precise point, he began to see what there was to be said on the other side—*his* side, as he now felt it to be.

VI

UPSTAIRS, in his brown firelit room, he threw himself into an armchair, and remembered . . .

Harvard first—then Oxford; then a year of wandering and rich initiation. Returning to New York, he had read law, and now had his desk in the office of the respectable firm in whose charge the Dagonet estate had mouldered for several generations. But his profession was the least real thing in his life. The realities lay about him now: the books jamming his old college bookcases and overflowing on chairs and tables; sketches too—he could do charming things, if only he had known how to finish them!—and, on the writing-table at his elbow, scattered sheets of prose and verse; charming things also, but, like the sketches, unfinished.

Nothing in the Dagonet and Marvell tradition was opposed to this desultory dabbling with life. For four or five generations it had been the rule of both houses that a young fellow should go to Columbia or Harvard, read law, and then lapse into more or less cultivated inaction. The only essential was that he should live 'like a gentleman'—that is, with a tranquil disdain for mere money-getting, a passive openness to the finer sensations, one or two fixed principles as to the quality of wine, and an archaic probity that had not yet learned to distinguish between private and 'business' honour.

No equipment could more thoroughly have unfitted the modern youth for getting on: it hardly needed the scribbled pages on the desk to complete the hopelessness of Ralph Marvell's case. He had accepted the fact with a humorous fatalism. Material resources were limited on both sides of the house, but there would always be enough for his frugal wants— enough to buy books (not 'editions'), and pay now and then for a holiday dash to the great centres of art and ideas. And meanwhile there was the world of wonders within him. As a boy at the sea-side, Ralph, between tides, had once come on a cave—a secret inaccessible place with glaucous lights, mysterious murmurs, and a single shaft of communication with the sky. He had kept his find from the other boys, not churlishly, for he was always an outspoken lad, but because he felt there were things about the cave that the others, good fellows as they all were, couldn't be expected to understand, and that, anyhow, it would never be quite his cave again after he had let his thick-set freckled cousins play smuggler and pirate in it.

And so with his inner world. Though so coloured by outer impressions, it wove a secret curtain about him, and he came and went in it with the same joy of furtive possession. One day, of course, some one would discover it and reign there with him—no, reign over it and him. Once or twice already a light foot had reached the threshold. His cousin Clare Dagonet, for instance: there had been a summer when her voice had sounded far down the windings . . . but he had run over to Spain for the autumn, and when he came back she was engaged to Peter Van Degen, and for a while it looked black in the cave. That was long ago, as time is reckoned under thirty; and for three years now he had felt for her only a half-contemptuous pity. To have stood at the mouth of his cave, and have turned from it to the Van Degen lair——!

Poor Clare repented, indeed—she wanted it clearly under- stood—but she repented in the Van Degen diamonds, and the Van Degen motor bore her broken heart from opera to ball. She had been subdued to what she worked in, and she could never again find her way to the enchanted cave . . . Ralph, since then, had reached the point of deciding that he would never marry; reached it not suddenly or dramatically, but with such sober advisedness as is urged on those about to take the opposite step. What he most wanted, now that the first flutter of being was over, was to learn and to do—to know what the great people had thought, think about their thinking, and then launch his own boat: write some good verse if possible; if not, then critical prose. A dramatic poem lay among the stuff at his elbow; but the prose critic was at his elbow too, and not to be satisfied about the poem; and poet and critic passed the nights in hot if unproductive debate. On the whole, it seemed likely that the critic would win the day, and the essay on 'The Rhythmical Structures of Walt Whitman' take shape before 'The Banished God.' Yet if the light in the cave was less supernaturally blue, the chant of its tides less laden with unimaginable music, it was still a thronged and echoing place when Undine Spragg appeared on its threshold . . .

His mother and sister of course wanted him to marry. They had the usual theory that he was 'made' for conjugal bliss: women always thought that of a fellow who didn't get drunk and have low tastes. Ralph smiled at the idea as he sat crouched among his secret treasures. Marry—but whom, in the name of light and freedom? The daughters of his own race sold themselves to the Invaders; the daughters of the Invaders bought their husbands as they bought an opera-box. It ought all to have been transacted on the Stock Exchange. His mother, he knew, had no such ambitions for him: she would have liked him to fancy a 'nice girl' like Harriet Ray. Harriet Ray was neither vulgar nor ambitious. She regarded Washington Square as the birthplace of Society, knew by heart all the cousinships of early New York, hated motor-cars, could not make herself understood on the telephone, and was determined, if she married, never to receive a divorced woman. As Mrs Marvell often said, such girls as Harriet were growing rare. Ralph was not sure about this. He was inclined to think that, certain modifications allowed for, there would always be plenty of Harriet Rays for unworldly mothers to commend to their sons; and he had no desire to diminish their number by removing one from the ranks of the marriageable. He had no desire to marry at all—that had been the whole truth of it till he met Undine Spragg. And now——? He lit a cigar, and began to recall his hour's conversation with Mrs Spragg.

Ralph had never taken his mother's social faiths very seriously. Surveying the march of civilization from a loftier angle, he had early mingled with the Invaders, and curiously observed their rites and customs. But most of those he had met had already been modified by contact with the indigenous: they spoke the same language as his, though on their lips it had often so different a meaning. Ralph had never seen them actually in the making, before they had acquired the speech of the conquered race. But Mrs Spragg still used the dialect of her people, and before the end of the visit Ralph had ceased to regret that her daughter was out. He felt obscurely that in the girl's presence—frank and simple as he thought her—he should have learned less of life in early Apex.

Mrs Spragg, once reconciled—or at least resigned—to the mysterious necessity of having to 'entertain' a friend of Undine's, had yielded to the first touch on the weak springs of her garrulity. She had not seen Mrs Heeny for two days, and this friendly young man with the gentle manner was almost as easy to talk to as the masseuse. And then she could tell him things that Mrs Heeny already knew, and Mrs Spragg liked to repeat her stories. To do so gave her almost her sole sense of permanence among the shifting scenes of life. So that, after she had lengthily deplored the untoward accident of Undine's absence, and her visitor, with a smile, and echoes of *divers et ondoyant** in his brain, had repeated her daughter's name after her, saying: 'It's a wonderful find—how could you tell it would be such a fit?'—it came to her quite easily to answer: 'Why, we called her after a hair-waver father put on the market the week she was born——' and then to explain, as he remained struck and silent: 'It's from *un*doolay, you know, the French for crimping; father always thought the name made it take. He was quite a scholar, and had the greatest knack for finding names. I remember the time he invented his Goliath Glue he sat up all night over the Bible to get the name . . . No, father didn't start *in* as a druggist,' she went on, expanding with the signs of Marvell's interest; 'he was educated for an undertaker, and built up a first-class business; but he was always a beautiful speaker, and after a while he sorter drifted into the ministry. Of course it didn't pay him anything like as well, so finally he opened a drug-store, and he did first-rate at that too, though his heart was always in the pulpit. But after he made such a success with his hair-waver he got speculating in land out at Apex, and somehow everything went—though Mr Spragg did all he *could*——.' Mrs Spragg, when she found herself embarked on a long sentence, always ballasted it by italicizing the last word.

Her husband, she continued, could not, at the time, do much for his father-in-law. Mr Spragg had come to Apex as a poor boy, and their early married life had been a protracted struggle, darkened by domestic affliction. Two of their three children had died of typhoid in the epidemic which devastated Apex before the new water-works were built; and this calamity, by causing Mr Spragg to resolve that thereafter Apex should drink pure water, had led directly to the founding of his fortunes.

'He had taken over some of poor father's land for a bad debt, and when he got up the Pure Water Move the company voted to buy the land and build the new reservoir up there: and after that we began to be better off, and it *did* seem as if it had come out so to comfort us some about the children.'

Mr Spragg, thereafter, had begun to be a power in Apex, and fat years had followed on the lean. Ralph Marvell was too little versed in affairs to read between the lines of Mrs Spragg's untutored narrative, and he understood no more than she the occult connection between Mr Spragg's domestic misfortunes and his business triumph. Mr Spragg had 'helped out' his ruined father-in-law, and had vowed on his children's graves that no Apex child should ever again drink poisoned water—and out of those two disinterested impulses, by some impressive law of compensation, material prosperity had come. What Ralph understood and appreciated was Mrs Spragg's unaffected frankness in talking of her early life. Here was no retrospective pretense of an opulent past, such as the other Invaders were given to parading before the bland but undeceived subject race. The Spraggs had been 'plain people' and had not yet learned to be ashamed of it. The fact drew them much closer to the Dagonet ideals than any sham elegance in the past tense. Ralph felt that his mother, who shuddered away from Mrs Harmon B. Driscoll, would understand and esteem Mrs Spragg.

But how long would their virgin innocence last? Popple's vulgar hands were on it already—Popple's and the unspeakable Van Degen's! Once they and theirs had begun the process of initiating Undine, there was no knowing—or rather there was too easy knowing—how it would end! It was incredible that she too should be destined to swell the ranks of the cheaply fashionable; yet were not her very freshness, her malleability, the mark of her fate? She was still at the age when the flexible soul offers itself to the first grasp. That the grasp should chance to be Van Degen's—that was what made Ralph's temples buzz, and swept away all his plans for his own future like a beaver's dam in a spring flood. To save her from Van Degen and Van Degenism: was that really to be his mission—the 'call' for which his life had obscurely waited? It was not in the least what he had meant to do with the fugitive flash of consciousness he called self; but all that he had purposed for that transitory being sank into insignificance under the pressure of Undine's claims.

Ralph Marvell's notion of women had been formed on the experiences common to good-looking young men of his kind. Women were drawn to him as much by his winning appealing quality, by the sense of a youthful warmth behind his light ironic exterior, as by his charms of face and mind. Except during Clare Dagonet's brief reign the depths in him had not been stirred; but in taking what each sentimental episode had to give he had preserved, through all his minor adventures, his faith in the great adventure to come. It was this faith that made him so easy a victim when love had at last appeared clad in the attributes of romance: the imaginative man's indestructible dream of a rounded passion.

The clearness with which he judged the girl and himself seemed the surest proof that his feeling was more than a surface thrill. He was not blind to her crudity and her limitations, but they were a part of her grace and her persuasion. *Diverse et ondoyante*—so he had seen her from the first. But was not that merely the sign of a quicker response to the world's manifold appeal? There was Harriet Ray, sealed up tight in the vacuum of inherited opinion, where not a breath of fresh sensation could get at her: there could be no call to rescue young ladies so secured from the perils of reality! Undine had no such traditional safeguards—Ralph guessed Mrs Spragg's opinions to be as fluid as her daughter's—and the girl's very sensitiveness to new impressions, combined with her obvious lack of any sense of relative values, would make her an easy prey to the powers of folly. He seemed to see her—as he sat there, pressing his fists into his temples—he seemed to see her like a lovely rock-bound Andromeda,* with the devouring monster Society careering up to make a mouthful of her; and himself whirling down on his winged horse—just Pegasus* turned Rosinante* for the nonce—to cut her bonds, snatch her up, and whirl her back into the blue . . .

VII

SOME two months later than the date of young Marvell's midnight vigil, Mrs Heeny, seated on a low chair at Undine's knee, gave the girl's left hand an approving pat as she laid aside her lapful of polishers.

'There! I guess you can put your ring on again,' she said with a laugh of jovial significance; and Undine echoing the laugh in a murmur of complacency, slipped on the fourth finger of her recovered hand a band of sapphires in an intricate setting.

Mrs Heeny took up the hand again. 'Them's old stones, Undine—they've got a different look,' she said, examining the ring while she rubbed her cushioned palm over the girl's brilliant finger-tips. 'And the setting's quaint—I wouldn't wonder but what it was one of old Gran'ma Dagonet's.'

Mrs Spragg, hovering near in fond beatitude, looked up quickly.

'Why, don't you s'pose he *bought* it for her, Mrs Heeny? It came in a Tiff'ny box.'

The manicure laughed again. 'Of course he's had Tiff'ny rub it up. Ain't you ever heard of ancestral jewels, Mrs Spragg? In the Eu-ropean aristocracy they never go out and *buy* engagement rings; and Undine's marrying into our aristocracy.'

Mrs Spragg looked relieved. 'Oh, I thought maybe they were trying to scrimp on the ring——'

Mrs Heeny, shrugging away this explanation, rose from her seat and rolled back her shiny black sleeves.

'Look at here, Undine, if you really want me to do your hair it's time we got to work.'

The girl swung about in her seat so that she faced the mirror on the dressing-table. Her shoulders shone through transparencies of lace and muslin which slipped back as she lifted her arms to draw the tortoise-shell pins from her hair.

'Of course you've got to do it—I want to look perfectly lovely!'

'Well—I dunno's my hand's in nowadays,' said Mrs Heeny in a tone that belied the doubt she cast on her own ability.

'Oh, you're an *artist*, Mrs Heeny—and I just couldn't have had that French maid 'round to-night,' sighed Mrs Spragg, sinking into a chair near the dressing-table.

Undine, with a backward toss of her head, scattered her loose locks about her. As they spread and sparkled under Mrs Heeny's touch, Mrs Spragg leaned back, drinking in through half-closed lids her daughter's loveliness. Some new quality seemed added to Undine's beauty: it had a milder bloom, a kind of melting grace, which might have been lent to it by the moisture in her mother's eyes.

'So you're to see the old gentleman for the first time at this dinner?' Mrs Heeny pursued, sweeping the live strands up into a loosely woven crown.

'Yes. I'm frightened to death!' Undine, laughing confidently, took up a hand-glass and scrutinized the small brown mole above the curve of her upper lip.

'I guess she'll know how to talk to him,' Mrs Spragg averred with a kind of quavering triumph.

'She'll know how to *look* at him, anyhow,' said Mrs Heeny; and Undine smiled at her own image.

'I hope he won't think I'm too awful!'

Mrs Heeny laughed. 'Did you read the description of yourself in the *Radiator* this morning? I wish't I'd 'a had time to cut it out. I guess I'll have to start a separate bag for *your* clippings soon.'

Undine stretched her arms luxuriously above her head and gazed through lowered lids at the foreshortened reflection of her face.

'Mercy! Don't jerk about like that. Am I to put in this rose? —There—you *are* lovely!' Mrs Heeny sighed, as the pink petals sank into the hair above the girl's forehead.

Undine pushed her chair back, and sat supporting her chin on her clasped hands while she studied the result of Mrs Heeny's manipulations.

'Yes—that's the way Mrs Peter Van Degen's flower was put in the other night; only hers was a camellia.—Do you think I'd look better with a camellia?'

'I guess if Mrs Van Degen looked like a rose she'd 'a worn a rose,' Mrs Heeny rejoined poetically. 'Sit still a minute longer,' she added. 'Your hair's so heavy I'd feel easier if I was to put in another pin.'

Undine remained motionless, and the manicure, suddenly laying both hands on the girl's shoulders, and bending over to peer at her reflection, said playfully: 'Ever been engaged before, Undine?'

A blush rose to the face in the mirror, spreading from chin to brow, and running rosily over the white shoulders from which their covering had slipped down.

'My! If he could see you now!' Mrs Heeny jested.

Mrs Spragg, rising noiselessly, glided across the room and became lost in a minute examination of the dress laid out on the bed.

With a supple twist Undine slipped from Mrs Heeny's hold.

'Engaged? Mercy, yes! Didn't you know? To the Prince of Wales. I broke it off because I wouldn't live in the Tower.'

Mrs Spragg, lifting the dress cautiously over her arm, advanced with a reassured smile.

'I s'pose Undie'll go to Europe now,' she said to Mrs Heeny.

'I guess Undie *will*!' the young lady herself declared. 'We're going to sail right afterward.—Here, mother, do be careful of my hair!' She ducked gracefully to slip into the lacy fabric which her mother held above her head.

As she rose Venus-like above its folds there was a tap on the door, immediately followed by its tentative opening.

'Mabel!' Undine muttered, her brows lowering like her father's; and Mrs Spragg, wheeling about to screen her daughter, addressed herself protestingly to the half-open door.

'Who's there? Oh, that *you*, Mrs Lipscomb? Well, I don't know as you *can*—Undie isn't half dressed yet——'

'Just like her—always pushing in!' Undine murmured as she slipped her arms into their transparent sleeves.

'Oh, that don't matter—I'll help dress her!' Mrs Lipscomb's large blond person surged across the threshold. 'Seems to me I ought to lend a hand to-night, considering I was the one that introduced them!'

Undine forced a smile, but Mrs Spragg, her soft wrinkles deepening with resentment, muttered to Mrs Heeny, as she bent down to shake out the girl's train: 'I guess my daughter's only got to show herself——'

The first meeting with old Mr Dagonet was less formidable than Undine had expected. She had been once before to the house in Washington Square, when, with her mother, she had returned Mrs Marvell's ceremonial visit; but on that occasion Ralph's grandfather had not been present. All the rites connected with her engagement were new and mysterious to Undine, and none more so than the unaccountable necessity of 'dragging'—as she phrased it—Mrs Spragg into the affair. It was an accepted article of the Apex creed that parental detachment should be completest at the moment when the filial fate was decided; and to find that New York reversed this rule was as puzzling to Undine as to her mother. Mrs Spragg was so unprepared for the part she was to play that on the occasion of her visit to Mrs Marvell her helplessness had infected Undine, and their half-hour in the sober faded drawing-room remained among the girl's most unsatisfactory memories.

She re-entered it alone with more assurance. Her confidence in her beauty had hitherto carried her through every ordeal; and it was fortified now by the feeling of power that came with the sense of being loved. If they would only leave her mother out she was sure, in her own phrase, of being able to 'run the thing'; and Mrs Spragg had providentially been left out of the Dagonet dinner.

It was to consist, it appeared, only of the small family group Undine had already met; and, seated at old Mr Dagonet's right, in the high dark dining-room with mahogany doors and dim portraits of 'Signers'* and their females, she felt a conscious joy in her ascendancy. Old Mr Dagonet—small, frail and softly sardonic—appeared to fall at once under her spell. If she felt, beneath his amenity, a kind of delicate dangerousness, like that of some fine surgical instrument, she ignored it as unimportant; for she had as yet no clear perception of forces that did not directly affect her.

Mrs Marvell, low-voiced, faded, yet impressive, was less responsive to her arts, and Undine divined in her the head of the opposition to Ralph's marriage. Mrs Heeny had reported that Mrs Marvell had other views for her son; and this was confirmed by such echoes of the short sharp struggle as reached the throbbing listeners at the Stentorian. But the conflict over, the air had immediately cleared, showing the enemy in the act of unconditional surrender. It surprised Undine that there had been no reprisals, no return on the points conceded. That was not her idea of warfare, and she could ascribe the completeness of the victory only to the effect of her charms.

Mrs Marvell's manner did not express entire subjugation; yet she seemed anxious to dispel any doubts of her good faith, and if she left the burden of the talk to her lively daughter it might have been because she felt more capable of showing indulgence by her silence than in her speech.

As for Mrs Fairford, she had never seemed more brilliantly bent on fusing the various elements under her hand. Undine had already discovered that she adored her brother, and had guessed that this would make her either a strong ally or a determined enemy. The latter alternative, however, did not alarm the girl. She thought Mrs Fairford 'bright,' and wanted to be liked by her; and she was in the state of dizzy self-assurance when it seemed easy to win any sympathy she chose to seek.

For the only other guests—Mrs Fairford's husband, and the elderly Charles Bowen who seemed to be her special friend—Undine had no attention to spare: they remained on a plane with the dim pictures hanging at her back. She had expected a larger party; but she was relieved, on the whole, that it was small enough to permit of her dominating it. Not that she wished to do so by any loudness of assertion. Her quickness in noting external differences had already taught her to modulate and lower her voice, and to replace 'The *i*-dea!' and 'I wouldn't wonder' by more polished locutions; and she had not been ten minutes at table before she found that to seem very much in love, and a little confused and subdued by the newness and intensity of the sentiment, was, to the Dagonet mind, the becoming attitude for a young lady in her situation. The part was not hard to play, for she *was* in love, of course. It was pleasant, when she looked across the table, to meet Ralph's grey eyes, with that new look in them, and to feel that she had kindled it; but it was only part of her larger pleasure in the general homage to her beauty, in the sensations of interest and curiosity excited by everything about her, from the family portraits overhead to the old Dagonet silver on the table— which were to be hers too, after all!

The talk, as at Mrs Fairford's, confused her by its lack of the personal allusion, its tendency to turn to books, pictures and politics. 'Politics,' to Undine, had always been like a kind of back-kitchen to business—the place where the refuse was thrown and the doubtful messes were brewed. As a drawing-room topic, and one to provoke disinterested sentiments, it had the hollowness of Fourth of July orations, and her mind wandered in spite of the desire to appear informed and competent.

Old Mr Dagonet, with his reedy staccato voice, that gave polish and relief to every syllable, tried to come to her aid by questioning her affably about her family and the friends she had made in New York. But the caryatid-parent, who exists simply as a filial prop, is not a fruitful theme, and Undine, called on for the first time to view her own progenitors as a subject of conversation, was struck by their lack of points. She had never paused to consider what her father and mother were 'interested' in, and, challenged to specify, could have named—with sincerity—only herself. On the subject of her New York friends it was not much easier to enlarge; for so far her circle had grown less rapidly than she expected. She had fancied Ralph's wooing would at once admit her to all his social privileges; but he had shown a puzzling reluctance to introduce her to the Van

Degen set, where he came and went with such familiarity; and the persons he seemed anxious to have her know—a few frumpy 'clever women' of his sister's age, and one or two brisk old ladies in shabby houses with mahogany furniture and Stuart portraits—did not offer the opportunities she sought.

'Oh, I don't know many people yet—I tell Ralph he's got to hurry up and take me round,' she said to Mr Dagonet, with a side-sparkle for Ralph, whose gaze, between the flowers and lights, she was aware of perpetually drawing.

'My daughter will take you—you must know his mother's friends,' the old gentleman rejoined while Mrs Marvell smiled noncommittally.

'But you have a great friend of your own—the lady who takes you into society,' Mr Dagonet pursued; and Undine had the sense that the irrepressible Mabel was again 'pushing in.'

'Oh, yes—Mabel Lipscomb. We were school-mates,' she said indifferently.

'Lipscomb? Lipscomb? What is Mr Lipscomb's occupation?'

'He's a broker,' said Undine, glad to be able to place her friend's husband in so handsome a light. The subtleties of a professional classification unknown to Apex had already taught her that in New York it is more distinguished to be a broker than a dentist; and she was surprised at Mr Dagonet's lack of enthusiasm.

'Ah? A broker?' He said it almost as Popple might have said 'A *dentist?*' and Undine found herself astray in a new labyrinth of social distinctions. She felt a sudden contempt for Harry Lipscomb, who had already struck her as too loud, and irrelevantly comic. 'I guess Mabel'll get a divorce pretty soon,' she added, desiring, for personal reasons, to present Mrs Lipscomb as favourably as possible.

Mr Dagonet's handsome eye-brows drew together. 'A divorce? H'm—that's bad. Has he been misbehaving himself?'

Undine looked innocently surprised. 'Oh, I guess not. They like each other well enough. But he's been a disappointment to her. He isn't in the right set, and I think Mabel realizes she'll never really get anywhere till she gets rid of him.'

These words, uttered in the high fluting tone that she rose to when sure of her subject, fell on a pause which prolonged and deepened itself to receive them, while every face at the table, Ralph Marvell's excepted, reflected in varying degree Mr Dagonet's pained astonishment.

'But, my dear young lady—what would your friend's own situation be if, as you put it, she "got rid" of her husband on so trivial a pretext?'

Undine, surprised at his dullness, tried to explain. 'Oh, that wouldn't be the reason *given*, of course. Any lawyer could fix it up for them. Don't they generally call it desertion?'

There was another, more palpitating, silence, broken by a laugh from Ralph.

'*Ralph!*' his mother breathed; then, turning to Undine, she said with a constrained smile: 'I believe in certain parts of the country such—unfortunate arrangements—are beginning to be tolerated. But in New York, in spite of our growing indifference, a divorced woman is still—thank heaven!—at a decided disadvantage.'

Undine's eyes opened wide. Here at last was a topic that really interested her, and one that gave another amazing glimpse into the camera obscura of New York society. 'Do you mean to say Mabel would be worse off, then? Couldn't she even go round as much as she does now?'

Mrs Marvell met this gravely. 'It would depend, I should say, on the kind of people she wished to see.'

'Oh, the very best, of course! That would be her only object.'

Ralph interposed with another laugh. 'You see, Undine, you'd better think twice before you divorce me!'

'*Ralph!*' his mother again breathed; but the girl, flushed and sparkling, flung back: 'Oh, it all depends on *you*! Out in Apex, if a girl marries a man who don't come up to what she expected, people consider it's to her credit to want to change. *You'd* better think twice of that!'

'If I were only sure of knowing what you expect!' he caught up her joke, tossing it back at her across the fascinated silence of their listeners.

'Why, *everything*!' she announced—and Mr Dagonet, turning, laid an intricately-veined old hand on hers, and said, with a change of tone that relaxed the tension of the listeners: 'My child, if you look like that you'll get it.'

VIII

IT was doubtless owing to Mrs Fairford's foresight that such possibilities of tension were curtailed, after dinner, by her carrying off Ralph and his betrothed to the theatre.

Mr Dagonet, it was understood, always went to bed after an hour's whist with his daughter; and the silent Mr Fairford gave his evenings to bridge at his club. The party, therefore, consisted only of Undine and Ralph, with Mrs Fairford and her attendant friend. Undine vaguely wondered why the grave and grey-haired Mr Bowen formed so invariable a part of that lady's train; but she concluded that it was the New York custom for married ladies to have gentlemen ''round' (as girls had in Apex), and that Mr Bowen was the sole survivor of Laura Fairford's earlier triumphs.

She had, however, little time to give to such conjectures, for the performance they were attending—the début of a fashionable London actress—had attracted a large audience in which Undine immediately recognized a number of familiar faces. Her engagement had been announced only the day before, and she had the delicious sense of being 'in all the papers,' and of focussing countless glances of interest and curiosity as she swept through the theatre in Mrs Fairford's wake. Their stalls were near the stage, and progress thither was slow enough to permit of prolonged enjoyment of this sensation. Before passing to her place she paused for Ralph to remove her cloak, and as he lifted it from her shoulders she heard a lady say behind her: 'There she is—the one in white, with the lovely back——' and a man answer: 'Gad! Where did he find anything as good as that?'

Anonymous approval was sweet enough; but she was to taste a moment more exquisite when, in the proscenium box across the house, she saw Clare Van Degen seated beside the prim figure of Miss Harriet Ray. 'They're here to see me with him—they hate it, but they couldn't keep away!' She turned and lifted a smile of possessorship to Ralph.

Mrs Fairford seemed also struck by the presence of the two ladies, and Undine heard her whisper to Mr Bowen: 'Do you see Clare over there—and Harriet with her? Harriet *would come*—I call it Spartan! And so like Clare to ask her!'

Her companion laughed. 'It's one of the deepest instincts in human nature. The murdered are as much given as the murderer to haunting the scene of the crime.'

Doubtless guessing Ralph's desire to have Undine to himself, Mrs Fairford had sent the girl in first; and Undine, as she seated herself, was aware that the occupant of the next stall half turned to her, as with a vague gesture of recognition. But just then the curtain rose, and she became absorbed in the development of the drama, especially as it tended to display the remarkable toilets which succeeded each other on the person of its leading lady. Undine, seated at Ralph Marvell's side, and feeling the thrill of his proximity as a subtler element in the general interest she was exciting, was at last repaid for the disappointment of her evening at the opera. It was characteristic of her that she remembered her failures as keenly as her triumphs, and that the passionate desire to obliterate, to 'get even' with them, was always among the latent incentives of her conduct. Now at last she was having what she wanted—she was in conscious possession of the 'real thing'; and through her other, more diffused, sensations Ralph's adoration gave her such a last refinement of pleasure as might have come to some warrior Queen borne in triumph by captive princes, and reading in the eyes of one the passion he dared not speak.

When the curtain fell this vague enjoyment was heightened by various acts of recognition. All the people she wanted to 'go with,' as they said in Apex, seemed to be about her in the stalls and boxes; and her eyes continued to revert with special satisfaction to the incongruous group formed by Mrs Peter Van Degen and Miss Ray. The sight made it irresistible to whisper to Ralph: 'You ought to go round and talk to your cousin. Have you told her we're engaged?'

'Clare? of course. She's going to call on you to-morrow.'

'Oh, she needn't put herself out—she's never been yet,' said Undine loftily.

He made no rejoinder, but presently asked: 'Who's that you're waving to?'

'Mr Popple. He's coming round to see us. You know he wants to paint me.' Undine fluttered and beamed as the brilliant Popple made his way across the stalls to the seat which her neighbour had momentarily left.

'First-rate chap next to you—whoever he is—to give me this chance,' the artist declared. 'Ha, Ralph, my boy, how did you pull it off? That's what we're all of us wondering.' He leaned over to give Marvell's hand the ironic grasp of celibacy. 'Well, you've left us lamenting: he has, you know, Miss Spragg. But I've got one pull over the others—I can paint you! He can't forbid that, can he? Not before marriage, anyhow!'

Undine divided her shining glances between the two. 'I guess he isn't going to treat me any different afterward,' she proclaimed with joyous defiance.

'Ah, well, there's no telling, you know. Hadn't we better begin at once? Seriously, I want awfully to get you into the spring show.'

'Oh, really? That would be too lovely!'

'*You* would be, certainly—the way I mean to do you. But I see Ralph getting glum. Cheer up, my dear fellow; I daresay you'll be invited to some of the sittings—that's for Miss Spragg to say.—Ah, here comes your neighbour back, confound him— You'll let me know when we can begin?'

As Popple moved away Undine turned eagerly to Marvell. 'Do you suppose there's time? I'd love to have him to do me!'

Ralph smiled. 'My poor child—he *would* "do" you, with a vengeance. Infernal cheek, his asking you to sit——'

She stared. 'But why? He's painted your cousin, and all the smart women.'

'Oh, if a "smart" portrait's all you want!'

'I want what the others want,' she answered, frowning and pouting a little.

She was already beginning to resent in Ralph the slightest sign of resistance to her pleasure; and her resentment took the form—a familiar one in Apex courtships—of turning on him, in the next entr'acte, a deliberately averted shoulder. The result of this was to bring her, for the first time, in more direct relation to her other neighbour. As she turned he turned too, showing her, above a shining shirt-front fastened with a large imitation pearl, a ruddy plump snub face without an angle in it, which yet looked sharper than a razor. Undine's eyes met his with a startled look, and for a long moment they remained suspended on each other's stare.

Undine at length shrank back with an unrecognizing face; but her movement made her opera-glass slip to the floor, and her neighbour bent down and picked it up.

'Well—don't you know me yet?' he said with a slight smile, as he restored the glass to her.

She had grown white to the lips, and when she tried to speak the effort produced only a faint click in her throat. She felt that the change in her appearance must be visible, and the dread of letting Marvell see it made her continue to turn her ravaged face to her other neighbour. The round black eyes set prominently in the latter's round glossy countenance had expressed at first only an impersonal and slightly ironic interest; but a look of surprise grew in them as Undine's silence continued.

'What's the matter? Don't you want me to speak to you?'

She became aware that Marvell, as if unconscious of her slight show of displeasure, had left his seat, and was making his way toward the aisle; and this assertion of independence, which a moment before she would so deeply have resented, now gave her a feeling of intense relief.

'No—don't speak to me, please. I'll tell you another time— I'll write.' Her neighbour continued to gaze at her, forming his lips into a noiseless whistle under his small dark moustache.

'Well, I—That's about the stiffest,' he murmured; and as she made no answer he added: 'Afraid I'll ask to be introduced to your friend?'

She made a faint movement of entreaty. 'I can't explain. I promise to see you; but I *ask* you not to talk to me now.'

He unfolded his programme, and went on speaking in a low tone while he affected to study it. 'Anything to oblige, of course. That's always been my motto. But *is* it a bargain—fair and square? You'll see me?'

She receded farther from him. 'I promise. I—I *want* to,' she faltered.

'All right, then. Call me up in the morning at the Driscoll Building. Seven-O-nine—got it?'

She nodded, and he added in a still lower tone: 'I suppose I can congratulate you, anyhow?' and then, without waiting for her reply, turned to study Mrs Van Degen's box through his opera-glass.

Clare, as if aware of the scrutiny fixed on her from below, leaned back and threw a question over her shoulder to Ralph Marvell, who had just seated himself behind her.

'Who's the funny man with the red face talking to Miss Spragg?'

Ralph bent forward. 'The man next to her? Never saw him before. But I think you're mistaken: she's not speaking to him.'

'She *was*—Wasn't she, Harriet?'

Miss Ray pinched her lips together without speaking, and Mrs Van Degen paused for the fraction of a second. 'Perhaps he's an Apex friend,' she then suggested.

'Very likely. Only I think she'd have introduced him if he had been.'

His cousin faintly shrugged. 'Shall you encourage that?'

Peter Van Degen, who had strayed into his wife's box for a moment, caught the colloquy, and lifted his opera-glass.

'The fellow next to Miss Spragg? (By George, Ralph, she's ripping to-night!) Wait a minute—I know his face. Saw him in old Harmon Driscoll's office the day of the Eubaw Mine meeting. This chap's his secretary, or something. Driscoll called him in to give some facts to the directors, and he seemed a mighty wide-awake customer.'

Clare Van Degen turned gaily to her cousin. 'If he has anything to do with the Driscolls you'd better cultivate him! That's the kind of acquaintance the Dagonets have always needed. I married to set them an example!'

Ralph rose with a laugh. 'You're right. I'll hurry back and make his acquaintance.' He held out his hand to his cousin, avoiding her disappointed eyes.

Undine, on entering her bedroom late that evening, was startled by the presence of a muffled figure which revealed itself, through the dimness, as the ungirded midnight outline of Mrs Spragg.

'*Mother?* What on earth——?' the girl exclaimed, as Mrs Spragg pressed the electric button and flooded the room with light. The idea of a mother's sitting up for her daughter was so foreign to Apex customs that it roused only mistrust and irritation in the object of the demonstration.

Mrs Spragg came forward deprecatingly to lift the cloak from her daughter's shoulders.

'I just *had* to, Undie—I told father I *had* to. I wanted to hear all about it.'

Undine shrugged away from her. 'Mercy! At this hour? You'll be as white as a sheet to-morrow, sitting up all night like this.'

She moved toward the toilet-table, and began to demolish with feverish hands the structure which Mrs Heeny, a few hours earlier, had so lovingly raised. But the rose caught in a mesh of hair, and Mrs Spragg, venturing timidly to release it, had a full view of her daughter's face in the glass.

'Why, Undie, *you're* as white as a sheet now! You look fairly sick. What's the matter, daughter?'

The girl broke away from her.

'Oh, can't you leave me alone, mother? There—do I look white *now*?' she cried, the blood flaming into her pale cheeks; and as Mrs Spragg shrank back, she added more mildly, in the tone of a parent rebuking a persistent child: 'It's enough to *make* anybody sick to be stared at that way!'

Mrs Spragg overflowed with compunction. 'I'm so sorry, Undie. I guess it was just seeing you in this glare of light.'

'Yes—the light's awful; do turn some off,' ordered Undine, for whom, ordinarily, no radiance was too strong; and Mrs Spragg, grateful to have commands laid upon her, hastened to obey.

Undine, after this, submitted in brooding silence to having her dress unlaced, and her slippers and dressing-gown brought to her. Mrs Spragg visibly yearned to say more, but she restrained the impulse lest it should provoke her dismissal.

'Won't you take just a sup of milk before you go to bed?' she suggested at length, as Undine sank into an armchair. 'I've got some for you right here in the parlour.'

Without looking up the girl answered: 'No. I don't want anything. Do go to bed.'

Her mother seemed to be struggling between the life-long instinct of obedience and a swift unformulated fear. 'I'm going, Undie.' She wavered. 'Didn't they receive you right, daughter?' she asked with sudden resolution.

'What nonsense! How *should* they receive me? Everybody was lovely to me.' Undine rose to her feet and went on with her undressing, tossing her clothes on the floor and shaking her hair over her bare shoulders.

Mrs Spragg stooped to gather up the scattered garments as they fell, folding them with a wistful caressing touch, and laying them on the lounge, without daring to raise her eyes to her daughter. It was not till she heard Undine throw herself on the bed that she went toward her and drew the coverlet up with deprecating hands.

'Oh, do put the light out—I'm dead tired,' the girl grumbled, pressing her face into the pillow.

Mrs Spragg turned away obediently; then, gathering all her scattered impulses into a passionate act of courage, she moved back to the bedside.

'Undie—you didn't see anybody—I mean at the theatre? *Anybody you didn't want to see?*'

Undine, at the question, raised her head and started upright against the tossed pillows, her white exasperated face close to her mother's twitching features. The two women examined each other a moment, fear and anger in their crossed glances; then Undine answered: 'No, nobody. Good-night.'

IX

UNDINE, late the next day, waited alone under the leafless trellising of a wistaria arbour on the west side of the Central Park. She had put on her plainest dress, and wound a closely patterned veil over her least vivid hat; but even thus toned down to the situation she was conscious of blazing out from it inconveniently.

The habit of meeting young men in sequestered spots was not unknown to her: the novelty was in feeling any embarrassment about it. Even now she was disturbed not so much by the unlikely chance of an accidental encounter with Ralph Marvell as by the remembrance of similar meetings, far from accidental, with the romantic Aaronson. Could it be that the hand now adorned with Ralph's engagement ring had once, in this very spot, surrendered itself to the riding-master's pressure? At the thought a wave of physical disgust passed over her, blotting out another memory as distasteful but more remote.

It was revived by the appearance of a ruddy middle-sized young man, his stoutish figure tightly buttoned into a square-shouldered over-coat, who presently approached along the path that led to the arbour. Silhouetted against the slope of the asphalt, the newcomer revealed an outline thick yet compact, with a round head set on a neck in which, at the first chance, prosperity would be likely to develop a red crease. His face, with its rounded surfaces, and the sanguine innocence of a complexion belied by prematurely astute black eyes, had a look of jovial cunning which Undine had formerly thought 'smart' but which now struck her as merely vulgar. She felt that in the Marvell set Elmer Moffatt would have been stamped as 'not a gentleman.' Nevertheless something in his look seemed to promise the capacity to develop into any character he might care to assume; though it did not seem probable that, for the present, that of a gentleman would be among them. He had always had a brisk swaggering step, and the faintly impudent tilt of the head that she had once thought 'dashing'; but whereas this look had formerly denoted a somewhat desperate defiance of the world and its judgments it now suggested an almost assured relation to these powers; and Undine's heart sank at the thought of what the change implied.

As he drew nearer, the young man's air of assurance was replaced by an expression of mildly humorous surprise.

'Well—this is white of you, Undine!' he said, taking her lifeless fingers into his dapperly gloved hand.

Through her veil she formed the words: 'I said I'd come.'

He laughed. 'That's so. And you see I believed you. Though I might not have——'

'I don't see the use of beginning like this,' she interrupted nervously.

'That's so too. Suppose we walk along a little ways? It's rather chilly standing round.'

He turned down the path that descended toward the Ramble and the girl moved on beside him with her long flowing steps.

When they had reached the comparative shelter of the inter-lacing trees Moffatt paused again to say: 'If we're going to talk I'd like to see you, Undine;' and after a first moment of reluc-tance she submissively threw back her veil.

He let his eyes rest on her in silence; then he said judicially: 'You've filled out some; but you're paler.' After another appre-ciative scrutiny he added: 'There's mighty few women as well worth looking at, and I'm obliged to you for letting me have the chance again.'

Undine's brows drew together, but she softened her frown to a quivering smile.

'I'm glad to see you too, Elmer—I am, *really*!'

He returned her smile while his glance continued to study her humorously. 'You didn't betray the fact last night, Miss Spragg.'

'I was so taken aback. I thought you were out in Alaska somewhere.'

The young man shaped his lips into the mute whistle by which he habitually vented his surprise. 'You *did*? Didn't Abner E. Spragg tell you he'd seen me down town?'

Undine gave him a startled glance. 'Father? Why, have you seen him? He never said a word about it!'

Her companion's whistle became audible. 'He's running yet!' he said gaily. 'I wish I could scare some people as easy as I can your father.'

The girl hesitated. 'I never felt toward you the way father did,' she hazarded at length; and he gave her another long look in return.

'Well, if they'd left you alone I don't believe you'd ever have acted mean to me,' was the conclusion he drew from it.

'I didn't mean to, Elmer. . . . I give you my word—but I was so young . . . I didn't know anything . . .'

His eyes had a twinkle of reminiscent pleasantry. 'No—I don't suppose it *would* teach a girl much to be engaged two years to a stiff like Millard Binch; and that was about all that had happened to you before I came along.'

Undine flushed to the forehead. 'Oh, Elmer—I was only a child when I was engaged to Millard——'

'That's a fact. And you went on being one a good while afterward. *The Apex Eagle* always head-lined you "The child-bride"——'

'I can't see what's the use—now——.'

'That ruled out of court too? See here, Undine—what *can* we talk about? I understood that was what we were here for.'

'Of course.' She made an effort at recovery. 'I only meant to say—what's the use of raking up things that are over?'

'Rake up? That's the idea, is it? Was that why you tried to cut me last night?'

'I—oh, Elmer! I didn't mean to; only, you see, I'm engaged.'

'Oh, I saw that fast enough. I'd have seen it even if I didn't read the papers.' He gave a short laugh. 'He was feeling pretty good, sitting there alongside of you, wasn't he? I don't wonder he was. I remember. But I don't see that that was a reason for cold-shouldering me. I'm a respectable member of society now—I'm one of Harmon B. Driscoll's private secretaries.' He brought out the fact with mock solemnity.

But to Undine, though undoubtedly impressive, the statement did not immediately present itself as a subject for pleasantry.

'Elmer Moffatt—you *are*?'

He laughed again. 'Guess you'd have remembered me last night if you'd known it.'

She was following her own train of thought with a look of pale intensity. 'You're *living* in New York, then—you're going to live here right along?'

'Well, it looks that way; as long as I can hang on to this job. Great men always gravitate to the metropolis. And I gravitated here just as Uncle Harmon B. was looking round for somebody who could give him an inside tip on the Eubaw mine deal—you know the Driscolls are pretty deep in Eubaw. I happened to go out there after our little unpleasantness at Apex, and it was just the time the deal went through. So in one way your folks did me a good turn when they made Apex too hot for me: funny to think of, ain't it?'

Undine, recovering herself, held out her hand impulsively.

'I'm real glad of it—I mean I'm real glad you've had such a stroke of luck!'

'Much obliged,' he returned. 'By the way, you might mention the fact to Abner E. Spragg next time you run across him.'

'Father'll be real glad too, Elmer.' She hesitated, and then went on: 'You must see now that it was natural father and mother should have felt the way they did——'

'Oh, the only thing that struck me as unnatural was their making you feel so too. But I'm free to admit I wasn't a promising case in those days.' His glance played over her for a moment. 'Say, Undine—it was good while it lasted, though, wasn't it?'

She shrank back with a burning face and eyes of misery.

'Why, what's the matter? That ruled out too? Oh, all right. Look at here, Undine, suppose you let me know what you *are* here to talk about, anyhow.'

She cast a helpless glance down the windings of the wooded glen in which they had halted.

'Just to ask you—to beg you—not to say anything of this kind again—*ever*——'

'Anything about you and me?'

She nodded mutely.

'Why, what's wrong? Anybody been saying anything against me?'

'Oh, no. It's not that!'

'What on earth *is* it, then—except that you're ashamed of me, one way or another?' She made no answer, and he stood digging the tip of his walking-stick into a fissure of the asphalt. At length he went on in a tone that showed a first faint trace of irritation: 'I don't want to break into your gilt-edged crowd, if it's that you're scared of.'

His tone seemed to increase her distress. 'No, no—you don't understand. All I want is that nothing shall be known.'

'Yes; but *why*? It was all straight enough, if you come to that.'

'It doesn't matter . . . whether it was straight . . . or . . . not . . .' He interpolated a whistle which made her add: 'What I mean is that out here in the East they don't even like it if a girl's been *engaged* before.'

This last strain on his credulity wrung a laugh from Moffatt. 'Gee! How'd they expect her fair young life to pass? Playing

"Holy City" on the melodeon, and knitting tidies for church fairs?'

'Girls are looked after here. It's all different. Their mothers go round with them.'

This increased her companion's hilarity and he glanced about him with a pretense of compunction. 'Excuse *me*! I ought to have remembered. Where's your chaperon, Miss Spragg?' He crooked his arm with mock ceremony. 'Allow me to escort you to the bew-fay. You see I'm onto the New York style myself.'

A sigh of discouragement escaped her. 'Elmer—if you really believe I never wanted to act mean to you, don't you act mean to me now!'

'Act mean?' He grew serious again and moved nearer to her. 'What is it you want, Undine? Why can't you say it right out?'

'What I told you. I don't want Ralph Marvell—or any of them—to know anything. If any of his folks found out, they'd never let him marry me—never! And he wouldn't want to: he'd be so horrified. And it would *kill* me, Elmer—it would just kill me!'

She pressed close to him, forgetful of her new reserves and repugnances, and impelled by the passionate absorbing desire to wring from him some definite pledge of safety.

'Oh, Elmer, if you ever liked me, help me now, and I'll help you if I get the chance!'

He had recovered his coolness as hers forsook her, and stood his ground steadily, though her entreating hands, her glowing face, were near enough to have shaken less sturdy nerves.

'That so, Puss? You just ask me to pass the sponge over Elmer Moffatt of Apex City? Cut the gentleman when we meet? That the size of it?'

'Oh, Elmer, it's my first chance—I can't lose it!' she broke out, sobbing.

'Nonsense, child! Of course you shan't. Here, look up, Undine—why, I never saw you cry before. Don't you be afraid of me—*I* ain't going to interrupt the wedding march.' He began to whistle a bar of Lohengrin. 'I only just want one little promise in return.'

She threw a startled look at him and he added reassuringly: 'Oh, don't mistake me. I don't want to butt into your set—not for social purposes, anyhow; but if ever it should come handy to know any of 'em in a business way, would you fix it up for me—*after you're married*?'

Their eyes met, and she remained silent for a tremulous moment or two; then she held out her hand. 'Afterward—yes. I promise. And *you* promise, Elmer?'

'Oh, to have and to hold!' he sang out, swinging about to follow her as she hurriedly began to retrace her steps.

The March twilight had fallen, and the Stentorian façade was all aglow, when Undine regained its monumental threshold. She slipped through the marble vestibule and soared skyward in the mirror-lined lift, hardly conscious of the direction she was taking. What she wanted was solitude, and the time to put some order into her thoughts; and she hoped to steal into her room without meeting her mother. Through her thick veil the clusters of lights in the Spragg drawing-room dilated and flowed together in a yellow blur, from which, as she entered, a figure detached itself; and with a start of annoyance she saw Ralph Marvell rise from the perusal of the 'fiction number' of a magazine which had replaced 'The Hound of the Baskervilles' on the onyx table.

'Yes; you told me not to come—and here I am.' He lifted her hand to his lips as his eyes tried to find hers through the veil.

She drew back with a nervous gesture. 'I told you I'd be awfully late.'

'I know—trying on! And you're horribly tired, and wishing with all your might I wasn't here.'

'I'm not so sure I'm not!' she rejoined, trying to hide her vexation in a smile.

'What a tragic little voice! You really *are* done up. I couldn't help dropping in for a minute; but of course if you say so I'll be off.' She was removing her long gloves, and he took her hands and drew her close. 'Only take off your veil, and let me see you.'

A quiver of resistance ran through her: he felt it and dropped her hands.

'Please don't tease. I never could bear it,' she stammered, drawing away.

'Till to-morrow, then; that is, if the dress-makers permit.'

She forced a laugh. 'If I showed myself now you might not come back to-morrow. I look perfectly hideous—it was so hot and they kept me so long.'

'All to make yourself more beautiful for a man who's blind with your beauty already?'

The words made her smile, and moving nearer she bent her head and stood still while he undid her veil. As he put it back their lips met, and his look of passionate tenderness was incense to her.

But the next moment his expression passed from worship to concern. 'Dear! Why, what's the matter? You've been crying!'

She put both hands to her hat in the instinctive effort to hide her face. His persistence was as irritating as her mother's.

'I told you it was frightfully hot—and all my things were horrid; and it made me so cross and nervous!' She turned to the looking-glass with a feint of smoothing her hair.

Marvell laid his hand on her arm. 'I can't bear to see you so done up. Why can't we be married to-morrow, and escape all these ridiculous preparations? I shall hate your fine clothes if they're going to make you so miserable.'

She dropped her hands, and swept about on him, her face lit up by a new idea. He was extraordinarily handsome and appealing, and her heart began to beat faster.

'I hate it all too! I wish we *could* be married right away!'

Marvell caught her to him joyously. 'Dearest—dearest! Don't, if you don't mean it! The thought's too glorious!'

Undine lingered in his arms, not with any intent of tenderness, but as if too deeply lost in a new train of thought to be conscious of his hold.

'I suppose most of the things *could* be got ready sooner—if I said they *must*,' she brooded, with a fixed gaze that travelled past him. 'And the rest—why shouldn't the rest be sent over to Europe after us? I want to go straight off with you, away from everything—ever so far away, where there'll be nobody but you and me alone!' She had a flash of illumination which made her turn her lips to his.

'Oh, my darling—my darling!' Marvell whispered.

X

Mr and Mrs Spragg were both given to such long periods of ruminating apathy that the student of inheritance might have wondered whence Undine derived her overflowing activity. The answer would have been obtained by observing her father's business life. From the moment he set foot in Wall Street Mr Spragg became another man. Physically the change revealed itself only by the subtlest signs. As he steered his way to his office through the jostling crowd of William Street his relaxed muscles did not grow more taut or his lounging gait less desultory. His shoulders were hollowed by the usual droop, and his rusty black waistcoat showed the same creased concavity at the waist, the same flabby prominence below. It was only in his face that the difference was perceptible, though even here it rather lurked behind the features than openly modified them: showing itself now and then in the cautious glint of half-closed eyes, the forward thrust of black brows, or a tightening of the lax lines of the mouth—as the gleam of a night-watchman's light might flash across the darkness of a shuttered house-front.

The shutters were more tightly barred than usual, when, on a morning some two weeks later than the date of the incidents last recorded, Mr Spragg approached the steel and concrete tower in which his office occupied a lofty pigeon-hole. Events had moved rapidly and somewhat surprisingly in the interval, and Mr Spragg had already accustomed himself to the fact that his daughter was to be married within the week, instead of awaiting the traditional post-Lenten date. Conventionally the change meant little to him; but on the practical side it presented unforeseen difficulties. Mr Spragg had learned within the last weeks that a New York marriage involved material obligations unknown to Apex. Marvell, indeed, had been loftily careless of such questions; but his grandfather, on the announcement of the engagement, had called on Mr Spragg and put before him, with polished precision, the young man's financial situation.

Mr Spragg, at the moment, had been inclined to deal with his visitor in a spirit of indulgent irony. As he leaned back in his revolving chair, with feet adroitly balanced against a tilted scrap basket, his air of relaxed power made Mr Dagonet's venerable elegance seem as harmless as that of an ivory jack-straw*—and his first replies to his visitor were made with the mildness of a kindly giant.

'Ralph don't make a living out of the law, you say? No, it didn't strike me he'd be likely to, from the talks I've had with him. Fact is, the law's a business that wants——' Mr Spragg broke off, checked by a protest from Mr Dagonet. 'Oh, a *profession*, you call it? It ain't a business?' His smile grew more indulgent as this novel distinction dawned on him. 'Why, I guess that's the whole trouble with Ralph. Nobody expects to make money in a *profession*; and if you've taught him to regard the law that way, he'd better go right into cooking-stoves and done with it.'

Mr Dagonet, within a narrower range, had his own play of humour; and it met Mr Spragg's with a leap. 'It's because I knew he would manage to make cooking-stoves as unremunerative as a profession that I saved him from so glaring a failure by putting him into the law.'

The retort drew a grunt of amusement from Mr Spragg; and the eyes of the two men met in unexpected understanding.

'That so? What *can* he do, then?' the future father-in-law enquired.

'He can write poetry—at least he tells me he can.' Mr Dagonet hesitated, as if aware of the inadequacy of the alternative, and then added: 'And he can count on three thousand a year from me.'

Mr Spragg tilted himself farther back without disturbing his subtly-calculated relation to the scrap basket.

'Does it cost anything like that to print his poetry?'

Mr Dagonet smiled again: he was clearly enjoying his visit. 'Dear, no—he doesn't go in for "luxe" editions. And now and then he gets ten dollars from a magazine.'

Mr Spragg mused. 'Wasn't he ever *taught* to work?'

'No; I really couldn't have afforded that.'

'I see. Then they've got to live on two hundred and fifty dollars a month.'

Mr Dagonet remained pleasantly unmoved. 'Does it cost anything like that to buy your daughter's dresses?'

A subterranean chuckle agitated the lower folds of Mr Spragg's waistcoat.

'I might put him in the way of something—I guess he's smart enough.'

Mr Dagonet made a gesture of friendly warning. 'It will pay us both in the end to keep him out of business,' he said, rising as if to show that his mission was accomplished.

The results of this friendly conference had been more serious than Mr Spragg could have foreseen—and the victory remained with his antagonist. It had not entered into Mr Spragg's calculations that he would have to give his daughter any fixed income on her marriage. He meant that she should have the 'handsomest' wedding the New York press had ever celebrated, and her mother's fancy was already afloat on a sea of luxuries— a motor, a Fifth Avenue house, and a tiara that should out-blaze Mrs Van Degen's; but these were movable benefits, to be conferred whenever Mr Spragg happened to be 'on the right side' of the market. It was a different matter to be called on, at such short notice, to bridge the gap between young Marvell's allowance and Undine's requirements; and her father's immediate conclusion was that the engagement had better be broken off. Such scissions were almost painless in Apex, and he had fancied it would be easy, by an appeal to the girl's pride, to make her see that she owed it to herself to do better.

'You'd better wait awhile and look round again,' was the way he had put it to her at the opening of the talk of which, even now, he could not recall the close without a tremor.

Undine, when she took his meaning, had been terrible. Everything had gone down before her, as towns and villages went down before one of the tornadoes of her native state. Wait awhile? Look round? Did he suppose she was marrying for *money*? Didn't he see it was all a question, now and here, of the kind of people she wanted to 'go with'? Did he want to throw her straight back into the Lipscomb set, to have her marry a

dentist and live in a West Side flat? Why hadn't they stayed in
Apex, if that was all he thought she was fit for? She might as well
have married Millard Binch, instead of handing him over to
Indiana Frusk! Couldn't her father understand that nice girls,
in New York, didn't regard getting married like going on a
buggy-ride? It was enough to ruin a girl's chances if she broke
her engagement to a man in Ralph Marvell's set. All kinds of
spiteful things would be said about her, and she would never be
able to go with the right people again. They had better go back
to Apex right off—it was they and not *she* who had wanted to
leave Apex, anyhow—she could call her mother to witness it.
She had always, when it came to that, done what her father and
mother wanted, but she'd given up trying to make out what
they were after, unless it was to make her miserable; and if that
was it, hadn't they had enough of it by this time? She had,
anyhow. But after this she meant to lead her own life; and they
needn't ask her where she was going, or what she meant to do,
because this time she'd die before she told them—and they'd
made life so hateful to her that she only wished she was dead
already.

Mr Spragg heard her out in silence, pulling at his beard with
one sallow wrinkled hand, while the other dragged down the
armhole of his waistcoat. Suddenly he looked up and said: 'Ain't
you in love with the fellow, Undie?'

The girl glared back at him, her splendid brows beetling like
an Amazon's. 'Do you think I'd care a cent for all the rest of it
if I wasn't?'

'Well, if you are, you and he won't mind beginning in a small
way.'

Her look poured contempt on his ignorance. 'Do you s'pose
I'd drag him down?' With a magnificent gesture she tore
Marvell's ring from her finger. 'I'll send this back this minute.
I'll tell him I thought he was a rich man, and now I see
I'm mistaken——' She burst into shattering sobs, rocking her
beautiful body back and forward in all the abandonment of
young grief; and her father stood over her, stroking her shoulder
and saying helplessly: 'I'll see what I can do, Undine——'

All his life, and at ever-diminishing intervals, Mr Spragg had
been called on by his womenkind to 'see what he could do'; and

the seeing had almost always resulted as they wished. Undine did not have to send back her ring, and in her state of trance-like happiness she hardly asked by what means her path had been smoothed, but merely accepted her mother's assurance that 'father had fixed everything all right.'

Mr Spragg accepted the situation also. A son-in-law who expected to be pensioned like a Grand Army veteran was a phenomenon new to his experience; but if that was what Undine wanted she should have it. Only two days later, however, he was met by a new demand—the young people had decided to be married 'right off,' instead of waiting till June. This change of plan was made known to Mr Spragg at a moment when he was peculiarly unprepared for the financial readjustment it necessitated. He had always declared himself able to cope with any crisis if Undine and her mother would 'go steady'; but he now warned them of his inability to keep up with the new pace they had set.

Undine, not deigning to return to the charge, had commissioned her mother to speak for her; and Mr Spragg was surprised to meet in his wife a firmness as inflexible as his daughter's.

'I can't do it, Loot—can't put my hand on the cash,' he had protested; but Mrs Spragg fought him inch by inch, her back to the wall—flinging out at last, as he pressed her closer: 'Well, if you want to know, she's seen Elmer.'

The bolt reached its mark, and her husband turned an agitated face on her.

'Elmer? What on earth—he didn't come *here*?'

'No; but he sat next to her the other night at the theatre, and she's wild with us for not having warned her.'

Mr Spragg's scowl drew his projecting brows together. 'Warned her of what? What's Elmer to her? Why's she afraid of Elmer Moffatt?'

'She's afraid of his talking.'

'Talking? What on earth can he say that'll hurt *her*?'

'Oh, I don't know,' Mrs Spragg wailed . 'She's so nervous I can hardly get a word out of her.'

Mr Spragg's whitening face showed the touch of a new fear. 'Is she afraid he'll get round her again—make up to her? Is that what she means by "talking"?'

'I don't know, I don't know. I only know she *is* afraid—she's afraid as death of him.'

For a long interval they sat silently looking at each other while their heavy eyes exchanged conjectures: then Mr Spragg rose from his chair, saying, as he took up his hat: 'Don't you fret, Leota; I'll see what I can do.'

He had been 'seeing' now for an arduous fortnight; and the strain on his vision had resulted in a state of tension such as he had not undergone since the epic days of the Pure Water Move at Apex. It was not his habit to impart his fears to Mrs Spragg and Undine, and they continued the bridal preparations, secure in their invariable experience that, once 'father' had been convinced of the impossibility of evading their demands, he might be trusted to satisfy them by means with which his womenkind need not concern themselves. Mr Spragg, as he approached his office on the morning in question, felt reasonably sure of fulfilling these expectations; but he reflected that a few more such victories would mean disaster.

He entered the vast marble vestibule of the Ararat Trust Building and walked toward the express elevator that was to carry him up to his office. At the door of the elevator a man turned to him, and he recognized Elmer Moffatt, who put out his hand with an easy gesture.

Mr Spragg did not ignore the gesture: he did not even withhold his hand. In his code the cut, as a conscious sign of disapproval, did not exist. In the south, if you had a grudge against a man you tried to shoot him; in the west, you tried to do him in a mean turn in business; but in neither region was the cut among the social weapons of offense. Mr Spragg, therefore, seeing Moffatt in his path, extended a lifeless hand while he faced the young man scowlingly. Moffatt met the hand and the scowl with equal coolness.

'Going up to your office? I was on my way there.'

The elevator door rolled back, and Mr Spragg, entering it, found his companion at his side. They remained silent during the ascent to Mr Spragg's threshold; but there the latter turned to enquire ironically of Moffatt: 'Anything left to say?'

Moffatt smiled. 'Nothing *left*—no; I'm carrying a whole new line of goods.'

Mr Spragg pondered the reply; then he opened the door and suffered Moffatt to follow him in. Behind an inner glazed enclosure, with its one window dimmed by a sooty perspective barred with chimneys, he seated himself at a dusty littered desk, and groped instinctively for the support of the scrap basket. Moffatt, uninvited, dropped into the nearest chair, and Mr Spragg said, after another silence: 'I'm pretty busy this morning.'

'I know you are: that's why I'm here,' Moffatt serenely answered. He leaned back, crossing his legs, and twisting his small stiff moustache with a plump hand adorned by a cameo.

'Fact is,' he went on, 'this is a coals-of-fire call.* You think I owe you a grudge, and I'm going to show you I'm not that kind. I'm going to put you onto a good thing—oh, not because I'm so fond of you; just because it happens to hit my sense of a joke.'

While Moffatt talked Mr Spragg took up the pile of letters on his desk and sat shuffling them like a pack of cards. He dealt them deliberately to two imaginary players; then he pushed them aside and drew out his watch.

'All right—I carry one too,' said the young man easily. 'But you'll find it's time gained to hear what I've got to say.'

Mr Spragg considered the vista of chimneys without speaking, and Moffatt continued: 'I don't suppose you care to hear the story of my life, so I won't refer you to the back numbers. You used to say out in Apex that I spent too much time loafing round the bar of the Mealey House; that was one of the things you had against me. Well, maybe I did—but it taught me to talk, and to listen to the other fellows too. Just at present I'm one of Harmon B. Driscoll's private secretaries, and some of that Mealey House loafing has come in more useful than any job I ever put my hand to. The old man happened to hear I knew something about the inside of the Eubaw deal, and took me on to have the information where he could get at it. I've given him good talk for his money; but I've done some listening too. Eubaw ain't the only commodity the Driscolls deal in.'

Mr Spragg restored his watch to his pocket and shifted his drowsy gaze from the window to his visitor's face.

'Yes,' said Moffatt, as if in reply to the movement, 'the Driscolls are getting busy out in Apex. Now they've got all the street railroads in their pocket they want the water-supply too—

but you know that as well as I do. Fact is, they've got to have it; and there's where you and I come in.'

Mr Spragg thrust his hands in his waistcoat arm-holes and turned his eyes back to the window.

'I'm out of that long ago,' he said indifferently.

'Sure,' Moffatt acquiesced; 'but you know what went on when you were in it.'

'Well?' said Mr Spragg, shifting one hand to the Masonic emblem on his watch-chain.

'Well, Representative James J. Rolliver, who was in it with you, ain't out of it yet. He's the man the Driscolls are up against. What d'you know about him?'

Mr Spragg twirled the emblem thoughtfully. 'Driscoll tell you to come here?'

Moffatt laughed. 'No, *sir*—not by a good many miles.'

Mr Spragg removed his feet from the scrap basket and straightened himself in his chair.

'Well—I didn't either; good morning, Mr Moffatt.'

The young man stared a moment, a humorous glint in his small black eyes; but he made no motion to leave his seat.

'Undine's to be married next week, isn't she?' he asked in a conversational tone.

Mr Spragg's face blackened and he swung about in his revolving chair.

'You go to——'

Moffatt raised a deprecating hand. 'Oh, you needn't warn me off. I don't want to be invited to the wedding. And I don't want to forbid the banns.'

There was a derisive sound in Mr Spragg's throat.

'But I *do* want to get out of Driscoll's office,' Moffatt imperturbably continued. 'There's no future there for a fellow like me. I see things big. That's the reason Apex was too tight a fit for me. It's only the little fellows that succeed in little places. New York's my size—without a single alteration. I could prove it to you to-morrow if I could put my hand on fifty thousand dollars.'

Mr Spragg did not repeat his gesture of dismissal: he was once more listening guardedly but intently. Moffatt saw it and continued.

'And I could put my hand on double that sum—yes, sir, *double*—if you'd just step round with me to old Driscoll's office before five p.m. See the connection, Mr Spragg?'

The older man remained silent while his visitor hummed a bar or two of 'In the Gloaming';* then he said: 'You want me to tell Driscoll what I know about James J. Rolliver?'

'I want you to tell the truth—I want you to stand for political purity in your native state. A man of your prominence owes it to the community, sir,' cried Moffatt.

Mr Spragg was still tormenting his Masonic emblem.

'Rolliver and I always stood together,' he said at last, with a tinge of reluctance.

'Well, how much have you made out of it? Ain't he always been ahead of the game?'

'I can't do it—I can't do it,' said Mr Spragg, bringing his clenched hand down on the desk, as if addressing an invisible throng of assailants.

Moffatt rose without any evidence of disappointment in his ruddy countenance. 'Well, so long,' he said, moving toward the door. Near the threshold he paused to add carelessly: 'Excuse my referring to a personal matter—but I understand Miss Spragg's wedding takes place next Monday.'

Mr Spragg was silent.

'How's that?' Moffatt continued unabashed. 'I saw in the papers the date was set for the end of June.'

Mr Spragg rose heavily from his seat. 'I presume my daughter has her reasons,' he said, moving toward the door in Moffatt's wake.

'I guess she has—same as I have for wanting you to step round with me to old Driscoll's. If Undine's reasons are as good as mine——'

'Stop right here, Elmer Moffatt!' the older man broke out with lifted hand.

Moffatt made a burlesque feint of evading a blow; then his face grew serious, and he moved close to Mr Spragg, whose arm had fallen to his side.

'See here, I know Undine's reasons. I've had a talk with her—didn't she tell you? *She* don't beat about the bush the way you do. She told me straight out what was bothering her. She wants the Marvells to think she's right out of Kindergarten. "No goods sent out on approval from this counter." And I see her point—*I* don't mean to publish my meemo'rs. Only a deal's a deal.' He paused a moment, twisting his fingers about the heavy gold watch-chain that crossed his waistcoat. 'Tell you what, Mr Spragg, I don't bear malice—not against Undine, anyway—and if I could have afforded it I'd have been glad enough to oblige her and forget old times. But you didn't hesitate to kick me when I was down and it's taken me a day or two to get on my legs again after that kicking. I see my way now to get there and keep there; and there's a kinder poetic justice in your being the man to help me up. If I can get hold of fifty thousand dollars within a day or so I don't care who's got the start of me. I've got a dead sure thing in sight, and you're the only man that can get it for me. Now do you see where we're coming out?'

Mr Spragg, during this discourse, had remained motionless, his hands in his pockets, his jaws moving mechanically, as though he mumbled a tooth-pick under his beard. His sallow cheek had turned a shade paler, and his brows hung threateningly over his half-closed eyes. But there was no threat—there was scarcely more than a note of dull curiosity—in the voice with which he said: 'You mean to talk?'

Moffatt's rosy face grew as hard as a steel safe. 'I mean *you* to talk—to old Driscoll.' He paused, and then added: 'It's a hundred thousand down, between us.'

Mr Spragg once more consulted his watch. 'I'll see you again,' he said with an effort.

Moffatt struck one fist against the other. 'No, *sir*—you won't! You'll only hear from me—through the Marvell family. Your news ain't worth a dollar to Driscoll if he don't get it to-day.'

He was checked by the sound of steps in the outer office, and Mr Spragg's stenographer appeared in the doorway.

'It's Mr Marvell,' she announced; and Ralph Marvell, glowing with haste and happiness, stood between the two men, holding out his hand to Mr Spragg.

'Am I awfully in the way, sir? Turn me out if I am—but first let me just say a word about this necklace I've ordered for Un——'

He broke off, made aware by Mr Spragg's glance of the presence of Elmer Moffatt, who, with unwonted discretion, had dropped back into the shadow of the door.

Marvell turned on Moffatt a bright gaze full of the instinctive hospitality of youth; but Moffatt looked straight past him at Mr Spragg.

The latter, as if in response to an imperceptible signal, mechanically pronounced his visitor's name; and the two young men moved toward each other.

'I beg your pardon most awfully—am I breaking up an important conference?' Ralph asked as he shook hands.

'Why, no—I guess we're pretty nearly through. I'll step outside and woo the blonde while you're talking,' Moffatt rejoined in the same key.

'Thanks so much—I shan't take two seconds.' Ralph broke off to scrutinize him. 'But haven't we met before? It seems to me I've seen you—just lately——'

Moffatt seemed about to answer, but his reply was checked by an abrupt movement on the part of Mr Spragg. There was a perceptible pause, during which Moffatt's bright black glance rested questioningly on Ralph; then he looked again at the older man, and their eyes held each other for a silent moment.

'Why, no—not as I'm aware of, Mr Marvell,' Moffatt said, addressing himself amicably to Ralph. 'Better late than never, though—and I hope to have the pleasure soon again.'

He divided a nod between the two men, and passed into the outer office, where they heard him addressing the stenographer in a strain of exaggerated gallantry.

BOOK TWO

XI

THE July sun enclosed in a ring of fire the ilex grove of a villa in the hills near Siena.

Below, by the roadside, the long yellow house seemed to waver and palpitate in the glare; but steep by steep, behind it, the cool ilex-dusk mounted to the ledge where Ralph Marvell, stretched on his back in the grass, lay gazing up at a black reticulation of branches between which bits of sky gleamed with the hardness and brilliancy of blue enamel.

Up there too the air was thick with heat; but compared with the white fire below it was a dim and tempered warmth, like that of the churches in which he and Undine sometimes took refuge at the height of the torrid days.

Ralph loved the heavy Italian summer, as he had loved the light spring days leading up to it: the long line of dancing days that had drawn them on and on ever since they had left their ship at Naples four months earlier. Four months of beauty, changeful, inexhaustible, weaving itself about him in shapes of softness and strength; and beside him, hand in hand with him, embodying that spirit of shifting magic, the radiant creature through whose eyes he saw it. This was what their hastened marriage had blessed them with, giving them leisure, before summer came, to penetrate to remote folds of the southern mountains, to linger in the shade of Sicilian orange-groves, and finally, travelling by slow stages to the Adriatic, to reach the central hill-country where even in July they might hope for a breathable air.

To Ralph the Sienese air was not only breathable but intoxicating. The sun, treading the earth like a vintager, drew from it heady fragrances, crushed out of it new colours. All the values of the temperate landscape were reversed: the noon high-lights were white, but the shadows had unimagined colour. On the blackness of cork and ilex and cypress lay the green and purple lustres, the coppery iridescences, of old bronze; and night after night the skies were wine-blue and bubbling with stars. Ralph said to himself that no one who had not seen Italy thus prostrate beneath the sun knew what secret treasures she could yield.

As he lay there, fragments of past states of emotion, fugitive felicities of thought and sensation, rose and floated on the surface of his thoughts. It was one of those moments when the accumulated impressions of life converge on heart and brain, elucidating, enlacing each other, in a mysterious confusion of beauty. He had had glimpses of such a state before, of such mergings of the personal with the general life that one felt one's self a mere wave on the wild stream of being, yet thrilled with a sharper sense of individuality than can be known within the mere bounds of the actual. But now he knew the sensation in its fulness, and with it came the releasing power of language. Words were flashing like brilliant birds through the boughs overhead; he had but to wave his magic wand to have them flutter down to him. Only they were so beautiful up there, weaving their fantastic flights against the blue, that it was pleasanter, for the moment, to watch them and let the wand lie.

He stared up at the pattern they made till his eyes ached with excess of light; then he changed his position and looked at his wife.

Undine, near by, leaned against a gnarled tree with the slightly constrained air of a person unused to sylvan abandonments. Her beautiful back could not adapt itself to the irregularities of the tree-trunk, and she moved a little now and then in the effort to find an easier position. But her expression was serene, and Ralph, looking up at her through drowsy lids, thought her face had never been more exquisite.

'You look as cool as a wave,' he said, reaching out for the hand on her knee. She let him have it, and he drew it closer, scrutinizing it as if it had been a bit of precious porcelain or ivory. It was small and soft, a mere featherweight, a puff-ball of a hand—not quick and thrilling, not a speaking hand, but one to be fondled and dressed in rings, and to leave a rosy blur in the brain. The fingers were short and tapering, dimpled at the base, with nails as smooth as rose-leaves. Ralph lifted them one by one, like a child playing with piano-keys, but they were inelastic and did not spring back far—only far enough to show the dimples.

He turned the hand over and traced the course of its blue veins from the wrist to the rounding of the palm below the fingers; then he put a kiss in the warm hollow between. The upper world had vanished: his universe had shrunk to the palm of a hand. But there was no sense of diminution. In the mystic depths whence his passion sprang, earthly dimensions were ignored and the curve of beauty was boundless enough to hold whatever the imagination could pour into it. Ralph had never felt more convinced of his power to write a great poem; but now it was Undine's hand which held the magic wand of expression.

She stirred again uneasily, answering his last words with a faint accent of reproach.

'I don't *feel* cool. You said there'd be a breeze up here.'

He laughed.

'You poor darling! Wasn't it ever as hot as this in Apex?'

She withdrew her hand with a slight grimace.

'Yes—but I didn't marry you to go back to Apex!'

Ralph laughed again; then he lifted himself on his elbow and regained the hand. 'I wonder what you *did* marry me for?'

'Mercy! It's too hot for conundrums.' She spoke without impatience, but with a lassitude less joyous than his.

He roused himself. 'Do you really mind the heat so much? We'll go, if you do.'

She sat up eagerly. 'Go to Switzerland, you mean?'

'Well, I hadn't taken quite as long a leap. I only meant we might drive back to Siena.'

She relapsed listlessly against her tree-trunk. 'Oh, Siena's hotter than this.'

'We could go and sit in the cathedral—it's always cool there at sunset.'

'We've sat in the cathedral at sunset every day for a week.'

'Well, what do you say to stopping at Lecceto* on the way? I haven't shown you Lecceto yet; and the drive back by moon-light would be glorious.'

This woke her to a slight show of interest. 'It might be nice— but where could we get anything to eat?'

Ralph laughed again. 'I don't believe we could. You're too practical.'

'Well, somebody's got to be. And the food in the hotel is too disgusting if we're not on time.'

'I admit that the best of it has usually been appropriated by the extremely good-looking cavalry-officer who's so keen to know you.'

Undine's face brightened. 'You know he's not a Count; he's a Marquis. His name's Roviano; his palace in Rome is in the guide-books, and he speaks English beautifully. Céleste found out about him from the head-waiter,' she said, with the security of one who treats of recognized values.

Marvell, sitting upright, reached lazily across the grass for his hat. 'Then there's all the more reason for rushing back to defend our share.' He spoke in the bantering tone which had become the habitual expression of his tenderness; but his eyes softened as they absorbed in a last glance the glimmering submarine light of the ancient grove, through which Undine's figure wavered nereid-like above him.

'You never looked your name more than you do now,' he said, kneeling at her side and putting his arm about her. She smiled back a little vaguely, as if not seizing his allusion, and being content to let it drop into the store of unexplained references which had once stimulated her curiosity but now merely gave her leisure to think of other things. But her smile was no less lovely for its vagueness, and indeed, to Ralph, the loveliness was enhanced by the latent doubt. He remembered afterward that at that moment the cup of life seemed to brim over.

'Come, dear—here or there—it's all divine!'

In the carriage, however, she remained insensible to the soft spell of the evening, noticing only the heat and dust, and saying, as they passed under the wooded cliff of Lecceto, that they might as well have stopped there after all, since with such a headache as she felt coming on she didn't care if she dined or not.

Ralph looked up yearningly at the long walls overhead; but Undine's mood was hardly favourable to communion with such scenes, and he made no attempt to stop the carriage. Instead he presently said: 'If you're tired of Italy, we've got the world to choose from.'

She did not speak for a moment; then she said: 'It's the heat I'm tired of. Don't people generally come here earlier?'

'Yes. That's why I chose the summer: so that we could have it all to ourselves.'

She tried to put a note of reasonableness into her voice. 'If you'd told me we were going everywhere at the wrong time, of course I could have arranged about my clothes.'

'You poor darling! Let us, by all means, go to the place where the clothes will be right: they're too beautiful to be left out of our scheme of life.'

Her lips hardened. 'I know you don't care how I look. But you didn't give me time to order anything before we were married, and I've got nothing but my last winter's things to wear.'

Ralph smiled. Even his subjugated mind perceived the inconsistency of Undine's taxing him with having hastened their marriage; but her variations on the eternal feminine still enchanted him.

'We'll go wherever you please—you make every place the one place,' he said, as if he were humouring an irresistible child.

'To Switzerland, then? Céleste says St Moritz is too heavenly,' exclaimed Undine, who gathered her ideas of Europe chiefly from the conversation of her experienced attendant.

'One can be cool short of the Engadine. Why not go south again—say to Capri?'

'Capri? Is that the island we saw from Naples, where the artists go?' She drew her brows together. 'It would be simply awful getting there in this heat.'

'Well, then, I know a little place in Switzerland where one can still get away from the crowd, and we can sit and look at a green water-fall while I lie in wait for adjectives.'

Mr Spragg's astonishment on learning that his son-in-law contemplated maintaining a household on the earnings of his Muse was still matter for pleasantry between the pair; and one of the humours of their first weeks together had consisted in picturing themselves as a primeval couple setting forth across a virgin continent and subsisting on the adjectives which Ralph was to trap for his epic. On this occasion, however, his wife did not take up the joke, and he remained silent while their carriage climbed the long dusty hill to the Fontebranda gate. He had seen her face droop as he suggested the possibility of an escape from the crowds in Switzerland, and it came to him, with the sharpness of a knife-thrust, that a crowd was what she wanted—that she was sick to death of being alone with him.

He sat motionless, staring ahead at the red-brown walls and towers on the steep above them. After all there was nothing sudden in his discovery. For weeks it had hung on the edge of consciousness, but he had turned from it with the heart's instinctive clinging to the unrealities by which it lives. Even now a hundred qualifying reasons rushed to his aid. They told him it was not of himself that Undine had wearied, but only of their present way of life. He had said a moment before, without conscious exaggeration, that her presence made any place the one place; yet how willingly would he have consented to share in such a life as she was leading before their marriage? And he had to acknowledge their months of desultory wandering from one remote Italian hill-top to another must have seemed as purposeless to her as balls and dinners would have been to him. An imagination like his, peopled with such varied images and associations, fed by so many currents from the long stream of human experience, could hardly picture the bareness of the small half-lit place in which his wife's spirit fluttered. Her mind was as destitute of beauty and mystery as the prairie schoolhouse in which she had been educated; and her ideals seemed to Ralph as pathetic as the ornaments made of corks and cigar-bands with which her infant hands had been taught to adorn it. He was beginning to understand this, and learning to adapt himself to the narrow compass of her experience. The task of opening new windows in her mind was inspiring enough to give him infinite patience; and he would not yet own to himself that her pliancy and variety were imitative rather than spontaneous.

Meanwhile he had no desire to sacrifice her wishes to his, and it distressed him that he dared not confess his real reason for avoiding the Engadine. The truth was that their funds were shrinking faster than he had expected. Mr Spragg, after bluntly opposing their hastened marriage on the ground that he was not prepared, at such short notice, to make the necessary provision for his daughter, had shortly afterward (probably, as Undine observed to Ralph, in consequence of a lucky 'turn' in the Street) met their wishes with all possible liberality, bestowing on them a wedding in conformity with Mrs Spragg's ideals and up to the highest standard of Mrs Heeny's clippings, and pledging himself to provide Undine with an income adequate to so brilliant a beginning. It was understood that Ralph, on their return, should renounce the law for some more paying business; but this seemed the smallest of sacrifices to make for the privilege of calling Undine his wife; and besides, he still secretly hoped that, in the interval, his real vocation might declare itself in some work which would justify his adopting the life of letters.

He had assumed that Undine's allowance, with the addition of his own small income, would be enough to satisfy their needs. His own were few, and had always been within his means; but his wife's daily requirements, combined with her intermittent outbreaks of extravagance, had thrown out all his calculations, and they were already seriously exceeding their income.

If any one had prophesied before his marriage that he would find it difficult to tell this to Undine he would have smiled at the suggestion; and during their first days together it had seemed as though pecuniary questions were the last likely to be raised between them. But his marital education had since made strides, and he now knew that a disregard for money may imply not the willingness to get on without it but merely a blind confidence that it will somehow be provided. If Undine, like the lilies of the field,* took no care, it was not because her wants were as few but because she assumed that care would be taken for her by those whose privilege it was to enable her to unite floral insouciance with Sheban elegance.

She had met Ralph's first note of warning with the assurance that she 'didn't mean to worry'; and her tone implied that it was his business to do so for her. He certainly wanted to guard her from this as from all other cares; he wanted also, and still more passionately after the topic had once or twice recurred between them, to guard himself from the risk of judging where he still adored. These restraints to frankness kept him silent during the remainder of the drive, and when, after dinner, Undine again complained of her headache, he let her go up to her room and wandered out into the dimly lit streets to renewed communion with his problems.

They hung on him insistently as darkness fell, and Siena grew vocal with that shrill diversity of sounds that breaks, on summer nights, from every cleft of the masonry in old Italian towns. Then the moon rose, unfolding depth by depth the lines of the antique land; and Ralph, leaning against an old brick parapet, and watching each silver-blue remoteness disclose itself between the dark masses of the middle distance, felt his spirit enlarged and pacified. For the first time, as his senses thrilled to the deep touch of beauty, he asked himself if out of these floating and fugitive vibrations he might not build something concrete and stable, if even such dull common cares as now oppressed him might not become the motive power of creation. If he could only, on the spot, do something with all the accumulated spoils of the last months—something that should both put money into his pocket and harmony into the rich confusion of his spirit! 'I'll write—I'll write: that must be what the whole thing means,' he said to himself, with a vague clutch at some solution which should keep him a little longer hanging half-way down the steep of disenchantment.

He would have stayed on, heedless of time, to trace the ramifications of his idea in the complex beauty of the scene, but for the longing to share his mood with Undine. For the last few months every thought and sensation had been instantly transmuted into such emotional impulses and, though the currents of communication between himself and Undine were neither deep nor numerous, each fresh rush of feeling seemed strong enough to clear a way to her heart. He hurried back, almost breathlessly, to the inn; but even as he knocked at her door the subtle emanation of other influences seemed to arrest and chill him.

She had put out the lamp, and sat by the window in the moonlight, her head propped on a listless hand. As Marvell entered she turned; then, without speaking, she looked away again.

He was used to this mute reception, and had learned that it had no personal motive, but was the result of an extremely simplified social code. Mr and Mrs Spragg seldom spoke to each other when they met, and words of greeting seemed almost unknown to their domestic vocabulary. Marvell, at first, had fancied that his own warmth would call forth a response from his wife, who had been so quick to learn the forms of worldly intercourse; but he soon saw that she regarded intimacy as a pretext for escaping from such forms into a total absence of expression.

To-night, however, he felt another meaning in her silence, and perceived that she intended him to feel it. He met it by silence, but of a different kind; letting his nearness speak for him as he knelt beside her and laid his cheek against hers. She seemed hardly aware of the gesture; but to that he was also used. She had never shown any repugnance to his tenderness, but such response as it evoked was remote and Ariel-like,* suggesting, from the first, not so much of the recoil of ignorance as the coolness of the element from which she took her name.

As he pressed her to him she seemed to grow less impassive and he felt her resign herself like a tired child. He held his breath, not daring to break the spell.

At length he whispered: 'I've just seen such a wonderful thing—I wish you'd been with me!'

'What sort of a thing?' She turned her head with a faint show of interest.

'A—I don't know—a vision . . . It came to me out there just now with the moonrise.'

'A vision?' Her interest flagged. 'I never cared much about spirits. Mother used to try to drag me to séances—but they always made me sleepy.'

Ralph laughed. 'I don't mean a dead spirit but a living one! I saw the vision of a book I mean to do. It came to me suddenly, magnificently, swooped down on me as that big white moon swooped down on the black landscape, tore at me like a great white eagle—like the bird of Jove!* After all, imagination *was* the eagle that devoured Prometheus!'*

She drew away abruptly, and the bright moonlight showed him the apprehension in her face. 'You're not going to write a book *here*?'

He stood up and wandered away a step or two; then he turned and came back. 'Of course not here. Wherever you

want. The main point is that it's come to me—no, that it's
come *back* to me! For it's all these months together, it's all our
happiness—it's the meaning of life that I've found, and it's you,
dearest, you who've given it to me!'

He dropped down beside her again; but she disengaged herself and he heard a little sob in her throat.

'Undine—what's the matter?'

'Nothing . . . I don't know . . . I suppose I'm homesick . . .'

'Homesick? You poor darling! You're tired of travelling?
What is it?'

'I don't know . . . I don't like Europe . . . it's not what I
expected, and I think it's all too dreadfully dreary!' The words
broke from her in a long wail of rebellion.

Marvell gazed at her perplexedly. It seemed strange that such
unguessed thoughts should have been stirring in the heart
pressed to his. 'It's less interesting than you expected—or less
amusing? Is that it?'

'It's dirty and ugly—all the towns we've been to are disgustingly dirty. I loathe the smells and the beggars. I'm sick and tired
of the stuffy rooms in the hotels. I thought it would all be so
splendid—but New York's ever so much nicer!'

'Not New York in July?'

'I don't care—there are the roof-gardens, anyway; and there
are always people round. All these places seem as if they were
dead. It's all like some awful cemetery.'

A sense of compunction checked Marvell's laughter. 'Don't
cry, dear—don't! I see, I understand. You're lonely and the heat
has tired you out. It *is* dull here; awfully dull; I've been stupid
not to feel it. But we'll start at once—we'll get out of it.'

She brightened instantly. 'We'll go up to Switzerland?'

'We'll go up to Switzerland.' He had a fleeting glimpse of
the quiet place with the green water-fall, where he might have
made tryst with his vision; then he turned his mind from it
and said: 'We'll go just where you want. How soon can you be
ready to start?'

'Oh, to-morrow—the first thing to-morrow! I'll make
Céleste get out of bed now and pack. Can we go right through
to St Moritz? I'd rather sleep in the train than in another of these
awful places.'

She was on her feet in a flash, her face alight, her hair waving and floating about her as though it rose on her happy heart-beats.

'Oh, Ralph, it's *sweet* of you, and I love you!' she cried out, letting him take her to his breast.

XII

IN the quiet place with the green water-fall Ralph's vision might have kept faith with him; but how could he hope to surprise it in the midsummer crowds of St Moritz?

Undine, at any rate, had found there what she wanted; and when he was at her side, and her radiant smile included him, every other question was in abeyance. But there were hours of solitary striding over bare grassy slopes, face to face with the ironic interrogation of sky and mountains, when his anxieties came back, more persistent and importunate. Sometimes they took the form of merely material difficulties. How, for instance, was he to meet the cost of their ruinous suite at the Engadine Palace while he awaited Mr Spragg's next remittance? And once the hotel bills were paid, what would be left for the journey back to Paris, the looming expenses there, the price of the passage to America? These questions would fling him back on the thought of his projected book, which was, after all, to be what the masterpieces of literature had mostly been—a pot-boiler. Well! Why not? Did not the worshipper always heap the rarest essences on the altar of his divinity? Ralph still rejoiced in the thought of giving back to Undine something of the beauty of their first months together. But even on his solitary walks the vision eluded him; and he could spare so few hours to its pursuit!

Undine's days were crowded, and it was still a matter of course that where she went he should follow. He had risen visibly in her opinion since they had been absorbed into the life of the big hotels, and she had seen that his command of foreign tongues put him at an advantage even in circles where English was generally spoken if not understood. Undine herself, ham-pered by her lack of languages, was soon drawn into the group of compatriots who struck the social pitch of their hotel. Their types were familiar enough to Ralph, who had taken their measure in former wanderings, and come across their duplicates in every scene of continental idleness. Foremost among them was Mrs Harvey Shallum, a showy Parisianized figure, with a small wax-featured husband whose ultra-fashionable clothes seemed a tribute to his wife's importance rather than the mark of his personal taste. Mr Shallum, in fact, could not be said to have any personal bent. Though he conversed with a colourless fluency in the principal European tongues, he seldom exercised his gift except in intercourse with hotel-managers and head-waiters; and his long silences were broken only by resigned allusions to the enormities he had suffered at the hands of this gifted but unscrupulous class.

Mrs Shallum, though in command of but a few verbs, all of which, on her lips, became irregular, managed to express a polyglot personality as vivid as her husband's was effaced. Her only idea of intercourse with her kind was to organize it into bands and subject it to frequent displacements; and society smiled at her for these exertions like an infant vigorously rocked. She saw at once Undine's value as a factor in her scheme, and the two formed an alliance on which Ralph refrained from shedding the cold light of depreciation. It was a point of honour with him not to seem to disdain any of Undine's amusements: the noisy interminable picnics, the hot promiscuous balls, the concerts, bridge-parties and theatricals which helped to disguise the difference between the high Alps and Paris or New York. He told himself that there is always a Narcissus-element in youth, and that what Undine really enjoyed was the image of her own charm mirrored in the general admiration. With her quick perceptions and adaptabilities she would soon learn to care more about the quality of the reflecting surface; and meanwhile no criticism of his should mar her pleasure.

The appearance at their hotel of the cavalry officer from Siena was a not wholly agreeable surprise but even after the handsome Marquis had been introduced to Undine, and had whirled her through an evening's dances, Ralph was not seriously disturbed. Husband and wife had grown closer to each other since they had come to St Moritz, and in the brief moments she could give him

Undine was now always gay and approachable. Her fitful humours had vanished, and she showed qualities of comradeship that seemed the promise of a deeper understanding. But this very hope made him more subject to her moods, more fearful of disturbing the harmony between them. Least of all could he broach the subject of money: he had too keen a memory of the way her lips could narrow, and her eyes turn from him as if he were a stranger.

It was a different matter that one day brought the look he feared to her face. She had announced her intention of going on an excursion with Mrs Shallum and three or four of the young men who formed the nucleus of their shifting circle, and for the first time she did not ask Ralph if he were coming; but he felt no resentment at being left out. He was tired of these noisy assaults on the high solitudes, and the prospect of a quiet after-noon turned his thoughts to his book. Now if ever there seemed a chance of recapturing the moonlight vision . . .

From his balcony he looked down on the assembling party. Mrs Shallum was already screaming bilingually at various windows in the long façade; and Undine presently came out of the hotel with the Marchese Roviano and two young English diplomatists. Slim and tall in her trim mountain garb, she made the ornate Mrs Shallum look like a piece of ambulant upholstery. The high air brightened her cheeks and struck new lights from her hair, and Ralph had never seen her so touched with morning freshness. The party was not yet complete, and he felt a movement of annoyance when he recognized, in the last person to join it, a Russian lady of cosmopolitan notoriety whom he had run across in his unmarried days, and as to whom he had already warned Undine. Knowing what strange speci-mens from the depths slip through the wide meshes of the watering-place world, he had foreseen that a meeting with the Baroness Adelschein was inevitable; but he had not expected her to become one of his wife's intimate circle.

When the excursionists had started he turned back to his writing-table and tried to take up his work; but he could not fix his thoughts: they were far away, in pursuit of Undine. He had been but five months married, and it seemed, after all, rather soon for him to be dropped out of such excursions as unquestioningly as poor Harvey Shallum. He smiled away this first twinge of jealousy, but the irritation it left found a pretext in his displeasure at Undine's choice of companions. Mrs Shallum grated on his taste, but she was as open to inspection as a shop-window, and he was sure that time would teach his wife the cheapness of what she had to show. Roviano and the English-men were well enough too: frankly bent on amusement, but pleasant and well-bred. But they would naturally take their tone from the women they were with; and Madame Adelschein's tone was notorious. He knew also that Undine's faculty of self-defense was weakened by the instinct of adapting herself to whatever company she was in, of copying 'the others' in speech and gesture as closely as she reflected them in dress; and he was disturbed by the thought of what her ignorance might expose her to.

She came back late, flushed with her long walk, her face all sparkle and mystery, as he had seen it in the first days of their courtship; and the look somehow revived his irritated sense of having been intentionally left out of the party.

'You've been gone forever. Was it the Adelschein who made you go such lengths?' he asked her, trying to keep to his usual joking tone.

Undine, as she dropped down on the sofa and unpinned her hat, shed on him the light of her guileless gaze.

'I don't know: everybody was amusing. The Marquis is awfully bright.'

'I'd no idea you or Bertha Shallum knew Madame Adelschein well enough to take her off with you in that way.'

Undine sat absently smoothing the tuft of glossy cock's-feathers in her hat.

'I don't see that you've got to know people particularly well to go for a walk with them. The Baroness is awfully bright too.'

She always gave her acquaintances their titles, seeming not, in this respect, to have noticed that a simpler form prevailed.

'I don't dispute the interest of what she says; but I've told you what decent people think of what she does,' Ralph retorted, exasperated by what seemed a wilful pretense of ignorance.

She continued to scrutinize him with her clear eyes, in which there was no shadow of offense.

'You mean they don't want to go round with her? You're mistaken: it's not true. She goes round with everybody. She dined last night with the Grand Duchess; Roviano told me so.'

This was not calculated to make Ralph take a more tolerant view of the question.

'Does he also tell you what's said of her?'

'What's said of her?' Undine's limpid glance rebuked him. 'Do you mean that disgusting scandal you told me about? Do you suppose I'd let him talk to me about such things? I meant you're mistaken about her social position. He says she goes everywhere.'

Ralph laughed impatiently. 'No doubt Roviano's an authority; but it doesn't happen to be his business to choose your friends for you.'

Undine echoed his laugh. 'Well, I guess I don't need anybody to do that: I can do it myself,' she said, with the good-humoured curtness that was the habitual note of intercourse with the Spraggs.

Ralph sat down beside her and laid a caressing touch on her shoulder. 'No, you can't, you foolish child. You know nothing of this society you're in; of its antecedents, its rules, its conventions; and it's my affair to look after you, and warn you when you're on the wrong track.'

'Mercy, what a solemn speech!' She shrugged away his hand without ill-temper. 'I don't believe an American woman needs to know such a lot about their old rules. They can see I mean to follow my own, and if they don't like it they needn't go with me.'

'Oh, they'll go with you fast enough, as you call it. They'll be too charmed to. The question is how far they'll make you go with *them*, and where they'll finally land you.'

She tossed her head back with the movement she had learned in 'speaking' school-pieces about freedom and the British tyrant.

'No one's ever yet gone any farther with me than I wanted!' she declared. She was really exquisitely simple.

'I'm not sure Roviano hasn't, in vouching for Madame Adelschein. But he probably thinks you know about her. To him this isn't "society" any more than the people in an omnibus are. Society, to everybody here, means the sanction of their own special group and of the corresponding groups elsewhere. The Adelschein goes about in a place like this because it's nobody's business to stop her; but the women who tolerate her here would drop her like a shot if she set foot on their own ground.'

The thoughtful air with which Undine heard him out made him fancy this argument had carried; and as he ended she threw him a bright look.

'Well, that's easy enough: I can drop her if she comes to New York.'

Ralph sat silent for a moment—then he turned away and began to gather up his scattered pages.

Undine, in the ensuing days, was no less often with Madame Adelschein, and Ralph suspected a challenge in her open frequentation of the lady. But if challenge there were, he let it lie. Whether his wife saw more or less of Madame Adelschein seemed no longer of much consequence: she had so amply shown him her ability to protect herself. The pang lay in the completeness of the proof—in the perfect functioning of her instinct of self-preservation. For the first time he was face to face with his hovering dread: he was judging where he still adored.

Before long more pressing cares absorbed him. He had already begun to watch the post for his father-in-law's monthly remittance, without precisely knowing how, even with its aid, he was to bridge the gulf of expense between St Moritz and New York. The non-arrival of Mr Spragg's cheque was productive of graver fears, and these were abruptly confirmed when, coming in one afternoon, he found Undine crying over a letter from her mother.

Her distress made him fear that Mr Spragg was ill, and he drew her to him soothingly; but she broke away with an impatient movement.

'Oh, they're all well enough—but father's lost a lot of money. He's been speculating, and he can't send us anything for at least three months.'

Ralph murmured reassuringly: 'As long as there's no one ill!'—but in reality he was following her despairing gaze down the long perspective of their barren quarter.

'Three months! Three months!'

Undine dried her eyes, and sat with set lips and tapping foot while he read her mother's letter.

'Your poor father! It's a hard knock for him. I'm sorry,' he said as he handed it back.

For a moment she did not seem to hear; then she said between her teeth: 'It's hard for *us*. I suppose now we'll have to go straight home.'

He looked at her with wonder. 'If that were all! In any case I should have to be back in a few weeks.'

'But we needn't have left here in August! It's the first place in Europe that I've liked, and it's just my luck to be dragged away from it!'

'I'm so awfully sorry, dearest. It's my fault for persuading you to marry a pauper.'

'It's father's fault. Why on earth did he go and speculate? There's no use his saying he's sorry now!' She sat brooding for a moment and then suddenly took Ralph's hand. 'Couldn't your people do something—help us out just this once, I mean?'

He flushed to the forehead: it seemed inconceivable that she should make such a suggestion.

'I couldn't ask them—it's not possible. My grandfather does as much as he can for me, and my mother has nothing but what he gives her.'

Undine seemed unconscious of his embarrassment. 'He doesn't give us nearly as much as father does,' she said; and, as Ralph remained silent, she went on: 'Couldn't you ask your sister, then? I must have some clothes to go home in.'

His heart contracted as he looked at her. What sinister change came over her when her will was crossed? She seemed to grow inaccessible, implacable—her eyes were like the eyes of an enemy.

'I don't know—I'll see,' he said, rising and moving away from her. At that moment the touch of her hand was repugnant. Yes—he might ask Laura, no doubt: and whatever she had would be his. But the necessity was bitter to him, and Undine's unconsciousness of the fact hurt him more than her indifference to her father's misfortune.

What hurt him most was the curious fact that for all her light irresponsibility, it was always she who made the practical suggestion, hit the nail of expediency on the head. No sentimental scruple made the blow waver or deflected her resolute aim. She had thought at once of Laura, and Laura was his only, his inevitable, resource. His anxious mind pictured his sister's wonder, and made him wince under the sting of Henley Fairford's irony: Fairford, who at the time of the marriage had sat silent and pulled his moustache while every one else argued and objected, yet under whose silence Ralph had felt a deeper protest than under all the reasoning of the others. It was no comfort to reflect that Fairford would probably continue to say nothing! But necessity made light of these twinges, and Ralph set his teeth and cabled.

Undine's chief surprise seemed to be that Laura's response, though immediate and generous, did not enable them to stay on at St Moritz. But she apparently read in her husband's look the uselessness of such a hope, for, with one of the sudden changes of mood that still disarmed him, she accepted the need of departure, and took leave philosophically of the Shallums and their band. After all, Paris was ahead, and in September one would have a chance to see the new models and surprise the secret councils of the dress-makers.

Ralph was astonished at the tenacity with which she held to her purpose. He tried, when they reached Paris, to make her feel the necessity of starting at once for home; but she complained of fatigue and of feeling vaguely unwell, and he had to yield to her desire for rest. The word, however, was to strike him as strangely misapplied, for from the day of their arrival she was in a state of perpetual activity. She seemed to have mastered her Paris by divination, and between the bounds of the Boulevards and the Place Vendôme she moved at once with supernatural ease.

'Of course,' she explained to him, 'I understand how little we've got to spend; but I left New York without a rag, and it was you who made me countermand my trousseau, instead of having it sent after us. I wish now I hadn't listened to you— father'd have had to pay for *that* before he lost his money. As it is, it will be cheaper in the end for me to pick up a few things here. The advantage of going to the French dress-makers is that they'll wait twice as long for their money as the people at home.

And they're all crazy to dress me—Bertha Shallum will tell you so: she says no one ever had such a chance! That's why I was willing to come to this stuffy little hotel—I wanted to save every scrap I could to get a few decent things. And over here they're accustomed to being bargained with—you ought to see how I've beaten them down! Have you any idea what a dinner-dress costs in New York——?'

So it went on, obtusely and persistently, whenever he tried to sound the note of prudence. But on other themes she was more than usually responsive. Paris enchanted her, and they had delightful hours at the theatres—the 'little' ones—amusing dinners at fashionable restaurants, and reckless evenings in haunts where she thrilled with simple glee at the thought of what she must so obviously be 'taken for.' All these familiar diversions regained, for Ralph, a fresh zest in her company. Her innocence, her high spirits, her astounding comments and credulities, renovated the old Parisian adventure and flung a veil of romance over its hackneyed scenes. Beheld through such a medium the future looked less near and implacable, and Ralph, when he had received a reassuring letter from his sister, let his conscience sleep and slipped forth on the high tide of pleasure. After all, in New York amusements would be fewer, and their life, for a time, perhaps more quiet. Moreover, Ralph's dim glimpses of Mr Spragg's past suggested that the latter was likely to be on his feet again at any moment, and atoning by redoubled prodigalities for his temporary straits; and beyond all these possibilities there was the book to be written—the book on which Ralph was sure he should get a real hold as soon as they settled down in New York.

Meanwhile the daily cost of living, and the bills that could not be deferred, were eating deep into Laura's subsidy. Ralph's anxieties returned, and his plight was brought home to him with a shock when, on going one day to engage passages, he learned that the prices were that of the 'rush season,' and one of the conditions immediate payment. At other times, he was told the rules were easier; but in September and October no exception could be made.

As he walked away with this fresh weight on his mind he caught sight of the strolling figure of Peter Van Degen—Peter lounging and luxuriating among the seductions of the Boulevard with the disgusting ease of a man whose wants are all measured by money, and who always has enough to gratify them.

His present sense of these advantages revealed itself in the affability of his greeting to Ralph, and in his off-hand request that the latter should 'look up Clare,' who had come over with him to get her winter finery.

'She's motoring to Italy next week with some of her long-haired friends—but I'm off for the other side; going back on the *Sorceress*. She's just been overhauled at Greenock, and we ought to have a good spin over. Better come along with me, old man.'

The *Sorceress* was Van Degen's steam-yacht, most huge and complicated of her kind: it was his habit, after his semi-annual flights to Paris and London, to take a joyous company back on her and let Clare return by steamer. The character of these parties made the invitation almost an offense to Ralph; but reflecting that it was probably a phrase distributed to every acquaintance when Van Degen was in a rosy mood, he merely answered: 'Much obliged, my dear fellow; but Undine and I are sailing immediately.'

Peter's glassy eye grew livelier. 'Ah, to be sure—you're not over the honeymoon yet. How's the bride? Stunning as ever? My regards to her, please. I suppose she's too deep in dress-making to be called on?—but don't you forget to look up Clare!' He hurried on in pursuit of a flitting petticoat and Ralph continued his walk home.

He prolonged it a little in order to put off telling Undine of his plight; for he could devise only one way of meeting the cost of the voyage, and that was to take it at once, and thus curtail their Parisian expenses. But he knew how unwelcome this plan would be, and he shrank the more from seeing Undine's face harden since, of late, he had so basked in its brightness.

When at last he entered the little *salon* she called 'stuffy' he found her in conference with a blond-bearded gentleman who wore the red ribbon in his lapel, and who, on Ralph's appearance—and at a sign, as it appeared, from Mrs Marvell—swept into his note-case some small objects that had lain on the table, and bowed himself out with a 'Madame—Monsieur' worthy of the highest traditions.

Ralph looked after him with amusement. 'Who's your friend—an Ambassador or a tailor?'

Undine was rapidly slipping on her rings, which, as he now saw, had also been scattered over the table.

'Oh, it was only that jeweller I told you about—the one Bertha Shallum goes to.'

'A jeweller? Good heavens, my poor girl! You're buying jewels?' The extravagance of the idea struck a laugh from him.

Undine's face did not harden: it took on, instead, an almost deprecating look. 'Of course not—how silly you are! I only wanted a few old things reset. But I won't if you'd rather not.'

She came to him and sat down at his side, laying her hand on his arm. He took the hand up and looked at the deep gleam of the sapphires in the old family ring he had given her.

'You won't have that reset?' he said, smiling and twisting the ring about on her finger; then he went on with his thankless explanation. 'It's not that I don't want you to do this or that; it's simply that, for the moment, we're rather strapped. I've just been to see the steamer people, and our passages will cost a good deal more than I thought.'

He mentioned the sum and the fact that he must give an answer the next day. Would she consent to sail that very Saturday? Or should they go a fortnight later, in a slow boat from Plymouth?

Undine frowned on both alternatives. She was an indifferent sailor and shrank from the possible 'nastiness' of the cheaper boat. She wanted to get the voyage over as quickly and luxuriously as possible—Bertha Shallum had told her that in a 'deck-suite' no one need be sea-sick—but she wanted still more to have another week or two of Paris; and it was always hard to make her see why circumstances could not be bent to her wishes.

'This week? But how on earth can I be ready? Besides, we're dining at Enghien with the Shallums on Saturday, and motoring to Chantilly with the Jim Driscolls on Sunday. I can't imagine how you thought we could go this week!'

But she still opposed the cheap steamer, and after they had carried the question on to Voisin's, and there unprofitably discussed it through a long luncheon, it seemed no nearer a solution.

'Well, think it over—let me know this evening,' Ralph said, proportioning the waiter's fee to a bill burdened by Undine's reckless choice of *primeurs*.

His wife was to join the newly-arrived Mrs Shallum in a round of the rue de la Paix; and he had seized the opportunity of slipping off to a classical performance at the Français. On their arrival in Paris he had taken Undine to one of these entertainments, but it left her too weary and puzzled for him to renew the attempt, and he had not found time to go back without her. He was glad now to shed his cares in such an atmosphere. The play was of the greatest, the interpretation that of the vanishing grand manner which lived in his first memories of the Parisian stage, and his surrender to such influences as complete as in his early days. Caught up in the fiery chariot of art, he felt once more the tug of its coursers in his muscles, and the rush of their flight still throbbed in him when he walked back late to the hotel.

XIII

HE had expected to find Undine still out; but on the stairs he crossed Mrs Shallum, who threw at him from under an immense hat-brim: 'Yes, she's in, but you'd better come and have tea with me at the Luxe. I don't think husbands are wanted!'

Ralph laughingly rejoined that that was just the moment for them to appear; and Mrs Shallum swept on, crying back: 'All the same, I'll wait for you!'

In the sitting-room Ralph found Undine seated behind a tea-table on the other side of which, in an attitude of easy intimacy, Peter Van Degen stretched his lounging length.

He did not move on Ralph's appearance, no doubt thinking their kinship close enough to make his nod and 'Hullo!' a sufficient greeting. Peter in intimacy was given to miscalculations of the sort, and Ralph's first movement was to glance at

Undine and see how it affected her. But her eyes gave out the vivid rays that noise and banter always struck from them; her face, at such moments, was like a theatre with all the lustres blazing. That the illumination should have been kindled by his cousin's husband was not precisely agreeable to Marvell, who thought Peter a bore in society and an insufferable nuisance on closer terms. But he was becoming blunted to Undine's lack of discrimination; and his own treatment of Van Degen was always tempered by his sympathy for Clare.

He therefore listened with apparent good-humour to Peter's suggestion of an evening at a *petit théâtre* with the Harvey Shallums, and joined in the laugh with which Undine declared: 'Oh, Ralph won't go—he only likes the theatres where they walk around in bath-towels and talk poetry.—Isn't that what you've just been seeing?' she added, with a turn of the neck that shed her brightness on him.

'What? One of those five-barrelled shows at the Français? Great Scott, Ralph—no wonder your wife's pining for the Folies Bergère!'

'She needn't, my dear fellow. We never interfere with each other's vices.'

Peter, unsolicited, was comfortably lighting a cigarette. 'Ah, there's the secret of domestic happiness. Marry somebody who likes all the things you don't, and make love to somebody who likes all the things you do.'

Undine laughed appreciatively. 'Only it dooms poor Ralph to such awful frumps. Can't you see the sort of woman who'd love his sort of play?'

'Oh, I can see her fast enough—my wife loves 'em,' said their visitor, rising with a grin; while Ralph threw out: 'So don't waste your pity on me!' and Undine's laugh had the slight note of asperity that the mention of Clare always elicited.

'To-morrow night, then, at Paillard's,' Van Degen concluded. 'And about the other business—that's a go too? I leave it to you to settle the date.'

The nod and laugh they exchanged seemed to hint at depths of collusion from which Ralph was pointedly excluded; and he wondered how large a programme of pleasure they had already had time to sketch out. He disliked the idea of Undine's being too frequently seen with Van Degen, whose Parisian reputation was not fortified by the connections that propped it up in New York; but he did not want to interfere with her pleasure, and he was still wondering what to say when, as the door closed, she turned to him gaily.

'I'm so glad you've come! I've got some news for you.' She laid a light touch on his arm.

Touch and tone were enough to disperse his anxieties, and he answered that he was in luck to find her already in when he had supposed her engaged, over a Nouveau Luxe tea-table, in repairing the afternoon's ravages.

'Oh, I didn't shop much—I didn't stay out long.' She raised a kindling face to him. 'And what do you think I've been doing? While you were sitting in your stuffy old theatre, worrying about the money I was spending (oh, you needn't fib—I know you were!) I was saving you hundreds and thousands. I've saved you the price of our passage!'

Ralph laughed in pure enjoyment of her beauty. When she shone on him like that what did it matter what nonsense she talked?

'You wonderful woman—how did you do it? By countermanding a tiara?'

'You know I'm not such a fool as you pretend!' She held him at arm's length with a nod of joyous mystery. 'You'll simply never guess! I've made Peter Van Degen ask us to go home on the *Sorceress*. What do you say to that?'

She flashed it out on a laugh of triumph, without appearing to have a doubt of the effect the announcement would produce.

Ralph stared at her. 'The *Sorceress*? You *made* him?'

'Well, I managed it, I worked him round to it! He's crazy about the idea now—but I don't think he'd thought of it before he came.'

'I should say not!' Ralph ejaculated. 'He never would have had the cheek to think of it.'

'Well, I've made him, anyhow! Did you ever know such luck?'

'Such luck?' He groaned at her obstinate innocence. 'Do you suppose I'll let you cross the ocean on the *Sorceress*?'

She shrugged impatiently. 'You say that because your cousin doesn't go on her.'

'If she doesn't, it's because it's no place for decent women.'

'It's Clare's fault if it isn't. Everybody knows she's crazy about you, and she makes him feel it. That's why he takes up with other women.'

Her anger reddened her cheeks and dropped her brows like a black bar above her glowing eyes. Even in his recoil from what she said Ralph felt the tempestuous heat of her beauty. But for the first time his latent resentments rose in him, and he gave her back wrath for wrath.

'Is that the precious stuff he tells you?'

'Do you suppose I had to wait for him to tell me? Everybody knows it—everybody in New York knew she was wild when you married. That's why she's always been so nasty to me. If you won't go on the *Sorceress* they'll all say it's because she was jealous of me and wouldn't let you.'

Ralph's indignation had already flickered down to disgust. Undine was no longer beautiful—she seemed to have the face of her thoughts. He stood up with an impatient laugh.

'Is that another of his arguments? I don't wonder they're convincing——' But as quickly as it had come the sneer dropped, yielding to a wave of pity, the vague impulse to silence and protect her. How could he have given way to the provocation of her weakness, when his business was to defend her from it and lift her above it? He recalled his old dreams of saving her from Van Degenism—it was not thus that he had imagined the rescue.

'Don't let's pay Peter the compliment of squabbling over him,' he said, turning away to pour himself a cup of tea.

When he had filled his cup he sat down beside Undine, with a smile. 'No doubt he was joking—and thought you were; but if you really made him believe we might go with him you'd better drop him a line.'

Undine's brow still gloomed. 'You refuse, then?'

'Refuse? I don't need to! Do you want to succeed to half the chorus-world of New York?'

'They won't be on board with us, I suppose!'

'The echoes of their conversation will. It's the only language Peter knows.'

'He told me he longed for the influence of a good woman——' She checked herself, reddening at Ralph's laugh.

'Well, tell him to apply again when he's been under it a month or two. Meanwhile we'll stick to the liners.'

Ralph was beginning to learn that the only road to her reason lay through her vanity, and he fancied that if she could be made to see Van Degen as an object of ridicule she might give up the idea of the *Sorceress* of her own accord. But her will hardened slowly under his joking opposition, and she became no less formidable as she grew more calm. He was used to women who, in such cases, yielded as a matter of course to masculine judgments: if one pronounced a man 'not decent' the question was closed. But it was Undine's habit to ascribe all interference with her plans to personal motives, and he could see that she attributed his opposition to the furtive machinations of poor Clare. It was odious to him to prolong the discussion, for the accent of recrimination was the one he most dreaded on her lips. But the moment came when he had to take the brunt of it, averting his thoughts as best he might from the glimpse it gave of a world of mean familiarities, of reprisals drawn from the vulgarist of vocabularies. Certain retorts sped through the air like the flight of household utensils, certain charges rang out like accusations of tampering with the groceries. He stiffened himself against such comparisons, but they stuck in his imagination and left him thankful when Undine's anger yielded to a burst of tears. He had held his own and gained his point. The trip on the *Sorceress* was given up, and a note of withdrawal despatched to Van Degen; but at the same time Ralph cabled his sister to ask if she could increase her loan. For he had conquered only at the cost of a concession: Undine was to stay in Paris till October, and they were to sail on a fast steamer, in a deck-suite, like the Harvey Shallums.

Undine's ill-humour was soon dispelled by any new distraction, and she gave herself to the untroubled enjoyment of Paris. The Shallums were the centre of a like-minded group, and in the hours the ladies could spare from their dress-makers the restaurants shook with their hilarity and the suburbs with the shriek of their motors. Van Degen, who had postponed his sailing, was a frequent sharer in these amusements; but Ralph counted on New York influences to detach him from Undine's train. He was learning to influence her through her social instincts where he had once tried to appeal to other sensibilities.

His worst moment came when he went to see Clare Van Degen, who, on the eve of departure, had begged him to come to her hotel. He found her less restless and rattling than usual, with a look in her eyes that reminded him of the days when she had haunted his thoughts. The visit passed off without vain returns to the past; but as he was leaving she surprised him by saying: 'Don't let Peter make a goose of your wife.'

Ralph reddened, but laughed.

'Oh, Undine's wonderfully able to defend herself, even against such seductions as Peter's.'

Mrs Van Degen looked down with a smile at the bracelets on her thin brown wrist. 'His personal seductions—yes. But as an inventor of amusements he's inexhaustible; and Undine likes to be amused.'

Ralph made no reply but showed no annoyance. He simply took her hand and kissed it as he said good-bye; and she turned from him without audible farewell.

As the day of departure approached, Undine's absorption in her dresses almost precluded the thought of amusement. Early and late she was closeted with fitters and packers—even the competent Céleste not being trusted to handle the treasures now pouring in—and Ralph cursed his weakness in not restraining her, and then fled for solace to museums and galleries.

He could not rouse in her any scruple about incurring fresh debts, yet he knew she was no longer unaware of the value of money. She had learned to bargain, pare down prices, evade fees, brow-beat the small tradespeople and wheedle concessions from the great—not, as Ralph perceived, from any effort to restrain her expenses, but only to prolong and intensify the pleasure of spending. Pained by the trait, he tried to laugh her out of it. He told her once that she had a miserly hand—showing her, in proof, that, for all their softness, the fingers would not bend back, or the pink palm open. But she retorted a little sharply that it was no wonder, since she'd heard nothing talked of since their marriage but economy; and this left him without any answer. So the purveyors continued to mount to their apartment, and Ralph, in the course of his frequent flights from it, found himself always dodging the corners of black glazed boxes and swaying pyramids of pasteboard; always lifting his hat to sidling milliners' girls, or effacing himself before slender *vendeuses** floating by in a mist of opopanax.* He felt incompetent to pronounce on the needs to which these visitors ministered; but the reappearance among them of the blond-bearded jeweller gave him ground for fresh fears. Undine had assured him that she had given up the idea of having her ornaments reset, and there had been ample time for their return; but on his questioning her she explained that there had been delays and 'bothers' and put him in the wrong by asking ironically if he supposed she was buying things 'for pleasure' when she knew as well as he that there wasn't any money to pay for them.

But his thoughts were not all dark. Undine's moods still infected him, and when she was happy he felt an answering lightness. Even when her amusements were too primitive to be shared he could enjoy their reflection in her face. Only, as he looked back, he was struck by the evanescence, the lack of substance, in their moments of sympathy, and by the permanent marks left by each breach between them. Yet he still fancied that some day the balance might be reversed, and that as she acquired a finer sense of values the depths in her would find a voice.

Something of this was in his mind when, the afternoon before their departure, he came home to help her with their last arrangements. She had begged him, for the day, to leave her alone in their cramped *salon*, into which belated bundles were still pouring; and it was nearly dark when he returned. The evening before she had seemed pale and nervous, and at the last moment had excused herself from dining with the Shallums at a suburban restaurant. It was so unlike her to miss any opportunity of the kind that Ralph had felt a little anxious. But with the arrival of the packers she was afoot and in command again, and he withdrew submissively, as Mr Spragg, in the early Apex days, might have fled from the spring storm of 'house-cleaning.'

When he entered the sitting-room, he found it still in disorder. Every chair was hidden under scattered dresses, tissue-paper surged from the yawning trunks and, prone among her heaped-up finery, Undine lay with closed eyes on the sofa.

She raised her head as he entered, and then turned listlessly away.

'My poor girl, what's the matter? Haven't they finished yet?'

Instead of answering she pressed her face into the cushion and began to sob. The violence of her weeping shook her hair down on her shoulders, and her hands, clenching the arm of the sofa, pressed it away from her as if any contact were insufferable.

Ralph bent over her in alarm. 'Why, what's wrong, dear? What's happened?'

Her fatigue of the previous evening came back to him—a puzzled hunted look in her eyes; and with the memory a vague wonder revived. He had fancied himself fairly disencumbered of the stock formulas about the hallowing effects of motherhood, and there were many reasons for not welcoming the news he suspected she had to give; but the woman a man loves is always a special case, and everything was different that befell Undine. If this was what had befallen her it was wonderful and divine: for the moment that was all he felt.

'Dear, tell me what's the matter,' he pleaded.

She sobbed on unheedingly and he waited for her agitation to subside. He shrank from the phrases considered appropriate to the situation, but he wanted to hold her close and give her the depth of his heart in a long kiss.

Suddenly she sat upright and turned a desperate face on him. 'Why on earth are you staring at me like that? Anybody can see what's the matter!'

He winced at her tone, but managed to get one of her hands in his; and they stayed thus in silence, eye to eye.

'Are you as sorry as all that?' he began at length, conscious of the flatness of his voice.

'Sorry—sorry? I'm—I'm——' She snatched her hand away, and went on weeping.

'But, Undine—dearest—bye and bye you'll feel differently—I know you will!'

'Differently? Differently? When? In a year? It *takes* a year— a whole year out of life! What do I care how I shall feel in a year?'

The chill of her tone struck in. This was more than a revolt of the nerves: it was a settled, a reasoned resentment. Ralph found himself groping for extenuations, evasions—anything to put a little warmth into her!

'Who knows? Perhaps, after all, it's a mistake.'

There was no answering light in her face. She turned her head from him wearily.

'Don't you think, dear, you may be mistaken?'

'Mistaken? How on earth can I be mistaken?'

Even in that moment of confusion he was struck by the cold competence of her tone, and wondered how she could be so sure.

'You mean you've asked—you've consulted——?'

The irony of it took him by the throat. They were the very words he might have spoken in some miserable secret colloquy—the words he was speaking to his wife!

She repeated dully: 'I know I'm not mistaken.'

There was another long silence. Undine lay still, her eyes shut, drumming on the arm of the sofa with a restless hand. The other lay cold in Ralph's clasp, and through it there gradually stole to him the benumbing influence of the thoughts she was thinking: the sense of the approach of illness, anxiety, and expense, and of the general unnecessary disorganization of their lives.

'That's all you feel, then?' he asked at length a little bitterly, as if to disguise from himself the hateful fact that he felt it too. He stood up and moved away. 'That's all?' he repeated.

'Why, what else do you expect me to feel? I feel horribly ill, if that's what you want.' He saw the sobs trembling up through her again.

'Poor dear—poor girl . . . I'm so sorry—so dreadfully sorry!'

The senseless reiteration seemed to exasperate her. He knew it by the quiver that ran through her like the premonitory ripple on smooth water before the coming of the wind. She turned about on him and jumped to her feet.

'Sorry—you're sorry? *You're* sorry? Why, what earthly difference will it make to *you*?' She drew back a few steps and lifted her slender arms from her sides. 'Look at me—see how I look—how I'm going to look! *You* won't hate yourself more and more every morning when you get up and see yourself in the glass! *Your* life's going on just as usual! But what's mine going to be for months and months? And just as I'd been to all this bother—fagging myself to death about all these things——' her tragic gesture swept the disordered room—'just as I thought I was going home to enjoy myself, and look nice, and see people again, and have a little pleasure after all our worries——' She dropped back on the sofa with another burst of tears. 'For all the good this rubbish will do me now! I loathe the very sight of it!' she sobbed with her face in her hands.

XIV

IT was one of the distinctions of Mr Claud Walsingham Popple that his studio was never too much encumbered with the attributes of his art to permit the installing, in one of its cushioned corners, of an elaborately furnished tea-table flanked by the most varied seductions in sandwiches and pastry.

Mr Popple, like all great men, had at first had his ups and downs; but his reputation had been permanently established by the verdict of a wealthy patron who, returning from an excursion into other fields of portraiture, had given it as the final fruit of his experience that Popple was the only man who could 'do pearls.' To sitters for whom this was of the first consequence it was another of the artist's merits that he always subordinated art to elegance, in life as well as in his portraits. The 'messy' element of production was no more visible in his expensively screened and tapestried studio than its results were perceptible in his painting; and it was often said, in praise of his work, that he was the only artist who kept his studio tidy enough for a lady to sit to him in a new dress.

Mr Popple, in fact, held that the personality of the artist should at all times be dissembled behind that of the man. It was his opinion that the essence of good-breeding lay in tossing off a picture as easily as you lit a cigarette. Ralph Marvell had once said of him that when he began a portrait he always turned back his cuffs and said: 'Ladies and gentlemen, you can see there's absolutely nothing here;' and Mrs Fairford supplemented the description by defining his painting as 'chafing-dish' art.

On a certain late afternoon of December, some four years after Mr Popple's first meeting with Miss Undine Spragg of Apex, even the symbolic chafing-dish was nowhere visible in his studio; the only evidence of its recent activity being the full-length portrait of Mrs Ralph Marvell, who, from her lofty easel and her heavily garlanded frame, faced the doorway with the air of having been invited to 'receive' for Mr Popple.

The artist himself, becomingly clad in mouse-coloured velveteen, had just turned away from the picture to hover above the tea-cups; but his place had been taken by the considerably broader bulk of Mr Peter Van Degen, who, tightly moulded into a coat of the latest cut, stood before the portrait in the attitude of a first arrival.

'Yes, it's good—it's damn good, Popp; you've hit the hair off rippingly; but the pearls ain't big enough,' he pronounced.

A slight laugh sounded from the raised dais behind the easel.

'Of course they're not! But it's not *his* fault, poor man; *he* didn't give them to me!' As she spoke Mrs Ralph Marvell rose from a monumental gilt arm-chair of pseudo-Venetian design and swept her long draperies to Van Degen's side.

'He might, then—for the privilege of painting you!' the latter rejoined, transferring his bulging stare from the counterfeit to the original. His eyes rested on Mrs Marvell's in what seemed a quick exchange of understanding; then they passed on to a critical inspection of her person. She was dressed for the sitting in something faint and shining, above which the long curves of her neck looked dead white in the cold light of the studio; and her hair, all a shadowless rosy gold, was starred with a hard glitter of diamonds.

'The privilege of painting me? Mercy, *I* have to pay for being painted! He'll tell you he's giving me the picture—but what do you suppose this cost?' She laid a finger-tip on her shimmering dress.

Van Degen's eye rested on her with cold enjoyment. 'Does the price come higher than the dress?'

She ignored the allusion. 'Of course what they charge for is the cut——'

'What they cut away? That's what they ought to charge for, ain't it, Popp?'

Undine took this with cool disdain, but Mr Popple's sensibilities were offended.

'My dear Peter—really—the artist, you understand, sees all this as a pure question of colour, of pattern; and it's a point of honour with the *man* to steel himself against the personal seduction.'

Mr Van Degen received this protest with a sound of almost vulgar derision, but Undine thrilled agreeably under the glance which her portrayer cast on her. She was flattered by Van Degen's notice, and thought his impertinence witty; but she glowed inwardly at Mr Popple's eloquence. After more than three years of social experience she still thought he 'spoke beautifully,' like the hero of a novel, and she ascribed to jealousy the lack of seriousness with which her husband's friends regarded him. His conversation struck her as intellectual, and his eagerness to have her share his thoughts was in flattering contrast to Ralph's growing tendency to keep his to himself. Popple's homage seemed the subtlest proof of what Ralph could have made of her if he had 'really understood' her. It was but another step to ascribe all her past mistakes to the lack of such understanding; and the satisfaction derived from this thought had once impelled her to tell the artist that he alone knew how to rouse her 'higher self.' He had assured her that the memory of her words would thereafter hallow his life; and as he hinted that it had been stained by the darkest errors she was moved at the thought of the purifying influence she exerted.

Thus it was that a man should talk to a true woman—but how few whom she had known possessed the secret! Ralph, in the first months of their marriage, had been eloquent too, had even gone the length of quoting poetry; but he disconcerted her by his baffling twists and strange allusions (she always scented ridicule in the unknown), and the poets he quoted were esoteric and abstruse. Mr Popple's rhetoric was drawn from more familiar sources, and abounded in favourite phrases and in moving reminiscences of the Fifth Reader.* He was moreover as literary as he was artistic; possessing an unequalled acquaintance with contemporary fiction, and dipping even into the lighter type of memoirs, in which the old acquaintances of history are served up in the disguise of 'A Royal Sorceress' or

'Passion in a Palace.'* The mastery with which Mr Popple discussed the novel of the day, especially in relation to the sensibilities of its hero and heroine, gave Undine a sense of intellectual activity which contrasted strikingly with Marvell's flippant estimate of such works. 'Passion,' the artist implied, would have been the dominant note of his life, had it not been held in check by a sentiment of exalted chivalry, and by the sense that a nature of such emotional intensity as his must always be 'ridden on the curb.'*

Van Degen was helping himself from the tray of iced cocktails which stood near the tea-table, and Popple, turning to Undine, took up the thread of his discourse. But why, he asked, why allude before others to feelings so few could understand? The average man—lucky devil!—(with a compassionate glance at Van Degen's back) the average man knew nothing of the fierce conflict between the lower and higher natures; and even the woman whose eyes had kindled it—how much did *she* guess of its violence? Did she know—Popple recklessly asked—how often the artist was forgotten in the man—how often the man would take the bit between his teeth, were it not that the look in her eyes recalled some sacred memory, some lesson learned perhaps beside his mother's knee?

'I say, Popp—was that where you learned to mix this drink? Because it does the old lady credit,' Van Degen called out, smacking his lips; while the artist, dashing a nervous hand through his hair, muttered: 'Hang it, Peter—is *nothing* sacred to you?'

It pleased Undine to feel herself capable of inspiring such emotions. She would have been fatigued by the necessity of maintaining her own talk on Popple's level, but she liked to listen to him, and especially to have others overhear what he said to her.

Her feeling for Van Degen was different. There was more similarity of tastes between them, though his manner flattered her vanity less than Popple's. She felt the strength of Van Degen's contempt for everything he did not understand or could not buy: that was the only kind of 'exclusiveness' that impressed her. And he was still to her, as in her inexperienced days, the master of the mundane science she had once imagined that Ralph Marvell possessed. During the three years since her marriage she had learned to make distinctions unknown to her girlish categories. She had found out that she had given herself to the exclusive and the dowdy when the future belonged to the showy and the promiscuous; that she was in the case of those who have cast in their lot with a fallen cause, or—to use an analogy more within her range—who have hired an opera box on the wrong night. It was all confusing and exasperating. Apex ideals had been based on the myth of 'old families' ruling New York from a throne of Revolutionary tradition, with the new millionaires paying them feudal allegiance. But experience had long since proved the delusiveness of the simile. Mrs Marvell's classification of the world into the visited and the unvisited was as obsolete as a mediaeval cosmogony. Some of those whom Washington Square left unvisited were the centre of social systems far outside its ken, and as indifferent to its opinions as the constellations to the reckonings of the astronomers; and all these systems joyously revolved about their central sun of gold.

There were moments after Undine's return to New York when she was tempted to class her marriage with the hateful early mistakes from the memories of which she had hoped it would free her. Since it was never her habit to accuse herself of such mistakes it was inevitable that she should gradually come to lay the blame on Ralph. She found a poignant pleasure, at this stage of her career, in the question: 'What does a young girl know of life?' And the poignancy was deepened by the fact that each of the friends to whom she put the question seemed convinced that—had the privilege been his—he would have known how to spare her the disenchantment it implied.

The conviction of having blundered was never more present to her than when, on this particular afternoon, the guests invited by Mr Popple to view her portrait began to assemble before it.

Some of the principal figures of Undine's group had rallied for the occasion, and almost all were in exasperating enjoyment of the privileges for which she pined. There was young Jim Driscoll, heir-apparent of the house, with his short stout mistrustful wife, who hated society, but went everywhere lest it might be thought she had been left out; the 'beautiful Mrs Beringer,' a lovely aimless being, who kept (as Laura Fairford said) a home for stray opinions, and could never quite tell them apart; little Dicky Bowles, whom every one invited because he was understood to 'say things' if one didn't; the Harvey Shallums, fresh from Paris, and dragging in their wake a bewildered nobleman vaguely designated as 'the Count,' who offered cautious conversational openings, like an explorer trying beads on savages; and, behind these more salient types, the usual filling in of those who are seen everywhere because they have learned to catch the social eye. Such a company was one to flatter the artist as much as his sitter, so completely did it represent that unanimity of opinion which constitutes social strength. Not one of the number was troubled by any personal theory of art: all they asked of a portrait was that the costume should be sufficiently 'life-like,' and the face not too much so; and a long experience in idealizing flesh and realizing dress-fabrics had enabled Mr Popple to meet both demands.

'Hang it,' Peter Van Degen pronounced, standing before the easel in an attitude of inspired interpretation, 'the great thing in a man's portrait is to catch the likeness—we all know that; but with a woman's it's different—a woman's picture has got to be pleasing. Who wants it about if it isn't? Those big chaps who blow about what they call realism—how do *their* portraits look in a drawing-room? Do you suppose they ever ask themselves that? *They* don't care—they're not going to live with the things! And what do they know of drawing-rooms, anyhow? Lots of them haven't even got a dress-suit. There's where old Popp has the pull over 'em—*he* knows how we live and what we want.'

This was received by the artist with a deprecating murmur, and by his public with warm expressions of approval.

'Happily in this case,' Popple began ('as in that of so many of my sitters,' he hastily put in), 'there has been no need to idealize—nature herself has outdone the artist's dream.'

Undine, radiantly challenging comparison with her portrait, glanced up at it with a smile of conscious merit, which deepened as young Jim Driscoll declared: 'By Jove, Mamie, you must be done exactly like that for the new music-room.'

His wife turned a cautious eye upon the picture.

'How big is it? For our house it would have to be a good deal bigger,' she objected; and Popple, fired by the thought of such a dimensional opportunity, rejoined that it would be the chance of all others to 'work in' a marble portico and a court-train: he had just done Mrs Lycurgus Ambler in a court-train and feathers, and as *that* was for Buffalo of course the pictures needn't clash.

'Well, it would have to be a good deal bigger than Mrs Ambler's,' Mrs Driscoll insisted; and on Popple's suggestion that in that case he might 'work in' Driscoll, in court-dress also— ('You've been presented? Well, you *will* be,—you'll *have* to, if I do the picture—which will make a lovely memento')—Van Degen turned aside to murmur to Undine: 'Pure bluff, you know—Jim couldn't pay for a photograph. Old Driscoll's high and dry since the Ararat investigation.'

She threw him a puzzled glance, having no time, in her crowded existence, to follow the perturbations of Wall Street save as they affected the hospitality of Fifth Avenue.

'You mean they've lost their money? Won't they give their fancy ball, then?'

Van Degen shrugged. 'Nobody knows how it's coming out. That queer chap Elmer Moffatt threatens to give old Driscoll a fancy ball—says he's going to dress him in stripes! It seems he knows too much about the Apex street-railways.'

Undine paled a little. Though she had already tried on her costume for the Driscoll ball her disappointment at Van Degen's announcement was effaced by the mention of Moffatt's name. She had not had the curiosity to follow the reports of the 'Ararat Trust Investigation,' but once or twice lately, in the snatches of smoking-room talk, she had been surprised by a vague allusion to Elmer Moffatt, as to an erratic financial influence, half ridiculed, yet already half redoubtable. Was it possible that the redoubtable element had prevailed? That the time had come when Elmer Moffatt—the Elmer Moffatt of Apex!—could, even for a moment, cause consternation in the Driscoll camp? He had always said he 'saw things big'; but no one had ever believed he was destined to carry them out on the same scale. Yet apparently in those idle Apex days, while he seemed to be 'loafing and fooling,' as her father called it, he had really been sharpening his weapons of aggression; there had been something, after all, in the effect of loose-drifting power she had always felt in him. Her heart beat faster, and she longed to question Van Degen; but she was afraid of betraying herself, and turned back to the group about the picture.

Mrs Driscoll was still presenting objections in a tone of small mild obstinacy. 'Oh, it's a *likeness*, of course—I can see that; but there's one thing I must say, Mr Popple. It looks like a last year's dress.'

The attention of the ladies instantly rallied to the picture, and the artist paled at the challenge.

'It doesn't look like a last year's face, anyhow—that's what makes them all wild,' Van Degen murmured.

Undine gave him back a quick smile. She had already forgotten about Moffatt. Any triumph in which she shared left a glow in her veins, and the success of the picture obscured all other impressions. She saw herself throning in a central panel at the spring exhibition, with the crowd pushing about the picture, repeating her name; and she decided to stop on the way home and telephone her press-agent to do a paragraph about Popple's tea.

But in the hall, as she drew on her cloak, her thoughts reverted to the Driscoll fancy ball. What a blow if it were given up after she had taken so much trouble about her dress! She was to go as the Empress Josephine, after the Prudhon portrait in the Louvre. The dress was already fitted and partly embroidered, and she foresaw the difficulty of persuading the dress-maker to take it back.

'Why so pale and sad, fair cousin? What's up?' Van Degen asked, as they emerged from the lift in which they had descended alone from the studio.

'I don't know—I'm tired of posing. And it was so frightfully hot.'

'Yes. Popple always keeps his place at low-neck temperature, as if the portraits might catch cold.' Van Degen glanced at his watch. 'Where are you off to?'

'West End Avenue, of course—if I can find a cab to take me there.'

It was not the least of Undine's grievances that she was still living in the house which represented Mr Spragg's first real-estate venture in New York. It had been understood, at the time of her marriage, that the young couple were to be established within the sacred precincts of fashion; but on their return from the honeymoon the still untenanted house in West End Avenue had been placed at their disposal, and in view of Mr Spragg's financial embarrassment even Undine had seen the folly of refusing it. That first winter, moreover, she had not regretted her exile: while she awaited her boy's birth she was glad to be out of sight of Fifth Avenue, and to take her hateful compulsory exercise where no familiar eye could fall on her. And the next year of course her father would give them a better house.

But the next year rents had risen in the Fifth Avenue quarter, and meanwhile little Paul Marvell, from his beautiful pink cradle, was already interfering with his mother's plans. Ralph, alarmed by the fresh rash of expenses, sided with his father-in-law in urging Undine to resign herself to West End Avenue; and thus after three years she was still submitting to the incessant pin-pricks inflicted by the incongruity between her social and geographical situation—the need of having to give a west side address to her tradesmen, and the deeper irritation of hearing her friends say: 'Do let me give you a lift home, dear—Oh, I'd forgotten! I'm afraid I haven't the time to go so far——'

It was bad enough to have no motor of her own, to be avowedly dependent on 'lifts,' openly and unconcealably in quest of them, and perpetually plotting to provoke their offer (she did so hate to be seen in a cab!); but to miss them, as often as not, because of the remoteness of her destination, emphasized the hateful sense of being 'out of things.'

Van Degen looked out at the long snow-piled street, down which the lamps were beginning to put their dreary yellow splashes.

'Of course you won't get a cab on a night like this. If you don't mind the open car, you'd better jump in with me. I'll run you out to the High Bridge* and give you a breath of air before dinner.'

The offer was tempting, for Undine's triumph in the studio had left her tired and nervous—she was beginning to learn that success may be as fatiguing as failure. Moreover, she was going to a big dinner that evening, and the fresh air would give her the eyes and complexion she needed: but in the back of her mind there lingered the vague sense of a forgotten engagement. As she tried to recall it she felt Van Degen raising the fur collar about her chin.

'Got anything you can put over your head? Will that lace thing do? Come along, then.' He pushed her through the swinging doors, and added with a laugh, as they reached the street: 'You're not afraid of being seen with me, are you? It's all right at this hour—Ralph's still swinging on a strap in the elevated.'

The winter twilight was deliciously cold, and as they swept through Central Park, and gathered impetus for their northward flight along the darkening Boulevard,* Undine felt the rush of physical joy that drowns scruples and silences memory. Her scruples, indeed, were not serious; but Ralph disliked her being too much with Van Degen, and it was her way to get what she wanted with as little 'fuss' as possible. Moreover, she knew it was a mistake to make herself too accessible to a man of Peter's sort: her impatience to enjoy was curbed by an instinct for holding off and biding her time that resembled the patient skill with which her father had conducted the sale of his 'bad' real estate in the Pure Water Move days. But now and then youth had its way—she could not always resist the present pleasure. And it was amusing, too, to be 'talked about' with Peter Van Degen, who was noted for not caring for 'nice women.' She enjoyed the thought of triumphing over meretricious charms: it ennobled her in her own eyes to influence such a man for good.

Nevertheless, as the motor flew on through the icy twilight, her present cares flew with it. She could not shake off the thought of the useless fancy dress which symbolized the other crowding expenses she had not dared confess to Ralph. Van Degen heard her sigh, and bent down, lowering the speed of the motor.

'What's the matter? Isn't everything all right?'

His tone made her suddenly feel that she could confide in him, and though she began by murmuring that it was nothing she did so with the conscious purpose of being persuaded to confess. And his extraordinary 'niceness' seemed to justify her and to prove that she had been right in trusting her instinct rather than in following the counsels of prudence. Heretofore, in their talks, she had never gone beyond the vaguest hint of material 'bothers'—as to which dissimulation seemed vain while one lived in West End Avenue! But now that the avowal of a definite worry had been wrung from her she felt the injustice of the view generally taken of poor Peter. For he had been neither too enterprising nor too cautious (though people said of him that he 'didn't care to part'); he had just laughed away, in bluff brotherly fashion, the gnawing thought of the fancy dress, had assured her he'd give a ball himself rather than miss seeing her wear it, and had added: 'Oh, hang waiting for the bill—won't a couple of thou' make it all right?' in a tone that showed what a small matter money was to any one who took the larger view of life.

The whole incident passed off so quickly and easily that within a few minutes she had settled down—with a nod for his 'Everything jolly again now?'—to untroubled enjoyment of the hour. Peace of mind, she said to herself, was all she needed to make her happy—and that was just what Ralph had never given her! At the thought his face seemed to rise before her, with the sharp lines of care between the eyes: it was almost like a part of his 'nagging' that he should thrust himself in at such a moment! She tried to shut her eyes to the face; but a moment later it was replaced by another, a small odd likeness of itself; and with a cry of compunction she started up from her furs.

'Mercy! It's the boy's birthday—I was to take him to his grandmother's. She was to have a cake for him, and Ralph was to come up town. I *knew* there was something I'd forgotten!'

XV

IN the Dagonet drawing-room the lamps had long been lit, and Mrs Fairford, after a last impatient turn, had put aside the curtains of worn damask to strain her eyes into the darkening square. She came back to the hearth, where Charles Bowen stood leaning between the prim caryatids of the white marble chimney-piece.

'No sign of her. She's simply forgotten.'

Bowen looked at his watch, and turned to compare it with the high-waisted Empire clock.

'Six o'clock. Why not telephone again? There must be some mistake. Perhaps she knew Ralph would be late.'

Laura laughed. 'I haven't noticed that she follows Ralph's movements so closely. When I telephoned just now the servant said she'd been out since two. The nurse waited till half-past four, not liking to come without orders; and now it's too late for Paul to come.'

She wandered away toward the farther end of the room, where, through half-open doors, a shining surface of mahogany reflected a flower-wreathed cake in which two candles dwindled.

'Put them out, please,' she said to some one in the background; then she shut the doors and turned back to Bowen.

'It's all so unlucky—my grandfather giving up his drive, and mother backing out of her hospital meeting, and having all the committee down on her. And Henley: I'd even coaxed Henley away from his bridge! He escaped again just before you came. Undine promised she'd have the boy here at four. It's not as if it had never happened before. She's always breaking her engagements.'

'She has so many that it's inevitable some should get broken.'

'Ah, if she'd only choose! Now that Ralph has had to go into business, and is kept in his office so late, it's cruel of her to drag him out every night. He told me the other day they hadn't dined at home for a month. Undine doesn't seem to notice how hard he works.'

Bowen gazed meditatively at the crumbling fire. 'No—why should she?'

'Why *should* she? Really, Charles——!'

'Why should she, when she knows nothing about it?'

'She may know nothing about his business; but she must know it's her extravagance that's forced him into it.' Mrs Fairford looked at Bowen reproachfully. 'You talk as if you were on her side!'

'Are there sides already? If so, I want to look down on them impartially from the heights of pure speculation. I want to get a general view of the whole problem of American marriages.'

Mrs Fairford dropped into her arm-chair with a sigh. 'If that's what you want you must make haste! Most of them don't last long enough to be classified.'

'I grant you it takes an active mind. But the weak point is so frequently the same that after a time one knows where to look for it.'

'What do you call the weak point?'

He paused. 'The fact that the average American looks down on his wife.'

Mrs Fairford was up with a spring. 'If that's where paradox lands you!'

Bowen mildly stood his ground. 'Well—doesn't he prove it? How much does he let her share in the real business of life? How much does he rely on her judgment and help in the conduct of serious affairs? Take Ralph, for instance—you say his wife's extravagance forces him to work too hard; but that's not what's wrong. It's normal for a man to work hard for a woman—what's abnormal is his not caring to tell her anything about it.'

'To tell Undine? She'd be bored to death if he did!'

'Just so; she'd even feel aggrieved. But why? Because it's against the custom of the country. And whose fault is that? The man's again—I don't mean Ralph, I mean the genus he belongs to: homo sapiens, Americanus. Why haven't we taught our women to take an interest in our work? Simply because we don't take enough interest in *them*.'

Mrs Fairford, sinking back into her chair, sat gazing at the vertiginous depths above which his thought seemed to dangle her.

'*You* don't? The American man doesn't—the most slaving, self-effacing, self-sacrificing——?'

'Yes; and the most indifferent: there's the point. The "slaving's" no argument against the indifference. To slave for women is part of the old American tradition; lots of people give their lives for dogmas they've ceased to believe in. Then again, in this country the passion for making money has preceded the knowing how to spend it, and the American man lavishes his fortune on his wife because he doesn't know what else to do with it.'

'Then you call it a mere want of imagination for a man to spend his money on his wife?'

'Not necessarily—but it's a want of imagination to fancy it's all he owes her. Look about you and you'll see what I mean. Why does the European woman interest herself so much more in what the men are doing? Because she's so important to them that they make it worth her while! She's not a parenthesis, as she is here—she's in the very middle of the picture. I'm not implying that Ralph isn't interested in his wife—he's a passionate, a pathetic exception. But even he has to conform to an environment where all the romantic values are reversed. Where does the real life of most American men lie? In some woman's drawing-room or in their offices? The answer's obvious, isn't it? The emotional centre of gravity's not the same in the two hemispheres. In the effete societies it's love, in our new one it's business. In America the real *crime passionnel* is a "big steal"—there's more excitement in wrecking railways than homes.'

Bowen paused to light another cigarette, and then took up his theme. 'Isn't that the key to our easy divorces? If we cared for women in the old barbarous possessive way do you suppose we'd give them up as readily as we do? The real paradox is the fact that the men who make, materially, the biggest sacrifices for their women, should do least for them ideally and romantically. And what's the result—how do the women avenge themselves? All my sympathy's with them, poor deluded dears, when I see their fallacious little attempts to trick out the leavings tossed them by the preoccupied male—the money and the motors and the clothes—and pretend to themselves and each other that *that's* what really constitutes life! Oh, I know what you're going to say—it's less and less of a pretense with them, I grant you; they're more and more succumbing to the force of the suggestion; but here and there I fancy there's one who still sees through the humbug, and knows that money and motors and clothes are simply the big bribe she's paid for keeping out of some man's way!'

Mrs Fairford presented an amazed silence to the rush of this tirade; but when she rallied it was to murmur: 'And is Undine one of the exceptions?'

Her companion took the shot with a smile. 'No—she's a monstrously perfect result of the system: the completest proof of its triumph. It's Ralph who's the victim and the exception.'

'Ah, poor Ralph!' Mrs Fairford raised her head quickly. 'I hear him now. I suppose,' she added in an undertone, 'we can't give him your explanation for his wife's having forgotten to come?'

Bowen echoed her sigh, and then seemed to toss it from him with his cigarette-end; but he stood in silence while the door opened and Ralph Marvell entered.

'Well, Laura! Hallo, Charles—have you been celebrating too?' Ralph turned to his sister. 'It's outrageous of me to be so late, and I daren't look my son in the face! But I stayed down town to make provision for his future birthdays.' He returned Mrs Fairford's kiss. 'Don't tell me the party's over, and the guest of honour gone to bed?'

As he stood before them, laughing and a little flushed, the strain of long fatigue sounding through his gaiety and looking out of his anxious eyes, Mrs Fairford threw a glance at Bowen and then turned away to ring the bell.

'Sit down, Ralph—you look tired. I'll give you some tea.'

He dropped into an arm-chair. 'I did have rather a rush to get here—but hadn't I better join the revellers? Where are they?'

He walked to the end of the room and threw open the dining-room doors. 'Hallo—where have they all gone to? What a jolly cake!' He went up to it. 'Why, it's never even been cut!'

Mrs Fairford called after him: 'Come and have your tea first.'

'No, no—tea afterward, thanks. Are they all upstairs with my grandfather? I must make my peace with Undine——'

His sister put her arm through his, and drew him back to the fire.

'Undine didn't come.'

'Didn't come? Who brought the boy, then?'

'He didn't come either. That's why the cake's not cut.'

Ralph frowned. 'What's the mystery? Is he ill, or what's happened?'

'Nothing's happened—Paul's all right. Apparently Undine forgot. She never went home for him, and the nurse waited till it was too late to come.'

She saw his eyes darken; but he merely gave a slight laugh and drew out his cigarette case. 'Poor little Paul—poor chap!' He moved toward the fire. 'Yes, please—some tea.'

He dropped back into his chair with a look of weariness, as if some strong stimulant had suddenly ceased to take effect on him; but before the tea-table was brought back he had glanced at his watch and was on his feet again.

'But this won't do. I must rush home and see the poor chap before dinner. And my mother—and my grandfather? I want to say a word to them—I must make Paul's excuses!'

'Grandfather's taking his nap. And mother had to rush out for a postponed committee meeting—she left as soon as we heard Paul wasn't coming.'

'Ah, I see.' He sat down again. 'Yes, make the tea strong, please. I've had a beastly fagging sort of day.'

He leaned back with half-closed eyes, his untouched cup in his hand. Bowen took leave, and Laura sat silent, watching her brother under lowered lids while she feigned to be busy with the kettle. Ralph presently emptied his cup and put it aside; then, sinking into his former attitude, he clasped his hands behind his head and lay staring apathetically into the fire. But suddenly he came to life and started up. A motor-horn had sounded outside, and there was a noise of wheels at the door.

'There's Undine! I wonder what could have kept her.' He jumped up and walked to the door; but it was Clare Van Degen who came in.

At sight of him she gave a little murmur of pleasure. 'What luck to find you! No, not luck—I came because I knew you'd be here. He never comes near me, Laura: I have to hunt him down to get a glimpse of him!'

Slender and shadowy in her long furs, she bent to kiss Mrs Fairford and then turned back to Ralph. 'Yes, I knew I'd catch you here. I knew it was the boy's birthday, and I've brought him a present: a vulgar expensive Van Degen offering. I've not enough imagination left to find the right thing, the thing it takes feeling and not money to buy. When I look for a present nowadays I never say to the shopman: "I want this or that"—I simply say: "Give me something that costs so much."' She drew a parcel from her muff. 'Where's the victim of my vulgarity? Let me crush him under the weight of my gold.'

Mrs Fairford sighed out 'Clare—Clare!' and Ralph smiled at his cousin.

'I'm sorry; but you'll have to depute me to present it. The birthday's over; you're too late.'

She looked surprised. 'Why, I've just left Mamie Driscoll, and she told me Undine was still at Popple's studio a few minutes ago: Popple's giving a tea to show the picture.'

'Popple's giving a tea?' Ralph struck an attitude of mock consternation. 'Ah, in that case——! In Popple's society who wouldn't forget the flight of time?'

He had recovered his usual easy tone, and Laura saw that Mrs Van Degen's words had dispelled his preoccupation. He turned to his cousin. 'Will you trust me with your present for the boy?'

Clare gave him the parcel. 'I'm sorry not to give it myself. I said what I did because I knew what you and Laura were thinking—but it's really a battered old Dagonet bowl that came down to me from our revered great-grandmother.'

'What—the heirloom you used to eat your porridge out of?' Ralph detained her hand to put a kiss on it. 'That's dear of you!'

She threw him one of her strange glances. 'Why not say: "That's like you?" But you don't remember what I'm like.' She turned away to glance at the clock. 'It's late, and I must be off. I'm going to a big dinner at the Chauncey Ellings'—but you must be going there too, Ralph? You'd better let me drive you home.'

In the motor Ralph leaned back in silence, while the rug was drawn over their knees, and Clare restlessly fingered the row of gold-topped objects in the rack at her elbow. It was restful to be swept through the crowded streets in this smooth fashion, and Clare's presence at his side gave him a vague sense of ease.

For a long time now feminine nearness had come to mean to him, not this relief from tension, but the ever-renewed dread of small daily deceptions, evasions, subterfuges. The change had come gradually, marked by one disillusionment after another; but there had been one moment that formed the point beyond which there was no returning. It was the moment, a month or two before his boy's birth, when, glancing over a batch of belated Paris bills, he had come on one from the jeweller he had once found in private conference with Undine. The bill was not large, but two of its items stood out sharply. 'Resetting pearl and diamond pendant. Resetting sapphire and diamond ring.' The pearl and diamond pendant was his mother's wedding present; the ring was the one he had given Undine on their engagement. That they were both family relics, kept unchanged through several generations, scarcely mattered to him at the time: he felt only the stab of his wife's deception. She had assured him in Paris that she had not had her jewels reset. He had noticed, soon after their return to New York, that she had left off her engagement-ring; but the others were soon discarded also, and in answer to his question she had told him that, in her ailing state, rings 'worried' her. Now he saw she had deceived him, and, forgetting everything else, he went to her, bill in hand. Her tears and distress filled him with immediate contrition. Was this a time to torment her about trifles? His anger seemed to cause her actual physical fear, and at the sight he abased himself in entreaties for forgiveness. When the scene ended she had pardoned him, and the reset ring was on her finger . . .

Soon afterward, the birth of the boy seemed to wipe out these humiliating memories; yet Marvell found in time that they were not effaced, but only momentarily crowded out of sight. In reality, the incident had a meaning out of proportion to its apparent seriousness, for it put in his hand a clue to a new side of his wife's character. He no longer minded her having lied about the jeweller; what pained him was that she had been unconscious of the wound she inflicted in destroying the identity of the jewels. He saw that, even after their explanation, she still supposed he was angry only because she had deceived him; and the discovery that she was completely unconscious of states of feeling on which so much of his inner life depended marked a new stage in their relation.

He was not thinking of all this as he sat beside Clare Van Degen; but it was part of the chronic disquietude which made him more alive to his cousin's sympathy, her shy unspoken understanding. After all, he and she were of the same blood and had the same traditions. She was light and frivolous, without

strength of will or depth of purpose; but she had the frankness
of her foibles, and she would never have lied to him or traded
on his tenderness.

Clare's nervousness gradually subsided, and she lapsed into a
low-voiced mood which seemed like an answer to his secret
thought. But she did not sound the personal note, and they
chatted quietly of commonplace things: of the dinner-dance at
which they were presently to meet, of the costume she had
chosen for the Driscoll fancy-ball, the recurring rumours of old
Driscoll's financial embarrassment, and the mysterious personality of Elmer Moffatt, on whose movements Wall Street was
beginning to fix a fascinated eye. When Ralph, the year after his
marriage, had renounced his profession to go into partnership
with a firm of real-estate agents, he had come in contact for the
first time with the drama of 'business,' and whenever he could
turn his attention from his own tasks he found a certain interest
in watching the fierce interplay of its forces. In the down-town
world he had heard things of Moffatt that seemed to single him
out from the common herd of money-makers: anecdotes of his
coolness, his lazy good-temper, the humorous detachment he
preserved in the heat of conflicting interests; and his figure was
enlarged by the mystery that hung about it—the fact that no
one seemed to know whence he came, or how he had acquired
the information which, for the moment, was making him so
formidable.

'I should like to see him,' Ralph said; 'he must be a good
specimen of the one of the few picturesque types we've got.'

'Yes—it might be amusing to fish him out; but the most
picturesque types in Wall Street are generally the tamest in a
drawing-room.' Clare considered. 'But doesn't Undine know
him? I seem to remember seeing them together.'

'Undine and Moffatt? Then *you* know him—you've met
him?'

'Not actually met him—but he's been pointed out to me. It
must have been some years ago. Yes—it was one night at the
theatre, just after you announced your engagement.' He fancied
her voice trembled slightly, as though she thought he might
notice her way of dating her memories. 'You came into our
box,' she went on, 'and I asked you the name of the red-faced

man who was sitting in the stall next to Undine. You didn't know, but some one told us it was Moffatt.'

Marvell was more struck by her tone than by what she was saying. 'If Undine knows him it's odd she's never mentioned it,' he answered indifferently.

The motor stopped at his door and Clare, as she held out her hand, turned a first full look on him.

'Why do you never come to see me? I miss you more than ever,' she said.

He pressed her hand without answering, but after the motor had rolled away he stood for a while on the pavement, looking after it.

When he entered the house the hall was still dark and the small over-furnished drawing-room empty. The parlour-maid told him that Mrs Marvell had not yet come in, and he went upstairs to the nursery. But on the threshold the nurse met him with the whispered request not to make a noise, as it had been hard to quiet the boy after the afternoon's disappointment, and she had just succeeded in putting him to sleep.

Ralph went down to his own room and threw himself in the old college arm-chair in which, four years previously, he had sat the night out, dreaming of Undine. He had no study of his own, and he had crowded into his narrow bed-room his prints and bookshelves, and the other relics of his youth. As he sat among them now the memory of that other night swept over him—the night when he had heard the 'call'! Fool as he had been not to recognize its meaning then, he knew himself triply mocked in being, even now, at its mercy. The flame of love that had played about his passion for his wife had died down to its embers; all the transfiguring hopes and illusions were gone, but they had left an unquenchable ache for her nearness, her smile, her touch. His life had come to be nothing but a long effort to win these mercies by one concession after another: the sacrifice of his literary projects, the exchange of his profession for an uncongenial business, and the incessant struggle to make enough money to satisfy her increasing exactions. That was where the 'call' had led him . . .

The clock struck eight, but it was useless to begin to dress till Undine came in, and he stretched himself out in his chair, reached for a pipe and took up the evening paper. His passing annoyance had died out; he was usually too tired after his day's work for such feelings to keep their edge long. But he was curious—disinterestedly curious—to know what pretext Undine would invent for being so late, and what excuse she would have found for forgetting the little boy's birthday.

He read on till half-past eight; then he stood up and sauntered to the window. The avenue below it was deserted; not a carriage or motor turned the corner around which he expected Undine to appear, and he looked idly in the opposite direction. There too the perspective was nearly empty, so empty that he singled out, a dozen blocks away, the blazing lamps of a large touring-car that was bearing furiously down the avenue from Morningside.* As it drew nearer its speed slackened, and he saw it hug the curb and stop at his door. By the light of the street lamp he recognized his wife as she sprang out and detected a familiar silhouette in her companion's fur-coated figure. Then the motor flew on and Undine ran up the steps.

Ralph went out on the landing. He saw her coming up quickly, as if to reach her room unperceived; but when she caught sight of him she stopped, her head thrown back and the light falling on her blown hair and glowing face.

'Well?' she said, smiling up at him.

'They waited for you all the afternoon in Washington Square—the boy never had his birthday,' he answered.

Her colour deepened, but she instantly rejoined: 'Why, what happened? Why didn't the nurse take him?'

'You said you were coming to fetch him, so she waited.'

'But I telephoned——'

He said to himself: 'Is *that* the lie?' and answered: 'Where from?'

'Why, the studio, of course——' She flung her cloak open, as if to attest her veracity. 'The sitting lasted longer than usual—there was something about the dress he couldn't get——'

'But I thought he was giving a tea.'

'He had tea afterward; he always does. And he asked some people in to see my portrait. That detained me too. I didn't know they were coming, and when they turned up I couldn't rush away. It would have looked as if I didn't like the picture.'

She paused and they gave each other a searching simultaneous glance. 'Who told you it was a tea?' she asked.

'Clare Van Degen. I saw her at my mother's.'

'So you weren't unconsoled after all——!'

'The nurse didn't get any message. My people were awfully disappointed; and the poor boy has cried his eyes out.'

'Dear me! What a fuss! But I might have known my message wouldn't be delivered. Everything always happens to put me in the wrong with your family.'

With a little air of injured pride she started to go to her room; but he put out a hand to detain her.

'You've just come from the studio?'

'Yes. Is it awfully late? I must go and dress. We're dining with the Ellings, you know.'

'I know . . . How did you come? In a cab?'

She faced him limpidly. 'No; I couldn't find one that would bring me—so Peter gave me a lift, like an angel. I'm blown to bits. He had his open car.'

Her colour was still high, and Ralph noticed that her lower lip twitched a little. He had led her to the point they had reached solely to be able to say: 'If you're straight from the studio, how was it that I saw you coming down from Morningside?'

Unless he asked her that there would be no point in his cross-questioning, and he would have sacrificed his pride without a purpose. But suddenly, as they stood there face to face, almost touching, she became something immeasurably alien and far off, and the question died on his lips.

'Is that all?' she asked with a slight smile.

'Yes; you'd better go and dress,' he said, and turned back to his room.

XVI

The turnings of life seldom show a sign-post; or rather, though the sign is always there, it is usually placed some distance back, like the notices that give warning of a bad hill or a level railway-crossing.

Ralph Marvell, pondering upon this, reflected that for him the sign had been set, more than three years earlier, in an Italian ilex-grove. That day his life had brimmed over—so he had put it at the time. He saw now that it had brimmed over indeed: brimmed to the extent of leaving the cup empty, or at least of uncovering the dregs beneath the nectar. He knew now that he should never hereafter look at his wife's hand without remembering something he had read in it that day. Its surface-language had been sweet enough, but under the rosy lines he had seen the warning letters.

Since then he had been walking with a ghost: the miserable ghost of his illusion. Only he had somehow vivified, coloured, substantiated it, by the force of his own great need—as a man might breathe a semblance of life into a dear drowned body that he cannot give up for dead. All this came to him with aching distinctness the morning after his talk with his wife on the stairs. He had accused himself, in midnight retrospect, of having failed to press home his conclusion because he dared not face the truth. But he knew this was not the case. It was not the truth he feared, it was another lie. If he had foreseen a chance of her saying: 'Yes, I was with Peter Van Degen, and for the reason you think,' he would have put it to the touch, stood up to the blow like a man; but he knew she would never say that. She would go on eluding and doubling, watching him as he watched her; and at that game she was sure to beat him in the end.

On their way home from the Elling dinner this certainty had become so insufferable that it nearly escaped him in the cry: 'You needn't watch me—I shall never again watch you!' But he had held his peace, knowing she would not understand. How little, indeed, she ever understood, had been made clear to him when, the same night, he had followed her upstairs through the sleeping house. She had gone on ahead while he stayed below to lock doors and put out lights, and he had supposed her to be already in her room when he reached the upper landing; but she stood there waiting, in the spot where he had waited for her a few hours earlier. She had shone her vividest at dinner, with the revolving brilliancy that collective approval always struck from her; and the glow of it still hung on her as she paused there in the dimness, her shining cloak dropped from her white shoulders.

'Ralphie——' she began; a soft hand on his arm.

He stopped, and she pulled him about so that their faces were close, and he saw her lips curving for a kiss. Every line of her face sought him, from the sweep of the narrowed eyelids to the dimples that played away from her smile. His eye received the picture with distinctness; but for the first time it did not pass into his veins. It was as if he had been struck with a subtle blindness that permitted images to give their colour to the eye but communicated nothing to the brain.

'Good-night,' he said, as he passed on.

When a man felt in that way about a woman he was surely in a position to deal with his case impartially. This came to Ralph as the joyless solace of the morning. At last the bandage was off and he could see. And what did he see? Only the uselessness of driving his wife to subterfuges that were no longer necessary. Was Van Degen her lover? Probably not—the suspicion died as it rose. She would not take more risks than she could help, and it was admiration, not love, that she wanted. She wanted to enjoy herself, and her conception of enjoyment was publicity, promiscuity—the band, the banners, the crowd, the close contact of covetous impulses, and the sense of walking among them in cool security. Any personal entanglement might mean 'bother,' and bother was the thing she most abhorred. Probably, as the queer formula went, his 'honour' was safe: he could count on the letter of her fidelity. At the moment the conviction meant no more to him than if he had been assured of the honesty of the first stranger he met in the street. A stranger—that was what she had always been to him. So malleable outwardly, she had remained insensible to the touch of the heart.

These thoughts accompanied him on his way to business the next morning. Then, as the routine took him back, the feeling of strangeness diminished. There he was again at his daily task—nothing tangible was altered. He was there for the same purpose as yesterday: to make money for his wife and child. The woman he had turned from on the stairs a few hours earlier was still his wife and the mother of Paul Marvell. She was an inherent part of his life; the inner disruption had not resulted in any outward upheaval. And with the sense of inevitableness there came a sudden wave of pity. Poor Undine! She was what the gods had made her—a creature of skin-deep reactions, a mote in the beam of pleasure. He had no desire to 'preach down' such heart as she had—he felt only a stronger wish to reach it, teach it, move it to something of the pity that filled his own. They were fellow-victims in the *noyade** of marriage, but if they ceased to struggle perhaps the drowning would be easier for both . . . Meanwhile the first of the month was at hand, with its usual batch of bills; and there was no time to think of any struggle less pressing than that connected with paying them . . .

Undine had been surprised, and a little disconcerted, at her husband's acceptance of the birthday incident. Since the resetting of her bridal ornaments the relations between Washington Square and West End Avenue had been more and more strained; and the silent disapproval of the Marvell ladies was more irritating to her than open recrimination. She knew how keenly Ralph must feel her last slight to his family, and she had been frightened when she guessed that he had seen her returning with Van Degen. He must have been watching from the window, since, credulous as he always was, he evidently had a reason for not believing her when she told him she had come from the studio. There was therefore something both puzzling and disturbing in his silence; and she made up her mind that it must be either explained or cajoled away.

These thoughts were with her as she dressed; but at the Ellings' they fled like ghosts before light and laughter. She had never been more open to the suggestions of immediate enjoyment. At last she had reached the envied situation of the pretty woman with whom society must reckon, and if she had only had the means to live up to her opportunities she would have been perfectly content with life, with herself and her husband. She still thought Ralph 'sweet' when she was not bored by his good advice or exasperated by his inability to pay her bills. The question of money was what chiefly stood between them; and now that this was momentarily disposed of by Van Degen's offer she looked at Ralph more kindly—she even felt a return of her first impersonal affection for him. Everybody could see that Clare Van Degen was 'gone' on him, and Undine always liked to know that what belonged to her was coveted by others.

Her reassurance had been fortified by the news she had heard at the Elling dinner—the published fact of Harmon B. Driscoll's unexpected victory. The Ararat investigation had been mysteriously stopped—quashed, in the language of the law—and Elmer Moffatt 'turned down,' as Van Degen (who sat next to her) expressed it.

'I don't believe we'll ever hear of that gentleman again,' he said contemptuously; and their eyes crossed gaily as she exclaimed: 'Then they'll give the fancy ball after all?'

'I should have given you one anyhow—shouldn't you have liked that as well?'

'Oh, you can give me one too!' she returned; and he bent closer to say: 'By Jove, I will—and anything else you want.'

But on the way home her fears revived. Ralph's indifference struck her as unnatural. He had not returned to the subject of Paul's disappointment, had not even asked her to write a word of excuse to his mother. Van Degen's way of looking at her at dinner—he was incapable of graduating his glances—had made it plain that the favour she had accepted would necessitate her being more conspicuously in his company (though she was still resolved that it should be on just such terms as she chose); and it would be extremely troublesome if, at this juncture, Ralph should suddenly turn suspicious and secretive.

Undine, hitherto, had found more benefits than drawbacks in her marriage; but now the tie began to gall. It was hard to be criticized for every grasp at opportunity by a man so avowedly unable to do the reaching for her! Ralph had gone into business to make more money for her; but it was plain that the 'more' would never be much, and that he would not achieve the quick rise to affluence which was man's natural tribute to woman's merits. Undine felt herself trapped, deceived; and it was intolerable that the agent of her disillusionment should presume to be the critic of her conduct.

Her annoyance, however, died out with her tears. Ralph, the morning after the Elling dinner, went his way as usual, and after nerving herself for the explosion which did not come she set down his indifference to the dulling effect of 'business.' No wonder poor women whose husbands were always 'down-town' had to look elsewhere for sympathy! Van Degen's cheque helped to calm her, and the weeks whirled on toward the Driscoll ball.

The ball was as brilliant as she had hoped, and her own part in it as thrilling as a page from one of the 'society novels' with which she had cheated the monotony of Apex days. She had no time for reading now: every hour was packed with what she would have called life, and the intensity of her sensations culminated on that triumphant evening. What could be more delightful than to feel that, while all the women envied her dress, the men did not so much as look at it? Their admiration was all for herself, and her beauty deepened under it as flowers take a warmer colour in the rays of sunset. Only Van Degen's glance weighed on her a little too heavily. Was it possible that he might become a 'bother' less negligible than those he had relieved her of? Undine was not greatly alarmed—she still had full faith in her powers of self-defense; but she disliked to feel the least crease in the smooth surface of existence. She had always been what her parents called 'sensitive.'

As the winter passed, material cares once more assailed her. In the thrill of liberation produced by Van Degen's gift she had been imprudent—had launched into fresh expenses. Not that she accused herself of extravagance: she had done nothing not really necessary. The drawing-room, for instance, cried out to be 'done over,' and Popple, who was an authority on decor-ation, had shown her, with a few strokes of his pencil, how easily it might be transformed into a French 'period' room, all curves and cupids: just the setting for a pretty woman and his portrait of her. But Undine, still hopeful of leaving West End Avenue, had heroically resisted the suggestion, and contented herself with the renewal of the curtains and carpet, and the purchase of some fragile gilt chairs which, as she told Ralph, would be 'so much to the good' when they moved—the explanation, as she made it, seemed an additional evidence of her thrift.

Partly as a result of these exertions she had a 'nervous break-down' toward the middle of the winter, and her physician having ordered massage and a daily drive it became necessary to secure Mrs Heeny's attendance and to engage a motor by the month. Other unforeseen expenses—the bills, that, at such times, seem to run up without visible impulsion—were added to by a severe illness of little Paul's: a long costly illness, with three nurses and frequent consultations. During these days Ralph's anxiety drove him to what seemed to Undine foolish excesses of expenditure and when the boy began to get better the doctors advised country air. Ralph at once hired a small house at Tuxedo* and Undine of course accompanied her son to the country; but she spent only the Sundays with him, running up to town during the week to be with her husband, as she explained. This necessitated the keeping up of two households, and even for so short a time the strain on Ralph's purse was severe. So it came about that the bill for the fancy-dress was still unpaid, and Undine left to wonder distractedly what had become of Van Degen's money. That Van Degen seemed also to wonder was becoming unpleasantly apparent: his cheque had evidently not brought in the return he expected, and he put his grievance to her frankly one day when he motored down to lunch at Tuxedo.

They were sitting, after luncheon, in the low-ceilinged drawing-room to which Undine had adapted her usual background of cushions, bric-a-brac and flowers—since one must make one's setting 'home-like,' however little one's habits happened to correspond with that particular effect. Undine, conscious of the intimate charm of her *mise-en-scène*, and of the recovered freshness and bloom which put her in harmony with it, had never been more sure of her power to keep her friend in the desired state of adoring submission. But Peter, as he grew more adoring, became less submissive; and there came a moment when she needed all her wits to save the situation. It was easy enough to rebuff him, the easier as his physical proximity always roused in her a vague instinct of resistance; but it was hard so to temper the rebuff with promise that the game of suspense should still delude him. He put it to her at last, standing squarely before her, his batrachian* sallowness unpleasantly flushed, and primitive man looking out of the eyes from which a frock-coated gentleman usually pined at her.

'Look here—the installment plan's all right; but ain't you a bit behind even on that?' (She had brusquely eluded a nearer approach.) 'Anyhow, I think I'd rather let the interest accumulate for a while. This is good-bye till I get back from Europe.'

The announcement took her by surprise. 'Europe? Why, when are you sailing?'

'On the first of April: good day for a fool to acknowledge his folly. I'm beaten, and I'm running away.'

She sat looking down, her hand absently occupied with the twist of pearls he had given her. In a flash she saw the peril of this departure. Once off on the *Sorceress*, he was lost to her—the power of old associations would prevail. Yet if she were as 'nice' to him as he asked—'nice' enough to keep him—the end might not be much more to her advantage. Hitherto she had let herself drift on the current of their adventure, but she now saw what port she had half-unconsciously been trying for. If she had striven so hard to hold him, had 'played' him with such patience and such skill, it was for something more than her passing amusement and convenience: for a purpose the more tenaciously cherished that she had not dared name it to herself. In the light of this discovery she saw the need of feigning complete indifference.

'Ah, you happy man! It's good-bye indeed, then,' she threw back at him, lifting a plaintive smile to his frown.

'Oh, you'll turn up in Paris later, I suppose—to get your things for Newport.'

'Paris? Newport? They're not on my map! When Ralph can get away we shall go to the Adirondacks for the boy. I hope I shan't need Paris clothes there! It doesn't matter, at any rate,' she ended, laughing, 'because nobody I care about will see me.'

Van Degen echoed her laugh. 'Oh, come—that's rough on Ralph!'

She looked down with a slight increase of colour. 'I oughtn't to have said it, ought I? But the fact is I'm unhappy—and a little hurt——'

'Unhappy? Hurt?' He was at her side again. 'Why, what's wrong?'

She lifted her eyes with a grave look. 'I thought you'd be sorrier to leave me.'

'Oh, it won't be for long—it needn't be, you know.' He was perceptibly softening. 'It's damnable, the way you're tied down. Fancy rotting all summer in the Adirondacks! Why do you stand it? You oughtn't to be bound for life by a girl's mistake.'

The lashes trembled slightly on her cheek. 'Aren't we all bound by our mistakes—we women? Don't let us talk of such things! Ralph would never let me go abroad without him.' She paused, and then, with a quick upward sweep of the lids: 'After all, it's better it should be good-bye—since I'm paying for another mistake in being so unhappy at your going.'

'Another mistake? Why do you call it that?'

'Because I've misunderstood you—or you me.' She continued to smile at him wistfully. 'And some things are best mended by a break.'

He met her smile with a loud sigh—she could feel him in the meshes again. '*Is* it to be a break between us?'

'Haven't you just said so? Anyhow, it might as well be, since we shan't be in the same place again for months.'

The frock-coated gentleman once more languished from his eyes: she thought she trembled on the edge of victory. 'Hang it,' he broke out, 'you ought to have a change—you're looking awfully pulled down. Why can't you coax your mother to run over to Paris with you? Ralph couldn't object to that.'

She shook her head. 'I don't believe she could afford it, even if I could persuade her to leave father. You know father hasn't done very well lately: I shouldn't like to ask him for the money.'

'You're so confoundedly proud!' He was edging nearer. 'It would all be so easy if you'd only be a little fond of me . . .'

She froze to her sofa-end. 'We women can't repair our mistakes. Don't make me more miserable by reminding me of mine.'

'Oh, nonsense! There's nothing cash won't do. Why won't you let me straighten things out for you?'

Her colour rose again, and she looked him quickly and consciously in the eye. It was time to play her last card. 'You seem to forget that I am—married,' she said.

Van Degen was silent—for a moment she thought he was swaying to her in the flush of surrender. But he remained doggedly seated, meeting her look with an odd clearing of his heated gaze, as if a shrewd businessman had suddenly replaced the pining gentleman at the window.

'Hang it—so am I!' he rejoined; and Undine saw that in the last issue he was still the stronger of the two.

XVII

NOTHING was bitterer to her than to confess to herself the failure of her power; but her last talk with Van Degen had taught her a lesson almost worth the abasement. She saw the mistake she had made in taking money from him, and understood that if she drifted into repeating that mistake her future would be irretrievably compromised. What she wanted was not a hand-to-mouth existence of precarious intrigue: to one with her gifts the privileges of life should come openly. Already in her short experience she had seen enough of the women who sacrifice future security for immediate success, and she meant to lay solid foundations before she began to build up the light superstructure of enjoyment.

Nevertheless it was galling to see Van Degen leave, and to know that for the time he had broken away from her. Over a nature so insensible to the spells of memory, the visible and tangible would always prevail. If she could have been with him again in Paris, where, in the shining spring days, every sight and sound ministered to such influences, she was sure she could have regained her hold. And the sense of frustration was intensified by the fact that every one she knew was to be there: her potential rivals were crowding the east-bound steamers. New York was a desert, and Ralph's seeming unconsciousness of the fact increased her resentment. She had had but one chance at Europe since her marriage, and that had been wasted through her husband's unaccountable perversity. She knew now with what packed hours of Paris and London they had paid for their empty weeks in Italy.

Meanwhile the long months of the New York spring stretched out before her in all their social vacancy to the measureless blank of a summer in the Adirondacks. In her girlhood she had plumbed the dim depths of such summers; but then she had been sustained by the hope of bringing some capture to the surface. Now she knew better: there were no 'finds' for her in that direction. The people she wanted would be at Newport or in Europe, and she was too resolutely bent on a definite object, too sternly animated by her father's business instinct, to turn aside in quest of casual distractions.

The chief difficulty in the way of her attaining any distant end had always been her reluctance to plod through the intervening stretches of dulness and privation. She had begun to see this, but she could not always master the weakness: never had she stood in greater need of Mrs Heeny's 'Go slow, Undine!' Her imagination was incapable of long flights. She could not cheat her impatience with the mirage of far-off satisfactions, and for the moment present and future seemed equally void. But her desire to go to Europe and to rejoin the little New York world that was reforming itself in London and Paris was fortified by reasons which seemed urgent enough to justify an appeal to her father.

She went down to his office to plead her case, fearing Mrs Spragg's intervention. For some time past Mr Spragg had been rather continuously overworked, and the strain was beginning to tell on him. He had never quite regained, in New York, the financial security of his Apex days. Since he had changed his base of operations his affairs had followed an uncertain course, and Undine suspected that his breach with his old political ally, the Representative Rolliver who had seen him through the muddiest reaches of the Pure Water Move, was not unconnected with his failure to get a footing in Wall Street. But all this was vague and shadowy to her. Even had 'business' been less of a mystery, she was too much absorbed in her own affairs to project herself into her father's case; and she thought she was sacrificing enough to delicacy of feeling in sparing him the 'bother' of Mrs Spragg's opposition.

When she came to him with a grievance he always heard her out with the same mild patience; but the long habit of 'managing' him had made her, in his own language, 'discount' this tolerance, and when she ceased to speak her heart throbbed with suspense as he leaned back, twirling an invisible toothpick under his sallow moustache. Presently he raised a hand to stroke the limp beard in which the moustache was merged; then he groped for the Masonic emblem that had lost itself in one of the folds of his depleted waistcoat.

He seemed to fish his answer from the same rusty depths, for as his fingers closed about the trinket he said: 'Yes, the heated term *is* trying in New York. That's why the Fresh Air Fund pulled my last dollar out of me last week.'

Undine frowned: there was nothing more irritating, in these encounters with her father, than his habit of opening the discussion with a joke.

'I wish you'd understand that I'm serious, father. I've never been strong since the baby was born, and I need a change. But it's not only that: there are other reasons for my wanting to go.'

Mr Spragg still held to his mild tone of banter. 'I never knew you short on reasons, Undie. Trouble is you don't always know other people's when you see 'em.'

His daughter's lips tightened. 'I know your reasons when I see them, father: I've heard them often enough. But you can't know mine because I haven't told you—not the real ones.'

'Jehoshaphat! I thought they were all real as long as you had a use for them.'

Experience had taught her that such protracted trifling usually concealed an exceptional vigour of resistance, and the suspense strengthened her determination.

'My reasons are all real enough,' she answered; 'but there's one more serious than the others.'

Mr Spragg's brows began to jut. 'More bills?'

'No.' She stretched out her hand and began to finger the dusty objects on his desk. 'I'm unhappy at home.'

'Unhappy——!' His start overturned the gorged waste-paper basket and shot a shower of paper across the rug. He stooped to put the basket back; then he turned his slow fagged eyes on his daughter. 'Why, he worships the ground you walk on, Undie.'

'That's not always a reason, for a woman——' It was the answer she would have given to Popple or Van Degen, but she saw in an instant the mistake of thinking it would impress her father. In the atmosphere of sentimental casuistry to which she had become accustomed, she had forgotten that Mr Spragg's private rule of conduct was as simple as his business morality was complicated.

He glowered at her under thrust-out brows. 'It isn't a reason, isn't it? I can seem to remember the time when you used to think it was equal to a whole carload of whitewash.'

She blushed a bright red, and her own brows were levelled at his above her stormy steel-grey eyes. The sense of her blunder made her angrier with him, and more ruthless.

'I can't expect you to understand—you never *have*, you or mother, when it came to my feelings. I suppose some people are born sensitive—I can't imagine anybody'd *choose* to be so. Because I've been too proud to complain you've taken it for granted that I was perfectly happy. But my marriage was a mistake from the beginning; and Ralph feels just as I do about it. His people hate me, they've always hated me; and he looks at everything as they do. They've never forgiven me for his having had to go into business—with their aristocratic ideas they look down on a man who works for his living. Of course it's all right for *you* to do it, because you're not a Marvell or a Dagonet; but they think Ralph ought to just lie back and let you support the baby and me.'

This time she had found the right note: she knew it by the tightening of her father's slack muscles and the sudden straightening of his back.

'By George, he pretty near does!' he exclaimed, bringing down his fist on the desk. 'They haven't been taking it out of you about that, have they?'

'They don't fight fair enough to say so. They just egg him on to turn against me. They only consented to his marrying me because they thought you were so crazy about the match you'd give us everything, and he'd have nothing to do but sit at home and write books.'

Mr Spragg emitted a derisive groan. 'From what I hear of the amount of business he's doing I guess he could keep the Poet's Corner going right along. I suppose the old man was right—he hasn't got it in him to make money.'

'Of course not; he wasn't brought up to it, and in his heart of hearts he's ashamed of having to do it. He told me it was killing a little more of him every day.'

'Do they back him up in that kind of talk?'

'They back him up in everything. Their ideas are all different from ours. They look down on us—can't you see that? Can't you guess how they treat me from the way they've acted to you and mother?'

He met this with a puzzled stare. 'The way they've acted to me and mother? Why, we never so much as set eyes on them.'

'That's just what I mean! I don't believe they've even called on mother this year, have they? Last year they just left their cards without asking. And why do you suppose they never invite you to dine? In their set lots of people older than you and mother dine out every night of the winter—society's full of them. The Marvells are ashamed to have you meet their friends: that's the reason. They're ashamed to have it known that Ralph married an Apex girl, and that you and mother haven't always had your own servants and carriages; and Ralph's ashamed of it too, now he's got over being crazy about me. If he was free I believe he'd turn round to-morrow and marry that Ray girl his mother's saving up for him.'

Mr Spragg listened with a heavy brow and pushed-out lip. His daughter's outburst seemed at last to have roused him to a faint resentment. After she had ceased to speak he remained silent, twisting an inky penhandle between his fingers; then he said: 'I guess mother and I can worry along without having Ralph's relatives drop in; but I'd like to make it clear to them that if you came from Apex your income came from there too. I presume they'd be sorry if Ralph was left to support you on *his*.'

She saw that she had scored in the first part of the argument, but every watchful nerve reminded her that the hardest stage was still ahead.

'Oh, they're willing enough he should take your money—that's only natural, they think.'

A chuckle sounded deep down under Mr Spragg's loose collar. 'There seems to be practical unanimity on that point,' he observed. 'But I don't see,' he continued, jerking round his bushy brows on her, 'how going to Europe is going to help you out.'

Undine leaned close enough for her lowered voice to reach him. 'Can't you understand that, knowing how they all feel about me—and how Ralph feels—I'd give almost anything to get away?'

Her father looked at her compassionately. 'I guess most of us feel that once in a way when we're young, Undine. Later on you'll see going away ain't much use when you've got to turn round and come back.'

She nodded at him with close-pressed lips, like a child in possession of some solemn secret.

'That's just it—that's the reason I'm so wild to go; because it *might* mean I wouldn't ever have to come back.'

'Not come back? What on earth are you talking about?'

'It might mean that I could get free—begin over again . . .'

He had pushed his seat back with a sudden jerk and cut her short by striking his palm on the arm of the chair.

'For the Lord's sake, Undine—do you know what you're saying?'

'Oh, yes, I know.' She gave him back a confident smile. 'If I can get away soon—go straight over to Paris . . . there's some one there who'd do anything . . . who *could* do anything . . . if I was free . . .'

Mr Spragg's hands continued to grasp his chair-arms. 'Good God, Undine Marvell—are you sitting there in your sane senses and talking to me of what you could do if you were *free*?'

Their glances met in an interval of speechless communion; but Undine did not shrink from her father's eyes and when she lowered her own it seemed to be only because there was nothing left for them to say.

'I know just what I could do if I were free. I could marry the right man,' she answered boldly.

He met her with a murmur of helpless irony. 'The right man? The right man? Haven't you had enough of trying for him yet?'

As he spoke the door behind them opened, and Mr Spragg looked up abruptly.

The stenographer stood on the threshold, and above her shoulder Undine perceived the ingratiating grin of Elmer Moffatt.

'"A little farther lend thy guiding hand"*—but I guess I can go the rest of the way alone,' he said, insinuating himself through the doorway with an airy gesture of dismissal; then he turned to Mr Spragg and Undine.

'I agree entirely with Mrs Marvell—and I'm happy to have the opportunity of telling her so,' he proclaimed, holding his hand out gallantly.

Undine stood up with a laugh. 'It sounded like old times, I suppose—you thought father and I were quarrelling? But we never quarrel any more: he always agrees with me.' She smiled at Mr Spragg and turned her shining eyes on Moffatt.

'I wish that treaty had been signed a few years sooner!' the latter rejoined in his usual tone of humorous familiarity.

Undine had not met him since her marriage, and of late the adverse turn of his fortunes had carried him quite beyond her thoughts. But his actual presence was always stimulating, and even through her self-absorption she was struck by his air of almost defiant prosperity. He did not look like a man who has been beaten; or rather he looked like a man who does not know when he is beaten; and his eye had the gleam of mocking confidence that had carried him unabashed through his lowest hours at Apex.

'I presume you're here to see me on business?' Mr Spragg enquired, rising from his chair with a glance that seemed to ask his daughter's silence.

'Why, yes, Senator,' rejoined Moffatt, who was given, in playful moments, to the bestowal of titles high-sounding. 'At least I'm here to ask you a little question that may lead to business.'

Mr Spragg crossed the office and held open the door. 'Step this way, please,' he said, guiding Moffatt out before him, though the latter hung back to exclaim: 'No family secrets, Mrs Marvell—anybody can turn the fierce white light on *me!*'

With the closing of the door Undine's thoughts turned back to her own preoccupations. It had not struck her as incongruous that Moffatt should have business dealings with her father: she was even a little surprised that Mr Spragg should still treat him so coldly. But she had no time to give to such considerations. Her own difficulties were too importunately present to her. She moved restlessly about the office, listening to the rise and fall of the two voices on the other side of the partition without once wondering what they were discussing.

What should she say to her father when he came back—what argument was most likely to prevail with him? If he really had no money to give her she was imprisoned fast—Van Degen was lost to her, and the old life must go on interminably . . . In her nervous pacings she paused before the blotched looking-glass that hung in a corner of the office under a steel engraving of Daniel Webster. Even that defective surface could not disfigure her, and she drew fresh hope from the sight of her beauty. Her few weeks of ill-health had given her cheeks a subtler curve and deepened the shadows beneath her eyes, and she was handsomer than before her marriage. No, Van Degen was not lost to her even! From narrowed lids to parted lips her face was swept by a smile like refracted sunlight. He was not lost to her while she could smile like that! Besides, even if her father had no money, there were always mysterious ways of 'raising' it—in the old Apex days he had often boasted of such feats. As the hope rose her eyes widened trustfully, and this time the smile that flowed up to them was as limpid as a child's. That was the way her father liked her to look at him . . .

The door opened, and she heard Mr Spragg say behind her: 'No, sir, I won't—that's final.'

He came in alone, with a brooding face, and lowered himself heavily into his chair. It was plain that the talk between the two men had had an abrupt ending. Undine looked at her father with a passing flicker of curiosity. Certainly it was an odd coincidence that Moffatt should have called while she was there . . .

'What did he want?' she asked, glancing back toward the door.

Mr Spragg mumbled his invisible toothpick. 'Oh, just another of his wild-cat schemes—some real-estate deal he's in.'

'Why did he come to *you* about it?'

He looked away from her, fumbling among the letters on the desk. 'Guess he'd tried everybody else first. He'd go and ring the devil's front-door bell if he thought he could get anything out of him.'

'I suppose he did himself a lot of harm by testifying in the Ararat investigation?'

'Yes, *sir*—he's down and out this time.'

He uttered the words with a certain satisfaction. His daughter did not answer, and they sat silent, facing each other across the littered desk. Under their brief talk about Elmer Moffatt currents of rapid intelligence seemed to be flowing between them. Suddenly Undine leaned over the desk, her eyes widening trustfully, and the limpid smile flowing up to them.

'Father, I did what you wanted that one time, anyhow—won't you listen to me and help me out now?'

XVIII

UNDINE stood alone on the landing outside her father's office.

Only once before had she failed to gain her end with him—and there was a peculiar irony in the fact that Moffatt's intrusion should have brought before her the providential result of her previous failure. Not that she confessed to any real resemblance between the two situations. In the present case she knew well enough what she wanted, and how to get it. But the analogy had served her father's purpose, and Moffatt's unlucky entrance had visibly strengthened his resistance.

The worst of it was that the obstacles in the way were real enough. Mr Spragg had not put her off with vague asseverations—somewhat against her will he had forced his proofs on her, showing her how much above his promised allowance he had contributed in the last three years to the support of her household. Since she could not accuse herself of extravagance—having still full faith in her gift of 'managing'—she could only conclude that it was impossible to live on what her father and Ralph could provide; and this seemed a practical reason for desiring her freedom. If she and Ralph parted he would of course return to his family, and Mr Spragg would no longer be burdened with a helpless son-in-law. But even this argument did not move him. Undine, as soon as she had risked Van Degen's name, found herself face to face with a code of domestic conduct as rigid as its exponent's business principles were elastic. Mr Spragg did not regard divorce as intrinsically wrong or even inexpedient; and of its social disadvantages he had never

even heard. Lots of women did it, as Undine said; and if their
reasons were adequate they were justified. If Ralph Marvell had
been a drunkard or 'unfaithful' Mr Spragg would have approved
Undine's desire to divorce him; but that it should be prompted
by her inclination for another man—and a man with a wife of
his own—was as shocking to him as it would have been to the
most uncompromising of the Dagonets and Marvells. Such
things happened, as Mr Spragg knew, but they should not
happen to any woman of his name while he had the power to
prevent it; and Undine recognized that for the moment he had
that power.

As she emerged from the elevator she was surprised to see
Moffatt in the vestibule. His presence was an irritating reminder
of her failure, and she walked past him with a rapid bow; but he
overtook her.

'Mrs Marvell—I've been waiting to say a word to you.'

If it had been any one else she would have passed on; but
Moffatt's voice had always a detaining power. Even now that
she knew him to be defeated and negligible the power asserted
itself, and she paused to say: 'I'm afraid I can't stop—I'm late for
an engagement.'

'I shan't make you much later; but if you'd rather have me call
round at your house——'

'Oh, I'm so seldom in.' She turned a wondering look on him.
'What is it you wanted to say?'

'Just two words. I've got an office in this building and the
shortest way would be to come up there for a minute.' As her
look grew distant he added: 'I think what I've got to say is worth
the trip.'

His face was serious, without underlying irony: the face he
wore when he wanted to be trusted.

'Very well,' she said, turning back.

Undine, glancing at her watch as she came out of Moffatt's
office, saw that he had been true to his promise of not keeping
her more than ten minutes. The fact was characteristic. Under
all his incalculableness there had always been a hard foundation
of reliability: it seemed to be a matter of choice with him
whether he let one feel that solid bottom or not. And in specific

matters the same quality showed itself in an accuracy of statement, a precision of conduct, that contrasted curiously with
his usual hyperbolic banter and his loose lounging manner. No
one could be more elusive yet no one could be firmer to the
touch.

Her face had cleared and she moved more lightly as she left
the building. Moffatt's communication had not been completely
clear to her, but she understood the outline of the plan he had
laid before her, and was satisfied with the bargain they had
struck. He had begun by reminding her of her promise to
introduce him to any friend of hers who might be useful in the
way of business. Over three years had passed since they had
made the pact, and Moffatt had kept loyally to his side of it.
With the lapse of time the whole matter had become less
important to her, but she wanted to prove her good faith, and
when he reminded her of her promise she at once admitted it.

'Well, then—I want you to introduce me to your husband.'

Undine was surprised; but beneath her surprise she felt a
quick sense of relief. Ralph was easier to manage than so many
of her friends—and it was a mark of his present indifference to
acquiesce in anything she suggested.

'My husband? Why, what can he do for you?'

Moffatt explained at once, in the fewest words, as his way was
when it came to business. He was interested in a big 'deal' which
involved the purchase of a piece of real estate held by a number
of wrangling heirs. The real-estate broker with whom Ralph
Marvell was associated represented these heirs, but Moffatt had
his reasons for not approaching him directly. And he didn't want
to go to Marvell with a 'business proposition'—it would be
better to be thrown with him socially, as if by accident. It was
with that object that Moffatt had just appealed to Mr Spragg, but
Mr Spragg, as usual, had 'turned him down,' without even
consenting to look into the case.

'He'd rather have you miss a good thing than have it come to
you through me. I don't know what on earth he thinks it's in
my power to do to you—or ever was, for that matter,' he added.
'Anyhow,' he went on to explain, 'the power's all on your side
now; and I'll show you how little the doing will hurt you as
soon as I can have a quiet chat with your husband.' He branched

off again into technicalities, nebulous projections of capital and
interest, taxes and rents, from which she finally extracted, and
clung to, the central fact that if the 'deal went through' it would
mean a commission of forty thousand dollars to Marvell's firm,
of which something over a fourth would come to Ralph.

'By Jove, that's an amazing fellow!' Ralph Marvell exclaimed,
turning back into the drawing-room, a few evenings later, at the
conclusion of one of their little dinners.

Undine looked up from her seat by the fire. She had had the
inspired thought of inviting Moffatt to meet Clare Van Degen,
Mrs Fairford and Charles Bowen. It had occurred to her that
the simplest way of explaining Moffatt was to tell Ralph that she
had unexpectedly discovered an old Apex acquaintance in the
protagonist of the great Ararat Trust fight. Moffatt's defeat had
not wholly divested him of interest. As a factor in affairs he no
longer inspired apprehension, but as the man who had dared to
defy Harmon B. Driscoll he was a conspicuous and, to some
minds, almost an heroic figure.

Undine remembered that Clare and Mrs Fairford had once
expressed a wish to see this braver of the Olympians, and her
suggestion that he should be asked to meet them gave Ralph
evident pleasure. It was long since she had made any conciliatory
sign to his family.

Moffatt's social gifts were hardly of a kind to please the two
ladies: he would have shone more brightly in Peter Van Degen's
set than in his wife's. But neither Clare nor Mrs Fairford had
expected a man of conventional cut, and Moffatt's loud easiness
was obviously less disturbing to them than to their hostess.
Undine felt only his crudeness, and the tacit criticism passed on
it by the mere presence of such men as her husband and Bowen;
but Mrs Fairford seemed to enjoy provoking him to fresh
excesses of slang and hyperbole. Gradually she drew him into
talking of the Driscoll campaign, and he became recklessly
explicit. He seemed to have nothing to hold back: all the details
of the prodigious exploit poured from him with Homeric
volume. Then he broke off abruptly, thrusting his hands into his
trouser-pockets and shaping his red lips to a whistle which he
checked as his glance met Undine's. To conceal his embarrass-

ment he leaned back in his chair, looked about the table with complacency, and said 'I don't mind if I do' to the servant who approached to re-fill his champagne glass.

The men sat long over their cigars; but after an interval Undine called Charles Bowen into the drawing-room to settle some question in dispute between Clare and Mrs Fairford, and thus gave Moffatt a chance to be alone with her husband. Now that their guests had gone she was throbbing with anxiety to know what had passed between the two; but when Ralph rejoined her in the drawing-room she continued to keep her eyes on the fire and twirl her fan listlessly.

'That's an amazing chap,' Ralph repeated, looking down at her. 'Where was it you ran across him—out at Apex?'

As he leaned against the chimney-piece, lighting his cigarette, it struck Undine that he looked less fagged and lifeless than usual, and she felt more and more sure that something important had happened during the moment of isolation she had contrived.

She opened and shut her fan reflectively. 'Yes—years ago; father had some business with him and brought him home to dinner one day.'

'And you've never seen him since?'

She waited, as if trying to piece her recollections together. 'I suppose I must have; but all that seems so long ago,' she said sighing. She had been given, of late, to such plaintive glances toward her happy girlhood; but Ralph seemed not to notice the allusion.

'Do you know,' he exclaimed after a moment, 'I don't believe the fellow's beaten yet.'

She looked up quickly. 'Don't you?'

'No; and I could see that Bowen didn't either. He strikes me as the kind of man who develops slowly, needs a big field, and perhaps makes some big mistakes, but gets where he wants to in the end. Jove, I wish I could put him in a book! There's something epic about him—a kind of epic effrontery.'

Undine's pulses beat faster as she listened. Was it not what Moffatt had always said of himself—that all he needed was time and elbow-room? How odd that Ralph, who seemed so dreamy and unobservant, should instantly have reached the same conclusion! But what she wanted to know was the practical result of their meeting.

'What did you and he talk about when you were smoking?'

'Oh, he got on the Driscoll fight again—gave us some extraordinary details. The man's a thundering brute, but he's full of observation and humour. Then, after Bowen joined you, he told me about a new deal he's gone into—rather a promising scheme, but on the same Titanic scale. It's just possible, by the way, that we may be able to do something for him: part of the property he's after is held in our office.' He paused, knowing Undine's indifference to business matters; but the face she turned to him was alive with interest.

'You mean you might sell the property to him?'

'Well, if the thing comes off. There would be a big commission if we did.' He glanced down on her half ironically. 'You'd like that, wouldn't you?'

She answered with a shade of reproach: 'Why do you say that? I haven't complained.'

'Oh, no; but I know I've been a disappointment as a money-maker.'

She leaned back in her chair, closing her eyes as if in utter weariness and indifference, and in a moment she felt him bending over her. 'What's the matter? Don't you feel well?'

'I'm a little tired. It's nothing.' She pulled her hand away and burst into tears.

Ralph knelt down by her chair and put his arm about her. It was the first time he had touched her since the night of the boy's birthday, and the sense of her softness woke a momentary warmth in his veins.

'What is it, dear? What is it?'

Without turning her head she sobbed out: 'You seem to think I'm too selfish and odious—that I'm just pretending to be ill.'

'No, no,' he assured her, smoothing back her hair. But she continued to sob on in a gradual crescendo of despair, till the vehemence of her weeping began to frighten him, and he drew her to her feet and tried to persuade her to let herself be led upstairs. She yielded to his arm, sobbing in short exhausted gasps, and leaning her whole weight on him as he guided her along the passage to her bedroom. On the lounge to which he lowered her she lay white and still, tears trickling through her lashes and her handkerchief pressed against her lips. He recognized the symptoms with a sinking heart: she was on the verge of a nervous attack such as she had had in the winter, and he foresaw with dismay the disastrous train of consequences, the doctors' and nurses' bills, and all the attendant confusion and expense. If only Moffatt's project might be realized—if for once he could feel a round sum in his pocket, and be freed from the perpetual daily strain!

The next morning Undine, though calmer, was too weak to leave her bed, and her doctor prescribed rest and absence of worry—later, perhaps, a change of scene. He explained to Ralph that nothing was so wearing to a high-strung nature as monotony, and that if Mrs Marvell were contemplating a Newport season it was necessary that she should be fortified to meet it. In such cases he often recommended a dash to Paris or London, just to tone up the nervous system.

Undine regained her strength slowly, and as the days dragged on the suggestion of the European trip recurred with increasing frequency. But it came always from her medical adviser: she herself had grown strangely passive and indifferent. She continued to remain upstairs on her lounge, seeing no one but Mrs Heeny, whose daily ministrations had once more been prescribed, and asking only that the noise of Paul's play should be kept from her. His scamperings overhead disturbed her sleep, and his bed was moved into the day nursery, above his father's room. The child's early romping did not trouble Ralph, since he himself was always awake before daylight. The days were not long enough to hold his cares, and they came and stood by him through the silent hours, when there was no other sound to drown their voices.

Ralph had not made a success of his business. The real-estate brokers who had taken him into partnership had done so only with the hope of profiting by his social connections; and in this respect the alliance had been a failure. It was in such directions that he most lacked facility, and so far he had been of use to his partners only as an office-drudge. He was resigned to the continuance of such drudgery, though all his powers cried out against it; but even for the routine of business his aptitude was small, and he began to feel that he was not considered an addition to the firm. The difficulty of finding another opening made him fear a break; and his thoughts turned hopefully to Elmer Moffatt's hint of a 'deal'. The success of the negotiation might bring advantages beyond the immediate pecuniary profit; and that, at the present juncture, was important enough in itself.

Moffatt reappeared two days after the dinner, presenting himself in West End Avenue in the late afternoon with the explanation that the business in hand necessitated discretion, and that he preferred not to be seen in Ralph's office. It was a question of negotiating with the utmost privacy for the purchase of a small strip of land between two large plots already acquired by purchasers cautiously designated by Moffatt as his 'parties.' How far he 'stood in' with the parties he left it to Ralph to conjecture; but it was plain that he had a large stake in the transaction, and that it offered him his first chance of recovering himself since Driscoll had 'thrown' him. The owners of the coveted plot did not seem anxious to sell, and there were personal reasons for Moffatt's not approaching them through Ralph's partners, who were the regular agents of the estate: so that Ralph's acquaintance with the conditions, combined with his detachments from the case, marked him out as a useful intermediary.

Their first talk left Ralph with a dazzled sense of Moffatt's strength and keenness, but with a vague doubt as to the 'straightness' of the proposed transaction. Ralph had never seen his way clearly in that dim underworld of affairs where men of the Moffatt and Driscoll type moved like shadowy destructive monsters beneath the darting small fry of the surface. He knew that 'business' has created its own special morality; and his musings on man's relation to his self-imposed laws had shown him how little human conduct is generally troubled about its own sanctions. He had a vivid sense of the things a man of his kind didn't do; but his inability to get a mental grasp on large financial problems made it hard to apply to them so simple a measure as this inherited standard. He only knew, as Moffatt's plan developed, that it seemed all right while he talked of it with its originator, but vaguely wrong when he thought it over afterward. It occurred to him to consult his grandfather; and if he renounced the idea for the obvious reason that Mr Dagonet's ignorance of business was as fathomless as his own, this was not his sole motive. Finally it occurred to him to put the case hypothetically to Mr Spragg. As far as Ralph knew, his father-in-law's business record was unblemished; yet one felt in him an elasticity of adjustment not allowed for in the Dagonet code.

Mr Spragg listened thoughtfully to Ralph's statement of the case, growling out here and there a tentative correction, and turning his cigar between his lips as he seemed to turn the problem over in the loose grasp of his mind.

'Well, what's the trouble with it?' he asked at length, stretching his big square-toed shoes against the grate of his son-in-law's dining-room, where, in the after-dinner privacy of a family evening, Ralph had seized the occasion to consult him.

'The trouble?' Ralph considered. 'Why, that's just what I should like you to explain to me.'

Mr Spragg threw back his head and stared at the garlanded French clock on the chimney-piece. Mrs Spragg was sitting upstairs in her daughter's bedroom, and the silence of the house seemed to hang about the two men like a listening presence.

'Well, I dunno but what I agree with the doctor who said there warn't any diseases, but only sick people. Every case is different, I guess.' Mr Spragg, munching his cigar, turned a ruminating glance on Ralph. 'Seems to me it all boils down to one thing. Was this fellow we're supposing about under any obligation to the other party—the one he was trying to buy the property from?'

Ralph hesitated. 'Only the obligation recognized between decent men to deal with each other decently.'

Mr Spragg listened to this with the suffering air of a teacher compelled to simplify upon his simplest questions.

'Any personal obligation, I meant. Had the other fellow done him a good turn any time?'

'No—I don't imagine them to have had any previous relations at all.'

His father-in-law stared. 'Where's your trouble, then?' He sat for a moment frowning at the embers. 'Even when it's the other way round it ain't always so easy to decide how far that kind of thing's binding . . . and they say shipwrecked fellows'll make a

meal of a friend as quick as they would of a total stranger.' He
drew himself together with a shake of his shoulders and pulled
back his feet from the grate. 'But I don't see the conundrum in
your case, I guess it's up to both parties to take care of their own
skins.'

He rose from his chair and wandered upstairs to Undine.

That was the Wall Street code: it all 'boiled down' to the
personal obligation, to the salt eaten in the enemy's tent. Ralph's
fancy wandered off on a long trail of speculation from which he
was pulled back with a jerk by the need of immediate action.
Moffatt's 'deal' could not wait: quick decisions were essential to
effective action, and brooding over ethical shades of difference
might work more ill than good in a world committed to swift
adjustments. The arrival of several unforeseen bills confirmed
this view, and once Ralph had adopted it he began to take a
detached interest in the affair.

In Paris, in his younger days, he had once attended a lesson in
acting given at the Conservatoire by one of the great lights of
the theatre, and had seen an apparently uncomplicated rôle of
the classic repertory, familiar to him through repeated performances, taken to pieces before his eyes, dissolved into its com-
ponent elements, and built up again with a minuteness of
elucidation and a range of reference that made him feel as
though he had been let into the secret of some age-long natural
process. As he listened to Moffatt the remembrance of that
lesson came back to him. At the outset the 'deal,' and his own
share in it, had seemed simple enough: he would have put on his
hat and gone out on the spot in the full assurance of being able
to transact the affair. But as Moffatt talked he began to feel as
blank and blundering as the class of dramatic students before
whom the great actor had analyzed his part. The affair was in fact
difficult and complex, and Moffatt saw at once just where
the difficulties lay and how the personal idiosyncrasies of 'the
parties' affected them. Such insight fascinated Ralph, and he
strayed off into wondering why it did not qualify every financier
to be a novelist, and what intrinsic barrier divided the two arts.

Both men had strong incentives for hastening the affair; and
within a fortnight after Moffatt's first advance Ralph was able to
tell him that his offer was accepted. Over and above his personal

satisfaction he felt the thrill of the agent whom some powerful negotiator has charged with a delicate mission: he might have been an eager young Jesuit carrying compromising papers to his superior. It had been stimulating to work with Moffatt, and to study at close range the large powerful instrument of his intelligence.

As he came out of Moffatt's office at the conclusion of this visit Ralph met Mr Spragg descending from his eyrie. He stopped short with a backward glance at Moffatt's door.

'Hallo—what were you doing in there with those cut-throats?'

Ralph judged discretion to be essential. 'Oh, just a little business for the firm.'

Mr Spragg said no more, but resorted to the soothing labial motion of revolving his phantom toothpick.

'How's Undie getting along?' he merely asked, as he and his son-in-law descended together in the elevator.

'She doesn't seem to feel much stronger. The doctor wants her to run over to Europe for a few weeks. She thinks of joining her friends the Shallums in Paris.'

Mr Spragg was again silent, but he left the building at Ralph's side, and the two walked along together toward Wall Street.

Presently the older man asked: 'How did you get acquainted with Moffatt?'

'Why, by chance—Undine ran across him somewhere and asked him to dine the other night.'

'Undine asked him to dine?'

'Yes: she told me you used to know him out at Apex.'

Mr Spragg appeared to search his memory for confirmation of the fact. 'I believe he used to be round there at one time. I've never heard any good of him yet.' He paused at a crossing and looked probingly at his son-in-law. 'Is she terribly set on this trip to Europe?'

Ralph smiled. 'You know how it is when she takes a fancy to do anything——'

Mr Spragg, by a slight lift of his brooding brows, seemed to convey a deep if unspoken response.

'Well, I'd let her do it this time—I'd let her do it,' he said as he turned down the steps of the Subway.

Ralph was surprised, for he had gathered from some frightened references of Mrs Spragg's that Undine's parents had wind of her European plan and were strongly opposed to it. He concluded that Mr Spragg had long since measured the extent of profitable resistance, and knew just when it became vain to hold out against his daughter or advise others to do so.

Ralph, for his own part, had no inclination to resist. As he left Moffatt's office his inmost feeling was one of relief. He had reached the point of recognizing that it was best for both that his wife should go. When she returned perhaps their lives would readjust themselves—but for the moment he longed for some kind of benumbing influence, something that should give relief to the dull daily ache of feeling her so near and yet so inaccessible. Certainly there were more urgent uses for their brilliant wind-fall: heavy arrears of household debts had to be met, and the summer would bring its own burden. But perhaps another stroke of luck might befall him: he was getting to have the drifting dependence on 'luck' of the man conscious of his inability to direct his life. And meanwhile it seemed easier to let Undine have what she wanted.

Undine, on the whole, behaved with discretion. She received the good news languidly and showed no unseemly haste to profit by it. But it was as hard to hide the light in her eyes as to dissemble the fact that she had not only thought out every detail of the trip in advance, but had decided exactly how her husband and son were to be disposed of in her absence. Her suggestion that Ralph should take Paul to his grandparents, and that the West End Avenue house should be let for the summer, was too practical not to be acted on; and Ralph found she had already put her hand on the Harry Lipscombs, who, after three years of neglect, were to be dragged back to favour and made to feel, as the first step in their reinstatement, the necessity of hiring for the summer months a cool airy house on the West Side. On her return from Europe, Undine explained, she would of course go straight to Ralph and the boy in the Adirondacks; and it seemed a foolish extravagance to let the house stand empty when the Lipscombs were so eager to take it.

As the day of departure approached it became harder for her to temper her beams; but her pleasure showed itself so amiably that Ralph began to think she might, after all, miss the boy and himself more than she imagined. She was tenderly preoccupied with Paul's welfare, and, to prepare for his translation to his grand-parents' she gave the household in Washington Square more of her time than she had accorded it since her marriage. She explained that she wanted Paul to grow used to his new surroundings; and with that object she took him frequently to his grandmother's, and won her way into old Mr Dagonet's sympathies by her devotion to the child and her pretty way of joining in his games.

Undine was not consciously acting a part: this new phase was as natural to her as the other. In the joy of her gratified desires she wanted to make everybody about her happy. If only every-one would do as she wished she would never be unreasonable. She much preferred to see smiling faces about her, and her dread of the reproachful and dissatisfied countenance gave the measure of what she would do to avoid it.

These thoughts were in her mind when, a day or two before sailing, she came out of the Washington Square house with her boy. It was a late spring afternoon, and she and Paul had lingered on till long past the hour sacred to his grandfather's nap. Now, as she came out into the square she saw that, however well Mr Dagonet had borne their protracted romp, it had left his playmate flushed and sleepy; and she lifted Paul in her arms to carry him to the nearest cab-stand.

As she raised herself she saw a thick-set figure approaching her across the square; and a moment later she was shaking hands with Elmer Moffatt. In the bright spring air he looked seasonably glossy and prosperous; and she noticed that he wore a bunch of violets in his buttonhole. His small black eyes twinkled with approval as they rested on her, and Undine reflected that, with Paul's arms about her neck, and his little flushed face against her own, she must present a not unpleasing image of young motherhood.

'That the heir apparent?' Moffatt asked; adding 'Happy to make your acquaintance, sir,' as the boy, at Undine's bidding, held out a fist sticky with sugar-plums.

'He's been spending the afternoon with his grandfather, and they played so hard that he's sleepy,' she explained. Little Paul, at that stage in his career, had a peculiar grace of wide-gazing deep-lashed eyes and arched cherubic lips, and Undine saw that Moffatt was not insensible to the picture she and her son composed. She did not dislike his admiration, for she no longer felt any shrinking from him—she would even have been glad to thank him for the service he had done her husband if she had known how to allude to it without awkwardness. Moffatt seemed equally pleased at the meeting, and they looked at each other almost intimately over Paul's tumbled curls.

'He's a mighty fine fellow and no mistake—but isn't he rather an armful for you?' Moffatt asked, his eyes lingering with real kindliness on the child's face.

'Oh, we haven't far to go. I'll pick up a cab at the corner.'

'Well, let me carry him that far anyhow,' said Moffatt.

Undine was glad to be relieved of her burden, for she was unused to the child's weight, and disliked to feel that her skirt was dragging on the pavement. 'Go to the gentleman, Pauly— he'll carry you better than mother,' she said.

The little boy's first movement was one of recoil from the ruddy sharp-eyed countenance that was so unlike his father's delicate face; but he was an obedient child, and after a moment's hesitation he wound his arms trustfully about the red gentle-man's neck.

'That's a good fellow—sit tight and I'll give you a ride,' Moffatt cried, hoisting the boy to his shoulder.

Paul was not used to being perched at such a height, and his nature was hospitable to new impressions. 'Oh, I like it up here—you're higher than father!' he exclaimed; and Moffatt hugged him with a laugh.

'It must feel mighty good to come uptown to a fellow like you in the evenings,' he said, addressing the child but looking at Undine, who also laughed a little.

'Oh, they're a dreadful nuisance, you know; but Paul's a very good boy.'

'I wonder if he knows what a friend I've been to him lately,' Moffatt went on, as they turned into Fifth Avenue.

Undine smiled: she was glad he should have given her an opening.

'He shall be told as soon as he's old enough to thank you. I'm so glad you came to Ralph about that business.'

'Oh, I gave him a leg up, and I guess he's given me one too. Queer the way things come round—he's fairly put me in the way of a fresh start.'

Their eyes met in a silence which Undine was the first to break. 'It's been awfully nice of you to do what you've done—right along. And this last thing has made a lot of difference to us.'

'Well, I'm glad you feel that way. I never wanted to be anything but "nice," as you call it.' Moffatt paused a moment and then added: 'If you're less scared of me than your father is I'd be glad to call round and see you once in a while.'

The quick blood rushed to her cheeks. There was nothing challenging, demanding in his tone—she guessed at once that if he made the request it was simply for the pleasure of being with her, and she liked the magnanimity implied. Nevertheless she was not sorry to have to answer: 'Of course I'll always be glad to see you—only, as it happens, I'm just sailing for Europe.'

'For Europe?' The word brought Moffatt to a stand so abruptly that little Paul lurched on his shoulder.

'For Europe?' he repeated. 'Why, I thought you said the other evening you expected to stay on in town till July. Didn't you think of going to the Adirondacks?'

Flattered by his evident disappointment, she became high and careless in her triumph. 'Oh, yes,—but that's all changed. Ralph and the boy are going; but I sail on Saturday to join some friends in Paris—and later I may do some motoring in Switzerland and Italy.'

She laughed a little in the mere enjoyment of putting her plans into words and Moffatt laughed too, but with an edge of sarcasm.

'I see—I see: everything's changed, as you say, and your husband can blow you off to the trip. Well, I hope you'll have a first-class time.'

Their glances crossed again, and something in his cool scrutiny impelled Undine to say, with a burst of candour: 'If I do, you know, I shall owe it all to you!'

'Well, I always told you I meant to act white by you,' he answered.

They walked on in silence, and presently he began again in his usual joking strain: 'See what one of the Apex girls has been up to?'

Apex was too remote for her to understand the reference, and he went on: 'Why, Millard Binch's wife—Indiana Frusk that was. Didn't you see in the papers that Indiana'd fixed it up with James J. Rolliver to marry her? They say it was easy enough squaring Millard Binch—you'd know it *would* be—but it cost Rolliver near a million to mislay Mrs R. and the children. Well, Indiana's pulled it off, anyhow; she always was a bright girl. But she never came up to you.'

'Oh——' she stammered with a laugh, astonished and agitated by his news. Indiana Frusk and Rolliver! It showed how easily the thing could be done. If only her father had listened to her! If a girl like Indiana Frusk could gain her end so easily, what might not Undine have accomplished? She knew Moffatt was right in saying that Indiana had never come up to her . . . She wondered how the marriage would strike Van Degen . . .

She signalled to a cab and they walked toward it without speaking. Undine was recalling with intensity that one of Indiana's shoulders was higher than the other, and that people in Apex had thought her lucky to catch Millard Binch, the druggist's clerk, when Undine herself had cast him off after a lingering engagement. And now Indiana Frusk was to be Mrs James J. Rolliver!

Undine got into the cab and bent forward to take little Paul.

Moffatt lowered his charge with exaggerated care, and a 'Steady there, steady,' that made the child laugh; then, stooping over, he put a kiss on Paul's lips before handing him over to his mother.

XIX

'THE PARISIAN DIAMOND COMPANY—Anglo-American branch.'

Charles Bowen, seated, one rainy evening of the Paris season, in a corner of the great Nouveau Luxe restaurant, was lazily trying to resolve his impressions of the scene into the phrases of a letter to his old friend Mrs Henley Fairford.

The long habit of unwritten communion with this lady—in no way conditioned by the short rare letters they actually exchanged—usually caused his notations, in absence, to fall into such terms when the subject was of a kind to strike an answering flash from her. And who but Mrs Fairford would see, from his own precise angle, the fantastic improbability, the layers on layers of unsubstantialness, on which the seemingly solid scene before him rested?

The dining-room of the Nouveau Luxe was at its fullest, and, having contracted on the garden side through stress of weather, had even overflowed to the farther end of the long hall beyond; so that Bowen, from his corner, surveyed a seemingly endless perspective of plumed and jewelled heads, of shoulders bare or black-coated, encircling the close-packed tables. He had come half an hour before the time he had named to his expected guest, so that he might have the undisturbed amusement of watching the picture compose itself again before his eyes. During some forty years' perpetual exercise of his perceptions he had never come across anything that gave them the special titillation produced by the sight of the dinner-hour at the Nouveau Luxe: the same sense of putting his hand on human nature's passion for the factitious, its incorrigible habit of imitating the imitation.

As he sat watching the familiar faces swept toward him on the rising tide of arrival—for it was one of the joys of the scene that the type was always the same even when the individual was not—he hailed with renewed appreciation this costly expression of a social ideal. The dining-room at the Nouveau Luxe represented, on such a spring evening, what unbounded material power had devised for the delusion of its leisure: a phantom 'society,' with all the rules, smirks, gestures of its model, but evoked out of promiscuity and incoherence while the other had been the product of continuity and choice. And the instinct which had driven a new class of world-compellers to bind themselves to slavish imitation of the superseded, and their prompt and reverent faith in the reality of the sham they had created, seemed to Bowen the most satisfying proof of human permanence.

With this thought in his mind he looked up to greet his guest. The Comte Raymond de Chelles, straight, slim and gravely smiling, came toward him with frequent pauses of salutation at the crowded tables; saying, as he seated himself and turned his pleasant eyes on the scene: '*Il n'y a pas à dire,**' my dear Bowen, it's charming and sympathetic and original—we owe America a debt of gratitude for inventing it!'

Bowen felt a last touch of satisfaction: they were the very words to complete his thought.

'My dear fellow, it's really you and your kind who are responsible. It's the direct creation of feudalism, like all the great social upheavals!'

Raymond de Chelles stroked his handsome brown moustache. 'I should have said, on the contrary, that one enjoyed it for the contrast. It's such a refreshing change from our institutions—which are, nevertheless, the necessary foundations of society. But just as one may have an infinite admiration for one's wife, and yet occasionally——' he waved a light hand toward the spectacle. 'This, in the social order, is the diversion, the permitted diversion, that your original race has devised: a kind of superior Bohemia, where one may be respectable without being bored.'

Bowen laughed. 'You've put it in a nutshell: the ideal of the American woman is to be respectable without being bored; and from that point of view this world they've invented has more originality than I gave it credit for.'

Chelles thoughtfully unfolded his napkin. 'My impression's a superficial one, of course—for as to what goes on under-neath——!' He looked across the room. 'If I married I shouldn't care to have my wife come here too often.'

Bowen laughed again. 'She'd be as safe as in a bank! Nothing ever goes on! Nothing that ever happens here is real.'

'*Ah, quant à cela*——'* the Frenchman murmured, inserting a fork into his melon.

Bowen looked at him with enjoyment—he was such a precious foot-note to the page! The two men, accidentally thrown together some years previously during a trip up the Nile, always met again with pleasure when Bowen returned to France. Raymond de Chelles, who came of a family of moderate fortune, lived for the greater part of the year on his father's estates in Burgundy; but he came up every spring to the *entresol** of the old Marquis's *hôtel** for a two months' study of human nature, applying to the pursuit the discriminating taste and transient ardour that give the finest bloom to pleasure. Bowen liked him as a companion and admired him as a charming specimen of the Frenchman of his class, embodying in his lean, fatigued and finished person that happy mean of simplicity and intelligence of which no other race has found the secret. If Raymond de Chelles had been English he would have been a mere fox-hunting animal, with appetites but without tastes; but in his lighter Gallic clay the wholesome territorial savour, the inherited passion for sport and agriculture, were blent with an openness to finer sensations, a sense of the come-and-go of ideas, under which one felt the tight hold of two or three inherited notions, religious, political, and domestic, in total contradiction to his surface attitude. That the inherited notions would in the end prevail, everything in his appearance declared, from the distinguished slant of his nose to the narrow forehead under his thinning hair; he was the kind of man who would inevitably 'revert' when he married. But meanwhile the surface he presented to the play of life was broad enough to take in the fantastic spectacle of the Nouveau Luxe; and to see its gestures reflected in a Latin consciousness was an endless entertainment to Bowen.

The tone of his guest's last words made him take them up. 'But is the lady you allude to more than a hypothesis? Surely you're not thinking of getting married?'

Chelles raised his eye-brows ironically. 'When hasn't one to think of it, in my situation? One hears of nothing else at home—one knows that, like death, it has to come.' His glance, which was still mustering the room, came to a sudden pause and kindled.

'Who's the lady over there—fair-haired, in white—the one who's just come in with the red-faced man? They seem to be with a party of your compatriots.'

Bowen followed his glance to a neighbouring table, where, at the moment, Undine Marvell was seating herself at Peter Van Degen's side, in the company of the Harvey Shallums, the beautiful Mrs Beringer and a dozen other New York figures.

She was so placed that as she took her seat she recognized Bowen and sent him a smile across the tables. She was more simply dressed than usual, and the pink lights, warming her cheeks and striking gleams from her hair, gave her face a dewy freshness that was new to Bowen. He had always thought her beauty too obvious, too bathed in the bright publicity of the American air; but to-night she seemed to have been brushed by the wing of poetry, and its shadow lingered in her eyes.

Chelles' gaze made it evident that he had received the same impression.

'One is sometimes inclined to deny your compatriots actual beauty—to charge them with producing the effect without having the features; but in this case—you say you know the lady?'

'Yes: she's the wife of an old friend.'

'The wife? She's married? There, again, it's so puzzling! Your young girls look so experienced, and your married women sometimes so—unmarried.'

'Well, they often are—in these days of divorce!'

The other's interest quickened. 'Your friend's divorced?'

'Oh, no; heaven forbid! Mrs Marvell hasn't been long married; and it was a love-match of the good old kind.'

'Ah—and the husband? Which is he?'

'He's not here—he's in New York.'

'Feverishly adding to a fortune already monstrous?'

'No; not precisely monstrous. The Marvells are not well off,' said Bowen, amused by his friend's interrogations.

'And he allows an exquisite being like that to come to Paris without him—and in company with the red-faced gentleman who seems so alive to his advantages?'

'We don't "allow" our women this or that; I don't think we set much store by the compulsory virtues.'

His companion received this with amusement. 'If you're as detached as that, why does the obsolete institution of marriage survive with you?'

'Oh, it still has its uses. One couldn't be divorced without it.'

Chelles laughed again; but his straying eye still followed the same direction, and Bowen noticed that the fact was not unremarked by the object of his contemplation. Undine's party was one of the liveliest in the room: the American laugh rose above the din of the orchestra as the American toilets dominated the less daring effects at the other tables. Undine, on entering, had seemed to be in the same mood as her companions; but Bowen saw that, as she became conscious of his friend's observation, she isolated herself in a kind of soft abstraction; and he admired the adaptability which enabled her to draw from such surroundings the contrasting graces of reserve.

They had greeted each other with all the outer signs of cordiality, but Bowen fancied she would not care to have him speak to her. She was evidently dining with Van Degen, and Van Degen's proximity was the last fact she would wish to have transmitted to the critics in Washington Square. Bowen was therefore surprised when, as he rose to leave the restaurant, he heard himself hailed by Peter.

'Hallo—hold on! When did you come over? Mrs Marvell's dying for the last news about the old homestead.'

Undine's smile confirmed the appeal. She wanted to know how lately Bowen had left New York, and pressed him to tell her when he had last seen her boy, how he was looking, and whether Ralph had been persuaded to go down to Clare's on Saturdays and get a little riding and tennis? And dear Laura—was she well too, and was Paul with her, or still with his grandmother? They were all dreadfully bad correspondents, and so was she, Undine laughingly admitted; and when Ralph had last written her these questions had still been undecided.

As she smiled up at Bowen he saw her glance stray to the spot where his companion hovered; and when the diners rose to move toward the garden for coffee she said, with a sweet note and a detaining smile: 'Do come with us—I haven't half finished.'

Van Degen echoed the request, and Bowen, amused by Undine's arts, was presently introducing Chelles, and joining with him in the party's transit to the terrace.

The rain had ceased, and under the clear evening sky the restaurant garden opened green depths that skilfully hid its narrow boundaries. Van Degen's company was large enough to surround two of the tables on the terrace, and Bowen noted the skill with which Undine, leaving him to Mrs Shallum's care, contrived to draw Raymond de Chelles to the other table. Still more noticeable was the effect of this stratagem on Van Degen, who also found himself relegated to Mrs Shallum's group. Poor Peter's state was betrayed by the irascibility which wreaked itself on a jostling waiter, and found cause for loud remonstrance in the coldness of the coffee and the badness of the cigars; and Bowen, with something more than the curiosity of the looker-on, wondered whether this were the real clue to Undine's conduct. He had always smiled at Mrs Fairford's fears for Ralph's domestic peace. He thought Undine too clear-headed to forfeit the advantages of her marriage; but it now struck him that she might have had a glimpse of larger opportunities. Bowen, at the thought, felt the pang of the sociologist over the individual havoc wrought by every social readjustment: it had so long been clear to him that poor Ralph was a survival, and destined, as such, to go down in any conflict with the rising forces.

XX

SOME six weeks later, Undine Marvell stood at the window smiling down on her recovered Paris.

Her hotel sitting-room had, as usual, been flowered, cushioned and lamp-shaded into a delusive semblance of stability; and she had really felt, for the last few weeks, that the life she was leading there must be going to last—it seemed so perfect an answer to all her wants!

As she looked out at the thronged street, on which the summer light lay like a blush of pleasure, she felt herself naturally akin to all the bright and careless freedom of the scene. She had been away from Paris for two days, and the spectacle before her seemed more rich and suggestive after her brief absence from it. Her senses luxuriated in all its material details: the thronging motors, the brilliant shops, the novelty and daring of the women's dresses, the piled-up colours of the ambulant flower-carts, the appetizing expanse of the fruiterers' windows, even the chromatic effects of the *petits fours* behind the plate-glass of the pastry-cooks: all the surface-sparkle and variety of the inexhaustible streets of Paris.

The scene before her typified to Undine her first real taste of life. How meagre and starved the past appeared in comparison with this abundant present! The noise, the crowd, the promiscuity beneath her eyes symbolized the glare and movement of her life. Every moment of her days was packed with excitement and exhilaration. Everything amused her: the long hours of bargaining and debate with dress-makers and jewellers, the crowded lunches at fashionable restaurants, the perfunctory dash through a picture-show or the lingering visit to the last new milliner; the afternoon motor-rush to some leafy suburb, where tea and music and sunset were hastily absorbed on a crowded terrace above the Seine; the whirl home through the Bois to dress for dinner and start again on the round of evening diversions; the dinner at the Nouveau Luxe or the Café de Paris, and the little play at the Capucines or the Variétés, followed, because the night was 'too lovely,' and it was a shame to waste it, by a breathless flight back to the Bois, with supper in one of its lamp-hung restaurants, or, if the weather forbade, a tumultuous progress through the midnight haunts where 'ladies' were not supposed to show themselves, and might consequently taste the thrill of being occasionally taken for their opposites.

As the varied vision unrolled itself, Undine contrasted it with the pale monotony of her previous summers. The one she most resented was the first after her marriage, the European summer out of whose joys she had been cheated by her own ignorance and Ralph's perversity. They had been free then, there had been no child to hamper their movements, their money anxieties had hardly begun, the face of life had been fresh and radiant, and she had been doomed to waste such opportunities on a succession of ill-smelling Italian towns. She still felt it to be her deepest grievance against her husband; and now that, after four years of petty household worries, another chance of escape had come, he already wanted to drag her back to bondage!

This fit of retrospection had been provoked by two letters which had come that morning. One was from Ralph, who began by reminding her that he had not heard from her for weeks, and went on to point out, in his usual tone of good-humoured remonstrance, that since her departure the drain on her letter of credit had been deep and constant. 'I wanted you,' he wrote, 'to get all the fun you could out of the money I made last spring; but I didn't think you'd get through it quite so fast. Try to come home without leaving too many bills behind you. Your illness and Paul's cost more than I expected, and Lipscomb has had a bad shock in Wall Street, and hasn't yet paid his first quarter . . .'

Always the same monotonous refrain! Was it her fault that she and the boy had been ill? Or that Harry Lipscomb had been 'on the wrong side' of Wall Street? Ralph seemed to have money on the brain: his business life had certainly deteriorated him. And, since he hadn't made a success of it after all, why shouldn't he turn back to literature and try to write his novel? Undine, the previous winter, had been dazzled by the figures which a well-known magazine editor whom she had met at dinner had named as within reach of the successful novelist. She perceived for the first time that literature was becoming fashionable, and instantly decided that it would be amusing and original if she and Ralph should owe their prosperity to his talent. She already saw herself, as the wife of a celebrated author, wearing 'artistic' dresses and doing the drawing-room over with Gothic tapestries and dim lights in altar candle-sticks. But when she suggested Ralph's taking up his novel he answered with a laugh that his brains were sold to the firm—that when he came back at night the tank was empty . . . And now he wanted her to sail for home in a week!

The other letter excited a deeper resentment. It was an appeal from Laura Fairford to return and look after Ralph. He was overworked and out of spirits, she wrote, and his mother and sister, reluctant as they were to interfere, felt they ought to urge Undine to come back to him. Details followed, unwelcome and officious. What right had Laura Fairford to preach to her of wifely obligations? No doubt Charles Bowen had sent home a highly-coloured report—and there was really a certain irony in Mrs Fairford's criticizing her sister-in-law's conduct on information obtained from such a source!

Undine turned from the window and threw herself down on her deeply cushioned sofa. She was feeling the pleasant fatigue consequent on her trip to the country, whither she and Mrs Shallum had gone with Raymond de Chelles to spend a night at the old Marquis's château. When her travelling companions, an hour earlier, had left her at her door, she had half-promised to rejoin them for a late dinner in the Bois; and as she leaned back among the cushions disturbing thoughts were banished by the urgent necessity of deciding what dress she should wear.

These bright weeks of the Parisian spring had given her a first real glimpse into the art of living. From the experts who had taught her to subdue the curves of her figure and soften her bright free stare with dusky pencillings, to the skilled purveyors of countless forms of pleasure—the theatres and restaurants, the green and blossoming suburbs, the whole shining shifting spectacle of nights and days—every sight and sound and word had combined to charm her perceptions and refine her taste. And her growing friendship with Raymond de Chelles had been the most potent of these influences.

Chelles, at once immensely 'taken,' had not only shown his eagerness to share in the helter-skelter motions of Undine's party, but had given her glimpses of another, still more brilliant existence, that life of the inaccessible 'Faubourg' of which the first tantalizing hints had but lately reached her. Hitherto she had assumed that Paris existed for the stranger, that its native life was merely an obscure foundation for the dazzling super-structure of hotels and restaurants in which her compatriots disported themselves. But lately she had begun to hear about other American women, the women who had married into the French aristocracy, and who led, in the high-walled houses beyond the Seine which she had once thought so dull and dingy, a life that made her own seem as undistinguished as the social existence of the Mealey House. Perhaps what most exasperated her was the discovery, in this impenetrable group, of the Miss Wincher who had poisoned her far-off summer at Potash Springs. To recognize her old enemy in the Marquise de Trézac who so frequently figured in the Parisian chronicle was the more irritating to Undine because her intervening social experiences had caused her to look back on Nettie Wincher as a frumpy girl who wouldn't have 'had a show' in New York.

Once more all the accepted values were reversed, and it turned out that Miss Wincher had been in possession of some key to success on which Undine had not yet put her hand. To know that others were indifferent to what she had thought important was to cheapen all present pleasure and turn the whole force of her desires in a new direction. What she wanted for the moment was to linger on in Paris, prolonging her flirtation with Chelles, and profiting by it to detach herself from her compatriots and enter doors closed to their approach. And Chelles himself attracted her: she thought him as 'sweet' as she had once thought Ralph, whose fastidiousness and refinement were blent in him with a delightful foreign vivacity. His chief value, however, lay in his power of exciting Van Degen's jealousy. She knew enough of French customs to be aware that such devotion as Chelles' was not likely to have much practical bearing on her future; but Peter had an alarming way of lapsing into security, and as a spur to his ardour she knew the value of other men's attentions.

It had become Undine's fixed purpose to bring Van Degen to a definite expression of his intentions. The case of Indiana Frusk, whose brilliant marriage the journals of two continents had recently chronicled with unprecedented richness of detail, had made less impression on him than she hoped. He treated it as a comic episode without special bearing on their case, and once, when Undine cited Rolliver's expensive fight for freedom as an instance of the power of love over the most invulnerable natures, had answered carelessly: 'Oh, his first wife was a laundress, I believe.'

But all about them couples were unpairing and pairing again with an ease and rapidity that encouraged Undine to bide her time. It was simply a question of making Van Degen want her enough, and of not being obliged to abandon the game before he wanted her as much as she meant he should. This was precisely what would happen if she were compelled to leave Paris now. Already the event had shown how right she had been to come abroad: the attention she attracted in Paris had reawakened Van Degen's fancy, and her hold over him was stronger

than when they had parted in America. But the next step must
be taken with coolness and circumspection; and she must not
throw away what she had gained by going away at a stage when
he was surer of her than she of him.

She was still intensely considering these questions when the
door behind her opened and he came in.

She looked up with a frown and he gave a deprecating laugh.
'Didn't I knock? Don't look so savage! They told me downstairs
you'd got back, and I just bolted in without thinking.'

He had widened and purpled since their first encounter, five
years earlier, but his features had not matured. His face was still
the face of a covetous bullying boy, with a large appetite for
primitive satisfactions and a sturdy belief in his intrinsic right
to them. It was all the more satisfying to Undine's vanity to see
his look change at her tone from command to conciliation,
and from conciliation to the entreaty of a capriciously-treated
animal.

'What a ridiculous hour for a visit!' she exclaimed, ignoring
his excuse.

'Well, if you disappear like that, without a word——'

'I told my maid to telephone you I was going away.'

'You couldn't make time to do it yourself, I suppose?'

'We rushed off suddenly; I'd hardly time to get to the station.'

'You rushed off where, may I ask?' Van Degen still lowered
down on her.

'Oh, didn't I tell you? I've been down staying at Chelles'
château in Burgundy.' Her face lit up and she raised herself
eagerly on her elbow.

'It's the most wonderful old house you ever saw: a real castle,
with towers, and water all round it, and a funny kind of bridge
they pull up. Chelles said he wanted me to see just how they
lived at home, and I did; I saw everything: the tapestries that
Louis Quinze gave them, and the family portraits, and the
chapel, where their own priest says mass, and they sit by themselves in a balcony with crowns all over it. The priest was a
lovely old man—he said he'd give anything to convert me. Do
you know, I think there's something very beautiful about the
Roman Catholic religion? I've even felt I might have been
happier if I'd had some religious influence in my life.'

She sighed a little, and turned her head away. She flattered herself that she had learned to strike the right note with Van Degen. At this crucial stage he needed a taste of his own methods, a glimpse of the fact that there were women in the world who could get on without him.

He continued to gaze down at her sulkily. 'Were the old people there? You never told me you knew his mother.'

'I don't. They weren't there. But it didn't make a bit of difference, because Raymond sent down a cook from the Luxe.'

'Oh, Lord,' Van Degen groaned, dropping down on the end of the sofa. 'Was the cook got down to chaperon you?'

Undine laughed. 'You talk like Ralph! I had Bertha with me.'

'*Bertha!*' His tone of contempt surprised her. She had supposed that Mrs Shallum's presence had made the visit perfectly correct.

'You went without knowing his parents, and without their inviting you? Don't you know what that sort of thing means out here? Chelles did it to brag about you at his club. He wants to compromise you—that's his game!'

'Do you suppose he does?' A flicker of a smile crossed her lips. 'I'm so unconventional: when I like a man I never stop to think about such things. But I ought to, of course—you're quite right.' She looked at Van Degen thoughtfully. 'At any rate, he's not a married man.'

Van Degen had got to his feet again and was standing accusingly before her; but as she spoke the blood rose to his neck and ears.

'What difference does that make?'

'It might make a good deal. I see,' she added, 'how careful I ought to be about going round with you.'

'With *me*?' His face fell at the retort; then he broke into a laugh. He adored Undine's 'smartness,' which was of precisely the same quality as his own. 'Oh, that's another thing: you can always trust me to look after you!'

'With your reputation? Much obliged!'

Van Degen smiled. She knew he liked such allusions, and was pleased that she thought him compromising.

'Oh, I'm as good as gold. You've made a new man of me!'

'Have I?' She considered him in silence for a moment. 'I wonder what you've done to me but make a discontented woman of me—discontented with everything I had before I knew you?'

The change of tone was thrilling to him. He forgot her mockery, forgot his rival, and sat down at her side, almost in possession of her waist. 'Look here,' he asked, 'where are we going to dine to-night?'

His nearness was not agreeable to Undine, but she liked his free way, his contempt for verbal preliminaries. Ralph's reserves and delicacies, his perpetual desire that he and she should be attuned to the same key, had always vaguely bored her; whereas in Van Degen's manner she felt a hint of the masterful way that had once subdued her in Elmer Moffatt. But she drew back, releasing herself.

'To-night? I can't—I'm engaged.'

'I know you are: engaged to *me*! You promised last Sunday you'd dine with me out of town to-night.'

'How can I remember what I promised last Sunday? Besides, after what you've said, I see I oughtn't to.'

'What do you mean by what I've said?'

'Why, that I'm imprudent; that people are talking——'

He stood up with an angry laugh. 'I suppose you're dining with Chelles. Is that it?'

'Is that the way you cross-examine Clare?'

'I don't care a hang what Clare does—I never have.'

'That must—in some ways—be rather convenient for her!'

'Glad you think so. *Are* you dining with him?'

She slowly turned the wedding-ring upon her finger. 'You know I'm *not* married to you—yet!'

He took a random turn through the room; then he came back and planted himself wrathfully before her. 'Can't you see the man's doing his best to make a fool of you?'

She kept her amused gaze on him. 'Does it strike you that it's such an awfully easy thing to do?'

The edges of his ears were purple. 'I sometimes think it's easier for these damned little dancing-masters than for one of us.'

Undine was still smiling up at him; but suddenly her face grew grave. 'What does it matter what I do or don't do, when Ralph has ordered me home next week?'

'Ordered you home?' His face changed. 'Well, you're not going, are you?'

'What's the use of saying such things?' She gave a disenchanted laugh. 'I'm a poor man's wife, and can't do the things my friends do. It's not because Ralph loves me that he wants me back—it's simply because he can't afford to let me stay!'

Van Degen's perturbation was increasing. 'But you mustn't go—it's preposterous! Why should a woman like you be sacrificed when a lot of dreary frumps have everything they want? Besides, you can't chuck me like this! Why, we're all to motor down to Aix next week, and perhaps take a dip into Italy——'

'*Oh, Italy*——' she murmured on a note of yearning.

He was closer now, and had her hands. 'You'd love that, wouldn't you? As far as Venice, anyhow; and then in August there's Trouville—you've never tried Trouville? There's an awfully jolly crowd there—and the motoring's ripping in Normandy. If you say so I'll take a villa there instead of going back to Newport. And I'll put the *Sorceress* in commission, and you can make up parties and run off whenever you like, to Scotland or Norway——' He hung above her. 'Don't dine with Chelles to-night! Come with me, and we'll talk things over; and next week we'll run down to Trouville to choose the villa.'

Undine's heart was beating fast, but she felt within her a strange lucid force of resistance. Because of that sense of security she left her hands in Van Degen's. So Mr Spragg might have felt at the tensest hour of the Pure Water Move. She leaned forward, holding her suitor off by the pressure of her bent-back palms.

'Kiss me good-bye, Peter; I sail on Wednesday,' she said.

It was the first time she had permitted him a kiss, and as his face darkened down on her she felt a moment's recoil. But her physical reactions were never very acute: she always vaguely wondered why people made 'such a fuss,' were so violently for or against such demonstrations. A cool spirit within her seemed to watch over and regulate her sensations, and leave her capable of measuring the intensity of those she provoked.

She turned to look at the clock. 'You must go now—I shall be hours late for dinner.'

'Go—after that?' He held her fast. 'Kiss me again,' he commanded.

It was wonderful how cool she felt—how easily she could slip out of his grasp! Any man could be managed like a child if he were really in love with one . . .

'Don't be a goose, Peter; do you suppose I'd have kissed you if——'

'If what—what—what?' he mimicked her ecstatically, not listening.

She saw that if she wished to make him hear her she must put more distance between them, and she rose and moved across the room. From the fireplace she turned to add—'if we hadn't been saying good-bye?'

'Good-bye—now? What's the use of talking like that?' He jumped up and followed her. 'Look here, Undine—I'll do anything on earth you want; only don't talk of going! If you'll only stay I'll make it all as straight and square as you please. I'll get Bertha Shallum to stop over with you for the summer; I'll take a house at Trouville and make my wife come out there. Hang it, she *shall*, if you say so! Only be a little good to me!'

Still she stood before him without speaking, aware that her implacable brows and narrowed lips would hold him off as long as she chose.

'What's the matter, Undine? Why don't you answer? You know you can't go back to that deadly dry-rot!'

She swept about on him with indignant eyes. 'I can't go on with my present life either. It's hateful—as hateful as the other. If I don't go home I've got to decide on something different.'

'What do you mean by "something different"?' She was silent, and he insisted: 'Are you really thinking of marrying Chelles?'

She started as if he had surprised a secret. 'I'll never forgive you if you speak of it——'

'Good Lord! Good Lord!' he groaned.

She remained motionless, with lowered lids, and he went up to her and pulled her about so that she faced him. 'Undine, honour bright—do you think he'll marry you?'

She looked at him with a sudden hardness in her eyes. 'I really can't discuss such things with you.'

'Oh, for the Lord's sake don't take that tone! I don't half know what I'm saying . . . but you mustn't throw yourself away a second time. I'll do anything you want—I swear I will!'

A knock on the door sent them apart, and a servant entered with a telegram.

Undine turned away to the window with the narrow blue slip. She was glad of the interruption: the sense of what she had at stake made her want to pause a moment and to draw breath.

The message was a long cable signed with Laura Fairford's name. It told her that Ralph had been taken suddenly ill with pneumonia, that his condition was serious and that the doctors advised his wife's immediate return.

Undine had to read the words over two or three times to get them into her crowded mind; and even after she had done so she needed more time to see their bearing on her own situation. If the message had concerned her boy her brain would have acted more quickly. She had never troubled herself over the possibility of Paul's falling ill in her absence, but she understood now that if the cable had been about him she would have rushed to the earliest steamer. With Ralph it was different. Ralph was always perfectly well—she could not picture him as being suddenly at death's door and in need of her. Probably his mother and sister had had a panic: they were always full of sentimental terrors. The next moment an angry suspicion flashed across her: what if the cable were a device of the Marvell women to bring her back? Perhaps it had been sent with Ralph's connivance? No doubt Bowen had written home about her—Washington Square had received some monstrous report of her doings! . . . Yes, the cable was clearly an echo of Laura's letter—mother and daughter had cooked it up to spoil her pleasure. Once the thought had occurred to her it struck root in her mind and began to throw out giant branches.

Van Degen followed her to the window, his face still flushed and working. 'What's the matter?' he asked, as she continued to stare silently at the telegram.

She crumpled the strip of paper in her hand. If only she had been alone, had had a chance to think out her answers!

'What on earth's the matter?' he repeated.

'Oh, nothing—nothing.'

'Nothing? When you're as white as a sheet?'

'Am I?' She gave a slight laugh. 'It's only a cable from home.'

'Ralph?'

She hesitated. 'No. Laura.'

'What the devil is *she* cabling you about?'

'She says Ralph wants me.'

'Now—at once?'

'At once.'

Van Degen laughed impatiently. 'Why don't he tell you so himself? What business is it of Laura Fairford's?'

Undine's gesture implied a 'What indeed?'

'Is that all she says?'

She hesitated again. 'Yes—that's all.' As she spoke she tossed the telegram into the basket beneath the writing-table. 'As if I didn't *have* to go anyhow?' she exclaimed.

With an aching clearness of vision she saw what lay before her—the hurried preparations, the long tedious voyage on a steamer chosen at haphazard, the arrival in the deadly July heat, and the relapse into all the insufferable daily fag of nursery and kitchen—she saw it and her imagination recoiled.

Van Degen's eyes still hung on her: she guessed that he was intensely engaged in trying to follow what was passing through her mind. Presently he came up to her again, no longer perilous and importunate, but awkwardly tender, ridiculously moved by her distress.

'Undine, listen: won't you let me make it all right for you to stay?'

Her heart began to beat more quickly, and she let him come close, meeting his eyes coldly but without anger.

'What do you call "making it all right"? Paying my bills? Don't you see that's what I hate, and will never let myself be dragged into again?' She laid her hand on his arm. 'The time has come when I must be sensible, Peter; that's why we must say good-bye.'

'Do you mean to tell me you're going back to Ralph?'

She paused a moment; then she murmured between her lips: 'I shall never go back to him.'

'Then you *do* mean to marry Chelles?'

'I've told you we must say good-bye. I've got to look out for my future.'

He stood before her, irresolute, tormented, his lazy mind and impatient senses labouring with a problem beyond their power. 'Ain't I here to look out for your future?' he said at last.

'No one shall look out for it in the way you mean. I'd rather never see you again——'

He gave her a baffled stare. 'Oh, damn it—if that's the way you feel!' He turned and flung away toward the door.

She stood motionless where he left her, every nerve strung to the highest pitch of watchfulness. As she stood there, the scene about her stamped itself on her brain with the sharpest precision. She was aware of the fading of the summer light outside, of the movements of her maid, who was laying out her dinner-dress in the room beyond, and of the fact that the tea-roses on her writing-table, shaken by Van Degen's tread, were dropping their petals over Ralph's letter, and down on the crumpled telegram which she could see through the trellised sides of the scrap-basket.

In another moment Van Degen would be gone. Worse yet, while he wavered in the doorway the Shallums and Chelles, after vainly awaiting her, might dash back from the Bois and break in on them. These and other chances rose before her, urging her to action; but she held fast, immovable, unwavering, a proud yet plaintive image of renunciation.

Van Degen's hand was on the door. He half-opened it and then turned back.

'That's all you've got to say, then?'

'That's all.'

He jerked the door open and passed out. She saw him stop in the ante-room to pick up his hat and stick, his heavy figure silhouetted against the glare of the wall-lights. A ray of the same light fell on her where she stood in the unlit sitting-room, and her reflection bloomed out like a flower from the mirror that faced her. She looked at the image and waited.

Van Degen put his hat on his head and slowly opened the door into the outer hall. Then he turned abruptly, his bulk eclipsing her reflection as he plunged back into the room and came up to her.

'I'll do anything you say, Undine; I'll do anything in God's world to keep you!'

She turned her eyes from the mirror and let them rest on his face, which looked as small and withered as an old man's, with a lower lip that trembled queerly . . .

BOOK THREE

XXI

THE spring in New York proceeded through more than its usual extremes of temperature to the threshold of a sultry June.

Ralph Marvell, wearily bent to his task, felt the fantastic humours of the weather as only one more incoherence in the general chaos of his case. It was strange enough, after four years of marriage, to find himself again in his old brown room in Washington Square. It was hardly there that he had expected Pegasus* to land him; and, like a man returning to the scenes of his childhood, he found everything on a much smaller scale than he had imagined. Had the Dagonet boundaries really narrowed, or had the breach in the walls of his own life let in a wider vision?

Certainly there had come to be other differences between his present and his former self than that embodied in the presence of his little boy in the next room. Paul, in fact, was now the chief link between Ralph and his past. Concerning his son he still felt and thought, in a general way, in the terms of the Dagonet tradition; he still wanted to implant in Paul some of the reserves and discriminations which divided that tradition from the new spirit of limitless concession. But for himself it was different. Since his transaction with Moffatt he had had the sense of living under a new dispensation. He was not sure that it was any worse than the other; but then he was no longer very sure about anything. Perhaps this growing indifference was merely the reaction from a long nervous strain: that his mother and sister thought it so was shown by the way in which they mutely watched and hovered. Their discretion was like the hushed tread about a sick-bed. They permitted themselves no criticism of Undine; he was asked no awkward questions, subjected to no ill-timed sympathy. They simply took him back, on his own terms, into the life he had left them to; and their silence had none of those subtle implications of disapproval which may be so much more wounding than speech.

For a while he received a weekly letter from Undine. Vague and disappointing though they were, these missives helped him through the days; but he looked forward to them rather as a pretext for replies than for their actual contents. Undine was never at a loss for the spoken word: Ralph had often wondered at her verbal range and her fluent use of terms outside the current vocabulary. She had certainly not picked these up in books, since she never opened one: they seemed rather like some odd transmission of her preaching grandparent's oratory. But in her brief and colourless letters she repeated the same bald statements in the same few terms. She was well, she had been 'round' with Bertha Shallum, she had dined with the Jim Driscolls or May Beringer or Dicky Bowles, the weather was too lovely or too awful; such was the gist of her news. On the last page she hoped Paul was well and sent him a kiss; but she never made a suggestion concerning his care or asked a question about his pursuits. One could only infer that, knowing in what good hands he was, she judged such solicitude superfluous; and it was thus that Ralph put the matter to his mother.

'Of course she's not worrying about the boy—why should she? She knows that with you and Laura he's as happy as a king.'

To which Mrs Marvell would answer gravely: 'When you write, be sure to say I shan't put on his thinner flannels as long as this east wind lasts.'

As for her husband's welfare, Undine's sole allusion to it consisted in the invariable expression of the hope that he was getting along all right: the phrase was always the same, and Ralph learned to know just how far down the third page to look for it. In a postscript she sometimes asked him to tell her mother about a new way of doing hair or cutting a skirt; and this was usually the most eloquent passage of the letter.

What satisfaction he extracted from these communications he would have found it hard to say; yet when they did not come he missed them hardly less than if they had given him all he craved. Sometimes the mere act of holding the blue or mauve sheet and breathing its scent was like holding his wife's hand and being enveloped in her fresh young fragrance: the sentimental disappointment vanished in the penetrating physical sensation. In other moods it was enough to trace the letters of the first line and the last for the desert of perfunctory phrases between the two to vanish, leaving him only the vision of their interlaced names, as of a mystic bond which her own hand had tied. Or else he saw her, closely, palpably before him, as she sat at her writing-table, frowning and a little flushed, her bent nape showing the light on her hair, her short lip pulled up by the effort of composition; and this picture had the violent reality of dream-images on the verge of waking. At other times, as he read her letter, he felt simply that at least in the moment of writing it she had been with him. But in one of the last she had said (to excuse a bad blot and an incoherent sentence): 'Everybody's talking to me at once, and I don't know what I'm writing.' That letter he had thrown into the fire . . .

After the first few weeks, the letters came less and less regularly: at the end of two months they ceased. Ralph had got into the habit of watching for them on the days when a foreign post was due, and as the weeks went by without a sign he began to invent excuses for leaving the office earlier and hurrying back to Washington Square to search the letter-box for a big tinted envelope with a straggling blotted superscription. Undine's departure had given him a momentary sense of liberation: at that stage in their relations any change would have brought relief. But now that she was gone he knew she could never really go. Though his feeling for her had changed, it still ruled his life. If he saw her in her weakness he felt her in her power: the power of youth and physical radiance that clung to his disenchanted memories as the scent she used clung to her letters. Looking back at their four years of marriage he began to ask himself if he had done all he could to draw her half-formed spirit from its sleep. Had he not expected too much at first, and grown too indifferent in the sequel? After all, she was still in the toy age; and perhaps the very extravagance of his love had retarded her growth, helped to imprison her in a little circle of frivolous illusions. But the last month had made a man of him, and when she came back he would know how to lift her to the height of his experience.

So he would reason, day by day, as he hastened back to Washington Square; but when he opened the door, and his first glance at the hall table showed him there was no letter there, his illusions shrivelled down to their weak roots. She had not written: she did not mean to write. He and the boy were no longer a part of her life. When she came back everything would be as it had been before, with the dreary difference that she had tasted new pleasures and that their absence would take the savour from all he had to give her. Then the coming of another foreign mail would lift his hopes, and as he hurried home he would imagine new reasons for expecting a letter . . .

Week after week he swung between the extremes of hope and dejection, and at last, when the strain had become unbearable, he cabled her. The answer ran: 'Very well best love writing'; but the promised letter never came . . .

He went on steadily with his work: he even passed through a phase of exaggerated energy. But his baffled youth fought in him for air. Was this to be the end? Was he to wear his life out in useless drudgery? The plain prose of it, of course, was that the economic situation remained unchanged by the sentimental catastrophe and that he must go on working for his wife and child. But at any rate, as it was mainly for Paul that he would henceforth work, it should be on his own terms and according to his inherited notions of 'straightness.' He would never again engage in any transaction resembling his compact with Moffatt. Even now he was not sure there had been anything crooked in that; but the fact of his having instinctively referred the point to Mr Spragg rather than to his grandfather implied a presumption against it.

His partners were quick to profit by his sudden spurt of energy, and his work grew no lighter. He was not only the youngest and most recent member of the firm, but the one who had so far added least to the volume of its business. His hours were the longest, his absences, as summer approached, the least frequent and the most grudgingly accorded. No doubt his associates knew that he was pressed for money and could not risk a break. They 'worked' him, and he was aware of it, and submitted because he dared not lose his job. But the long hours of mechanical drudgery were telling on his active body and undisciplined nerves. He had begun too late to subject himself to the persistent mortification of spirit and flesh which is a condition of the average business life; and after the long dull days in the office the evenings at his grandfather's whist-table did not give him the counter-stimulus he needed.

Almost every one had gone out of town; but now and then Miss Ray came to dine, and Ralph, seated beneath the family portraits and opposite the desiccated Harriet, who had already faded to the semblance of one of her own great-aunts, listened languidly to the kind of talk that the originals might have exchanged about the same table when New York gentility centred in the Battery and the Bowling Green.* Mr Dagonet was always pleasant to see and hear, but his sarcasms were growing faint and recondite: they had as little bearing on life as the humours of a Restoration comedy. As for Mrs Marvell and Miss Ray, they seemed to the young man even more spectrally remote: hardly anything that mattered to him existed for them, and their prejudices reminded him of sign-posts warning off trespassers who have long since ceased to intrude.

Now and then he dined at his club and went on to the theatre with some young men of his own age; but he left them afterward, half vexed with himself for not being in the humour to prolong the adventure. There were moments when he would have liked to affirm his freedom in however commonplace a way: moments when the vulgarest way would have seemed the most satisfying. But he always ended by walking home alone and tip-toeing upstairs through the sleeping house lest he should wake his boy . . .

On Saturday afternoons, when the business world was hurrying to the country for golf and tennis, he stayed in town and took Paul to see the Spraggs. Several times since his wife's departure he had tried to bring about closer relations between his own family and Undine's; and the ladies of Washington Square, in their eagerness to meet his wishes, had made various friendly advances to Mrs Spragg. But they were met by a mute resistance which made Ralph suspect that Undine's strictures on his family had taken root in her mother's brooding mind; and he gave up the struggle to bring together what had been so effectually put asunder.

If he regretted his lack of success it was chiefly because he was so sorry for the Spraggs. Soon after Undine's marriage they had abandoned their polychrome suite at the Stentorian, and since then their peregrinations had carried them through half the hotels of the metropolis. Undine, who had early discovered her mistake in thinking hotel life fashionable, had tried to persuade her parents to take a house of their own; but though they refrained from taxing her with inconsistency they did not act on her suggestion. Mrs Spragg seemed to shrink from the thought of 'going back to house-keeping,' and Ralph suspected that she depended on the transit from hotel to hotel as the one element of variety in her life. As for Mr Spragg, it was impossible to imagine any one in whom the domestic sentiments were more completely unlocalized and disconnected from any fixed habits; and he was probably aware of his changes of abode chiefly as they obliged him to ascend from the Subway, or descend from the 'Elevated,' a few blocks higher up or lower down.

Neither husband nor wife complained to Ralph of their frequent displacements, or assigned to them any cause save the vague one of 'guessing they could do better'; but Ralph noticed that the decreasing luxury of their life synchronized with Undine's growing demands for money. During the last few months they had transferred themselves to the 'Malibran,' a tall narrow structure resembling a grain-elevator divided into cells, where linoleum and lincrusta* simulated the stucco and marble of the Stentorian, and fagged business men and their families consumed the watery stews dispensed by 'coloured help' in the grey twilight of a basement dining-room.

Mrs Spragg had no sitting-room, and Paul and his father had to be received in one of the long public parlours, between ladies seated at rickety desks in the throes of correspondence and groups of listlessly conversing residents and callers.

The Spraggs were intensely proud of their grandson, and Ralph perceived that they would have liked to see Paul charging uproariously from group to group and thrusting his bright curls and cherubic smile upon the general attention. The fact that the boy preferred to stand between his grandfather's knees and play with Mr Spragg's Masonic emblem, or dangle his legs from the arm of Mrs Spragg's chair, seemed to his grandparents evidence of ill-health or undue repression, and he was subjected by Mrs Spragg to searching enquiries as to how his food set, and whether he didn't think his Popper was too strict with him. A more embarrassing problem was raised by the 'surprise' (in the shape of peanut candy or chocolate creams) which he was invited to hunt for in Gran'ma's pockets, and which Ralph had to confiscate on the way home lest the dietary rules of Washington Square should be too visibly infringed.

Sometimes Ralph found Mrs Heeny, ruddy and jovial, seated in the arm-chair opposite Mrs Spragg, and regaling her with selections from a new batch of clippings. During Undine's illness of the previous winter Mrs Heeny had become a familiar figure to Paul, who had learned to expect almost as much from her bag as from his grandmother's pockets; so that the intemperate Saturdays at the Malibran were usually followed by languid and abstemious Sundays in Washington Square.

Mrs Heeny, being unaware of this sequel to her bounties, formed the habit of appearing regularly on Saturdays, and while she chatted with his grandmother the little boy was encouraged to scatter the grimy carpet with face-creams and bunches of clippings in his thrilling quest for the sweets at the bottom of her bag.

'I declare, if he ain't in just as much of a hurry f'r everything as his mother!' she exclaimed one day in her rich rolling voice; and stooping to pick up a long strip of newspaper which Paul had flung aside she added, as she smoothed it out: 'I guess 'f he was a little mite older he'd be better pleased with this 'n with the candy. It's the very thing I was trying to find for you the other day, Mrs Spragg,' she went on, holding the bit of paper at arm's length; and she began to read out, with a loudness proportioned to the distance between her eyes and the text:

'With two such sprinters as "Pete" Van Degen and Dicky Bowles to set the pace, it's no wonder the New York set in Paris has struck a livelier gait than ever this spring. It's a high-pressure season and no mistake, and no one lags behind less than the fascinating Mrs Ralph Marvell, who is to be seen daily and nightly in all the smartest restaurants and naughtiest theatres, with so many devoted swains in attendance that the rival

beauties of both worlds are said to be making catty comments.
But then Mrs Marvell's gowns are almost as good as her looks—
and how can you expect the other women to stand for such a
monopoly?'

To escape the strain of these visits, Ralph once or twice tried
the experiment of leaving Paul with his grand-parents and
calling for him in the late afternoon; but one day, on re-entering
the Malibran, he was met by a small abashed figure clad in a
kaleidoscopic tartan and a green velvet cap with a silver thistle.
After this experience of the 'surprises' of which Gran'ma was
capable when she had a chance to take Paul shopping Ralph
did not again venture to leave his son, and their subsequent
Saturdays were passed together in the sultry gloom of the
Malibran.

Conversation with the Spraggs was almost impossible. Ralph
could talk with his father-in-law in his office, but in the hotel
parlour Mr Spragg sat in a ruminating silence broken only by
the emission of an occasional 'Well—well' addressed to his
grandson. As for Mrs Spragg, her son-in-law could not
remember having had a sustained conversation with her since
the distant day when he had first called at the Stentorian, and
had been 'entertained,' in Undine's absence, by her astonished
mother. The shock of that encounter had moved Mrs Spragg
to eloquence; but Ralph's entrance into the family, without
making him seem less of a stranger, appeared once for all to have
relieved her of the obligation of finding something to say to
him.

The one question she invariably asked: 'You heard from
Undie?' had been relatively easy to answer while his wife's
infrequent letters continued to arrive; but a Saturday came when
he felt the blood rise to his temples as, for the fourth consecutive
week, he stammered out, under the snapping eyes of Mrs
Heeny: 'No, not by this post either—I begin to think I must
have lost a letter'; and it was then that Mr Spragg, who had sat
silently looking up at the ceiling, cut short his wife's exclamation
by an enquiry about real estate in the Bronx. After that, Ralph
noticed, Mrs Spragg never again renewed her question; and he
understood that his father-in-law had guessed his embarrassment
and wished to spare it.

Ralph had never thought of looking for any delicacy of feeling under Mr Spragg's large lazy irony, and the incident drew the two men nearer together. Mrs Spragg, for her part, was certainly not delicate; but she was simple and without malice, and Ralph liked her for her silent acceptance of her diminished state. Sometimes, as he sat between the lonely primitive old couple, he wondered from what source Undine's voracious ambitions had been drawn: all she cared for, and attached importance to, was as remote from her parents' conception of life as her impatient greed from their passive stoicism.

One hot afternoon toward the end of June Ralph suddenly wondered if Clare Van Degen were still in town. She had dined in Washington Square some ten days earlier, and he remembered her saying that she had sent the children down to Long Island, but that she herself meant to stay on in town till the heat grew unbearable. She hated her big showy place on Long Island, she was tired of the spring trip to London and Paris, where one met at every turn the faces one had grown sick of seeing all winter, and she declared that in the early summer New York was the only place in which one could escape from New Yorkers . . . She put the case amusingly, and it was like her to take up any attitude that went against the habits of her set; but she lived at the mercy of her moods, and one could never tell how long any one of them would rule her.

As he sat in his office, with the noise and glare of the endless afternoon rising up in hot waves from the street, there wandered into Ralph's mind a vision of her shady drawing-room. All day it hung before him like the mirage of a spring before a dusty traveller: he felt a positive thirst for her presence, for the sound of her voice, the wide spaces and luxurious silences surrounding her.

It was perhaps because, on that particular day, a spiral pain was twisting around in the back of his head, and digging in a little deeper with each twist, and because the figures on the balance sheet before him were hopping about like black imps in an infernal forward-and-back, that the picture hung there so persistently. It was a long time since he had wanted anything as much as, at that particular moment, he wanted to be with Clare and hear her voice; and as soon as he had ground out the day's measure of work he rang up the Van Degen palace and learned that she was still in town.

The lowered awnings of her inner drawing-room cast a luminous shadow on old cabinets and consoles, and on the pale flowers scattered here and there in vases of bronze and porcelain. Clare's taste was as capricious as her moods, and the rest of the house was not in harmony with this room. There was, in particular, another drawing-room, which she now described as Peter's creation, but which Ralph knew to be partly hers: a heavily decorated apartment, where Popple's portrait of her throned over a waste of gilt furniture. It was characteristic that to-day she had had Ralph shown in by another way; and that, as she had spared him the polyphonic drawing-room, so she had skilfully adapted her own appearance to her soberer background. She sat near the window, reading, in a clear cool dress: and at his entrance she merely slipped a finger between the pages and looked up at him.

Her way of receiving him made him feel that her restlessness and stridency were as unlike her genuine self as the gilded drawing-room, and that this quiet creature was the only real Clare, the Clare who had once been so nearly his, and who seemed to want him to know that she had never wholly been any one else's.

'Why didn't you let me know you were still in town?' he asked, as he sat down in the sofa-corner near her chair.

Her dark smile deepened. 'I hoped you'd come and see.'

'One never knows, with you.'

He was looking about the room with a kind of confused pleasure in its pale shadows and spots of dark rich colour. The old lacquer screen behind Clare's head looked like a lustreless black pool with gold leaves floating on it; and another piece, a little table at her elbow, had the brown bloom and the pear-like curves of an old violin.

'I like to be here,' Ralph said.

She did not make the mistake of asking: 'Then why do you never come?' Instead, she turned away, and drew an inner curtain across the window to shut out the sunlight which was beginning to slant in under the awning.

The mere fact of her not answering, and the final touch of well-being which her gesture gave, reminded him of other summer days they had spent together, long rambling boy-and-girl days in the hot woods and sunny fields, when they had never thought of talking to each other unless there was something they particularly wanted to say. His tired fancy strayed off for a second to the thought of what it would have been like to come back, at the end of the day, to such a sweet community of silence; but his mind was too crowded with importunate facts for any lasting view of visionary distances. The thought faded, and he merely felt how restful it was to have her near . . .

'I'm glad you stayed in town: you must let me come again,' he said.

'I suppose you can't always get away,' she answered; and she began to listen, with grave intelligent eyes, to his description of his tedious days.

With her eyes on him he felt the exquisite relief of talking about himself as he had not dared to talk to any one since his marriage. He would not for the world have confessed his discouragement, his consciousness of incapacity; to Undine and in Washington Square any hint of failure would have been taken as a criticism of what his wife demanded of him. Only to Clare Van Degen could he cry out his present despondency and his loathing of the interminable task ahead.

'A man doesn't know till he tries it how killing uncongenial work is, and how it destroys the power of doing what one's fit for, even if there's time for both. But there's Paul to be looked out for, and I daren't chuck my job—I'm in mortal terror of its chucking me . . .'

Little by little he slipped into a detailed recital of all his lesser worries, the most recent of which was his experience with the Lipscombs, who, after a two months' tenancy of the West End Avenue house, had decamped without paying their rent.

Clare laughed contemptuously. 'Yes—I heard he'd come to grief and been suspended from the Stock Exchange, and I see in the papers that his wife's retort has been to sue for a divorce.'

Ralph knew that, like all their clan, his cousin regarded a divorce-suit as a vulgar and unnecessary way of taking the public into one's confidence. His mind flashed back to the family feast in Washington Square in celebration of his engagement. He recalled his grandfather's chance allusion to Mrs Lipscomb, and Undine's answer, fluted out on her highest note: 'Oh, I guess she'll get a divorce pretty soon. He's been a disappointment to her.'

Ralph could still hear the horrified murmur with which his mother had rebuked his laugh. For he had laughed—had thought Undine's speech fresh and natural! Now he felt the ironic rebound of her words. Heaven knew he had been a disappointment to her; and what was there in her own feeling, or in her inherited prejudices, to prevent her seeking the same redress as Mabel Lipscomb? He wondered if the same thought were in his cousin's mind . . .

They began to talk of other things: books, pictures, plays; and one by one the closed doors opened and light was let into dusty shuttered places. Clare's mind was neither keen nor deep: Ralph, in the past, had often smiled at her rash ardours and vague intensities. But she had his own range of allusions, and a great gift of momentary understanding; and he had so long beaten his thoughts out against a blank wall of incomprehension that her sympathy seemed full of insight.

She began by a question about his writing, but the subject was distasteful to him, and he turned the talk to a new book in which he had been interested. She knew enough of it to slip in the right word here and there; and thence they wandered on to kindred topics. Under the warmth of her attention his torpid ideas awoke again, and his eyes took their fill of pleasure as she leaned forward, her thin brown hands clasped on her knees and her eager face reflecting all his feelings.

There was a moment when the two currents of sensation were merged in one, and he began to feel confusedly that he was young and she was kind, and that there was nothing he would like better than to go on sitting there, not much caring what she said or how he answered, if only she would let him look at her and give him one of her thin brown hands to hold. Then the corkscrew in the back of his head dug into him again with a deeper thrust, and she seemed suddenly to recede to a great distance and be divided from him by a fog of pain. The fog lifted after a minute, but it left him queerly remote from her, from the cool room with its scents and shadows, and from all the objects which, a moment before, had so sharply impinged upon his senses. It was as though he looked at it all through a rain-blurred pane, against which his hand would strike if he held it out to her . . .

That impression passed also, and he found himself thinking how tired he was and how little anything mattered. He recalled the unfinished piece of work on his desk, and for a moment had the odd illusion that it was there before him . . .

She exclaimed: 'But are you going?' and her exclamation made him aware that he had left his seat and was standing in front of her . . . He fancied there was some kind of appeal in her brown eyes; but she was so dim and far off that he couldn't be sure of what she wanted, and the next moment he found himself shaking hands with her, and heard her saying something kind and cold about its having been so nice to see him . . .

Half way up the stairs little Paul, shining and rosy from supper, lurked in ambush for his evening game. Ralph was fond of stooping down to let the boy climb up his outstretched arms to his shoulders, but to-day, as he did so, Paul's hug seemed to crush him in a vice, and the shout of welcome that accompanied it racked his ears like an explosion of steam-whistles. The queer distance between himself and the rest of the world was annihilated again: everything stared and glared and clutched him. He tried to turn away his face from the child's hot kisses; and as he did so he caught sight of a mauve envelope among the hats and sticks on the hall table.

Instantly he passed Paul over to his nurse, stammered out a word about being tired, and sprang up the long flights to his study. The pain in his head had stopped, but his hands trembled as he tore open the envelope. Within it was a second letter bearing a French stamp and addressed to himself. It looked like a business communication and had apparently been sent to Undine's hotel in Paris and forwarded to him by her hand.

'Another bill!' he reflected grimly, as he threw it aside and felt in the outer envelope for her letter. There was nothing there, and after a first sharp pang of disappointment he picked up the enclosure and opened it.

Inside was a lithographed circular, headed 'Confidential' and bearing the Paris address of a firm of private detectives who undertook, in conditions of attested and inviolable discretion, to investigate 'delicate' situations, look up doubtful antecedents, and furnish reliable evidence of misconduct—all on the most reasonable terms.

For a long time Ralph sat and stared at this document; then he began to laugh and tossed it into the scrap-basket. After that, with a groan, he dropped his head against the edge of his writing-table.

XXII

When he woke, the first thing he remembered was the fact of having cried.

He could not think how he had come to be such a fool. He hoped to heaven no one had seen him. He supposed he must have been worrying about the unfinished piece of work at the office: where was it, by the way, he wondered? Why—where he had left it the day before, of course! What a ridiculous thing to worry about—but it seemed to follow him about like a dog . . .

He said to himself that he must get up presently and go down to the office. Presently—when he could open his eyes. Just now there was a dead weight on them; he tried one after another in vain. The effort set him weakly trembling, and he wanted to cry again. Nonsense! He must get out of bed.

He stretched his arms out, trying to reach something to pull himself up by; but everything slipped away and evaded him. It was like trying to catch at bright short waves. Then suddenly his fingers clasped themselves about something firm and warm. A hand: a hand that gave back his pressure! The relief was inexpressible. He lay still and let the hand hold him, while

mentally he went through the motions of getting up and beginning to dress. So indistinct were the boundaries between
thought and action that he really felt himself moving about the
room, in a queer disembodied way, as one treads the air in sleep.
Then he felt the bed-clothes over him and the pillows under
his head.

'I *must* get up,' he said, and pulled at the hand.

It pressed him down again: down into a dim deep pool of
sleep. He lay there for a long time, in a silent blackness far below
light and sound; then he gradually floated to the surface with the
buoyancy of a dead body. But his body had never been more
alive. Jagged strokes of pain tore through it, hands dragged at it
with nails that bit like teeth. They wound thongs about him,
bound him, tied weights to him, tried to pull him down with
them; but still he floated, floated, danced on the fiery waves
of pain, with barbed light pouring down on him from an
arrowy sky.

Charmed intervals of rest, blue sailings on melodious seas,
alternated with the anguish. He became a leaf on the air, a
feather on a current, a straw on the tide, the spray of the wave
spinning itself to sunshine as the wave toppled over into gulfs of
blue . . .

He woke on a stony beach, his legs and arms still lashed to his
sides and the thongs cutting into him; but the fierce sky was
hidden, and hidden by his own languid lids. He felt the ecstasy
of decreasing pain, and courage came to him to open his eyes
and look about him . . .

The beach was his own bed; the tempered light lay on
familiar things, and some one was moving about in a shadowy
way between bed and window. He was thirsty, and some one
gave him a drink. His pillow burned, and some one turned the
cool side out. His brain was clear enough now for him to
understand that he was ill, and to want to talk about it; but his
tongue hung in his throat like a clapper in a bell. He must wait
till the rope was pulled . . .

So time and life stole back on him, and his thoughts laboured
weakly with dim fears. Slowly he cleared a way through them,
adjusted himself to his strange state, and found out that he was
in his own room, in his grandfather's house, that alternating

with the white-capped faces about him were those of his mother
and sister, and that in a few days—if he took his beef-tea and
didn't fret—Paul would be brought up from Long Island,
whither, on account of the great heat, he had been carried off by
Clare Van Degen.

No one named Undine to him, and he did not speak of her.
But one day, as he lay in bed in the summer twilight, he had a
vision of a moment, a long way behind him—at the beginning
of his illness, it must have been—when he had called out for her
in his anguish, and some one had said: 'She's coming: she'll be
here next week.'

Could it be that next week was not yet here? He supposed
that illness robbed one of all sense of time, and he lay still, as if
in ambush, watching his scattered memories come out one by
one and join themselves together. If he watched long enough he
was sure he should recognize one that fitted into his picture of
the day when he had asked for Undine. And at length a face
came out of the twilight: a freckled face, benevolently bent
over him under a starched cap. He had not seen the face for a
long time, but suddenly it took shape and fitted itself into the
picture . . .

Laura Fairford sat near by, a book on her knee. At the sound
of his voice she looked up.

'What was the name of the first nurse?'

'The first——?'

'The one that went away.'

'Oh—Miss Hicks, you mean?'

'How long is it since she went?'

'It must be three weeks. She had another case.'

He thought this over carefully; then he spoke again. 'Call
Undine.'

She made no answer, and he repeated irritably: 'Why don't
you call her? I want to speak to her.'

Mrs Fairford laid down her book and came to him.

'She's not here—just now.'

He dealt with this also, laboriously. 'You mean she's out—
she's not in the house?'

'I mean she hasn't come yet.'

As she spoke Ralph felt a sudden strength and hardness in his
brain and body. Everything in him became as clear as noon.

'But it was before Miss Hicks left that you told me you'd sent for her, and that she'd be here the following week. And you say Miss Hicks has been gone three weeks.'

This was what he had worked out in his head, and what he meant to say to his sister; but something seemed to snap shut in his throat, and he closed his eyes without speaking.

Even when Mr Spragg came to see him he said nothing. They talked about his illness, about the hot weather, about the rumours that Harmon B. Driscoll was again threatened with indictment; and then Mr Spragg pulled himself out of his chair and said: 'I presume you'll call round at the office before you leave the city.'

'Oh, yes: as soon as I'm up,' Ralph answered. They understood each other.

Clare had urged him to come down to Long Island and complete his convalescence there, but he preferred to stay in Washington Square till he should be strong enough for the journey to the Adirondacks, whither Laura had already preceded him with Paul. He did not want to see any one but his mother and grandfather till his legs could carry him to Mr Spragg's office.

It was an oppressive day in mid-August, with a yellow mist of heat in the sky, when at last he entered the big office-building. Swirls of dust lay on the mosaic floor, and a stale smell of decayed fruit and salt air and steaming asphalt filled the place like a fog. As he shot up in the elevator some one slapped him on the back, and turning he saw Elmer Moffatt at his side, smooth and rubicund under a new straw hat.

Moffatt was loudly glad to see him. 'I haven't laid eyes on you for months. At the old stand still?'

'So am I,' he added, as Ralph assented. 'Hope to see you there again some day. Don't forget it's *my* turn this time: glad if I can be any use to you. So long.' Ralph's weak bones ached under his handshake.

'How's Mrs Marvell?' he turned back from his landing to call out; and Ralph answered: 'Thanks; she's very well.'

Mr Spragg sat alone in his murky inner office, the fly-blown engraving of Daniel Webster above his head and the congested scrap-basket beneath his feet. He looked fagged and sallow, like the day.

Ralph sat down on the other side of the desk. For a moment his throat contracted as it had when he had tried to question his sister; then he asked: 'Where's Undine?'

Mr Spragg glanced at the calendar that hung from a hat-peg on the door. Then he released the Masonic emblem from his grasp, drew out his watch and consulted it critically.

'If the train's on time I presume she's somewhere between Chicago and Omaha round about now.'

Ralph stared at him, wondering if the heat had gone to his head.

'I don't understand.'

'The Twentieth Century's* generally considered the best route to Dakota,' explained Mr Spragg, who pronounced the word *rowt*.

'Do you mean to say Undine's in the United States?'

Mr Spragg's lower lip groped for the phantom tooth-pick. 'Why, let me see: hasn't Dakota* been a state a year or two now?'

'Oh, God——' Ralph cried, pushing his chair back violently and striding across the narrow room.

As he turned, Mr Spragg stood up and advanced a few steps. He had given up the quest for the tooth-pick, and his drawn-in lips were no more than a narrow depression in his beard. He stood before Ralph, absently shaking the loose change in his trouser-pockets.

Ralph felt the same hardness and lucidity that had come to him when he had heard his sister's answer.

'She's gone, you mean? Left me? With another man?'

Mr Spragg drew himself up with a kind of slouching majesty. 'My daughter is not that style. I understand Undine thinks there have been mistakes on both sides. She considers the tie was formed too hastily. I believe desertion is the usual plea in such cases.'

Ralph stared about him, hardly listening. He did not resent his father-in-law's tone. In a dim way he guessed that Mr Spragg was suffering hardly less than himself. But nothing was clear to him save the monstrous fact suddenly upheaved in his path. His wife had left him, and the plan for her evasion had been made and executed while he lay helpless: she had seized the opportunity of his illness to keep him in ignorance of her design. The humour of it suddenly struck him and he laughed.

'Do you mean to tell me that Undine's divorcing *me*?'

'I presume that's her plan,' Mr Spragg admitted.

'For desertion?' Ralph pursued, still laughing.

His father-in-law hesitated a moment; then he answered: 'You've always done all you could for my daughter. There wasn't any other plea she could think of. She presumed this would be the most agreeable to your family.'

'It was good of her to think of that!'

Mr Spragg's only comment was a sigh.

'Does she imagine I won't fight it?' Ralph broke out with sudden passion.

His father-in-law looked at him thoughtfully. 'I presume you realize it ain't easy to change Undine, once she's set on a thing.'

'Perhaps not. But if she really means to apply for a divorce I can make it a little less easy for her to get.'

'That's so,' Mr Spragg conceded. He turned back to his revolving chair, and seating himself in it began to drum on the desk with cigar-stained fingers.

'And by God, I will!' Ralph thundered. Anger was the only emotion in him now. He had been fooled, cheated, made a mock of; but the score was not settled yet. He turned back and stood before Mr Spragg.

'I suppose she's gone with Van Degen?'

'My daughter's gone alone, sir. I saw her off at the station. I understood she was to join a lady friend.'

At every point Ralph felt his hold slip off the surface of his father-in-law's impervious fatalism.

'Does she suppose Van Degen's going to marry her?'

'Undine didn't mention her future plans to me.' After a moment Mr Spragg appended: 'If she had, I should have declined to discuss them with her.'

Ralph looked at him curiously, perceiving that he intended in this negative way to imply his disapproval of his daughter's course.

'I shall fight it—I shall fight it!' the young man cried again. 'You may tell her I shall fight it to the end!'

Mr Spragg pressed the nib of his pen against the dust-coated inkstand. 'I suppose you would have to engage a lawyer. She'll know it that way,' he remarked.

'She'll know it—you may count on that!'

Ralph had begun to laugh again. Suddenly he heard his own laugh and it pulled him up. What was he laughing about? What was he talking about? The thing was to act—to hold his tongue and act. There was no use uttering windy threats to this broken-spirited old man. A fury of action burned in Ralph, pouring light into his mind and strength into his muscles. He caught up his hat and turned to the door.

As he opened it Mr Spragg rose again and came forward with his slow shambling step. He laid his hand on Ralph's arm.

'I'd 'a' given anything—anything short of my girl herself—not to have this happen to you, Ralph Marvell.'

'Thank you, sir,' said Ralph.

They looked at each other for a moment; then Mr Spragg added: 'But it *has* happened, you know. Bear that in mind. Nothing you can do will change it. Time and again, I've found that a good thing to remember.'

XXIII

IN the Adirondacks Ralph Marvell sat day after day on the balcony of his little house above the lake, staring at the great white cloud-reflections in the water and at the dark line of trees that closed them in. Now and then he got into the canoe and paddled himself through a winding chain of ponds to some lonely clearing in the forest; and there he lay on his back in the pine-needles and watched the great clouds form and dissolve themselves above his head.

All his past life seemed to be symbolized by the building-up and breaking-down of those fluctuating shapes, which incalculable wind-currents perpetually shifted and remodelled or swept from the zenith like a pinch of dust.

His sister told him that he looked well—better than he had in years; and there were moments when his listlessness, his stony insensibility to the small pricks and frictions of daily life, might have passed for the serenity of recovered health.

There was no one with whom he could speak of Undine. His family had thrown over the whole subject a pall of silence which even Laura Fairford shrank from raising. As for his mother, Ralph had seen at once that the idea of talking over the situation was positively frightening to her. There was no provision for such emergencies in the moral order of Washington Square. The affair was a 'scandal,' and it was not in the Dagonet tradition to acknowledge the existence of scandals. Ralph recalled a dim memory of his childhood, the tale of a misguided friend of his mother's who had left her husband for a more congenial companion, and who, years later, returning ill and friendless to New York, had appealed for sympathy to Mrs Marvell. The latter had not refused to give it; but she had put on her black cashmere and two veils when she went to see her unhappy friend, and had never mentioned these errands of mercy to her husband.

Ralph suspected that the constraint shown by his mother and sister was partly due to their having but a dim and confused view of what had happened. In their vocabulary the word 'divorce' was wrapped in such a dark veil of innuendo as no ladylike hand would care to lift. They had not reached the point of differentiating divorces, but classed them indistinctively as disgraceful incidents, in which the woman was always to blame, but the man, though her innocent victim, was yet inevitably contaminated. The time involved in the 'proceedings' was viewed as a penitential season during which it behoved the family of the persons concerned to behave as if they were dead; yet any open allusion to the reason for adopting such an attitude would have been regarded as the height of indelicacy.

Mr Dagonet's notion of the case was almost as remote from reality. All he asked was that his grandson should 'thrash' some-body, and he could not be made to understand that the modern drama of divorce is sometimes cast without a Lovelace.*

'You might as well tell me there was nobody but Adam in the garden when Eve picked the apple. You say your wife was discontented? No woman ever knows she's discontented till some man tells her so. My God! I've seen smash-ups before now; but I never yet saw a marriage dissolved like a business partnership. Divorce without a lover? Why, it's—it's as unnatural as getting drunk on lemonade.'

After this first explosion Mr Dagonet also became silent; and Ralph perceived that what annoyed him most was the fact of the 'scandal's' not being one in any gentlemanly sense of the word. It was like some nasty business mess, about which Mr Dagonet couldn't pretend to have an opinion, since such things didn't happen to men of his kind. That such a thing should have happened to his only grandson was probably the bitterest experience of his pleasantly uneventful life; and it added a touch of irony to Ralph's unhappiness to know how little, in the whole affair, he was cutting the figure Mr Dagonet expected him to cut.

At first he had chafed under the taciturnity surrounding him: had passionately longed to cry out his humiliation, his rebellion, his despair. Then he began to feel the tonic effect of silence; and the next stage was reached when it became clear to him that there was nothing to say. There were thoughts and thoughts: they bubbled up perpetually from the black springs of his hidden misery, they stole on him in the darkness of night, they blotted out the light of day; but when it came to putting them into words and applying them to the external facts of the case, they seemed totally unrelated to it. One more white and sun-touched glory had gone from his sky; but there seemed no way of connecting that with such practical issues as his being called on to decide whether Paul was to be put in knickerbockers or trousers, and whether he should go back to Washington Square for the winter or hire a small house for himself and his son.

The latter question was ultimately decided by his remaining under his grandfather's roof. November found him back in the office again, in fairly good health, with an outer skin of indifference slowly forming over his lacerated soul. There had been a hard minute to live through when he came back to his old brown room in Washington Square. The walls and tables were covered with photographs of Undine: effigies of all shapes and sizes, expressing every possible sentiment dear to the photographic tradition. Ralph had gathered them all up when he had moved from West End Avenue after Undine's departure for

Europe, and they throned over his other possessions as her image had throned over his future the night he had sat in that very room and dreamed of soaring up with her into the blue . . .

It was impossible to go on living with her photographs about him; and one evening, going up to his room after dinner, he began to unhang them from the walls, and to gather them up from book-shelves and mantel-piece and tables. Then he looked about for some place in which to hide them. There were drawers under his book-cases; but they were full of old discarded things, and even if he emptied the drawers, the photographs, in their heavy frames, were almost all too large to fit into them. He turned next to the top shelf of his cupboard; but here the nurse had stored Paul's old toys, his sand-pails, shovels and croquet-box. Every corner was packed with the vain impedimenta of living, and the mere thought of clearing a space in the chaos was too great an effort.

He began to replace the pictures one by one; and the last was still in his hand when he heard his sister's voice outside. He hurriedly put the portrait back in its usual place on his writing-table, and Mrs Fairford, who had been dining in Washington Square, and had come up to bid him good night, flung her arms about him in a quick embrace and went down to her carriage.

The next afternoon, when he came home from the office, he did not at first see any change in his room; but when he had lit his pipe and thrown himself into his arm-chair he noticed that the photograph of his wife's picture by Popple no longer faced him from the mantel-piece. He turned to his writing-table, but her image had vanished from there too; then his eye, making the circuit of the walls, perceived that they also had been stripped. Not a single photograph of Undine was left; yet so adroitly had the work of elimination been done, so ingeniously the remaining objects readjusted, that the change attracted no attention.

Ralph was angry, sore, ashamed. He felt as if Laura, whose hand he instantly detected, had taken a cruel pleasure in her work, and for an instant he hated her for it. Then a sense of relief stole over him. He was glad he could look about him without meeting Undine's eyes, and he understood that what had been done to his room he must do to his memory and his imagination: he must so readjust his mind that, whichever way he turned his thoughts, her face should no longer confront him. But that was a task that Laura could not perform for him, a task to be accomplished only by the hard continuous tension of his will.

With the setting in of the mood of silence all desire to fight his wife's suit died out. The idea of touching publicly on anything that had passed between himself and Undine had become unthinkable. Insensibly he had been subdued to the point of view about him, and the idea of calling on the law to repair his shattered happiness struck him as even more grotesque than it was degrading. Nevertheless, some contradictory impulse of his divided spirit made him resent, on the part of his mother and sister, a too-ready acceptance of his attitude. There were moments when their tacit assumption that his wife was banished and forgotten irritated him like the hushed tread of sympathizers about the bed of an invalid who will not admit that he suffers.

His irritation was aggravated by the discovery that Mrs Marvell and Laura had already begun to treat Paul as if he were an orphan. One day, coming unnoticed into the nursery, Ralph heard the boy ask when his mother was coming back; and Mrs Fairford, who was with him, answered: 'She's not coming back, dearest; and you're not to speak of her to father.'

Ralph, when the boy was out of hearing, rebuked his sister for her answer. 'I don't want you to talk of his mother as if she were dead. I don't want you to forbid Paul to speak of her.'

Laura, though usually so yielding, defended herself. 'What's the use of encouraging him to speak of her when he's never to see her? The sooner he forgets her the better.'

Ralph pondered. 'Later—if she asks to see him—I shan't refuse.'

Mrs Fairford pressed her lips together to check the answer: 'She never will!'

Ralph heard it, nevertheless, and let it pass. Nothing gave him so profound a sense of estrangement from his former life as the conviction that his sister was probably right. He did not really believe that Undine would ever ask to see her boy; but if she did he was determined not to refuse her request.

Time wore on, the Christmas holidays came and went, and the winter continued to grind out the weary measure of its days. Toward the end of January Ralph received a registered letter, addressed to him at his office, and bearing in the corner of the envelope the names of a firm of Sioux Falls attorneys. He instantly divined that it contained the legal notification of his wife's application for divorce, and as he wrote his name in the postman's book he smiled grimly at the thought that the stroke of his pen was doubtless signing her release. He opened the letter, found it to be what he had expected, and locked it away in his desk without mentioning the matter to any one.

He supposed that with the putting away of this document he was thrusting the whole subject out of sight; but not more than a fortnight later, as he sat in the Subway on his way down-town, his eye was caught by his own name on the first page of the heavily head-lined paper which the unshaved occupant of the next seat held between grimy fists. The blood rushed to Ralph's forehead as he looked over the man's arm and read: 'Society Leader Gets Decree,' and beneath it the subordinate clause: 'Says Husband Too Absorbed In Business To Make Home Happy.' For weeks afterward, wherever he went, he felt that blush upon his forehead. For the first time in his life the coarse fingering of public curiosity had touched the secret places of his soul, and nothing that had gone before seemed as humiliating as this trivial comment on his tragedy. The paragraph continued on its way through the press, and whenever he took up a news-paper he seemed to come upon it, slightly modified, variously developed, but always reverting with a kind of unctuous irony to his financial preoccupations and his wife's consequent loneliness. The phrase was even taken up by the paragraph writer, called forth excited letters from similarly situated victims, was commented on in humorous editorials and served as a text for pulpit denunciations of the growing craze for wealth; and finally, at his dentist's, Ralph came across it in a Family Weekly, as one of the 'Heart problems' propounded to subscribers, with a Gramophone, a Straight-front Corset and a Vanity-box among the prizes offered for its solution.

XXIV

'IF you'd only had the sense to come straight to me, Undine Spragg! There isn't a tip I couldn't have given you—not one!'

This speech, in which a faintly contemptuous compassion for her friend's case was blent with the frankest pride in her own, probably represented the nearest approach to 'tact' that Mrs James J. Rolliver had yet acquired. Undine was impartial enough to note in it a distinct advance on the youthful methods of Indiana Frusk; yet it required a good deal of self-control to take the words to herself with a smile, while they seemed to be laying a visible scarlet welt across the pale face she kept valiantly turned to her friend. The fact that she must permit herself to be pitied by Indiana Frusk gave her the uttermost measure of the depth to which her fortunes had fallen.

This abasement was inflicted on her in the staring gold apartment of the Hôtel Nouveau Luxe in which the Rollivers had established themselves on their recent arrival in Paris. The vast drawing-room, adorned only by two high-shouldered gilt baskets of orchids drooping on their wires, reminded Undine of the 'Looey suite' in which the opening scenes of her own history had been enacted; and the resemblance and the difference were emphasized by the fact that the image of her past self was not inaccurately repeated in the triumphant presence of Indiana Rolliver.

'There isn't a tip I couldn't have given you—not one!' Mrs Rolliver reproachfully repeated; and all Undine's superiorities and discriminations seemed to shrivel up in the crude blaze of the other's solid achievement.

There was little comfort in noting, for one's private delectation, that Indiana spoke of her husband as 'Mr Rolliver,' that she twanged a piercing r, that one of her shoulders was still higher than the other, and that her striking dress was totally unsuited to the hour, the place and the occasion. She still did and was all that Undine had so sedulously learned not to be and to do; but to dwell on these obstacles to her success was but to be more deeply impressed by the fact that she had nevertheless succeeded.

Not much more than a year had elapsed since Undine Marvell, sitting in the drawing-room of another Parisian hotel, had heard the immense orchestral murmur of Paris rise through the open windows like the ascending movement of her own hopes. The immense murmur still sounded on, deafening and implacable as some elemental force; and the discord in her fate no more disturbed it than the motor wheels rolling by under the windows were disturbed by the particles of dust that they ground to finer powder as they passed.

'I could have told you one thing right off,' Mrs Rolliver went on with her ringing energy. 'And that is, to get your divorce first thing. A divorce is always a good thing to have: you never can tell when you may want it. You ought to have attended to that before you even *began* with Peter Van Degen.'

Undine listened, irresistibly impressed. 'Did *you?*' she asked; but Mrs Rolliver, at this, grew suddenly veiled and sibylline. She wound her big bejewelled hand through her pearls—there were ropes and ropes of them—and leaned back, modestly sinking her lids.

'I'm here, anyhow,' she rejoined, with '*Circumspice!*'* in look and tone.

Undine, obedient to the challenge, continued to gaze at the pearls. They were real; there was no doubt about that. And so was Indiana's marriage—if she kept out of certain states.

'Don't you see,' Mrs Rolliver continued, 'that having to leave him when you did, and rush off to Dakota for six months, was—was giving him too much time to think; and giving it at the wrong time, too?'

'Oh, I see. But what could I do? I'm not an immoral woman.'

'Of course not, dearest. You were merely thoughtless—that's what I meant by saying you ought to have had your divorce ready.'

A flicker of self-esteem caused Undine to protest. 'It wouldn't have made any difference. His wife would never have given him up.'

'She's so crazy about him?'

'No: she hates him so. And she hates me too, because she's in love with my husband.'

Indiana bounced out of her lounging attitude and struck her hands together with a rattle of rings.

'In love with your husband? What's the matter, then? Why on earth didn't the four of you fix it up together?'

'You don't understand.' (It was an undoubted relief to be able, at last, to say that to Indiana!) 'Clare Van Degen thinks divorce wrong—or rather awfully vulgar.'

'*Vulgar?*' Indiana flamed. 'If that isn't just too much! A woman who's in love with another woman's husband? What does she think refined, I'd like to know? Having a lover, I suppose—like the women in these nasty French plays? I've told Mr Rolliver I won't go to the theatre with him again in Paris—it's too utterly low. And the swell society's just as bad: it's simply rotten. Thank goodness I was brought up in a place where there's some sense of decency left!' She looked compassionately at Undine. 'It was New York that demoralized you—and I don't blame you for it. Out at Apex you'd have acted different. You never *never* would have given way to your feelings before you'd got your divorce.'

A slow blush rose to Undine's forehead.

'He seemed so unhappy——' she murmured.

'Oh, I *know!*' said Indiana in a tone of cold competence. She gave Undine an impatient glance. 'What was the understanding between you, when you left Europe last August to go out to Dakota?'

'Peter was to go to Reno in the autumn—so that it wouldn't look too much as if we were acting together. I was to come to Chicago to see him on his way out there.'

'And he never came?'

'No.'

'And he stopped writing?'

'Oh, he never writes.'

Indiana heaved a deep sigh of intelligence. 'There's one perfectly clear rule: never let out of your sight a man who doesn't write.'

'I know. That's why I stayed with him—those few weeks last summer . . .'

Indiana sat thinking, her fine shallow eyes fixed unblinkingly on her friend's embarrassed face.

'I suppose there isn't anybody else——?'

'Anybody——?'

'Well—now you've got your divorce: anybody else it would come in handy for?'

This was harder to bear than anything that had gone before: Undine could not have borne it if she had not had a purpose. 'Mr Van Degen owes it to me——' she began with an air of wounded dignity.

'Yes, yes: I know. But that's just talk. If there *is* anybody else——'

'I can't imagine what you think of me, Indiana!'

Indiana, without appearing to resent this challenge, again lost herself in meditation.

'Well, I'll tell him he's just *got* to see you,' she finally emerged from it to say.

Undine gave a quick upward look: this was what she had been waiting for ever since she had read, a few days earlier, in the columns of her morning journal, that Mr Peter Van Degen and Mr and Mrs James J. Rolliver had been fellow-passengers on board the *Semantic*.* But she did not betray her expectations by as much as the tremor of an eye-lash. She knew her friend well enough to pour out to her the expected tribute of surprise.

'Why, do you mean to say you know him, Indiana?'

'Mercy, yes! He's round here all the time. He crossed on the steamer with us, and Mr Rolliver's taken a fancy to him,' Indiana explained, in the tone of the absorbed bride to whom her husband's preferences are the sole criterion.

Undine turned a tear-suffused gaze on her. 'Oh, Indiana, if I could only see him again I know it would be all right! He's awfully, awfully fond of me; but his family have influenced him against me——'

'I know what *that* is!' Mrs Rolliver interjected.

'But perhaps,' Undine continued, 'it would be better if I could meet him first without his knowing beforehand—with-

out your telling him . . . I love him too much to reproach him!'
she added nobly.

Indiana pondered: it was clear that, though the nobility of the
sentiment impressed her, she was disinclined to renounce the
idea of taking a more active part in her friend's rehabilitation.
But Undine went on: 'Of course you've found out by this time
that he's just a big spoiled baby. Afterward—when I've seen
him—if you'd talk to him; or if you'd only just let him *be* with
you, and see how perfectly happy you and Mr Rolliver are!'

Indiana seized on this at once. 'You mean that what he wants
is the influence of a home like ours? Yes, yes, I understand. I tell
you what I'll do: I'll just ask him round to dine, and let you
know the day, without telling him beforehand that you're
coming.'

'Oh, Indiana!' Undine held her in a close embrace, and then
drew away to say: 'I'm so glad I found you. You must go round
with me everywhere. There are lots of people here I want you
to know.'

Mrs Rolliver's expression changed from vague sympathy to
concentrated interest. 'I suppose it's awfully gay here? Do you
go round a great deal with the American set?'

Undine hesitated for a fraction of a moment. 'There are a few
of them who are rather jolly. But I particularly want you to meet
my friend the Marquis Roviano—he's from Rome; and a lovely
Austrian woman, Baroness Adelschein.'

Her friend's face was brushed by a shade of distrust. 'I
don't know as I care much about meeting foreigners,' she said
indifferently.

Undine smiled: it was agreeable at last to be able to give
Indiana a 'point' as valuable as any of hers on divorce.

'Oh, some of them are awfully attractive; and *they'll* make you
meet the Americans.'

Indiana caught this on the bound: one began to see why she
had got on in spite of everything.

'Of course I'd love to know your friends,' she said, kissing
Undine; who answered, giving back the kiss: 'You know there's
nothing on earth I wouldn't do for you.'

Indiana drew back to look at her with a comic grimace under
which a shade of anxiety was visible. 'Well, that's a pretty large

order. But there's just one thing you *can* do, dearest: please to let
Mr Rolliver alone!'

'Mr Rolliver, my dear?' Undine's laugh showed that she took
this for unmixed comedy. 'That's a nice way to remind me that
you're heaps and heaps better-looking than I am!'

Indiana gave her an acute glance. 'Millard Binch didn't think
so—not even at the very end.'

'Oh, poor Millard!' The women's smiles mingled easily over
the common reminiscence, and once again, on the threshold,
Undine enfolded her friend.

In the light of the autumn afternoon she paused a moment at
the door of the Nouveau Luxe, and looked aimlessly forth at
the brave spectacle in which she seemed no longer to have a
stake.

Many of her old friends had already returned to Paris: the
Harvey Shallums, May Beringer, Dicky Bowles and other west-
ward-bound nomads lingering on for a glimpse of the autumn
theatres and fashions before hurrying back to inaugurate the
New York season. A year ago Undine would have had no
difficulty in introducing Indiana Rolliver to this group—a
group above which her own aspirations already beat an impatient wing. Now her place in it had become too precarious for
her to force an entrance for her protectress. Her New York
friends were at no pains to conceal from her that in their opinion
her divorce had been a blunder. Their logic was that of Apex
reversed. Since she had not been 'sure' of Van Degen, why in
the world, they asked, had she thrown away a position she *was*
sure of? Mrs Harvey Shallum, in particular, had not scrupled to
put the question squarely. 'Chelles was awfully taken—he
would have introduced you everywhere. I thought you were
wild to know smart French people; I thought Harvey and I
weren't good enough for you any longer. And now you've
done your best to spoil everything! Of course I feel for you
tremendously—that's the reason why I'm talking so frankly.
You must be horribly depressed. Come and dine to-night—or
no, if you don't mind I'd rather you chose another evening. I'd
forgotten that I'd asked the Jim Driscolls, and it might be
uncomfortable—for *you* . . .'

In another world she was still welcome, at first perhaps even more so than before: the world, namely, to which she had proposed to present Indiana Rolliver. Roviano, Madame Adelschein, and a few of the freer spirits of her old St Moritz band, reappearing in Paris with the close of the watering-place season, had quickly discovered her and shown a keen interest in her liberation. It appeared in some mysterious way to make her more available for their purpose, and she found that, in the character of the last American divorcée, she was even regarded as eligible to the small and intimate inner circle of their loosely-knit association. At first she could not make out what had entitled her to this privilege, and increasing enlightenment produced a revolt of the Apex puritanism which, despite some odd accommodations and compliances, still carried its head so high in her.

Undine had been perfectly sincere in telling Indiana Rolliver that she was not 'an immoral woman.' The pleasures for which her sex took such risks had never attracted her, and she did not even crave the excitement of having it thought that they did. She wanted, passionately and persistently, two things which she believed should subsist together in any well-ordered life: amusement and respectability; and despite her surface-sophistication her notion of amusement was hardly less innocent than when she had hung on the plumber's fence with Indiana Frusk.

It gave her, therefore, no satisfaction to find herself included among Madame Adelschein's intimates. It embarrassed her to feel that she was expected to be 'queer' and 'different,' to respond to pass-words and talk in innuendo, to associate with the equivocal and the subterranean and affect to despise the ingenuous daylight joys which really satisfied her soul. But the business shrewdness which was never quite dormant in her suggested that this was not the moment for such scruples. She must make the best of what she could get and wait her chance of getting something better; and meanwhile the most practical use to which she could put her shady friends was to flash their authentic nobility in the dazzled eyes of Mrs Rolliver.

With this object in view she made haste, in a fashionable tea-room of the rue de Rivoli, to group about Indiana the most titled members of the band; and the felicity of the occasion would have been unmarred had she not suddenly caught sight of Raymond de Chelles sitting on the other side of the room.

She had not seen Chelles since her return to Paris. It had seemed preferable to leave their meeting to chance, and the present chance might have served as well as another but for the fact that among his companions were two or three of the most eminent ladies of the proud quarter beyond the Seine. It was what Undine, in moments of discouragement, characterized as 'her luck' that one of these should be the hated Miss Wincher of Potash Springs, who had now become the Marquise de Trézac. Undine knew that Chelles and his compatriots, however scandalized at her European companions, would be completely indifferent to Mrs Rolliver's appearance; but one gesture of Madame de Trézac's eye-glass would wave Indiana to her place and thus brand the whole party as 'wrong.'

All this passed through Undine's mind in the very moment of her noting the change of expression with which Chelles had signalled his recognition. If their encounter could have occurred in happier conditions it might have had far-reaching results. As it was, the crowded state of the tea-room, and the distance between their tables, sufficiently excused his restricting his greeting to an eager bow; and Undine went home heavy-hearted from this first attempt to reconstruct her past.

Her spirits were not lightened by the developments of the next few days. She kept herself well in the foreground of Indiana's life, and cultivated toward the rarely-visible Rolliver a manner in which impersonal admiration for the statesman was tempered with the politest indifference to the man. Indiana seemed to do justice to her efforts and to be reassured by the result; but still there came no hint of a reward. For a time Undine restrained the question on her lips; but one afternoon, when she had inducted Indiana into the deepest mysteries of Parisian complexion-making, the importance of the service and the confidential mood it engendered seemed to warrant a discreet allusion to their bargain.

Indiana leaned back among her cushions with an embarrassed laugh.

'Oh, my dear, I've been meaning to tell you—it's off, I'm afraid. The dinner is, I mean. You see, Mr Van Degen has seen you 'round with me, and the very minute I asked him to come and dine he guessed——'

'He guessed—and he wouldn't?'

'Well, no. He wouldn't. I hate to tell you.'

'Oh——' Undine threw off a vague laugh. 'Since you're intimate enough for him to tell you *that* he must have told you more—told you something to justify his behaviour. He couldn't—even Peter Van Degen couldn't—just simply have said to you: "I won't see her."'

Mrs Rolliver hesitated, visibly troubled to the point of regretting her intervention.

'He *did* say more?' Undine insisted. 'He gave you a reason?'

'He said you'd know.'

'Oh, how base—how base!' Undine was trembling with one of her little-girl rages, the storms of destructive fury before which Mr and Mrs Spragg had cowered when she was a charming golden-curled cherub. But life had administered some of the discipline which her parents had spared her, and she pulled herself together with a gasp of pain. 'Of course he's been turned against me. His wife has the whole of New York behind her, and I've no one; but I know it would be all right if I could only see him.'

Her friend made no answer, and Undine pursued, with an irrepressible outbreak of her old vehemence: 'Indiana Rolliver, if you won't do it for me I'll go straight off to his hotel this very minute. I'll wait there in the hall till he sees me!'

Indiana lifted a protesting hand. 'Don't, Undine—not that!'

'Why not?'

'Well—I wouldn't, that's all.'

'You wouldn't? Why wouldn't you? You must have a reason.' Undine faced her with levelled brows. 'Without a reason you can't have changed so utterly since our last talk. You were positive enough then that I had a right to make him see me.'

Somewhat to her surprise, Indiana made no effort to elude the challenge. 'Yes, I did think so then. But I know now that it wouldn't do you the least bit of good.'

'Have they turned him so completely against me? I don't care if they have! I know him—I can get him back.'

'That's the trouble.' Indiana shed on her a gaze of cold compassion. 'It's not that any one has turned him against you. It's worse than that——'

'What can be?'

'You'll hate me if I tell you.'

'Then you'd better make him tell me himself!'

'I can't. I tried to. The trouble is that it was *you*—something you did, I mean. Something he found out about you——'

Undine, to restrain a spring of anger, had to clutch both arms of her chair. 'About me? How fearfully false! Why, I've never even *looked* at anybody——!'

'It's nothing of that kind.' Indiana's mournful head-shake seemed to deplore, in Undine, an unsuspected moral obtuseness. 'It's the way you acted to your own husband.'

'I—my—to Ralph? *He* reproaches me for that? Peter Van Degen does?'

'Well, for one particular thing. He says that the very day you went off with him last year you got a cable from New York telling you to come back at once to Mr Marvell, who was desperately ill.'

'How on earth did he know?' The cry escaped Undine before she could repress it.

'It's true, then?' Indiana exclaimed. 'Oh, Undine——'

Undine sat speechless and motionless, the anger frozen to terror on her lips.

Mrs Rolliver turned on her the reproachful gaze of the deceived benefactress. 'I didn't believe it when he told me; I'd never have thought it of you. Before you'd even applied for your divorce!'

Undine made no attempt to deny the charge or to defend herself. For a moment she was lost in the pursuit of an unseizable clue—the explanation of this monstrous last perversity of fate. Suddenly she rose to her feet with a set face.

'The Marvells must have told him—the beasts!' It relieved her to be able to cry it out.

'It was your husband's sister—what did you say her name was? When you didn't answer her cable, she cabled Mr Van

Degen to find out where you were and tell you to come straight
back.'

Undine stared. 'He never did!'

'No.'

'Doesn't that show you the story's all trumped up?'

Indiana shook her head. 'He said nothing to you about it
because he was with you when you received the first cable, and
you told him it was from your sister-in-law, just worrying you
as usual to go home; and when he asked if there was anything
else in it you said there wasn't another thing.'

Undine, intently following her, caught at this with a spring.
'Then he knew it all along—he admits that? And it made
no earthly difference to him at the time?' She turned almost
victoriously on her friend. 'Did he happen to explain *that*, I
wonder?'

'Yes.' Indiana's longanimity* grew almost solemn. 'It came
over him gradually, he said. One day when he wasn't feeling
very well he thought to himself: "Would she act like that to *me*
if I was dying?" And after that he never felt the same to you.'
Indiana lowered her empurpled lids. 'Men have their feelings
too—even when they're carried away by passion.' After a pause
she added: 'I don't know as I can blame him, Undine. You see,
you were his ideal.'

XXV

Undine Marvell, for the next few months, tasted all the
accumulated bitterness of failure. After January the drifting
hordes of her compatriots had scattered to the four quarters of
the globe, leaving Paris to resume, under its low grey sky, its
compacter winter personality. Noting, from her more and more
deserted corner, each least sign of the social revival, Undine felt
herself as stranded and baffled as after the ineffectual summers of
her girlhood. She was not without possible alternatives; but the
sense of what she had lost took the savour from all that was left.
She might have attached herself to some migratory group
winged for Italy or Egypt; but the prospect of travel did not in

itself appeal to her, and she was doubtful of its social benefit. She lacked the adventurous curiosity which seeks its occasion in the unknown; and though she could work doggedly for a given object the obstacles to be overcome had to be as distinct as the prize.

Her one desire was to get back an equivalent of the precise value she had lost in ceasing to be Ralph Marvell's wife. Her new visiting-card, bearing her Christian name in place of her husband's, was like the coin of a debased currency testifying to her diminished trading capacity. Her restricted means, her vacant days, all the minor irritations of her life, were as nothing compared to this sense of a lost advantage. Even in the narrowed field of a Parisian winter she might have made herself a place in some more or less extra-social world; but her experiments in this line gave her no pleasure proportioned to the possible derogation. She feared to be associated with 'the wrong people,' and scented a shade of disrespect in every amicable advance. The more pressing attentions of one or two men she had formerly known filled her with a glow of outraged pride, and for the first time in her life she felt that even solitude might be preferable to certain kinds of society.

Since ill health was the most plausible pretext for seclusion, it was almost a relief to find that she was really growing 'nervous' and sleeping badly. The doctor she summoned advised her trying a small quiet place on the Riviera, not too near the sea; and thither, in the early days of December, she transported herself with her maid and an omnibus-load of luggage.

The place disconcerted her by being really small and quiet, and for a few days she struggled against the desire for flight. She had never before known a world as colourless and negative as that of the large white hotel where everybody went to bed at nine, and donkey-rides over stony hills were the only alternative to slow drives along dusty roads. Many of the dwellers in this temple of repose found even these exercises too stimulating, and preferred to sit for hours under the palms in the garden, playing Patience, embroidering, or reading odd volumes of Tauchnitz.* Undine, driven by despair to an inspection of the hotel book-shelves, discovered that scarcely any work they contained was complete; but this did not seem to trouble the readers, who continued to feed their leisure with mutilated fiction, from which they occasionally raised their eyes to glance mistrustfully at the new arrival sweeping the garden gravel with her frivolous draperies. The inmates of the hotel were of different nationalities, but their racial differences were levelled by the stamp of a common mediocrity. All differences of tongue, of custom, of physiognomy, disappeared in this deep community of insignificance, which was like some secret bond, with the manifold signs and pass-words of its ignorances and its imperceptions. It was not the heterogeneous mediocrity of the American summer hotel, where the lack of any standard is the nearest approach to a tie, but an organized codified dulness, in conscious possession of its rights, and strong in the voluntary ignorance of any others.

It took Undine a long time to accustom herself to such an atmosphere, and meanwhile she fretted, fumed and flaunted, or abandoned herself to long periods of fruitless brooding. Sometimes a flame of anger shot up in her, dismally illuminating the path she had travelled and the blank wall to which it led. At other moments past and present were enveloped in a dull fog of rancour which distorted and faded even the image she presented to her morning mirror. There were days when every young face she saw left in her a taste of poison. But when she compared herself with the specimens of her sex who plied their languid industries under the palms, or looked away as she passed them in hall or staircase, her spirits rose, and she rang for her maid and dressed herself in her newest and vividest. These were unprofitable triumphs, however. She never made one of her attacks on the organized disapproval of the community without feeling she had lost ground by it; and the next day she would lie in bed and send down capricious orders for food, which her maid would presently remove untouched, with instructions to transmit her complaints to the landlord.

Sometimes the events of the past year, ceaselessly revolving through her brain, became no longer a subject for criticism or justification but simply a series of pictures monotonously unrolled. Hour by hour, in such moods, she re-lived the incidents of her flight with Peter Van Degen: the part of her career that, since it had proved a failure, seemed least like herself and most difficult to justify. She had gone away with him, and had lived with him for two months: she, Undine Marvell, to whom respectability was the breath of life, to whom such follies had always been unintelligible and therefore inexcusable.—She had done this incredible thing, and she had done it from a motive that seemed, at the time, as clear, as logical, as free from the distorting mists of sentimentality, as any of her father's financial enterprises. It had been a bold move, but it had been as carefully calculated as the happiest Wall Street 'stroke.' She had gone away with Peter because, after the decisive scene in which she had put her power to the test, to yield to him seemed the surest means of victory. Even to her practical intelligence it was clear that an immediate dash to Dakota might look too calculated; and she had preserved her self-respect by telling herself that she was really his wife, and in no way to blame if the law delayed to ratify the bond.

She was still persuaded of the justness of her reasoning; but she now saw that it had left certain risks out of account. Her life with Van Degen had taught her many things. The two had wandered from place to place, spending a great deal of money, always more and more money; for the first time in her life she had been able to buy everything she wanted. For a while this had kept her amused and busy; but presently she began to perceive that her companion's view of their relation was not the same as hers. She saw that he had always meant it to be an unavowed tie, screened by Mrs Shallum's companionship and Clare's careless tolerance; and that on those terms he would have been ready to shed on their adventure the brightest blaze of notoriety. But since Undine had insisted on being carried off like a sentimental school-girl he meant to shroud the affair in mystery, and was as zealous in concealing their relation as she was bent on proclaiming it. In the 'powerful' novels which Popple was fond of lending her she had met with increasing frequency the type of heroine who scorns to love clandestinely, and proclaims the sanctity of passion and the moral duty of obeying its call. Undine had been struck by these arguments as justifying and even ennobling her course, and had let Peter understand that she had been actuated by the highest motives in openly associating her life with his; but he had opposed a placid insensibility to these allusions, and had persisted in treating her as though their journey were the kind of escapade that a man of the world is bound to hide. She had expected him to take her to all the showy places where couples like themselves are relieved from a too sustained contemplation of nature by the distractions of the restaurant and the gaming-table; but he had carried her from one obscure corner of Europe to another, shunning fashionable hotels and crowded watering-places, and displaying an ingenuity in the discovery of the unvisited and the out-of-season that gave their journey an odd resemblance to her melancholy wedding-tour.

She had never for a moment ceased to remember that the Dakota divorce-court was the objective point of this later honeymoon, and her allusions to the fact were as frequent as prudence permitted. Peter seemed in no way disturbed by them. He responded with expressions of increasing tenderness, or the purchase of another piece of jewelry; and though Undine could not remember his ever voluntarily bringing up the subject of their marriage he did not shrink from her recurring mention of it. He seemed merely too steeped in present well-being to think of the future; and she ascribed this to the fact that his faculty of enjoyment could not project itself beyond the moment. Her business was to make each of their days so agreeable that when the last came he should be conscious of a void to be bridged over as rapidly as possible; and when she thought this point had been reached she packed her trunks and started for Dakota.

The next picture to follow was that of the dull months in the western divorce-town, where, to escape loneliness and avoid comment, she had cast in her lot with Mabel Lipscomb, who had lately arrived there on the same errand.

Undine, at the outset, had been sorry for the friend whose new venture seemed likely to result so much less brilliantly than her own; but compassion had been replaced by irritation as Mabel's unpruned vulgarities, her enormous encroaching satisfaction with herself and her surroundings, began to pervade every corner of their provisional household. Undine, during the first months of her exile, had been sustained by the fullest confidence in her future. When she had parted from Van Degen she had felt sure he meant to marry her, and the fact that Mrs

Lipscomb was fortified by no similar hope made her easier to bear with. Undine was almost ashamed that the unwooed Mabel should be the witness of her own felicity, and planned to send her off on a trip to Denver when Peter should announce his arrival; but the weeks passed, and Peter did not come. Mabel, on the whole, behaved well in this contingency. Undine, in her first exultation, had confided all her hopes and plans to her friend, but Mabel took no undue advantage of the confidence. She was even tactful in her loud fond clumsy way, with a tact that insistently boomed and buzzed about its victim's head. But one day she mentioned that she had asked to dinner a gentleman from Little Rock who had come to Dakota with the same object as themselves, and whose acquaintance she had made through her lawyer.

The gentleman from Little Rock came to dine, and within a week Undine understood that Mabel's future was assured. If Van Degen had been at hand Undine would have smiled with him at poor Mabel's infatuation and her suitor's crudeness. But Van Degen was not there. He made no sign, he sent no excuse; he simply continued to absent himself; and it was Undine who, in due course, had to make way for Mrs Lipscomb's caller, and sit upstairs with a novel while the drawing-room below was given up to the enacting of an actual love-story.

Even then, even to the end, Undine had to admit that Mabel had behaved 'beautifully.' But it is comparatively easy to behave beautifully when one is getting what one wants, and when some one else, who has not always been altogether kind, is not. The net result of Mrs Lipscomb's magnanimity was that when, on the day of parting, she drew Undine to her bosom with the hand on which her new engagement-ring blazed, Undine hated her as she hated everything else connected with her vain exile in the wilderness.

XXVI

THE next phase in the unrolling vision was the episode of her return to New York. She had gone to the Malibran, to her parents—for it was a moment in her career when she clung passionately to the conformities, and when the fact of being able to say: 'I'm here with my father and mother' was worth paying for even in the discomfort of that grim abode. Nevertheless, it was another thorn in her pride that her parents could not—for the meanest of material reasons—transfer themselves at her coming to one of the big Fifth Avenue hotels. When she had suggested it Mr Spragg had briefly replied that, owing to the heavy expenses of her divorce suit, he couldn't for the moment afford anything better; and this announcement cast a deeper gloom over the future.

It was not an occasion for being 'nervous,' however; she had learned too many hard facts in the last few months to think of having recourse to her youthful methods. And something told her that if she made the attempt it would be useless. Her father and mother seemed much older, seemed tired and defeated, like herself.

Parents and daughter bore their common failure in a common silence, broken only by Mrs Spragg's occasional tentative allusions to her grandson. But her anecdotes of Paul left a deeper silence behind them. Undine did not want to talk of her boy. She could forget him when, as she put it, things were 'going her way,' but in moments of discouragement the thought of him was an added bitterness, subtly different from her other bitter thoughts, and harder to quiet. It had not occurred to her to try to gain possession of the child. She was vaguely aware that the courts had given her his custody; but she had never seriously thought of asserting this claim. Her parents' diminished means and her own uncertain future made her regard the care of Paul as an additional burden, and she quieted her scruples by thinking of him as 'better off' with Ralph's family, and of herself as rather touchingly disinterested in putting his welfare before her own. Poor Mrs Spragg was pining for him, but Undine rejected her artless suggestion that Mrs Heeny should be sent to 'bring him round.' 'I wouldn't ask them a favour for the world—they're just waiting for a chance to be hateful to me,' she scornfully declared; but it pained her that her boy should be so near, yet inaccessible, and for the first time she was visited by unwonted questionings as to her share in the misfortunes that had befallen her. She had voluntarily stepped out of her social frame, and the only person on whom she could with any satisfaction have laid the blame was the person to whom her mind now turned with a belated tenderness. It was thus, in fact, that she thought of Ralph. His pride, his reserve, all the secret expressions of his devotion, the tones of his voice, his quiet manner, even his disconcerting irony: these seemed, in contrast to what she had since known, the qualities essential to her happiness. She could console herself only by regarding it as part of her sad lot that poverty, and the relentless animosity of his family, should have put an end to so perfect a union: she gradually began to look on herself and Ralph as the victims of dark machinations, and when she mentioned him she spoke forgivingly, and implied that 'everything might have been different' if 'people' had not 'come between' them.

She had arrived in New York in midseason, and the dread of seeing familiar faces kept her shut up in her room at the Malibran, reading novels and brooding over possibilities of escape. She tried to avoid the daily papers, but they formed the staple diet of her parents, and now and then she could not help taking one up and turning to the 'Society Column.' Its perusal produced the impression that the season must be the gayest New York had ever known. The Harmon B. Driscolls, young Jim and his wife, the Thurber Van Degens, the Chauncey Ellings, and all the other Fifth Avenue potentates, seemed to have their doors perpetually open to a stream of feasters among whom the familiar presences of Grace Beringer, Bertha Shallum, Dicky Bowles and Claud Walsingham Popple came and went with the irritating sameness of the figures in a stage-procession.

Among them also Peter Van Degen presently appeared. He had been on a tour around the world, and Undine could not look at a newspaper without seeing some allusion to his progress. After his return she noticed that his name was usually coupled with his wife's: he and Clare seemed to be celebrating his home-coming in a series of festivities, and Undine guessed that he had reasons for wishing to keep before the world the evidences of his conjugal accord.

Mrs Heeny's clippings supplied her with such items as her own reading missed; and one day the masseuse appeared with a long article from the leading journal of Little Rock, describing the brilliant nuptials of Mabel Lipscomb—now Mrs Homer Branney—and her departure for 'the Coast' in the bridegroom's private car. This put the last touch to Undine's irritation, and the next morning she got up earlier than usual, put on her most effective dress, went for a quick walk around the Park, and told her father when she came in that she wanted him to take her to the opera that evening.

Mr Spragg stared and frowned. 'You mean you want me to go round and hire a box for you?'

'Oh, no.' Undine coloured at the infelicitous allusion: besides, she knew now that the smart people who were 'musical' went in stalls.

'I only want two good seats. I don't see why I should stay shut up. I want you to go with me,' she added.

Her father received the latter part of the request without comment: he seemed to have gone beyond surprise. But it appeared that evening at dinner in a creased and loosely fitting dress-suit which he had probably not put on since the last time he had dined with his son-in-law, and he and Undine drove off together, leaving Mrs Spragg to gaze after them with the pale stare of Hecuba.*

Their stalls were in the middle of the house, and around them swept the great curve of boxes at which Undine had so often looked up in the remote Stentorian days. Then all had been one indistinguishable glitter, now the scene was full of familiar details: the house was thronged with people she knew, and every box seemed to contain a parcel of her past. At first she had shrunk from recognition; but gradually, as she perceived that no one noticed her, that she was merely part of the invisible crowd out of range of the exploring opera glasses, she felt a defiant desire to make herself seen. When the performance was over her father wanted to leave the house by the door at which they had entered, but she guided him toward the stockholders' entrance, and pressed her way among the furred and jewelled ladies waiting for their motors. 'Oh, it's the wrong door—never mind, we'll walk to the corner and get a cab,' she exclaimed, speaking loudly enough to be overheard. Two or three heads turned, and she met Dicky Bowles's glance, and returned his laughing bow. The woman talking to him looked around, coloured slightly, and made a barely perceptible motion of her head. Just beyond her, Mrs Chauncey Elling, plumed and purple, stared, parted her lips, and turned to say something important to young Jim Driscoll, who looked up involuntarily and then squared his shoulders and gazed fixedly at a distant point, as people do at a funeral. Behind them Undine caught sight of Clare Van Degen; she stood alone, and her face was pale and listless. 'Shall I go up and speak to her?' Undine wondered. Some intuition told her that, alone of all the women present, Clare might have greeted her kindly; but she hung back, and Mrs Harmon Driscoll surged by on Popple's arm. Popple crimsoned, coughed, and signalled despotically to Mrs Driscoll's footman. Over his shoulder Undine received a bow from Charles Bowen, and behind Bowen she saw two or three other men she knew, and read in their faces surprise, curiosity, and the wish to show their pleasure at seeing her. But she grasped her father's arm and drew him out among the entangled motors and vociferating policemen.

Neither she nor Mr Spragg spoke a word on the way home; but when they reached the Malibran her father followed her up to her room. She had dropped her cloak and stood before the wardrobe mirror studying her reflection when he came up behind her and she saw that he was looking at it too.

'Where did that necklace come from?'

Undine's neck grew pink under the shining circlet. It was the first time since her return to New York that she had put on a low dress and thus uncovered the string of pearls she always wore. She made no answer, and Mr Spragg continued: 'Did your husband give them to you?'

'*Ralph!*' She could not restrain a laugh.

'Who did, then?'

Undine remained silent. She really had not thought about the pearls, except in so far as she consciously enjoyed the pleasure of possessing them; and her father, habitually so unobservant, had seemed the last person likely to raise the awkward question of their origin.

'Why——' she began, without knowing what she meant to say.

'I guess you better send 'em back to the party they belong to,' Mr Spragg continued, in a voice she did not know.

'They belong to me!' she flamed up.

He looked at her as if she had grown suddenly small and insignificant. 'You better send 'em back to Peter Van Degen the first thing to-morrow morning,' he said as he went out of the room.

As far as Undine could remember, it was the first time in her life that he had ever ordered her to do anything; and when the door closed on him she had the distinct sense that the question had closed with it, and that she would have to obey. She took the pearls off and threw them from her angrily. The humiliation her father had inflicted on her was merged with the humiliation to which she had subjected herself in going to the opera, and she had never before hated her life as she hated it then.

All night she lay sleepless, wondering miserably what to do; and out of her hatred of her life, and her hatred of Peter Van Degen, there gradually grew a loathing of Van Degen's pearls. How could she have kept them, how have continued to wear them about her neck? Only her absorption in other cares could have kept her from feeling the humiliation of carrying about with her the price of her shame. Her novel-reading had filled her mind with the vocabulary of outraged virtue, and with pathetic allusions to woman's frailty, and while she pitied herself she thought her father heroic. She was proud to think that she had such a man to defend her, and rejoiced that it was in her power to express her scorn of Van Degen by sending back his jewels.

But her righteous ardour gradually cooled, and she was left once more to face the dreary problem of the future. Her evening at the opera had shown her the impossibility of remaining in New York. She had neither the skill nor the power to fight the forces of indifference leagued against her: she must get away at once, and try to make a fresh start. But, as usual, the lack of money hampered her. Mr Spragg could no longer afford to make her the allowance she had intermittently received from him during the first years of her marriage, and since she was now without child or household she could hardly make it a grievance that he had reduced her income. But what he allowed her, even with the addition of her alimony, was absurdly insufficient. Not that she looked far ahead; she had always felt herself predestined to ease and luxury, and the possibility of a future adapted to her present budget did not occur to her. But she desperately wanted enough money to carry her without anxiety through the coming year.

When her breakfast tray was brought in she sent it away untouched and continued to lie in her darkened room. She knew that when she got up she must send back the pearls; but there was no longer any satisfaction in the thought, and she lay listlessly wondering how she could best transmit them to Van Degen.

As she lay there she heard Mrs Heeny's voice in the passage. Hitherto she had avoided the masseuse, as she did every one else associated with her past. Mrs Heeny had behaved with extreme discretion, refraining from all direct allusions to Undine's misadventure; but her silence was obviously the criticism of a superior mind. Once again Undine had disregarded her injunction to 'go slow,' with results that justified the warning. Mrs Heeny's very reserve, however, now marked her as a safe adviser; and Undine sprang up and called her in.

'My sakes, Undine! You look's if you'd been setting up all night with a remains!' the masseuse exclaimed in her round rich tones.

Undine, without answering, caught up the pearls and thrust them into Mrs Heeny's hands.

'Good land alive!' The masseuse dropped into a chair and let the twist slip through her fat flexible fingers. 'Well, you got a fortune right round your neck whenever you wear them, Undine Spragg.'

Undine murmured something indistinguishable. 'I want you to take them——' she began.

'Take 'em? Where to?'

'Why, to——' She was checked by the wondering simplicity of Mrs Heeny's stare. The masseuse must know where the pearls had come from, yet it had evidently not occurred to her that Mrs Marvell was about to ask her to return them to their donor. In the light of Mrs Heeny's unclouded gaze the whole episode took on a different aspect, and Undine began to be vaguely astonished at her immediate submission to her father's will. The pearls were hers, after all!

'To be re-strung?' Mrs Heeny placidly suggested. 'Why, you'd oughter to have it done right here before your eyes, with pearls that are worth what these are.'

As Undine listened, a new thought shaped itself. She could not continue to wear the pearls: the idea had become intolerable. But for the first time she saw what they might be converted into, and what they might rescue her from; and suddenly she brought out: 'Do you suppose I could get anything for them?'

'Get anything? Why, what——'

'Anything like what they're worth, I mean. They cost a lot of money: they came from the biggest place in Paris.' Under Mrs Heeny's simplifying eye it was comparatively easy to make these explanations. 'I want you to try and sell them for me—I want you to do the best you can with them. I can't do it myself—but you must swear you'll never tell a soul,' she pressed on breathlessly.

'Why, you poor child—it ain't the first time,' said Mrs Heeny, coiling the pearls in her big palm. 'It's a pity too: they're such beauties. But you'll get others,' she added, as the necklace vanished into her bag.

A few days later there appeared from the same receptacle a bundle of banknotes considerable enough to quiet Undine's last scruples. She no longer understood why she had hesitated. Why should she have thought it necessary to give back the pearls to Van Degen? His obligation to her represented far more than the relatively small sum she had been able to realize on the necklace. She hid the money in her dress, and when Mrs Heeny had gone on to Mrs Spragg's room she drew the packet out, and counting the bills over, murmured to herself: 'Now I can get away!'

Her one thought was to return to Europe; but she did not want to go alone. The vision of her solitary figure adrift in the spring mob of trans-Atlantic pleasure-seekers depressed and mortified her. She would be sure to run across acquaintances, and they would infer that she was in quest of a new opportunity, a fresh start, and would suspect her of trying to use them for the purpose. The thought was repugnant to her newly awakened pride, and she decided that if she went to Europe her father and mother must go with her. The project was a bold one, and when she broached it she had to run the whole gamut of Mr Spragg's irony. He wanted to know what she expected to do with him when she got him there; whether she meant to introduce him to 'all those old Kings,' how she thought he and her mother would look in court dress, and how she supposed he was going to get on without his New York paper. But Undine had been aware of having what he himself would have called 'a pull' over her father since, the day after their visit to the opera, he had taken her aside to ask: 'You sent back those pearls?' and she had answered coldly: 'Mrs Heeny's taken them.'

After a moment of half-bewildered resistance her parents, perhaps secretly flattered by this first expression of her need for them, had yielded to her entreaty, packed their trunks, and stoically set out for the unknown. Neither Mr Spragg nor his wife had ever before been out of their country; and Undine had not understood, till they stood beside her tongue-tied and help-less on the dock at Cherbourg, the task she had undertaken in uprooting them. Mr Spragg had never been physically active, but on foreign shores he was seized by a strange restlessness, and a helpless dependence on his daughter. Mrs Spragg's long habit of apathy was overcome by her dread of being left alone when her husband and Undine went out, and she delayed and impeded their expeditions by insisting on accompanying them; so that, much as Undine disliked sightseeing, there seemed no alternative between 'going round' with her parents and shutting herself up with them in the crowded hotels to which she successively transported them.

The hotels were the only European institutions that really interested Mr Spragg. He considered them manifestly inferior to those at home; but he was haunted by a statistical curiosity as to their size, their number, their cost and their capacity for housing and feeding the incalculable hordes of his countrymen. He went through galleries, churches and museums in a stolid silence like his daughter's; but in the hotels he never ceased to enquire and investigate, questioning every one who could speak English, comparing bills, collecting prospectuses and computing the cost of construction and the probable return on the investment. He regarded the non-existence of the cold-storage system as one more proof of European inferiority, and no longer wondered, in the absence of the room-to-room telephone, that foreigners hadn't yet mastered the first principles of time-saving.

After a few weeks it became evident to both parents and daughter that their unnatural association could not continue much longer. Mrs Spragg's shrinking from everything new and unfamiliar had developed into a kind of settled terror, and Mr Spragg had begun to be depressed by the incredible number of the hotels and their simply incalculable housing capacity.

'It ain't that they're any great shakes in themselves, any one of 'em; but there's such a darned lot of 'em: they're as thick as mosquitoes, every place you go.' And he began to reckon up, on slips of paper, on the backs of bills and the margins of old newspapers, the number of travellers who could be simultaneously lodged, bathed and boarded on the continent of Europe. 'Five hundred bedrooms—three hundred bath-rooms—no; three hundred and fifty bath-rooms, that one has: that makes, supposing two-thirds of 'em double up—do you s'pose as many as that do, Undie? That porter at Lucerne told me the Germans slept three in a room—well, call it eight hundred people; and three meals a day per head; no, four meals, with that afternoon tea they take; and the last place we were at—'way up on that mountain there—why, there were seventy-five hotels in that one spot alone, and all jam full— well, it beats me to know where all the people come from . . .'

He had gone on in this fashion for what seemed to his daughter an endless length of days; and then suddenly he had roused himself to say: 'See here, Undie, I got to go back and make the money to pay for all this.'

There had been no question on the part of any of the three of Undine's returning with them; and after she had conveyed them to their steamer, and seen their vaguely relieved faces merged in the handkerchief-waving throng along the taffrail,* she had returned alone to Paris and made her unsuccessful attempt to enlist the aid of Indiana Rolliver.

XXVII

SHE was still brooding over this last failure when one afternoon, as she loitered on the hotel terrace, she was approached by a

young woman whom she had seen sitting near the wheeled
chair of an old lady wearing a crumpled black bonnet under a
funny fringed parasol with a jointed handle.

The young woman, who was small, slight and brown, was
dressed with a disregard of the fashion which contrasted oddly
with the mauve powder on her face and the traces of artificial
colour in her dark untidy hair. She looked as if she might have
several different personalities, and as if the one of the moment
had been hanging up a long time in her wardrobe and been
hurriedly taken down as probably good enough for the present
occasion.

With her hands in her jacket pockets, and an agreeable smile
on her boyish face, she strolled up to Undine and asked, in a
pretty variety of Parisian English, if she had the pleasure of
speaking to Mrs Marvell.

On Undine's assenting, the smile grew more alert and the
lady continued: 'I think you know my friend Sacha Adelschein?'

No question could have been less welcome to Undine. If
there was one point on which she was doggedly and puritani-
cally resolved, it was that no extremes of social adversity should
ever again draw her into the group of people among whom
Madame Adelschein too conspicuously figured. Since her unsuccessful attempt to win over Indiana by introducing her to
that group, Undine had been righteously resolved to remain
aloof from it; and she was drawing herself up to her loftiest
height of disapproval when the stranger, as if unconscious of it,
went on: 'Sacha speaks of you so often—she admires you so
much.—I think you know also my cousin Chelles,' she added,
looking into Undine's eyes. 'I am the Princess Estradina. I've
come here with my mother for the air.'

The murmur of negation died on Undine's lips. She found
herself grappling with a new social riddle, and such surprises
were always stimulating. The name of the untidy-looking young
woman she had been about to repel was one of the most
eminent in the impregnable quarter beyond the Seine. No one
figured more largely in the Parisian chronicle than the Princess
Estradina, and no name more impressively headed the list at
every marriage, funeral and philanthropic entertainment of the
Faubourg Saint Germain than that of her mother, the Duchesse

de Dordogne, who must be no other than the old woman sitting
in the Bath-chair with the crumpled bonnet and the ridiculous
sunshade.

But it was not the appearance of the two ladies that surprised
Undine. She knew that social gold does not always glitter, and
that the lady she had heard spoken of as Lili Estradina was
notoriously careless of the conventions; but that she should boast
of her intimacy with Madame Adelschein, and use it as a pretext
for naming herself, overthrew all Undine's hierarchies.

'Yes—it's hideously dull here, and I'm dying of it. Do come
over and speak to my mother. She's dying of it too; but don't
tell her so, because she hasn't found it out. There were so many
things our mothers never found out,' the Princess rambled on,
with her half-mocking half-intimate smile; and in another
moment Undine, thrilled at having Mrs Spragg thus coupled
with a Duchess, found herself seated between mother and
daughter, and responding by a radiant blush to the elder lady's
amiable opening: 'You know my nephew Raymond—he's
your great admirer.'

How had it happened, whither would it lead, how long could
it last? The questions raced through Undine's brain as she sat
listening to her new friends—they seemed already too friendly
to be called acquaintances!—replying to their enquiries, and
trying to think far enough ahead to guess what they would
expect her to say, and what tone it would be well to take. She
was used to such feats of mental agility, and it was instinctive
with her to become, for the moment, the person she thought
her interlocutors expected her to be; but she had never had
quite so new a part to play at such short notice. She took her
cue, however, from the fact that the Princess Estradina, in her
mother's presence, made no farther allusion to her dear friend
Sacha, and seemed somehow, though she continued to chat on
in the same easy strain, to look differently and throw out
different implications. All these shades of demeanour were
immediately perceptible to Undine, who tried to adapt herself
to them by combining in her manner a mixture of Apex dash
and New York dignity; and the result was so successful that
when she rose to go the Princess, with a hand on her arm, said
almost wistfully: 'You're staying on too? Then do take pity on

us! We might go on some trips together; and in the evenings we could make a bridge.'

A new life began for Undine. The Princess, chained to her mother's side, and frankly restive under her filial duty, clung to her new acquaintance with a persistence too flattering to be analyzed. 'My dear, I was on the brink of suicide when I saw your name in the visitors' list,' she explained; and Undine felt like answering that she had nearly reached the same pass when the Princess's thin little hand had been held out to her. For the moment she was dizzy with the effect of that random gesture. Here she was, at the lowest ebb of her fortunes, miraculously rehabilitated, reinstated, and restored to the old victorious sense of her youth and her power! Her sole graces, her unaided personality, had worked the miracle; how should she not trust in them hereafter?

Aside from her feeling of concrete attainment, Undine was deeply interested in her new friends. The Princess and her mother, in their different ways, were different from any one else she had known. The Princess, who might have been of any age between twenty and forty, had a small triangular face with caressing impudent eyes, a smile like a silent whistle and the gait of a baker's boy balancing his basket. She wore either baggy shabby clothes like a man's, or rich draperies that looked as if they had been rained on; and she seemed equally at ease in either style of dress, and carelessly unconscious of both. She was extremely familiar and unblushingly inquisitive, but she never gave Undine the time to ask her any questions or the opportunity to venture on any freedom with her. Nevertheless she did not scruple to talk of her sentimental experiences, and seemed surprised, and rather disappointed, that Undine had so few to relate in return. She playfully accused her beautiful new friend of being *cachottière*,* and at the sight of Undine's blush cried out: 'Ah, you funny Americans! Why do you all behave as if love were a secret infirmity?'

The old Duchess was even more impressive, because she fitted better into Undine's preconceived picture of the Faubourg Saint Germain, and was more like the people with whom she pictured the former Nettie Wincher as living in privileged intimacy. The Duchess was, indeed, more amiable and accessible than Undine's conception of a Duchess, and displayed a curiosity as great as her daughter's, and much more puerile, concerning her new friend's history and habits. But through her mild prattle, and in spite of her limited perceptions, Undine felt in her the same clear impenetrable barrier that she ran against occasionally in the Princess; and she was beginning to understand that this barrier represented a number of things about which she herself had yet to learn. She would not have known this a few years earlier, nor would she have seen in the Duchess anything but the ruin of an ugly woman, dressed in clothes that Mrs Spragg wouldn't have touched. The Duchess certainly looked like a ruin; but Undine now saw that she looked like the ruin of a castle.

The Princess, who was unofficially separated from her husband, had with her two little girls. She seemed extremely attached to both—though avowing for the younger a preference she frankly ascribed to the interesting accident of its parentage—and she could not understand that Undine, as to whose domestic difficulties she minutely informed herself, should have consented to leave her child to strangers. 'For, to one's child, every one but one's self is a stranger; and whatever your *égarements**——' she began, breaking off with a stare when Undine interrupted her to explain that the courts had ascribed all the wrongs in the case to her husband. 'But then—but then——' murmured the Princess, turning away from the subject as if checked by too deep an abyss of difference.

The incident had embarrassed Undine, and though she tried to justify herself by allusions to her boy's dependence on his father's family, and to the duty of not standing in his way, she saw that she made no impression. 'Whatever one's errors, one's child belongs to one,' her hearer continued to repeat; and Undine, who was frequently scandalized by the Princess's conversation, now found herself in the odd position of having to set a watch upon her own in order not to scandalize the Princess.

Each day, nevertheless, strengthened her hold on her new friends. After her first flush of triumph she began indeed to suspect that she had been a slight disappointment to the Princess, had not completely justified the hopes raised by the doubtful honour of being one of Sacha Adelschein's intimates. Undine

guessed that the Princess had expected to find her more amusing, 'queerer,' more startling in speech and conduct. Though
by instinct she was none of these things, she was eager to go
as far as was expected; but she felt that her audacities were on
lines too normal to be interesting, and that the Princess thought
her rather school-girlish and old-fashioned. Still, they had in
common their youth, their boredom, their high spirits and their
hunger for amusement; and Undine was making the most of
these ties when one day, coming back from a trip to Monte-
Carlo with the Princess, she was brought up short by the sight
of a lady—evidently a new arrival—who was seated in an
attitude of respectful intimacy beside the old Duchess's chair.
Undine, advancing unheard over the fine gravel of the garden
path, recognized at a glance the Marquise de Trézac's drooping
nose and disdainful back, and at the same moment heard her say:
'—And her husband?'

'Her husband? But she's an American—she's divorced,' the
Duchess replied, as if she were merely stating the same fact in
two different ways; and Undine stopped short with a pang of
apprehension.

The Princess came up behind her. 'Who's the solemn person
with Mamma? Ah, that old bore of a Trézac!' She dropped her
long eye-glass with a laugh. 'Well, she'll be useful—she'll stick
to Mamma like a leech, and we shall get away oftener. Come,
let's go and be charming to her.'

She approached Madame de Trézac effusively, and after an
interchange of exclamations Undine heard her say: 'You know
my friend Mrs Marvell? No? How odd! Where do you manage
to hide yourself, *chère Madame*? Undine, here's a compatriot who
hasn't the pleasure——'

'I'm such a hermit, dear Mrs Marvell—the Princess shows me
what I miss,' the Marquise de Trézac murmured, rising to give
her hand to Undine, and speaking in a voice so different from
that of the supercilious Miss Wincher that only her facial angle
and the droop of her nose linked her to the hated vision of
Potash Springs.

Undine felt herself dancing on a flood-tide of security. For
the first time the memory of Potash Springs became a thing to
smile at, and with the Princess's arm through hers she shone

back triumphantly on Madame de Trézac, who seemed to have grown suddenly obsequious and insignificant, as though the waving of the Princess's wand had stripped her of all her false advantages.

But upstairs, in her own room, Undine's courage fell. Madame de Trézac had been civil, effusive even, because for the moment she had been taken off her guard by finding Mrs Marvell on terms of intimacy with the Princess Estradina and her mother. But the force of facts would reassert itself. Far from continuing to see Undine through her French friends' eyes she would probably invite them to view her compatriot through the searching lens of her own ampler information. 'The old hypocrite—she'll tell them everything,' Undine murmured, wincing at the recollection of the dentist's assistant from Deposit, and staring miserably at her reflection in the dressing-table mirror. Of what use were youth and grace and good looks, if one drop of poison distilled from the envy of a narrow-minded woman was enough to paralyze them? Of course Madame de Trézac knew and remembered, and, secure in her own impregnable position, would never rest till she had driven out the intruder.

XXVIII

'WHAT do you say to Nice to-morrow, dearest?' the Princess suggested a few evenings later, as she followed Undine upstairs after a languid evening at bridge with the Duchess and Madame de Trézac.

Half-way down the passage she stopped to open a door and, putting her finger to her lip, signed to Undine to enter. In the taper-lit dimness stood two small white beds, each surmounted by a crucifix and a palm-branch, and each containing a small brown sleeping child with a mop of hair and a curiously finished little face. As the Princess stood gazing on their innocent slumbers she seemed for a moment like a third little girl, scarcely bigger and browner than the others; and the smile with which she watched them was as clear as theirs.

'*Ah, si seulement je pouvais choisir leurs amants!*'* she sighed as she turned away.

'—Nice to-morrow,' she repeated, as she and Undine walked on to their rooms with linked arms. 'We may as well make hay while the Trézac shines. She bores Mamma frightfully, but Mamma won't admit it because they belong to the same *œuvres*. Shall it be the eleven train, dear? We can lunch at the *Royal* and look in the shops—we may meet somebody amusing. Anyhow, it's better than staying here!'

Undine was sure the trip to Nice would be delightful. Their previous expeditions had shown her the Princess's faculty for organizing such adventures. At Monte-Carlo, a few days before, they had run across two or three amusing but unassorted people, and the Princess, having fused them in a jolly lunch, had followed it up by a bout at baccarat, and, finally hunting down an eminent composer who had just arrived to rehearse a new production, had insisted on his asking the party to tea, and treating them to fragments of his opera.

A few days earlier, Undine's hope of renewing such pleasures would have been clouded by the dread of leaving Madame de Trézac alone with the Duchess. But she had no longer any fear of Madame de Trézac. She had discovered that her old rival of Potash Springs was in actual dread of her disfavour, and nervously anxious to conciliate her, and the discovery gave her such a sense of the heights she had scaled, and the security of her footing, that all her troubled past began to seem like the result of some providential 'design,' and vague impulses of piety stirred in her as she and the Princess whirled toward Nice through the blue and gold glitter of the morning.

They wandered about the lively streets, they gazed into the beguiling shops, the Princess tried on hats and Undine bought them, and they lunched at the *Royal* on all sorts of succulent dishes prepared under the head-waiter's special supervision. But as they were savouring their 'double' coffee and liqueurs, and Undine was wondering what her companion would devise for the afternoon, the Princess clapped her hands together and cried out: 'Dearest, I'd forgotten! I must desert you.'

She explained that she'd promised the Duchess to look up a friend who was ill—a poor wretch who'd been sent to Cimiez for her lungs—and that she must rush off at once, and would be back as soon as possible—well, if not in an hour, then in two at latest. She was full of compunction, but she knew Undine would forgive her, and find something amusing to fill up the time: she advised her to go back and buy the black hat with the osprey, and try on the crêpe de Chine they'd thought so smart: for any one as good-looking as herself the woman would probably alter it for nothing; and they could meet again at the Palace Tea-Rooms at four.

She whirled away in a cloud of explanations, and Undine, left alone, sat down on the Promenade des Anglais. She did not believe a word the Princess had said. She had seen in a flash why she was being left, and why the plan had not been divulged to her beforehand; and she quivered with resentment and humiliation. 'That's what she's wanted me for . . . that's why she made up to me. She's trying it to-day, and after this it'll happen regularly . . . she'll drag me over here every day or two . . . at least she thinks she will!'

A sincere disgust was Undine's uppermost sensation. She was as much ashamed as Mrs Spragg might have been at finding herself used to screen a clandestine adventure.

'I'll let her see . . . I'll make her understand,' she repeated angrily; and for a moment she was half-disposed to drive to the station and take the first train back. But the sense of her precarious situation withheld her; and presently, with bitterness in her heart, she got up and began to stroll toward the shops.

To show that she was not a dupe, she arrived at the designated meeting-place nearly an hour later than the time appointed; but when she entered the Tea-Rooms the Princess was nowhere to be seen. The rooms were crowded, and Undine was guided toward a small inner apartment where isolated couples were absorbing refreshments in an atmosphere of intimacy that made it seem incongruous to be alone. She glanced about for a face she knew, but none was visible, and she was just giving up the search when she beheld Elmer Moffatt shouldering his way through the crowd.

The sight was so surprising that she sat gazing with unconscious fixity at the round black head and glossy reddish face which kept appearing and disappearing through the intervening jungle of aigrettes.* It was long since she had either heard of Moffatt or thought about him, and now, in her loneliness and exasperation, she took comfort in the sight of his confident capable face, and felt a longing to hear his voice and unbosom her woes to him. She had half risen to attract his attention when she saw him turn back and make way for a companion, who was cautiously steering her huge feathered hat between the tea-tables. The woman was of the vulgarest type; everything about her was cheap and gaudy. But Moffatt was obviously elated: he stood aside with a flourish to usher her in, and as he followed he shot out a pink shirt-cuff with jewelled links, and gave his moustache a gallant twist. Undine felt an unreasoning irritation: she was vexed with him both for not being alone and for being so vulgarly accompanied. As the couple seated themselves she caught Moffatt's glance and saw him redden to the edge of his white forehead; but he elaborately avoided her eye—he evidently wanted her to see him do it—and proceeded to minister to his companion's wants with an air of experienced gallantry.

The incident, trifling as it was, filled up the measure of Undine's bitterness. She thought Moffatt pitiably ridiculous, and she hated him for showing himself in such a light at that particular moment. Her mind turned back to her own grievance, and she was just saying to herself that nothing on earth should prevent her letting the Princess know what she thought of her, when the lady in question at last appeared. She came hurriedly forward and behind her Undine perceived the figure of a slight quietly dressed man, as to whom her immediate impression was that he made every one else in the room look as common as Moffatt. An instant later the colour had flown to her face and her hand was in Raymond de Chelles', while the Princess, murmuring: 'Cimiez's such a long way off; but you *will* forgive me?' looked into her eyes with a smile that added: 'See how I pay for what I get!'

Her first glance showed Undine how glad Raymond de Chelles was to see her. Since their last meeting his admiration for her seemed not only to have increased but to have acquired a different character. Undine, at an earlier stage in her career, might not have known exactly what the difference signified; but it was as clear to her now as if the Princess had said—what her beaming eyes seemed, in fact, to convey—'I'm only too glad to do my cousin the same kind of turn you're doing me.'

But Undine's increased experience, if it had made her more vigilant, had also given her a clearer measure of her power. She saw at once that Chelles, in seeking to meet her again, was not in quest of a mere passing adventure. He was evidently deeply drawn to her, and her present situation, if it made it natural to regard her as more accessible, had not altered the nature of his feeling. She saw and weighed all this in the first five minutes during which, over tea and muffins, the Princess descanted on her luck in happening to run across her cousin, and Chelles, his enchanted eyes on Undine, expressed his sense of his good fortune. He was staying, it appeared, with friends at Beaulieu, and had run over to Nice that afternoon by the merest chance: he added that, having just learned of his aunt's presence in the neighbourhood, he had already planned to present his homage to her.

'Oh, don't come to us—we're too dull!' the Princess exclaimed. 'Let us run over occasionally and call on you: we're dying for a pretext, aren't we?' she added, smiling at Undine.

The latter smiled back vaguely, and looked across the room. Moffatt, looking flushed and foolish, was just pushing back his chair. To carry off his embarrassment he put on an additional touch of importance; and, as he swaggered out behind his companion, Undine said to herself, with a shiver: 'If he'd been alone they would have found me taking tea with him.'

Undine, during the ensuing weeks, returned several times to Nice with the Princess; but, to the latter's surprise, she absolutely refused to have Raymond de Chelles included in their luncheon-parties, or even apprised in advance of their expeditions.

The Princess, always impatient of unnecessary dissimulation, had not attempted to keep up the feint of the interesting invalid at Cimiez. She confessed to Undine that she was drawn to Nice by the presence there of the person without whom, for the moment, she found life intolerable, and whom she could not well receive under the same roof with her little girls and her mother. She appealed to Undine's sisterly heart to feel for her in her difficulty, and implied that—as her conduct had already proved—she would always be ready to render her friend a like service.

It was at this point that Undine checked her by a decided word. 'I understand your position, and I'm very sorry for you, of course,' she began (the Princess stared at the 'sorry'). 'Your secret's perfectly safe with me, and I'll do anything I can for you . . . but if I go to Nice with you again you must promise not to ask your cousin to meet us.'

The Princess's face expressed the most genuine astonishment. 'Oh, my dear, do forgive me if I've been stupid! He admires you so tremendously; and I thought——'

'You'll do as I ask, please—won't you?' Undine went on, ignoring the interruption and looking straight at her under level brows; and the Princess, with a shrug, merely murmured: 'What a pity! I fancied you liked him.'

XXIX

THE early spring found Undine once more in Paris.

She had every reason to be satisfied with the result of the course she had pursued since she had pronounced her ultimatum on the subject of Raymond de Chelles. She had continued to remain on the best of terms with the Princess, to rise in the estimation of the old Duchess, and to measure the rapidity of her ascent in the upward gaze of Madame de Trézac; and she had given Chelles to understand that, if he wished to renew their acquaintance, he must do so in the shelter of his venerable aunt's protection.

To the Princess she was careful to make her attitude equally clear. 'I like your cousin very much—he's delightful, and if I'm in Paris this spring I hope I shall see a great deal of him. But I know how easy it is for a woman in my position to get talked about—and I have my little boy to consider.'

Nevertheless, whenever Chelles came over from Beaulieu to spend a day with his aunt and cousin—an excursion he not infrequently repeated—Undine was at no pains to conceal her pleasure. Nor was there anything calculated in her attitude. Chelles seemed to her more charming than ever, and the warmth of his wooing was in flattering contrast to the cool reserve of his manners. At last she felt herself alive and young again, and it became a joy to look in her glass and to try on her new hats and dresses . . .

The only menace ahead was the usual one of the want of money. While she had travelled with her parents she had been at relatively small expense, and since their return to America Mr Spragg had sent her allowance regularly; yet almost all the money she had received for the pearls was already gone, and she knew her Paris season would be far more expensive than the quiet weeks on the Riviera.

Meanwhile the sense of reviving popularity, and the charm of Chelles' devotion, had almost effaced the ugly memories of failure, and refurbished that image of herself in other minds which was her only notion of self-seeing. Under the guidance of Madame de Trézac she had found a prettily furnished apartment in a not too inaccessible quarter, and in its light bright drawing-room she sat one June afternoon listening, with all the forbearance of which she was capable, to the counsels of her newly-acquired guide.

'Everything but marriage——' Madame de Trézac was repeating, her long head slightly tilted, her features wearing the rapt look of an adept reciting a hallowed formula.

Raymond de Chelles had not been mentioned by either of the ladies, and the former Miss Wincher was merely imparting to her young friend one of the fundamental dogmas of her social creed; but Undine was conscious that the air between them vibrated with an unspoken name. She made no immediate answer, but her glance, passing by Madame de Trézac's dull countenance, sought her own reflection in the mirror behind her visitor's chair. A beam of spring sunlight touched the living masses of her hair and made the face beneath as radiant as a girl's. Undine smiled faintly at the promise her own eyes gave her, and then turned them back to her friend. 'What can such women know about anything?' she thought compassionately.

'There's everything against it,' Madame de Trézac continued in a tone of patient exposition. She seemed to be doing her best to make the matter clear. 'In the first place, between people in society a religious marriage is necessary; and, since the Church doesn't recognize divorce, that's obviously out of the question. In France, a man of position who goes through the form of civil marriage with a divorced woman is simply ruining himself and her. They might much better—from her point of view as well as his—be 'friends,' as it's called over here: such arrangements are understood and allowed for. But when a Frenchman marries he wants to marry as his people always have. He knows there are traditions he can't fight against—and in his heart he's glad there are.'

'Oh, I know: they've so much religious feeling. I admire that in them: their religion's so beautiful.' Undine looked thoughtfully at her visitor. 'I suppose even money—a great deal of money—wouldn't make the least bit of difference?'

'None whatever, except to make matters worse,' Madame de Trézac decisively rejoined. She returned Undine's look with something of Miss Wincher's contemptuous authority. 'But,' she added, softening to a smile, 'between ourselves—I can say it, since we're neither of us children—a woman with tact, who's not in a position to remarry, will find society extremely indulgent . . . provided, of course, she keeps up appearances . . .'

Undine turned to her with the frown of a startled Diana. 'We don't look at things that way out at Apex,' she said coldly; and the blood rose in Madame de Trézac's sallow cheek.

'Oh, my dear, it's so refreshing to hear you talk like that! Personally, of course, I've never quite got used to the French view——'

'I hope no American woman ever does,' said Undine.

She had been in Paris for about two months when this conversation took place, and in spite of her reviving self-confidence she was beginning to recognize the strength of the forces opposed to her. It had taken a long time to convince her that even money could not prevail against them; and, in the intervals of expressing her admiration for the Catholic creed, she now had violent reactions of militant Protestantism, during which she talked of the tyranny of Rome and recalled school stories of immoral Popes and persecuting Jesuits.

Meanwhile her demeanour to Chelles was that of the incorruptible but fearless American woman, who cannot even conceive of love outside of marriage, but is ready to give her devoted friendship to the man on whom, in happier circumstances, she might have bestowed her hand. This attitude was provocative of many scenes, during which her suitor's unfailing powers of expression—his gift of looking and saying all the desperate and devoted things a pretty woman likes to think she inspires—gave Undine the thrilling sense of breathing the very air of French fiction. But she was aware that too prolonged tension of these cords usually ends in their snapping, and that Chelles' patience was probably in inverse ratio to his ardour.

When Madame de Trézac had left her these thoughts remained in her mind. She understood exactly what each of her new friends wanted of her. The Princess, who was fond of her cousin, and had the French sense of family solidarity, would have liked to see Chelles happy in what seemed to her the only imaginable way. Madame de Trézac would have liked to do what she could to second the Princess's efforts in this or any other line; and even the old Duchess—though piously desirous of seeing her favourite nephew married—would have thought it not only natural but inevitable that, while awaiting that happy event, he should try to induce an amiable young woman to mitigate the drawbacks of celibacy. Meanwhile, they might one and all weary of her if Chelles did; and a persistent rejection of his suit would probably imperil her scarcely-gained footing among his friends. All this was clear to her, yet it did not shake her resolve. She was determined to give up Chelles unless he was willing to marry her; and the thought of her renunciation moved her to a kind of wistful melancholy.

In this mood her mind reverted to a letter she had just received from her mother. Mrs Spragg wrote more fully than usual, and the unwonted flow of her pen had been occasioned by an event for which she had long yearned. For months she had pined for a sight of her grandson, had tried to screw up her courage to write and ask permission to visit him, and, finally breaking through her sedentary habits, had begun to haunt the neighbourhood of Washington Square, with the result that one afternoon she had had the luck to meet the little boy coming out of the house with his nurse. She had spoken to him, and he had remembered her and called her 'Granny'; and the next day she had received a note from Mrs Fairford saying that Ralph would be glad to send Paul to see her. Mrs Spragg enlarged on the delights of the visit and the growing beauty and cleverness of her grandson. She described to Undine exactly how Paul was dressed, how he looked and what he said, and told her how he had examined everything in the room, and, finally coming upon his mother's photograph, had asked who the lady was; and, on being told, had wanted to know if she was a very long way off, and when Granny thought she would come back.

As Undine re-read her mother's pages, she felt an unusual tightness in her throat and two tears rose to her eyes. It was dreadful that her little boy should be growing up far away from her, perhaps dressed in clothes she would have hated; and wicked and unnatural that when he saw her picture he should have to be told who she was. 'If I could only meet some good man who would give me a home and be a father to him,' she thought—and the tears overflowed and ran down.

Even as they fell, the door was thrown open to admit Raymond de Chelles, and the consciousness of the moisture still glistening on her cheeks perhaps strengthened her resolve to resist him, and thus made her more imperiously to be desired. Certain it is that on that day her suitor first alluded to a possibility which Madame de Trézac had prudently refrained from suggesting, and there fell upon Undine's attentive ears the magic phrase 'annulment of marriage.'

Her alert intelligence immediately set to work in this new direction; but almost at the same moment she became aware of a subtle change of tone in the Princess and her mother, a change reflected in the corresponding decline of Madame de Trézac's cordiality. Undine, since her arrival in Paris, had necessarily been less in the Princess's company, but when they met she had found her as friendly as ever. It was manifestly not a failing of the Princess's to forget past favours, and though increasingly absorbed by the demands of town life she treated her new friend with the same affectionate frankness, and Undine was given frequent opportunities to enlarge her Parisian acquaintance, not only in the Princess's intimate circle but in the majestic drawing-rooms of the Hôtel de Dordogne. Now, however, there was a perceptible decline in these signs of hospitality, and Undine, on calling one day on the Duchess, noticed that her appearance sent a visible flutter of discomfort through the circle about her hostess's chair. Two or three of the ladies present looked away from the new-comer and at each other, and several of them seemed spontaneously to encircle without approaching her, while another—grey-haired, elderly and slightly frightened—with an 'Adieu, ma bonne tante'* to the Duchess, was hastily aided in her retreat down the long line of old gilded rooms.

The incident was too mute and rapid to have been noticeable had it not been followed by the Duchess's resuming her conversation with the ladies nearest her as though Undine had just gone out of the room instead of entering it. The sense of having been thus rendered invisible filled Undine with a vehement desire to make herself seen, and an equally strong sense that all attempts to do so would be vain; and when, a few minutes later, she issued from the portals of the Hôtel de Dordogne it was with the fixed resolve not to enter them again till she had had an explanation with the Princess.

She was spared the trouble of seeking one by the arrival, early the next morning, of Madame de Trézac, who, entering almost with the breakfast tray, mysteriously asked to be allowed to communicate something of importance.

'You'll understand, I know, the Princess's not coming her-self——' Madame de Trézac began, sitting up very straight on the edge of the arm-chair over which Undine's lace dressing-gown hung.

'If there's anything she wants to say to me, I don't,' Undine answered, leaning back among her rosy pillows, and reflecting compassionately that the face opposite her was just the colour of the café au lait she was pouring out.

'There are things that are . . . that might seem too pointed . . . if one said them one's self,' Madame de Trézac continued. 'Our dear Lili's so good-natured . . . she so hates to do anything unfriendly; but she naturally thinks first of her mother . . .'

'Her mother? What's the matter with her mother?'

'I told her I knew you didn't understand. I was sure you'd take it in good part . . .'

Undine raised herself on her elbow. 'What did Lili tell you to tell me?'

'Oh, not to *tell* you . . . simply to ask if, just for the present, you'd mind avoiding the Duchess's Thursdays . . . calling on any other day, that is.'

'Any other day? She's not at home on any other. Do you mean she doesn't want me to call?'

'Well—not while the Marquise de Chelles is in Paris. She's the Duchess's favourite niece—and of course they all hang together. That kind of family feeling is something you naturally don't——'

Undine had a sudden glimpse of hidden intricacies.

'That was Raymond de Chelles' mother I saw there yesterday? The one they hurried out when I came in?'

'It seems she was very much upset. She somehow heard your name.'

'Why shouldn't she have heard my name? And why in the world should it upset her?'

Madame de Trézac heaved a hesitating sigh. 'Isn't it better to be frank? She thinks she has reason to feel badly—they all do.'

'To feel badly? Because her son wants to marry me?'

'Of course they know that's impossible.' Madame de Trézac smiled compassionately. 'But they're afraid of your spoiling his other chances.'

Undine paused a moment before answering. 'It won't be impossible when my marriage is annulled,' she said.

The effect of this statement was less electrifying than she had hoped. Her visitor simply broke into a laugh. 'My dear child! Your marriage annulled? Who can have put such a mad idea into your head?'

Undine's gaze followed the pattern she was tracing with a lustrous nail on her embroidered bedspread. 'Raymond himself,' she let fall.

This time there was no mistaking the effect she produced. Madame de Trézac, with a murmured 'Oh,' sat gazing before her as if she had lost the thread of her argument; and it was only after a considerable interval that she recovered it sufficiently to exclaim: 'They'll never hear of it—absolutely never!'

'But they can't prevent it, can they?'

'They can prevent its being of any use to you.'

'I see,' Undine pensively assented.

She knew the tone she had taken was virtually a declaration of war; but she was in a mood when the act of defiance, apart from its strategic value, was a satisfaction in itself. Moreover, if she could not gain her end without a fight it was better that the battle should be engaged while Raymond's ardour was at its height. To provoke immediate hostilities she sent for him the same afternoon, and related, quietly and without comment, the incident of her visit to the Duchess, and the mission with which Madame de Trézac had been charged. In the circumstances, she went on to explain, it was manifestly impossible that she should continue to receive his visits; and she met his wrathful comments on his relatives by the gently but firmly expressed resolve not to be the cause of any disagreement between himself and his family.

XXX

A few days after her decisive conversation with Raymond de Chelles, Undine, emerging from the doors of the Nouveau Luxe, where she had been to call on the newly-arrived Mrs Homer Branney, once more found herself face to face with Elmer Moffatt.

This time there was no mistaking his eagerness to be recognized. He stopped short as they met, and she read such pleasure in his eyes that she too stopped, holding out her hand.

'I'm glad you're going to speak to me,' she said, and Moffatt reddened at the allusion.

'Well, I very nearly didn't. I didn't know you. You look about as old as you did when I first landed at Apex—remember?'

He turned back and began to walk at her side in the direction of the Champs Elysées.

'Say—this is all right!' he exclaimed; and she saw that his glance had left her and was ranging across the wide silvery square ahead of them to the congregated domes and spires beyond the river.

'Do you like Paris?' she asked, wondering what theatres he had been to.

'It beats everything.' He seemed to be breathing in deeply the impression of fountains, sculpture, leafy avenues and long-drawn architectural distances fading into the afternoon haze.

'I suppose you've been to that old church over there?' he went on, his gold-topped stick pointing toward the towers of Notre Dame.

'Oh, of course; when I used to sightsee. Have you never been to Paris before?'

'No, this is my first look-round. I came across in March.'

'In March?' she echoed inattentively. It never occurred to her that other people's lives went on when they were out of her range of vision, and she tried in vain to remember what she had last heard of Moffatt. 'Wasn't that a bad time to leave Wall Street?'

'Well, so-so. Fact is, I was played out: needed a change.' Nothing in his robust mien confirmed the statement, and he did not seem inclined to develop it. 'I presume you're settled here now?' he went on. 'I saw by the papers——'

'Yes,' she interrupted; adding, after a moment: 'It was all a mistake from the first.'

'Well, I never thought he was your form,' said Moffatt.

His eyes had come back to her, and the look in them struck her as something she might use to her advantage; but the next moment he had glanced away with a furrowed brow, and she felt she had not wholly fixed his attention.

'I live at the other end of Paris. Why not come back and have tea with me?' she suggested, half moved by a desire to know more of his affairs, and half by the thought that a talk with him might help to shed some light on hers.

In the open taxi-cab he seemed to recover his sense of well-being, and leaned back, his hands on the knob of his stick, with the air of a man pleasantly aware of his privileges. 'This Paris is a thundering good place,' he repeated once or twice as they rolled on through the crush and glitter of the afternoon; and when they had descended at Undine's door, and he stood in her drawing-room, and looked out on the horse-chestnut trees rounding their green domes under the balcony, his satisfaction culminated in the comment: 'I guess this lays out West End Avenue!'

His eyes met Undine's with their old twinkle, and their expression encouraged her to murmur: 'Of course there are times when I'm very lonely.'

She sat down behind the tea-table, and he stood at a little distance, watching her pull off her gloves with a queer comic twitch of his elastic mouth. 'Well, I guess it's only when you want to be,' he said, grasping a lyre-backed chair by its gilt cords, and sitting down astride of it, his light grey trousers stretching too tightly over his plump thighs. Undine was perfectly aware that he was a vulgar over-dressed man, with a red crease of fat above his collar and an impudent swaggering eye; yet she liked to see him there, and was conscious that he stirred the fibres of a self she had forgotten but had not ceased to understand.

She had fancied her avowal of loneliness might call forth some sentimental phrase; but though Moffatt was clearly pleased to be with her she saw that she was not the centre of his thoughts, and the discovery irritated her.

'I don't suppose *you've* known what it is to be lonely since you've been in Europe?' she continued as she held out his tea-cup.

'Oh,' he said jocosely, 'I don't always go round with a guide'; and she rejoined on the same note: 'Then perhaps I shall see something of you.'

'Why, there's nothing would suit me better; but the fact is, I'm probably sailing next week.'

'Oh, are you? I'm sorry.' There was nothing feigned in her regret.

'Anything I can do for you across the pond?'

She hesitated. 'There's something you can do for me right off.'

He looked at her more attentively, as if his practised eye had passed through the surface of her beauty to what might be going on behind it. 'Do you want my blessing again?' he asked with sudden irony.

Undine opened her eyes with a trustful look. 'Yes—I do.'

'Well—I'll be damned!' said Moffatt gaily.

'You've always been so awfully nice,' she began; and he leaned back, grasping both sides of the chair-back, and shaking it a little with his laugh.

He kept the same attitude while she proceeded to unfold her case, listening to her with the air of sober concentration that his frivolous face took on at any serious demand on his attention. When she had ended he kept the same look during an interval of silent pondering. 'Is it the fellow who was over at Nice with you that day?'

She looked at him with surprise. 'How did you know?'

'Why, I liked his looks,' said Moffatt simply.

He got up and strolled toward the window. On the way he stopped before a table covered with showy trifles, and after looking at them for a moment singled out a dim old brown and golden book which Chelles had given her. He examined it lingeringly, as though it touched the spring of some choked-up sensibility for which he had no language. 'Say——' he began: it was the usual prelude to his enthusiasms; but he laid the book down and turned back.

'Then you think if you had the cash you could fix it up all right with the Pope?'

Her heart began to beat. She remembered that he had once put a job in Ralph's way, and had let her understand that he had done it partly for her sake.

'Well,' he continued, relapsing into hyperbole, 'I wish I could send the old gentleman my cheque to-morrow morning: but the fact is I'm high and dry.' He looked at her with a sudden odd intensity. 'If I *wasn't*, I dunno but what——' The phrase was lost in his familiar whistle. 'That's an awfully fetching way you do your hair,' he said.

It was a disappointment to Undine to hear that his affairs were not prospering, for she knew that in his world 'pull' and solvency were closely related, and that such support as she had hoped he might give her would be contingent on his own situation. But she had again a fleeting sense of his mysterious power of accomplishing things in the teeth of adversity; and she answered: 'What I want is your advice.'

He turned away and wandered across the room, his hands in his pockets. On her ornate writing desk he saw a photograph of Paul, bright-curled and sturdy-legged, in a manly reefer,* and bent over it with a murmur of approval. 'Say—what a fellow! Got him with you?'

Undine coloured. 'No——' she began; and seeing his look of surprise, she embarked on her usual explanation. 'I can't tell you how I miss him,' she ended, with a ring of truth that carried conviction to her own ears if not to Moffatt's.

'Why don't you get him back, then?'

'Why, I——'

Moffatt had picked up the frame and was looking at the photograph more closely. 'Pants!' he chuckled. 'I declare!'

He turned back to Undine. 'Who *does* he belong to, anyhow?'

'Belong to?'

'Who got him when you were divorced? Did you?'

'Oh, I got everything,' she said, her instinct of self-defense on the alert.

'So I thought.' He stood before her, stoutly planted on his short legs, and speaking with an aggressive energy. 'Well, I know what I'd do if he was mine.'

'If he was yours?'

'And you tried to get him away from me. Fight you to a finish! If it cost me down to my last dollar I would.'

The conversation seemed to be wandering from the point, and she answered, with a touch of impatience: 'It wouldn't cost you anything like that. I haven't got a dollar to fight back with.'

'Well, you ain't got to fight. Your decree gave him to you, didn't it? Why don't you send right over and get him? That's what I'd do if I was you.'

Undine looked up. 'But I'm awfully poor; I can't afford to have him here.'

'You couldn't, up to now; but now you're going to get married. You're going to be able to give him a home and a

father's care—and the foreign languages. That's what I'd say if
I was you . . . His father takes considerable stock in him, don't
he?'

She coloured, a denial on her lips; but she could not shape it.
'We're both awfully fond of him, of course . . . His father'd
never give him up!'

'Just so.' Moffatt's face had grown as sharp as glass. 'You've
got the Marvells running. All you've got to do's to sit tight and
wait for their cheque.' He dropped back to his equestrian seat on
the lyre-backed chair.

Undine stood up and moved uneasily toward the window.
She seemed to see her little boy as though he were in the room
with her; she did not understand how she could have lived
so long without him . . . She stood for a long time without
speaking, feeling behind her the concentrated irony of Moffatt's
gaze.

'You couldn't lend me the money—manage to borrow it for
me, I mean?' she finally turned back to ask.

He laughed. 'If I could manage to borrow any money at this
particular minute—well, I'd have to lend every dollar of it to
Elmer Moffatt, Esquire. I'm stone-broke, if you want to know.
And wanted for an Investigation too. That's why I'm over here
improving my mind.'

'Why, I thought you were going home next week?'

He grinned. 'I am, because I've found out there's a party
wants me to stay away worse than the courts want me back.
Making the trip just for my private satisfaction—there won't be
any money in it, I'm afraid.'

Leaden disappointment descended on Undine. She had felt
almost sure of Moffatt's helping her, and for an instant she
wondered if some long-smouldering jealousy had flamed up
under its cold cinders. But another look at his face denied her
this solace; and his evident indifference was the last blow to her
pride. The twinge it gave her prompted her to ask: 'Don't you
ever mean to get married?'

Moffatt gave her a quick look. 'Why, I shouldn't wonder—
one of these days. Millionaires always collect something; but
I've got to collect my millions first.'

He spoke coolly and half-humorously, and before he had ended she had lost all interest in his reply. He seemed aware of the fact, for he stood up and held out his hand.

'Well, so long, Mrs Marvell. It's been uncommonly pleasant to see you; and you'd better think over what I've said.'

She laid her hand sadly in his. 'You've never had a child,' she replied.

BOOK FOUR

XXXI

NEARLY two years had passed since Ralph Marvell, waking
from his long sleep in the hot summer light of Washington
Square, had found that the face of life was changed for him.

In the interval he had gradually adapted himself to the new
order of things; but the months of adaptation had been a time of
such darkness and confusion that, from the vantage-ground of
his recovered lucidity, he could not yet distinguish the stages by
which he had worked his way out; and even now his footing
was not secure.

His first effort had been to readjust his values—to take an
inventory of them, and reclassify them, so that one at least might
be made to appear as important as those he had lost; otherwise
there could be no reason why he should go on living. He
applied himself doggedly to this attempt; but whenever he
thought he had found a reason that his mind could rest in, it
gave way under him, and the old struggle for a foot-hold began
again. His two objects in life were his boy and his book. The
boy was incomparably the stronger argument, yet the less
serviceable in filling the void. Ralph felt his son all the while,
and all through his other feelings; but he could not think about
him actively and continuously, could not forever exercise his
eager empty dissatisfied mind on the relatively simple problem
of clothing, educating and amusing a little boy of six. Yet Paul's
existence was the all-sufficient reason for his own; and he turned
again, with a kind of cold fervour, to his abandoned literary
dream. Material needs obliged him to go on with his regular
business; but, the day's work over, he was possessed of a leisure
as bare and as blank as an unfurnished house, yet that was at least
his own to furnish as he pleased.

Meanwhile he was beginning to show a presentable face to
the world, and to be once more treated like a man in whose case
no one is particularly interested. His men friends ceased to say:

'Hallo, old chap, I never saw you looking fitter!' and elderly ladies no longer told him they were sure he kept too much to himself, and urged him to drop in any afternoon for a quiet talk. People left him to his sorrow as a man is left to an incurable habit, an unfortunate tie: they ignored it, or looked over its head if they happened to catch a glimpse of it at his elbow.

These glimpses were given to them more and more rarely. The smothered springs of life were bubbling up in Ralph, and there were days when he was glad to wake and see the sun in his window, and when he began to plan his book, and to fancy that the planning really interested him. He could even maintain the delusion for several days—for intervals each time appreciably longer—before it shrivelled up again in a scorching blast of disenchantment. The worst of it was that he could never tell when these hot gusts of anguish would overtake him. They came sometimes just when he felt most secure, when he was saying to himself: 'After all, things are really worth while——' sometimes even when he was sitting with Clare Van Degen, listening to her voice, watching her hands, and turning over in his mind the opening chapters of his book.

'You ought to write'; they had one and all said it to him from the first; and he fancied he might have begun sooner if he had not been urged on by their watchful fondness. Everybody wanted him to write—everybody had decided that he ought to, that he would, that he must be persuaded to; and the incessant imperceptible pressure of encouragement—the assumption of those about him that because it would be good for him to write he must naturally be able to—acted on his restive nerves as a stronger deterrent than disapproval.

Even Clare had fallen into the same mistake; and one day, as he sat talking with her on the verandah of Laura Fairford's house on the Sound—where they now most frequently met—Ralph had half-impatiently rejoined: 'Oh, if you think it's literature I need——!'

Instantly he had seen her face change, and the speaking hands tremble on her knee. But she achieved the feat of not answering him, or turning her steady eyes from the dancing mid-summer water at the foot of Laura's lawn. Ralph leaned a little nearer, and for an instant his hand imagined the flutter of hers. But instead of clasping it he drew back, and rising from his chair wandered away to the other end of the verandah . . . No, he didn't feel as Clare felt. If he loved her—as he sometimes thought he did—it was not in the same way. He had a great tenderness for her, he was more nearly happy with her than with any one else; he liked to sit and talk with her, and watch her face and her hands, and he wished there were some way—some different way—of letting her know it; but he could not conceive that tenderness and desire could ever again be one for him: such a notion as that seemed part of the monstrous sentimental muddle on which his life had gone aground.

'I shall write—of course I shall write some day,' he said, turning back to his seat. 'I've had a novel in the back of my head for years; and now's the time to pull it out.'

He hardly knew what he was saying; but before the end of the sentence he saw that Clare had understood what he meant to convey, and henceforth he felt committed to letting her talk to him as much as she pleased about his book. He himself, in consequence, took to thinking about it more consecutively; and just as his friends ceased to urge him to write, he sat down in earnest to begin.

The vision that had come to him had no likeness to any of his earlier imaginings. Two or three subjects had haunted him, pleading for expression, during the first years of his marriage; but these now seemed either too lyrical or too tragic. He no longer saw life on the heroic scale: he wanted to do something in which men should look no bigger than the insects they were. He contrived in the course of time to reduce one of his old subjects to these dimensions, and after nights of brooding he made a dash at it, and wrote an opening chapter that struck him as not too bad. In the exhilaration of this first attempt he spent some pleasant evenings revising and polishing his work; and gradually a feeling of authority and importance developed in him. In the morning, when he woke, instead of his habitual sense of lassitude, he felt an eagerness to be up and doing, and a conviction that his individual task was a necessary part of the world's machinery. He kept his secret with the beginner's deadly fear of losing his hold on his half-real creations if he let in any outer light on them; but he went about with a more

assured step, shrank less from meeting his friends, and even
began to dine out again, and to laugh at some of the jokes he
heard.

Laura Fairford, to get Paul away from town, had gone early to
the country; and Ralph, who went down to her every Saturday,
usually found Clare Van Degen there. Since his divorce he had
never entered his cousin's pinnacled palace; and Clare had never
asked him why he stayed away. This mutual silence had been
their sole allusion to Van Degen's share in the catastrophe,
though Ralph had spoken frankly of its other aspects. They
talked, however, most often of impersonal subjects—books,
pictures, plays, or whatever the world that interested them was
doing—and she showed no desire to draw him back to his own
affairs. She was again staying late in town—to have a pretext, as
he guessed, for coming down on Sundays to the Fairfords'—
and they often made the trip together in her motor; but he had
not yet spoken to her of having begun his book. One May
evening, however, as they sat alone in the verandah, he suddenly
told her that he was writing. As he spoke his heart beat like a
boy's; but once the words were out they gave him a feeling of
self-confidence, and he began to sketch his plan, and then to go
into its details. Clare listened devoutly, her eyes burning on him
through the dusk like the stars deepening above the garden; and
when she got up to go in he followed her with a new sense of
reassurance.

The dinner that evening was unusually pleasant. Charles
Bowen, just back from his usual spring travels, had come straight
down to his friends from the steamer; and the fund of impressions he brought with him gave Ralph a desire to be up
and wandering. And why not—when the book was done? He
smiled across the table at Clare.

'Next summer you'll have to charter a yacht, and take us all
off to the Aegean. We can't have Charles condescending to us
about the out-of-the-way places he's been seeing.'

Was it really he who was speaking, and his cousin who was
sending him back her dusky smile? Well—why not, again? The
seasons renewed themselves, and he too was putting out a new
growth. 'My book—my book—my book,' kept repeating itself
under all his thoughts, as Undine's name had once perpetually

murmured there. That night as he went up to bed he said to himself that he was actually ceasing to think about his wife . . .

As he passed Laura's door she called him in, and put her arms about him.

'You look so well, dear!'

'But why shouldn't I?' he answered gaily, as if ridiculing the fancy that he had ever looked otherwise. Paul was sleeping behind the next door, and the sense of the boy's nearness gave him a warmer glow. His little world was rounding itself out again, and once more he felt safe and at peace in its circle.

His sister looked as if she had something more to say; but she merely kissed him good night, and he went up whistling to his room.

The next morning he was to take a walk with Clare, and while he lounged about the drawing-room, waiting for her to come down, a servant came in with the Sunday papers. Ralph picked one up, and was absently unfolding it when his eye fell on his own name: a sight he had been spared since the last echoes of his divorce had subsided. His impulse was to fling the paper down, to hurl it as far from him as he could; but a grim fascination tightened his hold and drew his eyes back to the hated head-line.

NEW YORK BEAUTY WEDS FRENCH NOBLEMAN

Mrs Undine Marvell Confident Pope Will Annul Previous Marriage

MRS MARVELL TALKS ABOUT HER CASE

There it was before him in all its long-drawn horror—an 'interview'—an 'interview' of Undine's about her coming marriage! Ah, she talked about her case indeed! Her confidences filled the greater part of a column, and the only detail she seemed to have omitted was the name of her future husband, who was referred to by herself as 'my fiancé' and by the interviewer as 'the Count' or 'a prominent scion of the French nobility.'

Ralph heard Laura's step behind him. He threw the paper aside and their eyes met.

'Is this what you wanted to tell me last night?'

'Last night?—Is it in the papers?'

'Who told you? Bowen? What else has he heard?'

'Oh, Ralph, what does it matter—what can it matter?'

'Who's the man? Did he tell you that?' Ralph insisted. He saw her growing agitation. 'Why can't you answer? Is it any one I know?'

'He was told in Paris it was his friend Raymond de Chelles.'

Ralph laughed, and his laugh sounded in his own ears like an echo of the dreary mirth with which he had filled Mr Spragg's office the day he had learned that Undine intended to divorce him. But now his wrath was seasoned with a wholesome irony. The fact of his wife's having reached another stage in her ascent fell into its place as a part of the huge human buffoonery.

'Besides,' Laura went on, 'it's all perfect nonsense, of course. How in the world can she have her marriage annulled?'

Ralph pondered: this put the matter in another light. 'With a great deal of money I suppose she might.'

'Well, she certainly won't get that from Chelles. He's far from rich, Charles tells me.' Laura waited, watching him, before she risked: 'That's what convinces me she wouldn't have him if she could.'

Ralph shrugged. 'There may be other inducements. But she won't be able to manage it.' He heard himself speaking quite collectedly. Had Undine at last lost her power of wounding him?

Clare came in, dressed for their walk, and under Laura's anxious eyes he picked up the newspaper and held it out with a careless: 'Look at this!'

His cousin's glance flew down the column, and he saw the tremor of her lashes as she read. Then she lifted her head. 'But you'll be free!' Her face was as vivid as a flower.

'Free? I'm free now, as far as that goes!'

'Oh, but it will go so much farther when she has another name—when she's a different person altogether! Then you'll really have Paul to yourself.'

'Paul?' Laura intervened with a nervous laugh. 'But there's never been the least doubt about his having Paul!'

They heard the boy's laughter on the lawn, and she went out to join him. Ralph was still looking at his cousin.

'You're glad, then?' came from him involuntarily; and she startled him by bursting into tears. He bent over and kissed her on the cheek.

XXXII

RALPH, as the days passed, felt that Clare was right: if Undine married again he would possess himself more completely, be more definitely rid of his past. And he did not doubt that she would gain her end: he knew her violent desires and her cold tenacity. If she had failed to capture Van Degen it was probably because she lacked experience of that particular type of man, of his huge immediate wants and feeble vacillating purposes; most of all, because she had not yet measured the strength of the social considerations that restrained him. It was a mistake she was not likely to repeat, and her failure had probably been a useful preliminary to success. It was a long time since Ralph had allowed himself to think of her, and as he did so the overwhelming fact of her beauty became present to him again, no longer as an element of his being but as a power dispassionately estimated. He said to himself: 'Any man who can feel at all will feel it as I did'; and the conviction grew in him that Raymond de Chelles, of whom he had formed an idea through Bowen's talk, was not the man to give her up, even if she failed to obtain the release his religion exacted.

Meanwhile Ralph was gradually beginning to feel himself freer and lighter. Undine's act, by cutting the last link between them, seemed to have given him back to himself; and the mere fact that he could consider his case in all its bearings, impartially and ironically, showed him the distance he had travelled, the extent to which he had renewed himself. He had been moved, too, by Clare's cry of joy at his release. Though the nature of his feeling for her had not changed he was aware of a new quality in their friendship. When he went back to his book again his sense of power had lost its asperity, and the spectacle of life seemed less like a witless dangling of limp dolls. He was well on in his second chapter now.

This lightness of mood was still on him when, returning one afternoon to Washington Square, full of projects for a long evening's work, he found his mother awaiting him with a strange face. He followed her into the drawing-room, and she explained that there had been a telephone message she didn't understand—something perfectly crazy about Paul—of course it was all a mistake . . .

Ralph's first thought was of an accident, and his heart contracted. 'Did Laura telephone?'

'No, no; not Laura. It seemed to be a message from Mrs Spragg: something about sending some one here to fetch him—a queer name like Heeny—to fetch him to a steamer on Saturday. I was to be sure to have his things packed . . . but of course it's a misunderstanding . . .' She gave an uncertain laugh, and looked up at Ralph as though entreating him to return the reassurance she had given him.

'Of course, of course,' he echoed.

He made his mother repeat her statement; but the unforeseen always flurried her, and she was confused and inaccurate. She didn't actually know who had telephoned: the voice hadn't sounded like Mrs Spragg's . . . A woman's voice; yes—oh, not a lady's! And there was certainly something about a steamer . . . but he knew how the telephone bewildered her . . . and she was sure she was getting a little deaf. Hadn't he better call up the Malibran? Of course it was all a mistake—but . . . well, perhaps he *had* better go there himself . . .

As he reached the front door a letter clinked in the box, and he saw his name on an ordinary looking business envelope. He turned the door-handle, paused again, and stooped to take out the letter. It bore the address of the firm of lawyers who had represented Undine in the divorce proceedings and as he tore open the envelope Paul's name started out at him.

Mrs Marvell had followed him into the hall, and her cry broke the silence. 'Ralph—Ralph—is it anything she's done?'

'Nothing—it's nothing.' He stared at her. 'What's the day of the week?'

'Wednesday. Why, what——?' She suddenly seemed to understand. 'She's not going to take him away from us?'

Ralph dropped into a chair, crumpling the letter in his hand. He had been in a dream, poor fool that he was—a dream about his child! He sat gazing at the type-written phrases that spun themselves out before him. 'My client's circumstances now happily permitting . . . at last in a position to offer her son a home . . . long separation . . . a mother's feelings . . . every social and educational advantage' . . . and then, at the end, the poisoned dart that struck him speechless: 'The courts having awarded her the sole custody . . .'

The sole custody! But that meant that Paul was hers, hers only, hers for always: that his father had no more claim on him than any casual stranger in the street! And he, Ralph Marvell, a sane man, young, able-bodied, in full possession of his wits, had assisted at the perpetration of this abominable wrong, had passively forfeited his right to the flesh of his body, the blood of his being! But it couldn't be—of course it couldn't be. The preposterousness of it proved that it wasn't true. There was a mistake somewhere; a mistake his own lawyer would instantly rectify. If a hammer hadn't been drumming in his head he could have recalled the terms of the decree—but for the moment all the details of the agonizing episode were lost in a blur of uncertainty.

To escape his mother's silent anguish of interrogation he stood up and said: 'I'll see Mr Spragg—of course it's a mistake.' But as he spoke he retravelled the hateful months during the divorce proceedings, remembering his incomprehensible lassitude, his acquiescence in his family's determination to ignore the whole episode, and his gradual lapse into the same state of apathy. He recalled all the old family catchwords, the full and elaborate vocabulary of evasion: 'delicacy,' 'pride,' 'personal dignity,' 'preferring not to know about such things'; Mrs Marvell's: 'All I ask is that you won't mention the subject to your grandfather,' Mr Dagonet's: 'Spare your mother, Ralph, whatever happens,' and even Laura's terrified: 'Of course, for Paul's sake, there must be no scandal.'

For Paul's sake! And it was because, for Paul's sake, there must be no scandal, that he, Paul's father, had tamely abstained from defending his rights and contesting his wife's charges, and had thus handed the child over to her keeping!

As his cab whirled him up Fifth Avenue, Ralph's whole body throbbed with rage against the influences that had reduced him to such weakness. Then, gradually, he saw that the weakness was innate in him. He had been eloquent enough, in his free youth, against the conventions of his class; yet when the moment came to show his contempt for them they had mysteriously mastered him, deflecting his course like some hidden hereditary failing. As he looked back it seemed as though even his great disaster had been conventionalized and sentimentalized by this inherited attitude: that the thoughts he had thought about it were only those of generations of Dagonets, and that there had been nothing real and his own in his life but the foolish passion he had been trying so hard to think out of existence.

Halfway to the Malibran he changed his direction, and drove to the house of the lawyer he had consulted at the time of his divorce. The lawyer had not yet come up town, and Ralph had a half hour of bitter meditation before the sound of a latch-key brought him to his feet. The visit did not last long. His host, after an affable greeting, listened without surprise to what he had to say, and when he had ended reminded him with somewhat ironic precision that, at the time of the divorce, he had asked for neither advice nor information—had simply declared that he wanted to 'turn his back on the whole business' (Ralph recognized the phrase as one of his grandfather's), and, on hearing that in that case he had only to abstain from action, and was in no need of legal services, had gone away without farther enquiries.

'You led me to infer you had your reasons——' the slighted counsellor concluded; and, in reply to Ralph's breathless question, he subjoined, 'Why, you see, the case is closed, and I don't exactly know on what ground you can re-open it—unless, of course, you can bring evidence showing that the irregularity of the mother's life is such . . .'.

'She's going to marry again,' Ralph threw in.

'Indeed? Well, that in itself can hardly be described as irregular. In fact, in certain circumstances it might be construed as an advantage to the child.'

'Then I'm powerless?'

'Why—unless there's an ulterior motive—through which pressure might be brought to bear.'

'You mean that the first thing to do is to find out what she's up to?'

'Precisely. Of course, if it should prove to be a genuine case of maternal feeling, I won't conceal from you that the outlook's bad. At most, you could probably arrange to see your boy at stated intervals.'

To see his boy at stated intervals! Ralph wondered how a sane man could sit there, looking responsible and efficient, and talk such rubbish . . . As he got up to go the lawyer detained him to add: 'Of course there's no immediate cause for alarm. It will take time to enforce the provision of the Dakota decree in New York, and till it's done your son can't be taken from you. But there's sure to be a lot of nasty talk in the papers; and you're bound to lose in the end.'

Ralph thanked him and left.

He sped northward to the Malibran, where he learned that Mr and Mrs Spragg were at dinner. He sent his name down to the subterranean restaurant, and Mr Spragg presently appeared between the limp portières of the 'Adam' writing-room. He had grown older and heavier, as if illness instead of health had put more flesh on his bones, and there were greyish tints in the hollows of his face.

'What's this about Paul?' Ralph exclaimed. 'My mother's had a message we can't make out.'

Mr Spragg sat down, with the effect of immersing his spinal column in the depths of the arm-chair he selected. He crossed his legs, and swung one foot to and fro in its high wrinkled boot with elastic sides.

'Didn't you get a letter?' he asked.

'From my—from Undine's lawyers? Yes.' Ralph held it out. 'It's queer reading. She hasn't hitherto been very keen to have Paul with her.'

Mr Spragg, adjusting his glasses, read the letter slowly, restored it to the envelope and gave it back. 'My daughter has intimated that she wishes these gentlemen to act for her. I haven't received any additional instructions from her,' he said, with none of the curtness of tone that his stiff legal vocabulary implied.

'But the first communication I received was from you—at least from Mrs Spragg.'

Mr Spragg drew his beard through his hand. 'The ladies are apt to be a trifle hasty. I believe Mrs Spragg had a letter yesterday instructing her to select a reliable escort for Paul; and I suppose she thought——'

'Oh, this is all too preposterous!' Ralph burst out, springing from his seat. 'You don't for a moment imagine, do you—any of you—that I'm going to deliver up my son like a bale of goods in answer to any instructions in God's world?—Oh, yes, I know—I let him go—I abandoned my right to him . . . but I didn't know what I was doing . . . I was sick with grief and misery. My people were awfully broken up over the whole business, and I wanted to spare them. I wanted, above all, to spare my boy when he grew up. If I'd contested the case you know what the result would have been. I let it go by default—I made no conditions—all I wanted was to keep Paul, and never to let him hear a word against his mother!'

Mr Spragg received this passionate appeal in a silence that implied not so much disdain or indifference, as the total inability to deal verbally with emotional crises. At length, he said, a slight unsteadiness in his usually calm tones: 'I presume at the time it was optional with you to demand Paul's custody.'

'Oh, yes—it was optional,' Ralph sneered.

Mr Spragg looked at him compassionately. 'I'm sorry you didn't do it,' he said.

XXXIII

THE upshot of Ralph's visit was that Mr Spragg, after considerable deliberation, agreed, pending farther negotiations between the opposing lawyers, to undertake that no attempt should be made to remove Paul from his father's custody. Nevertheless, he seemed to think it quite natural that Undine, on the point of making a marriage which would put it in her power to give her child a suitable home, should assert her claim on him. It was more disconcerting to Ralph to learn that Mrs Spragg, for once departing from her attitude of passive impartiality, had eagerly abetted her daughter's move; he had somehow felt that Undine's desertion of the child had established a kind of mute understanding between himself and his mother-in-law.

'I thought Mrs Spragg would know there's no earthly use trying to take Paul from me,' he said with a desperate awkwardness of entreaty, and Mr Spragg startled him by replying: 'I presume his grandma thinks he'll belong to her more if we keep him in the family.'

Ralph, abruptly awakened from his dream of recovered peace, found himself confronted on every side by indifference or hostility: it was as though the June fields in which his boy was playing had suddenly opened to engulf him. Mrs Marvell's fears and tremors were almost harder to bear than the Spraggs' antagonism; and for the next few days Ralph wandered about miserably, dreading some fresh communication from Undine's lawyers, yet racked by the strain of hearing nothing more from them. Mr Spragg had agreed to cable his daughter asking her to await a letter before enforcing her demands; but on the fourth day after Ralph's visit to the Malibran a telephone message summoned him to his father-in-law's office.

Half an hour later their talk was over and he stood once more on the landing outside Mr Spragg's door. Undine's answer had come and Paul's fate was sealed. His mother refused to give him up, refused to await the arrival of her lawyer's letter, and reiterated, in more peremptory language, her demand that the child should be sent immediately to Paris in Mrs Heeny's care.

Mr Spragg, in face of Ralph's entreaties, remained pacific but remote. It was evident that, though he had no wish to quarrel with Ralph, he saw no reason for resisting Undine. 'I guess she's got the law on her side,' he said; and in response to Ralph's passionate remonstrances he added fatalistically: 'I presume you'll have to leave the matter to my daughter.'

Ralph had gone to the office resolved to control his temper and keep on the watch for any shred of information he might glean; but it soon became clear that Mr Spragg knew as little as himself of Undine's projects, or of the stage her plans had reached. All she had apparently vouchsafed her parent was the statement that she intended to re-marry, and the command to send Paul over; and Ralph reflected that his own betrothal to her had probably been announced to Mr Spragg in the same curt fashion.

The thought brought back an overwhelming sense of the past. One by one the details of that incredible moment revived, and he felt in his veins the glow of rapture with which he had first approached the dingy threshold he was now leaving. There came back to him with peculiar vividness the memory of his rushing up to Mr Spragg's office to consult him about a necklace for Undine. Ralph recalled the incident because his eager appeal for advice had been received by Mr Spragg with the very phrase he had just used: 'I presume you'll have to leave the matter to my daughter.'

Ralph saw him slouching in his chair, swung sideways from the untidy desk, his legs stretched out, his hands in his pockets, his jaws engaged on the phantom tooth-pick; and, in a corner of the office, the figure of a middle-sized red-faced young man who seemed to have been interrupted in the act of saying something disagreeable.

'Why, it must have been then that I first saw Moffatt,' Ralph reflected; and the thought suggested the memory of other, subsequent meetings in the same building, and of frequent ascents to Moffatt's office during the ardent weeks of their mysterious and remunerative 'deal.'

Ralph wondered if Moffatt's office were still in the Ararat; and on the way out he paused before the black tablet affixed to the wall of the vestibule and sought and found the name in its familiar place.

The next moment he was again absorbed in his own cares. Now that he had learned the imminence of Paul's danger, and the futility of pleading for delay, a thousand fantastic projects were contending in his head. To get the boy away—that seemed the first thing to do: to put him out of reach, and then invoke the law, get the case re-opened, and carry the fight from court to court till his rights should be recognized. It would cost a lot of money—well, the money would have to be found. The first step was to secure the boy's temporary safety; after that, the question of ways and means would have to be considered . . . Had there ever been a time, Ralph wondered, when that question hadn't been at the root of all the others?

He had promised to let Clare Van Degen know the result of his visit, and half an hour later he was in her drawing-room. It was the first time he had entered it since his divorce; but Van Degen was tarpon-fishing* in California—and besides, he had to see Clare. His one relief was in talking to her, in feverishly turning over with her every possibility of delay and obstruction; and he marvelled at the intelligence and energy she brought to the discussion of these questions. It was as if she had never before felt strongly enough about anything to put her heart or her brains into it; but now everything in her was at work for him.

She listened intently to what he told her; then she said: 'You tell me it will cost a great deal; but why take it to the courts at all? Why not give the money to Undine instead of to your lawyers?'

Ralph looked at her in surprise, and she continued: 'Why do you suppose she's suddenly made up her mind she must have Paul?'

'That's comprehensible enough to any one who knows her. She wants him because he'll give her the appearance of respectability. Having him with her will prove, as no mere assertions can, that all the rights are on her side and the "wrongs" on mine.'

Clare considered. 'Yes; that's the obvious answer. But shall I tell you what I think, my dear? You and I are both completely out-of-date. I don't believe Undine cares a straw for "the appearance of respectability." What she wants is the money for her annulment.'

Ralph uttered an incredulous exclamation. 'But don't you see?' she hurried on. 'It's her only hope—her last chance. She's much too clever to burden herself with the child merely to annoy you. What she wants is to make you buy him back from her.' She stood up and came to him with outstretched hands. 'Perhaps I can be of use to you at last!'

'You?' He summoned up a haggard smile. 'As if you weren't always—letting me load you with all my bothers!'

'Oh, if only I've hit on the way out of this one! Then there wouldn't be any others left!' Her eyes followed him intently as he turned away to the window and stood staring down at the sultry prospect of Fifth Avenue. As he turned over her conjecture its probability became more and more apparent. It put into logical relation all the incoherencies of Undine's recent conduct, completed and defined her anew as if a sharp line had been drawn about her fading image.

'If it's that, I shall soon know,' he said, turning back into the room. His course had instantly become plain. He had only to resist and Undine would have to show her hand. Simultaneously with this thought there sprang up in his mind the remembrance of the autumn afternoon in Paris when he had come home and found her, among her half-packed finery, desperately bewailing her coming motherhood.

Clare's touch was on his arm. 'If I'm right—you *will* let me help?'

He laid his hand on hers without speaking, and she went on:

'It will take a lot of money: all these law-suits do. Besides, she'd be ashamed to sell him cheap. You must be ready to give her anything she wants. And I've got a lot saved up—money of my own, I mean . . .'

'Your own?' As he looked at her the rare blush rose under her brown skin.

'My very own. Why shouldn't you believe me? I've been hoarding up my scrap of an income for years, thinking that some day I'd find I couldn't stand this any longer . . .' Her gesture embraced their sumptuous setting. 'But now I know I shall never budge. There are the children; and besides, things are easier for me since——' she paused, embarrassed.

'Yes, yes; I know.' He felt like completing her phrase: 'Since my wife has furnished you with the means of putting pressure on your husband——' but he simply repeated: 'I know.'

'And you *will* let me help?'

'Oh, we must get at the facts first.' He caught her hands in his with sudden energy. 'As you say, when Paul's safe there won't be another bother left!'

XXXIV

THE means of raising the requisite amount of money became, during the next few weeks, the anxious theme of all Ralph's thoughts. His lawyers' enquiries soon brought the confirmation of Clare's surmise, and it became clear that—for reasons swathed in all the ingenuities of legal verbiage—Undine might, in return for a substantial consideration, be prevailed on to admit that it was for her son's advantage to remain with his father.

The day this admission was communicated to Ralph his first impulse was to carry the news to his cousin. His mood was one of pure exaltation; he seemed to be hugging his boy to him as he walked. Paul and he were to belong to each other forever: no mysterious threat of separation could ever menace them again! He had the blissful sense of relief that the child himself might have had on waking out of a frightened dream and finding the jolly daylight in his room.

Clare at once renewed her entreaty to be allowed to aid in ransoming her little cousin, but Ralph tried to put her off by explaining that he meant to 'look about.'

'Look where? In the Dagonet coffers? Oh, Ralph, what's the use of pretending? Tell me what you've got to give her.' It was amazing how his cousin suddenly dominated him. But as yet he couldn't go into the details of the bargain. That the reckoning between himself and Undine should be settled in dollars and cents seemed the last bitterest satire on his dreams: he felt himself miserably diminished by the smallness of what had filled his world.

Nevertheless, the looking about had to be done; and a day came when he found himself once more at the door of Elmer Moffatt's office. His thoughts had been drawn back to Moffatt by the insistence with which the latter's name had lately been put forward by the press in connection with a revival of the Ararat investigation. Moffatt, it appeared, had been regarded as one of the most valuable witnesses for the State; his return from Europe had been anxiously awaited, his unreadiness to testify caustically criticized; then at last he had arrived, had gone on to Washington—and had apparently had nothing to tell.

Ralph was too deep in his own troubles to waste any wonder over this anticlimax; but the frequent appearance of Moffatt's name in the morning papers acted as an unconscious suggestion. Besides, to whom else could he look for help? The sum his wife demanded could be acquired only by 'a quick turn,' and the fact that Ralph had once rendered the same kind of service to Moffatt made it natural to appeal to him now. The market, moreover, happened to be booming, and it seemed not unlikely that so experienced a speculator might have a 'good thing' up his sleeve.

Moffatt's office had been transformed since Ralph's last visit. Paint, varnish and brass railings gave an air of opulence to the outer precincts, and the inner room, with its mahogany bookcases containing morocco-bound 'sets' and its wide blue leather arm-chairs, lacked only a palm or two to resemble the lounge of a fashionable hotel. Moffatt himself, as he came forward, gave Ralph the impression of having been done over by the same hand: he was smoother, broader, more supremely tailored, and his whole person exhaled the faintest whiff of an expensive scent.

He installed his visitor in one of the blue arm-chairs, and sitting opposite, an elbow on his impressive 'Washington' desk, listened attentively while Ralph made his request.

'You want to be put onto something good in a damned hurry?' Moffatt twisted his moustache between two plump square-tipped fingers with a little black growth on their lower joints. 'I don't suppose,' he remarked, 'there's a sane man between here and San Francisco who isn't consumed by that yearning.'

Having permitted himself this pleasantry he passed on to business. 'Yes—it's a first-rate time to buy: no doubt of that. But you say you want to make a quick turn-over? Heard of a soft thing that won't wait, I presume? That's apt to be the way with soft things—all kinds of 'em. There's always other fellows after them.' Moffatt's smile was playful. 'Well, I'd go considerably out of my way to do you a good turn, because you did me one when I needed it mighty bad. "In youth you sheltered me."* Yes, sir, that's the kind I am.' He stood up, sauntered to the other side of the room, and took a small object from the top of the bookcase.

'Fond of these pink crystals?' He held the oriental toy against the light. 'Oh, I ain't a judge—but now and then I like to pick up a pretty thing.' Ralph noticed that his eyes caressed it.

'Well—now let's talk. You say you've got to have the funds for your—your investment within three weeks. That's quick work. And you want a hundred thousand. Can you put up fifty?'

Ralph had been prepared for the question, but when it came he felt a moment's tremor. He knew he could count on half the amount from his grandfather; could possibly ask Fairford for a small additional loan—but what of the rest? Well, there was Clare. He had always known there would be no other way. And after all, the money was Clare's—it was Dagonet money. At least she said it was. All the misery of his predicament was distilled into the short silence that preceded his answer: 'Yes— I think so.'

'Well, I guess I can double it for you.' Moffatt spoke with an air of Olympian modesty. 'Anyhow, I'll try. Only don't tell the other girls!'

He proceeded to develop his plan to ears which Ralph tried to make alert and attentive, but in which perpetually, through the intricate concert of facts and figures, there broke the shout of a small boy racing across a suburban lawn. 'When I pick him up to-night he'll be mine for good!' Ralph thought as Moffatt summed up: 'There's the whole scheme in a nutshell; but you'd better think it over. I don't want to let you in for anything you ain't quite sure about.'

'Oh, if you're sure——' Ralph was already calculating the time it would take to dash up to Clare Van Degen's on his way to catch the train for the Fairfords'.

His impatience made it hard to pay due regard to Moffatt's parting civilities. 'Glad to have seen you,' he heard the latter assuring him with a final hand-grasp. 'Wish you'd dine with me some evening at my club'; and, as Ralph murmured a vague acceptance: 'How's that boy of yours, by the way?' Moffatt continued. 'He was a stunning chap last time I saw him.—

Excuse me if I've put my foot in it; but I understood you kept him with you . . . ? Yes: that's what I thought . . . Well, so long.'

Clare's inner sitting-room was empty; but the servant, presently returning, led Ralph into the gilded and tapestried wilderness where she occasionally chose to receive her visitors. There, under Popple's effigy of herself, she sat, small and alone, on a monumental sofa behind a tea-table laden with gold plate; while from his lofty frame, on the opposite wall Van Degen, portrayed by a 'powerful' artist, cast on her the satisfied eye of proprietorship.

Ralph, swept forward on the blast of his excitement, felt as in a dream the frivolous perversity of her receiving him in such a setting instead of in their usual quiet corner; but there was no room in his mind for anything but the cry that broke from him: 'I believe I've done it!'

He sat down and explained to her by what means, trying, as best he could, to restate the particulars of Moffatt's deal; and her manifest ignorance of business methods had the effect of making his vagueness appear less vague.

'Anyhow, he seems to be sure it's a safe thing. I understand he's in with Rolliver now, and Rolliver practically controls Apex. This is some kind of a scheme to buy up all the works of public utility at Apex. They're practically sure of their charter, and Moffatt tells me I can count on doubling my investment within a few weeks. Of course I'll go into the details if you like——'

'Oh, no; you've made it all so clear to me!' She really made him feel he had. 'And besides, what on earth does it matter? The great things is that it's done.' She lifted her sparkling eyes. 'And now—my share—you haven't told me . . .'

He explained that Mr Dagonet, to whom he had already named the amount demanded, had at once promised him twenty-five thousand dollars, to be eventually deducted from his share of the estate. His mother had something put by that she insisted on contributing; and Henley Fairford, of his own accord, had come forward with ten thousand: it was awfully decent of Henley . . .

'Even Henley!' Clare sighed. 'Then I'm the only one left out?'

Ralph felt the colour in his face. 'Well, you see, I shall need as much as fifty——'

Her hands flew together joyfully. 'But then you've got to let me help! Oh, I'm so glad—so glad! I've twenty thousand waiting.'

He looked about the room, checked anew by all its oppressive implications. 'You're a darling . . . but I couldn't take it.'

'I've told you it's mine, every penny of it!'

'Yes; but supposing things went wrong?'

'Nothing *can*—if you'll only take it . . .'

'I may lose it——'

'*I* sha'n't, if I've given it to you!' Her look followed his about the room and then came back to him. 'Can't you imagine all it will make up for?'

The rapture of the cry caught him up with it. Ah, yes, he could imagine it all! He stooped his head above her hands. 'I accept,' he said; and they stood and looked at each other like radiant children.

She followed him to the door, and as he turned to leave he broke into a laugh. 'It's queer, though, its happening in this room!'

She was close beside him, her hand on the heavy tapestry curtaining the door; and her glance shot past him to her husband's portrait. Ralph caught the look, and a flood of old tendernesses and hates welled up in him. He drew her under the portrait and kissed her vehemently.

XXXV

WITHIN forty-eight hours Ralph's money was in Moffatt's hands, and the interval of suspense had begun.

The transaction over, he felt the deceptive buoyancy that follows on periods of painful indecision. It seemed to him that now at last life had freed him from all trammelling delusions, leaving him only the best thing in its gift—his boy.

The things he meant Paul to do and to be filled his fancy with happy pictures. The child was growing more and more interesting—throwing out countless tendrils of feeling and perception that delighted Ralph but preoccupied the watchful Laura.

'He's going to be exactly like you, Ralph——' she paused and then risked it: 'For his own sake, I wish there were just a drop or two of Spragg in him.'

Ralph laughed, understanding her. 'Oh, the plodding citizen I've become will keep him from taking after the lyric idiot who begot him. Paul and I, between us, are going to turn out something first-rate.'

His book too was spreading and throwing out tendrils, and he worked at it in the white heat of energy which his factitious exhilaration produced. For a few weeks everything he did and said seemed as easy and unconditioned as the actions in a dream.

Clare Van Degen, in the light of this mood, became again the comrade of his boyhood. He did not see her often, for she had gone down to the country with her children, but they communicated daily by letter or telephone, and now and then she came over to the Fairfords' for a night. There they renewed the long rambles of their youth, and once more the summer fields and woods seemed full of magic presences. Clare was no more intelligent, she followed him no farther in his flights; but some of the qualities that had become most precious to him were as native to her as its perfume to a flower. So, through the long June afternoons, they ranged together over many themes; and if her answers sometimes missed the mark it did not matter, because her silences never did.

Meanwhile Ralph, from various sources, continued to pick up a good deal of more or less contradictory information about Elmer Moffatt. It seemed to be generally understood that Moffatt had come back from Europe with the intention of testifying in the Ararat investigation, and that his former patron, the great Harmon B. Driscoll, had managed to silence him; and it was implied that the price of this silence, which was set at a considerable figure, had been turned to account in a series of speculations likely to lift Moffatt to permanent eminence among the rulers of Wall Street. The stories as to his latest achievement, and the theories as to the man himself, varied with the visual angle of each reporter: and whenever any attempt was made to focus his hard sharp personality some guardian divinity seemed to throw a veil of mystery over him. His detractors, however, were the first to own that there was 'something about him'; it was felt that he had passed beyond the meteoric stage, and the business world was unanimous in recognizing that he had 'come to stay.' A dawning sense of his stability was even beginning to make itself felt in Fifth Avenue. It was said that he had bought a house in Seventy-second Street, then that he meant to build near the Park; one or two people (always 'taken by a friend') had been to his flat in the Pactolus, to see his Chinese porcelains and Persian rugs; now and then he had a few important men to dine at a Fifth Avenue restaurant; his name began to appear in philanthropic reports and on municipal committees (there were even rumours of its having been put up at a well-known club); and the rector of a wealthy parish, who was raising funds for a chantry, was known to have met him at dinner and to have stated afterward that 'the man was not wholly a materialist.'

All these converging proofs of Moffatt's solidity strengthened Ralph's faith in his venture. He remembered with what astuteness and authority Moffatt had conducted their real estate transaction—how far off and unreal it all seemed!—and awaited events with the passive faith of a sufferer in the hands of a skilful surgeon.

The days moved on toward the end of June, and each morning Ralph opened his newspaper with a keener thrill of expectation. Any day now he might read of the granting of the Apex charter: Moffatt had assured him it would 'go through' before the close of the month. But the announcement did not appear, and after what seemed to Ralph a decent lapse of time he telephoned to ask for news. Moffatt was away, and when he came back a few days later he answered Ralph's enquiries evasively, with an edge of irritation in his voice. The same day Ralph received a letter from his lawyer, who had been reminded by Mrs Marvell's representatives that the latest date agreed on for the execution of the financial agreement was the end of the following week.

Ralph, alarmed, betook himself at once to the Ararat, and his first glimpse of Moffatt's round common face and fastidiously dressed person gave him an immediate sense of reassurance. He felt that under the circle of baldness on top of that carefully brushed head lay the solution of every monetary problem that could beset the soul of man. Moffatt's voice had recovered its usual cordial note, and the warmth of his welcome dispelled Ralph's last apprehension.

'Why, yes, everything's going along first-rate. They thought they'd hung us up last week—but they haven't. There may be another week's delay; but we ought to be opening a bottle of wine on it by the Fourth.'

An office-boy came in with a name on a slip of paper, and Moffatt looked at his watch and held out a hearty hand. 'Glad you came. Of course I'll keep you posted . . . No, this way . . . Look in again . . .' and he steered Ralph out by another door.

July came, and passed into its second week. Ralph's lawyer had obtained a postponement from the other side, but Undine's representatives had given him to understand that the transaction must be closed before the first of August. Ralph telephoned once or twice to Moffatt, receiving genially-worded assurances that everything was 'going their way'; but he felt a certain embarrassment in returning again to the office, and let himself drift through the days in a state of hungry apprehension. Finally one afternoon Henley Fairford, coming back from town (which Ralph had left in the morning to join his boy over Sunday), brought word that the Apex consolidation scheme had failed to get its charter. It was useless to attempt to reach Moffatt on Sunday, and Ralph wore on as he could through the succeeding twenty-four hours. Clare Van Degen had come down to stay with her youngest boy, and in the afternoon she and Ralph took the two children for a sail. A light breeze brightened the waters of the Sound, and they ran down the shore before it and then tacked out toward the sunset, coming back at last, under a failing breeze, as the summer sky passed from blue to a translucid green and then into the accumulating greys of twilight.

As they left the landing and walked up behind the children across the darkening lawn, a sense of security descended again on Ralph. He could not believe that such a scene and such a mood could be the disguise of any impending evil, and all his doubts and anxieties fell away from him.

The next morning, he and Clare travelled up to town together, and at the station he put her in the motor which was to take her to Long Island, and hastened down to Moffatt's office. When he arrived he was told that Moffatt was 'engaged,' and he had to wait for nearly half an hour in the outer office, where, to the steady click of the type-writer and the spasmodic buzzing of the telephone, his thoughts again began their restless circlings. Finally the inner door opened, and he found himself in the sanctuary. Moffatt was seated behind his desk, examining another little crystal vase somewhat like the one he had shown Ralph a few weeks earlier. As his visitor entered, he held it up against the light, revealing on its dewy sides an incised design as frail as the shadow of grass-blades on water.

'Ain't she a peach?' He put the toy down and reached across the desk to shake hands. 'Well, well,' he went on, leaning back in his chair, and pushing out his lower lip in a half-comic pout, 'they've got us in the neck this time and no mistake. Seen this morning's *Radiator*? I don't know how the thing leaked out—but the reformers somehow got a smell of the scheme, and whenever they get swishing round something's bound to get spilt.'

He talked gaily, genially, in his roundest tones and with his easiest gestures; never had he conveyed a completer sense of unhurried power; but Ralph noticed for the first time the crow's-feet about his eyes, and the sharpness of the contrast between the white of his forehead and the redness of the fold of neck above his collar.

'Do you mean to say it's not going through?'

'Not this time, anyhow. We're high and dry.'

Something seemed to snap in Ralph's head, and he sat down in the nearest chair. 'Has the common stock dropped a lot?'

'Well, you've got to lean over to see it.' Moffatt pressed his finger-tips together and added thoughtfully: 'But it's *there* all right. We're bound to get our charter in the end.'

'What do you call the end?'

'Oh, before the Day of Judgment, sure: next year, I guess.'

'Next year?' Ralph flushed. 'What earthly good will that do me?'

'I don't say it's as pleasant as driving your best girl home by moonlight. But that's how it is. And the stuff's safe enough any way—I've told you that right along.'

'But you've told me all along I could count on a rise before August. You knew I had to have the money now.'

'I knew you *wanted* to have the money now; and so did I, and several of my friends. I put you onto it because it was the only thing in sight likely to give you the return you wanted.'

'You ought at least to have warned me of the risk!'

'Risk? I don't call it much of a risk to lie back in your chair and wait another few months for fifty thousand to drop into your lap. I tell you the thing's as safe as a bank.'

'How do I know it is? You've misled me about it from the first.'

Moffatt's face grew dark red to the forehead: for the first time in their acquaintance Ralph saw him on the verge of anger.

'Well, if you get stuck so do I. I'm in it a good deal deeper than you. That's about the best guarantee I can give; unless you won't take my word for that either.' To control himself Moffatt spoke with extreme deliberation, separating his syllables like a machine cutting something into even lengths.

Ralph listened through a cloud of confusion; but he saw the madness of offending Moffatt, and tried to take a more conciliatory tone. 'Of course I take your word for it. But I can't—I simply can't afford to lose . . .'

'You ain't going to lose: I don't believe you'll even have to put up any margin. It's *there* safe enough, I tell you . . .'

'Yes, yes; I understand. I'm sure you wouldn't have advised me——' Ralph's tongue seemed swollen, and he had difficulty in bringing out the words. 'Only, you see—I can't wait; it's not possible; and I want to know if there isn't a way——'

Moffatt looked at him with a sort of resigned compassion, as a doctor looks at a despairing mother who will not understand what he has tried to imply without uttering the word she dreads. Ralph understood the look, but hurried on.

'You'll think I'm mad, or an ass, to talk like this; but the fact is, I must have the money.' He waited and drew a hard breath. 'I must have it: that's all. Perhaps I'd better tell you——'

Moffatt, who had risen, as if assuming that the interview was over, sat down again and turned an attentive look on him. 'Go ahead,' he said, more humanly than he had hitherto spoken.

'My boy . . . you spoke of him the other day . . . I'm awfully fond of him——' Ralph broke off, deterred by the impossibility of confiding his feeling for Paul to this coarse-grained man with whom he hadn't a sentiment in common.

Moffatt was still looking at him. 'I should say you would be! He's as smart a little chap as I ever saw; and I guess he's the kind that gets better every day.'

Ralph had collected himself, and went on with sudden resolution: 'Well, you see—when my wife and I separated, I never dreamed she'd want the boy: the question never came up. If it had, of course—but she'd left him with me when she went away two years before, and at the time of the divorce I was a fool . . . I didn't take the proper steps . . .'

'You mean she's got sole custody?'

Ralph made a sign of assent, and Moffatt pondered. 'That's bad—bad.'

'And now I understand she's going to marry again—and of course I can't give up my son.'

'She's wants you to, eh?'

Ralph again assented.

Moffatt swung his chair about and leaned back in it, stretching out his plump legs and contemplating the tips of his varnished boots. He hummed a low tune behind inscrutable lips.

'That's what you want the money for?' he finally raised his head to ask.

The word came out of the depths of Ralph's anguish: 'Yes.'

'And why you want it in such a hurry. I see.' Moffatt reverted to the study of his boots. 'It's a lot of money.'

'Yes. That's the difficulty. And I . . . she . . .'

Ralph's tongue was again too thick for his mouth. 'I'm afraid she won't wait . . . or take less . . .'

Moffatt, abandoning the boots, was scrutinizing him through half-shut lids. 'No,' he said slowly, 'I don't believe Undine Spragg'll take a single cent less.'

Ralph felt himself whiten. Was it insolence or ignorance that had prompted Moffatt's speech? Nothing in his voice or face showed the sense of any shades of expression or of feeling: he seemed to apply to everything the measure of the same crude flippancy. But such considerations could not curb Ralph now. He said to himself 'Keep your temper—keep your temper——' and his anger suddenly boiled over.

'Look here, Moffatt,' he said, getting to his feet, 'the fact that I've been divorced from Mrs Marvell doesn't authorize any one to take that tone to me in speaking of her.'

Moffatt met the challenge with a calm stare under which there were dawning signs of surprise and interest. 'That so? Well, if that's the case I presume I ought to feel the same way: I've been divorced from her myself.'

For an instant the words conveyed no meaning to Ralph; then they surged up into his brain and flung him forward with half-raised arm. But he felt the grotesqueness of the gesture and his arm dropped back to his side. A series of unimportant and irrelevant things raced through his mind; then obscurity settled down on it. '*This* man . . . *this* man . . .' was the one fiery point in his darkened consciousness . . . 'What on earth are you talking about?' he brought out.

'Why, facts,' said Moffatt, in a cool half-humorous voice. 'You didn't know? I understood from Mrs Marvell your folks had a prejudice against divorce, so I suppose she kept quiet about that early episode. The truth is,' he continued amicably, 'I wouldn't have alluded to it now if you hadn't taken rather a high tone with me about our little venture; but now it's out I guess you may as well hear the whole story. It's mighty wholesome for a man to have a round now and then with a few facts. Shall I go on?'

Ralph had stood listening without a sign, but as Moffatt ended he made a slight motion of acquiescence. He did not otherwise change his attitude, except to grasp with one hand the back of the chair that Moffatt pushed toward him.

'Rather stand? . . .' Moffatt himself dropped back into his seat and took the pose of easy narrative. 'Well, it was this way. Undine Spragg and I were made one at Opake, Nebraska, just nine years ago last month. My! She was a beauty then. Nothing

much had happened to her before but being engaged for a year
or two to a soft called Millard Binch; the same she passed on to
Indiana Rolliver; and—well, I guess she liked the change. We
didn't have what you'd called a society wedding: no best man or
bridesmaids or Voice that Breathed o'er Eden.* Fact is, Pa and
Ma didn't know about it till it was over. But it was a marriage
fast enough, as they found out when they tried to undo it.
Trouble was, they caught on too soon; we only had a fortnight.
Then they hauled Undine back to Apex, and—well, I hadn't
the cash or the pull to fight 'em. Uncle Abner was a pretty big
man out there then; and he had James J. Rolliver behind him.
I always know when I'm licked; and I was licked that time. So
we unlooped the loop, and they fixed it up for me to make a trip
to Alaska. Let me see—that was the year before they moved
over to New York. Next time I saw Undine I sat alongside of
her at the theatre the day your engagement was announced.'

He still kept to his half-humorous minor key, as though he
were in the first stages of an after-dinner speech; but as he went
on his bodily presence, which hitherto had seemed to Ralph the
mere average garment of vulgarity, began to loom, huge and
portentous as some monster released from a magician's bottle.
His redness, his glossiness, his baldness, and the carefully brushed
ring of hair encircling it; the square line of his shoulders, the too
careful fit of his clothes, the prominent lustre of his scarf-pin, the
growth of short black hair on his manicured hands, even the tiny
cracks and crow's-feet beginning to show in the hard close
surface of his complexion: all these solid witnesses to his reality
and his proximity pressed on Ralph with the mounting pang of
physical nausea.

'*This* man . . . *this* man . . .' he couldn't get beyond the
thought: whichever way he turned his haggard thought, there
was Moffatt bodily blocking the perspective . . . Ralph's eyes
roamed toward the crystal toy that stood on the desk beside
Moffatt's hand. Faugh! That such a hand should have touched it!

Suddenly he heard himself speaking. 'Before my marriage—
did you know they hadn't told me?'

'Why, I understood as much . . .'

Ralph pushed on: 'You knew it the day I met you in Mr
Spragg's office?'

Moffatt considered a moment, as if the incident had escaped him. 'Did we meet there?' He seemed benevolently ready for enlightenment. But Ralph had been assailed by another memory; he recalled that Moffatt had dined one night in his house, that he and the man who now faced him had sat at the same table, their wife between them . . .

He was seized with another dumb gust of fury; but it died out and left him face to face with the uselessness, the irrelevance of all the old attitudes of appropriation and defiance. He seemed to be stumbling about in his inherited prejudices like a modern man in mediæval armour . . . Moffatt still sat at his desk, unmoved and apparently uncomprehending. 'He doesn't even know what I'm feeling,' flashed through Ralph; and the whole archaic structure of his rites and sanctions tumbled down about him.

Through the noise of the crash he heard Moffatt's voice going on without perceptible change of tone: 'About that other matter now . . . you can't feel any meaner about it than I do, I can tell you that . . . but all we've got to do is to sit tight . . .'

Ralph turned from the voice, and found himself outside on the landing, and then in the street below.

XXXVI

HE stood at the corner of Wall Street, looking up and down its hot summer perspective. He noticed the swirls of dust in the cracks of the pavement, the rubbish in the gutters, the ceaseless stream of perspiring faces that poured by under tilted hats.

He found himself, next, slipping northward between the glazed walls of the Subway, another languid crowd in the seats about him and the nasal yelp of the stations ringing through the car like some repeated ritual wail. The blindness within him seemed to have intensified his physical perceptions, his sensitiveness to the heat, the noise, the smells of the dishevelled midsummer city; but combined with the acuter perception of these offenses was a complete indifference to them, as though he were some vivisected animal deprived of the power of discrimination.

Now he had turned into Waverly Place, and was walking westward toward Washington Square. At the corner he pulled himself up, saying half-aloud: 'The office—I ought to be at the office.' He drew out his watch and stared at it blankly. What the devil had he taken it out for? He had to go through a laborious process of readjustment to find out what it had to say . . . Twelve o'clock . . . Should he turn back to the office? It seemed easier to cross the square, go up the steps of the old house and slip his key into the door . . .

The house was empty. His mother, a few days previously, had departed with Mr Dagonet for their usual two months on the Maine coast, where Ralph was to join them with his boy . . . The blinds were all drawn down, and the freshness and silence of the marble-paved hall laid soothing hands on him . . . He said to himself: 'I'll jump into a cab presently, and go and lunch at the club——' He laid down his hat and stick and climbed the carpetless stairs to his room. When he entered it he had the shock of feeling himself in a strange place: it did not seem like anything he had ever seen before. Then, one by one, all the old stale usual things in it confronted him, and he longed with a sick intensity to be in a place that was really strange.

'How on earth can I go on living here?' he wondered.

A careless servant had left the outer shutters open, and the sun was beating on the window-panes. Ralph pushed open the windows, shut the shutters, and wandered toward his arm-chair. Beads of perspiration stood on his forehead: the temperature of the room reminded him of the heat under the ilexes of the Sienese villa where he and Undine had sat through a long July afternoon. He saw her before him, leaning against the tree-trunk in her white dress, limpid and inscrutable . . . 'We were made one at Opake, Nebraska . . .' Had she been thinking of it that afternoon at Siena, he wondered? Did she ever think of it at all? . . . It was she who had asked Moffatt to dine. She had said: 'Father brought him home one day at Apex . . . I don't remember ever having seen him since'—and the man she spoke of had had her in his arms . . . and perhaps it was really all she remembered!

She had lied to him—lied to him from the first . . . there hadn't been a moment when she hadn't lied to him, deliberately, ingeniously and inventively. As he thought of it, there came to him, for the first time in months, that overwhelming sense of her physical nearness which had once so haunted and tortured him. Her freshness, her fragrance, the luminous haze of her youth, filled the room with a mocking glory; and he dropped his head on his hands to shut it out . . .

The vision was swept away by another wave of hurrying thoughts. He felt it was intensely important that he should keep the thread of every one of them, that they all represented things to be said or done, or guarded against; and his mind, with the unwondering versatility and tireless haste of the dreamer's brain, seemed to be pursuing them all simultaneously. Then they became as unreal and meaningless as the red specks dancing behind the lids against which he had pressed his fists clenched, and he had the feeling that if he opened his eyes they would vanish, and the familiar daylight look in on him . . .

A knock disturbed him. The old parlour-maid who was always left in charge of the house had come up to ask if he wasn't well, and if there was anything she could do for him. He told her no . . . he was perfectly well . . . or, rather, no, he wasn't . . . he supposed it must be the heat; and he began to scold her for having forgotten to close the shutters.

It wasn't her fault, it appeared, but Eliza's: her tone implied that he knew what one had to expect of Eliza . . . and wouldn't he go down to the nice cool shady dining-room, and let her make him an iced drink and a few sandwiches?

'I've always told Mrs Marvell I couldn't turn my back for a second but what Eliza'd find a way to make trouble,' the old woman continued, evidently glad of the chance to air a perennial grievance. 'It's not only the things she *forgets* to do,' she added significantly; and it dawned on Ralph that she was making an appeal to him, expecting him to take sides with her in the chronic conflict between herself and Eliza. He said to himself that perhaps she was right . . . that perhaps there was something he ought to do . . . that his mother was old, and didn't always see things; and for a while his mind revolved this problem with feverish intensity . . .

'Then you'll come down, sir?'

'Yes.'

The door closed, and he heard her heavy heels along the passage.

'But the money—where's the money to come from?' The question sprang out from some denser fold of the fog in his brain. The money—how on earth was he to pay it back? How could he have wasted his time in thinking of anything else while that central difficulty existed?

'But I can't . . . I can't . . . it's gone . . . and even if it weren't . . .' He dropped back in his chair and took his head between his hands. He had forgotten what he wanted the money for. He made a great effort to regain hold of the idea, but all the whirring, shuttling, flying had abruptly ceased in his brain, and he sat with his eyes shut, staring straight into darkness . . .

The clock struck, and he remembered that he had said he would go down to the dining-room. 'If I don't she'll come up——' He raised his head and sat listening for the sound of the old woman's step: it seemed to him perfectly intolerable that any one should cross the threshold of the room again.

'Why can't they leave me alone?' he groaned . . . At length through the silence of the empty house, he fancied he heard a door opening and closing far below; and he said to himself: 'She's coming.'

He got to his feet and went to the door. He didn't feel anything now except the insane dread of hearing the woman's steps come nearer. He bolted the door and stood looking about the room. For a moment he was conscious of seeing it in every detail with a distinctness he had never before known; then everything in it vanished but the single narrow panel of a drawer under one of the bookcases. He went up to the drawer, knelt down and slipped his hand into it.

As he raised himself he listened again, and this time he distinctly heard the old servant's steps on the stairs. He passed his left hand over the side of his head, and down the curve of the skull behind the ear. He said to himself: 'My wife . . . this will make it all right for her . . .' and a last flash of irony twitched through him. Then he felt again, more deliberately, for the spot he wanted, and put the muzzle of his revolver against it.

BOOK FIVE

XXXVII

IN a drawing-room hung with portraits of high-nosed personages in perukes and orders, a circle of ladies and gentlemen, looking not unlike every-day versions of the official figures above their heads, sat examining with friendly interest a little boy in mourning.

The boy was slim, fair and shy, and his small black figure, islanded in the middle of the wide lustrous floor, looked curiously lonely and remote. This effect of remoteness seemed to strike his mother as something intentional, and almost naughty, for after having launched him from the door, and waited to judge of the impression he produced, she came forward and, giving him a slight push, said impatiently: 'Paul! Why don't you go and kiss your new granny?'

The boy, without turning to her, or moving, sent his blue glance gravely about the circle. 'Does she want me to?' he asked, in a tone of evident apprehension; and on his mother's answering: 'Of course, you silly!' he added earnestly: 'How many more do you think there'll be?'

Undine blushed to the ripples of her brilliant hair. 'I never knew such a child! They've turned him into a perfect little savage!'

Raymond de Chelles advanced from behind his mother's chair.

'He won't be a savage long with me,' he said, stooping down so that his fatigued finely-drawn face was close to Paul's. Their eyes met and the boy smiled. 'Come along, old chap,' Chelles continued in English, drawing the little boy after him.

'*Il est bien beau*,'* the Marquise de Chelles observed, her eyes turning from Paul's grave face to her daughter-in-law's vivid countenance.

'Do be nice, darling! Say, "*bonjour, Madame*,"' Undine urged.

An odd mingling of emotions stirred in her while she stood watching Paul make the round of the family group under her husband's guidance. It was 'lovely' to have the child back, and to find him, after their three years' separation, grown into so endearing a figure: her first glimpse of him when, in Mrs Heeny's arms, he had emerged that morning from the steamer train, had shown what an acquisition he would be. If she had had any lingering doubts on the point, the impression produced on her husband would have dispelled them. Chelles had been instantly charmed, and Paul, in a shy confused way, was already responding to his advances. The Count and Countess Raymond had returned but a few weeks before from their protracted wedding journey, and were staying—as they were apparently to do whenever they came to Paris—with the old Marquis, Raymond's father, who had amicably proposed that little Paul Marvell should also share the hospitality of the Hôtel de Chelles. Undine, at first, was somewhat dismayed to find that she was expected to fit the boy and his nurse into a corner of her contracted *entresol*. But the possibility of a mother's not finding room for her son, however cramped her own quarters, seemed not to have occurred to her new relations, and the preparing of her dressing-room and boudoir for Paul's occupancy was carried on by the household with a zeal which obliged her to dissemble her lukewarmness.

Undine had supposed that on her marriage one of the great suites of the Hôtel de Chelles would be emptied of its tenants and put at her husband's disposal; but she had since learned that, even had such a plan occurred to her parents-in-law, considerations of economy would have hindered it. The old Marquis and his wife, who were content, when they came up from Burgundy in the spring, with a modest set of rooms looking out on the court of their ancestral residence, expected their son and his wife to fit themselves into the still smaller apartment which had served as Raymond's bachelor lodging. The rest of the fine old mouldering house—the tall-windowed *premier* on the garden, and the whole of the floor above—had been let for years to old-fashioned tenants who would have been more surprised than their landlord had he suddenly proposed to dispossess them. Undine, at first, had regarded these arrangements as merely provisional. She was persuaded that, under her influence, Raymond would soon convert his parents to more modern ideas, and meanwhile she was still in the flush of a completer well-being than she had ever known, and disposed, for the moment, to make light of any inconveniences connected with it. The three months since her marriage had been more nearly like what she had dreamed of than any of her previous experiments in happiness. At last she had what she wanted, and for the first time the glow of triumph was warmed by a deeper feeling. Her husband was really charming (it was odd how he reminded her of Ralph!), and after her bitter two years of loneliness and humiliation it was delicious to find herself once more adored and protected.

The very fact that Raymond was more jealous of her than Ralph had ever been—or at any rate less reluctant to show it—gave her a keener sense of recovered power. None of the men who had been in love with her before had been so frankly possessive, or so eager for reciprocal assurances of constancy. She knew that Ralph had suffered deeply from her intimacy with Van Degen, but he had betrayed his feeling only by a more studied detachment; and Van Degen, from the first, had been contemptuously indifferent to what she did or felt when she was out of his sight. As to her earlier experiences, she had frankly forgotten them: her sentimental memories went back no farther than the beginning of her New York career.

Raymond seemed to attach more importance to love, in all its manifestations, than was usual or convenient in a husband; and she gradually began to be aware that her domination over him involved a corresponding loss of independence. Since their return to Paris she had found that she was expected to give a circumstantial report of every hour she spent away from him. She had nothing to hide, and no designs against his peace of mind except those connected with her frequent and costly sessions at the dress-makers'; but she had never before been called upon to account to any one for the use of her time, and after the first amused surprise at Raymond's always wanting to know where she had been and whom she had seen she began to be oppressed by so exacting a devotion. Her parents, from her tenderest youth, had tacitly recognized her inalienable right to

'go round,' and Ralph—though from motives which she divined to be different—had shown the same respect for her
freedom. It was therefore disconcerting to find that Raymond
expected her to choose her friends, and even her acquaintances,
in conformity not only with his personal tastes but with a
definite and complicated code of family prejudices and traditions; and she was especially surprised to discover that he viewed
with disapproval her intimacy with the Princess Estradina.

'My cousin's extremely amusing, of course, but utterly mad
and very *mal entourée*.* Most of the people she has about her
ought to be in prison or Bedlam: especially that unspeakable
Madame Adelschein, who's a candidate for both. My aunt's an
angel, but she's been weak enough to let Lili turn the Hôtel de
Dordogne into an annex of Montmartre.* Of course you'll have
to show yourself there now and then: in these days families like
ours must hold together. But go to the *réunions de famille* rather
than to Lili's intimate parties; go with me, or with my mother;
don't let yourself be seen there alone. You're too young and
good-looking to be mixed up with that crew. A woman's
classed—or rather unclassed—by being known as one of Lili's
set.'

Agreeable as it was to Undine that an appeal to her discretion
should be based on the ground of her youth and good-looks, she
was dismayed to find herself cut off from the very circle she
had meant them to establish her in. Before she had become
Raymond's wife there had been a moment of sharp tension in
her relations with the Princess Estradina and the old Duchess.
They had done their best to prevent her marrying their cousin,
and had gone so far as openly to accuse her of being the cause
of a breach between themselves and his parents. But Ralph
Marvell's death had brought about a sudden change in her
situation. She was now no longer a divorced woman struggling
to obtain ecclesiastical sanction for her remarriage, but a widow
whose conspicuous beauty and independent situation made her
the object of lawful aspirations. The first person to seize on this
distinction and make the most of it was her old enemy the
Marquise de Trézac. The latter, who had been loudly charged
by the house of Chelles with furthering her beautiful compatriot's designs, had instantly seen a chance of vindicating

herself by taking the widowed Mrs Marvell under her wing and favouring the attentions of other suitors. These were not lacking, and the expected result had followed. Raymond de Chelles, more than ever infatuated as attainment became less certain, had claimed a definite promise from Undine, and his family, discouraged by his persistent bachelorhood, and their failure to fix his attention on any of the amiable maidens obviously designed to continue the race, had ended by withdrawing their opposition and discovering in Mrs Marvell the moral and financial merits necessary to justify their change of front.

'A good match? If she isn't, I should like to know what the Chelles call one!' Madame de Trézac went about indefatigably proclaiming. 'Related to the best people in New York—well, by marriage, that is; and her husband left much more money than was expected. It goes to the boy, of course; but as the boy is with his mother she naturally enjoys the income. And her father's a rich man—much richer than is generally known; I mean what *we* call rich in America, you understand!'

Madame de Trézac had lately discovered that the proper attitude for the American married abroad was that of a militant patriotism; and she flaunted Undine Marvell in the face of the Faubourg like a particularly showy specimen of her national banner. The success of the experiment emboldened her to throw off the most sacred observances of her past. She took up Madame Adelschein, she entertained the James J. Rollivers, she resuscitated Creole dishes, she patronized negro melodists, she abandoned her weekly teas for impromptu afternoon dances, and the prim drawing-room in which dowagers had droned echoed with a cosmopolitan hubbub.

Even when the period of tension was over, and Undine had been officially received into the family of her betrothed, Madame de Trézac did not at once surrender. She laughingly professed to have had enough of the proprieties, and declared herself bored by the social rites she had hitherto so piously performed. 'You'll always find a corner of home here, dearest, when you get tired of their ceremonies and solemnities,' she said as she embraced the bride after the wedding breakfast; and Undine hoped that the devoted Nettie would in fact provide a refuge from the extreme domesticity of her new state. But since her return to Paris, and her taking up her domicile in the Hôtel de Chelles, she had found Madame de Trézac less and less disposed to abet her in any assertion of independence.

'My dear, a woman must adopt her husband's nationality whether she wants to or not. It's the law, and it's the custom besides. If you wanted to amuse yourself with your Nouveau Luxe friends you oughtn't to have married Raymond—but of course I say that only in joke. As if any woman would have hesitated who'd had your chance! Take my advice—keep out of Lili's set just at first. Later . . . well, perhaps Raymond won't be so particular; but meanwhile you'd make a great mistake to go against his people——' and Madame de Trézac, with a '*Chère Madame*,' swept forward from her tea-table to receive the first of the returning dowagers.

It was about this time that Mrs Heeny arrived with Paul; and for a while Undine was pleasantly absorbed in her boy. She kept Mrs Heeny in Paris for a fortnight, and between her more pressing occupations it amused her to listen to the masseuse's New York gossip and her comments on the social organization of the old world. It was Mrs Heeny's first visit to Europe, and she confessed to Undine that she had always wanted to 'see something of the aristocracy'—using the phrase as a naturalist might, with no hint of personal pretensions. Mrs Heeny's democratic ease was combined with the strictest professional discretion, and it would never have occurred to her to regard herself, or to wish others to regard her, as anything but a manipulator of muscles; but in that character she felt herself entitled to admission to the highest circles.

'They certainly do things with style over here—but it's kinder one-horse after New York, ain't it? Is this what they call their season? Why, you dined home two nights last week. They ought to come over to New York and see!' And she poured into Undine's half-envious ear a list of the entertainments which had illuminated the last weeks of the New York winter. 'I suppose you'll begin to give parties as soon as ever you get into a house of your own. You're not going to have one? Oh, well, then you'll give a lot of big week-ends at your place down in the Shatter-country*—that's where the swells all go to in the summer time, ain't it? But I dunno what your ma would say if she knew you were going to live on with *his* folks after you're done honey-mooning. Why, we read in the papers you were going to live in some grand hotel or other—oh, they call their houses *hotels*, do they? That's funny: I suppose it's because they let out part of 'em. Well, you look handsomer than ever, Undine; I'll take *that* back to your mother, anyhow. And he's dead in love, I can see that; reminds me of the way——' but she broke off suddenly, as if something in Undine's look had silenced her.

Even to herself, Undine did not like to call up the image of Ralph Marvell; and any mention of his name gave her a vague sense of distress. His death had released her, had given her what she wanted; yet she could honestly say to herself that she had not wanted him to die—at least not to die like that . . . People said at the time that it was the hot weather—his own family had said so: he had never quite got over his attack of pneumonia, and the sudden rise of temperature—one of the fierce 'heat-waves' that devastate New York in summer—had probably affected his brain: the doctors said such cases were not uncommon . . . She had worn black for a few weeks—not quite mourning, but something decently regretful (the dress-makers were beginning to provide a special garb for such cases); and even since her remarriage, and the lapse of a year, she continued to wish that she could have got what she wanted without having had to pay that particular price for it.

This feeling was intensified by an incident—in itself far from unwelcome—which had occurred about three months after Ralph's death. Her lawyers had written to say that the sum of a hundred thousand dollars had been paid over to Marvell's estate by the Apex Consolidation Company; and as Marvell had left a will bequeathing everything he possessed to his son, this unexpected windfall handsomely increased Paul's patrimony. Undine had never relinquished her claim on her child; she had merely, by the advice of her lawyers, waived the assertion of her right for a few months after Marvell's death, with the express stipulation that her doing so was only a temporary concession to the feelings of her husband's family; and she had held out against all attempts to induce her to surrender Paul permanently. Before her marriage she had somewhat conspicuously adopted her husband's creed, and the Dagonets, picturing Paul as the prey of the Jesuits, had made the mistake of appealing to the courts for his custody. This had confirmed Undine's resistance, and her determination to keep the child. The case had been decided in her favour, and she had thereupon demanded, and obtained, an allowance of five thousand dollars, to be devoted to the bringing up and education of her son. This sum, added to what Mr Spragg had agreed to give her, made up an income which had appreciably bettered her position, and justified Madame de Trézac's discreet allusions to her wealth. Nevertheless, it was one of the facts about which she least liked to think when any chance allusion evoked Ralph's image. The money was hers, of course; she had a right to it, and she was an ardent believer in 'rights.' But she wished she could have got it in some other way—she hated the thought of it as one more instance of the perverseness with which things she was entitled to always came to her as if they had been stolen.

The approach of summer, and the culmination of the Paris season, swept aside such thoughts. The Countess Raymond de Chelles, contrasting her situation with that of Mrs Undine Marvell, and the fulness and animation of her new life with the vacant dissatisfied days which had followed on her return from Dakota, forgot the smallness of her apartment, the inconvenient proximity of Paul and his nurse, the interminable round of visits with her mother-in-law, and the long dinners in the solemn hôtels of all the family connection. The world was radiant, the lights were lit, the music playing; she was still young, and better-looking than ever, with a Countess's coronet, a famous château and a handsome and popular husband who adored her. And then suddenly the lights went out and the music stopped when one day Raymond, putting his arm about her, said in his tenderest tones: 'And now, my dear, the world's had you long enough and it's my turn. What do you say to going down to Saint Désert?'

XXXVIII

IN a window of the long gallery of the château de Saint Désert the new Marquise de Chelles stood looking down the poplar avenue into the November rain. It had been raining heavily and persistently for a longer time than she could remember. Day after day the hills beyond the park had been curtained by motionless clouds, the gutters of the long steep roofs had gurgled with a perpetual overflow, the opaque surface of the moat been peppered by a continuous pelting of big drops. The water lay in glassy stretches under the trees and along the sodden edges of the garden-paths, it rose in a white mist from the fields beyond, it exuded in a chill moisture from the brick flooring of the passages and from the walls of the rooms on the lower floor. Everything in the great empty house smelt of dampness: the stuffing of the chairs, the threadbare folds of the faded curtains, the splendid tapestries, that were fading too, on the walls of the room in which Undine stood, and the wide bands of crape which her husband had insisted on her keeping on her black dresses till the last hour of her mourning for the old Marquis.

The summer had been more than usually inclement, and since her first coming to the country Undine had lived through many periods of rainy weather; but none which had gone before had so completely epitomized, so summed up in one vast monotonous blur, the image of her long months at Saint Désert.

When, the year before, she had reluctantly suffered herself to be torn from the joys of Paris, she had been sustained by the belief that her exile would not be of long duration. Once Paris was out of sight, she had even found a certain lazy charm in the long warm days at Saint Désert. Her parents-in-law had remained in town, and she enjoyed being alone with her husband, exploring and appraising the treasures of the great half-abandoned house, and watching her boy scamper over the June meadows or trot about the gardens on the pony his stepfather had given him. Paul, after Mrs Heeny's departure, had grown fretful and restive, and Undine had found it more and more difficult to fit his small exacting personality into her cramped rooms and crowded life. He irritated her by pining for his Aunt Laura, his Marvell granny, and old Mr Dagonet's funny stories about gods and fairies; and his wistful allusions to his games with Clare's children sounded like a lesson he might have been drilled in to make her feel how little he belonged to her. But once released from Paris, and blessed with rabbits, a pony and the freedom of the fields, he became again all that a charming child should be, and for a time it amused her to share in his romps and rambles. Raymond seemed enchanted at the picture they made, and the quiet weeks of fresh air and outdoor activity gave her back a bloom that reflected itself in her tranquillized mood. She was the more resigned to this interlude because she was so sure of its not lasting. Before they left Paris a doctor had been found to say that Paul—who was certainly looking pale and pulled-down—was in urgent need of sea air, and Undine had nearly convinced her husband of the expediency of hiring a châlet at Deauville for July and August, when this plan, and with it every other prospect of escape, was dashed by the sudden death of the old Marquis.

Undine, at first, had supposed that the resulting change could not be other than favourable. She had been on too formal terms with her father-in-law—a remote and ceremonious old gentleman to whom her own personality was evidently an insoluble enigma—to feel more than the merest conventional pang at his death; and it was certainly 'more fun' to be a marchioness than a countess, and to know that one's husband was the head of the house. Besides, now they would have the château to themselves—or at least the old Marquise, when she came, would be there as a guest and not a ruler—and visions of smart house-parties and big shoots lit up the first weeks of Undine's enforced seclusion. Then, by degrees, the inexorable conditions of French mourning closed in on her. Immediately after the long-drawn funeral observances the bereaved family—mother, daughters, sons and sons-in-law—came down to seclude themselves at Saint Désert; and Undine, through the slow hot crape-smelling months, lived encircled by shrouded images of woe in which the only live points were the eyes constantly fixed on her least movements. The hope of escaping to the seaside with Paul vanished in the pained stare with which her mother-in-law received the suggestion. Undine learned the next day that it had cost the old Marquise a sleepless night, and might have had more distressing results had it not been explained as a harmless instance of transatlantic oddness. Raymond entreated his wife to atone for her involuntary *légèreté** by submitting with a good grace to the usages of her adopted country; and he seemed to regard the remaining months of the summer as hardly long enough for this act of expiation. As Undine looked back on them, they appeared to have been composed of an interminable succession of identical days, in which attendance at early mass (in the coroneted gallery she had once so glowingly depicted to Van Degen) was followed by a great deal of conversational sitting about, a great deal of excellent eating, an occasional drive to the nearest town behind a pair of heavy draft horses, and long evenings in a lamp-heated drawing-room with all the windows shut, and the stout curé making an asthmatic fourth at the Marquise's card-table.

Still, even these conditions were not permanent, and the discipline of the last years had trained Undine to wait and dissemble. The summer over, it was decided—after a protracted family conclave—that the state of the old Marquise's health made it advisable for her to spend the winter with the married daughter who lived near Pau. The other members of the family returned to their respective estates, and Undine once more found herself alone with her husband. But she knew by this time that there was to be no thought of Paris that winter, or even the next spring. Worse still, she was presently to discover that Raymond's accession of rank brought with it no financial advantages. Having but the vaguest notion of French testamentary law, she was dismayed to learn that the compulsory division of property made it impossible for a father to benefit his eldest son at the expense of the others. Raymond was therefore little richer than before, and with the debts of honour of a troublesome younger brother to settle, and Saint Désert to keep up, his available income was actually reduced. He held out, indeed, the hope of eventual improvement, since the old Marquis had managed his estates with a lofty contempt for modern methods, and the application of new principles of agriculture and forestry were certain to yield profitable results. But for a year or two, at any rate, this very change of treatment would necessitate the owner's continual supervision, and would not in the meanwhile produce any increase of income.

To *faire valoir** the family acres had always, it appeared, been Raymond's deepest-seated purpose, and all his frivolities dropped from him with the prospect of putting his hand to the

plough. He was not, indeed, inhuman enough to condemn his
wife to perpetual exile. He meant, he assured her, that she
should have her annual spring visit to Paris—but he stared in
dismay at her suggestion that they should take possession of the
coveted *premier** of the Hôtel de Chelles. He was gallant enough
to express the wish that it were in his power to house her on
such a scale; but he could not conceal his surprise that she had
ever seriously expected it. She was beginning to see that he felt
her constitutional inability to understand anything about money
as the deepest difference between them. It was a proficiency no
one had ever expected her to acquire, and the lack of which
she had even been encouraged to regard as a grace and to use as
a pretext. During the interval between her divorce and her
remarriage she had learned what things cost, but not how to
do without them; and money still seemed to her like some
mysterious and uncertain stream which occasionally vanished
underground but was sure to bubble up again at one's feet.
Now, however, she found herself in a world where it represented not the means of individual gratification but the
substance binding together whole groups of interests, and
where the uses to which it might be put in twenty years were
considered before the reasons for spending it on the spot. At first
she was sure she could laugh Raymond out of his prudence or
coax him round to her point of view. She did not understand
how a man so romantically in love could be so unpersuadable on
certain points. Hitherto she had had to contend with personal
moods, now she was arguing against a policy; and she was
gradually to learn that it was as natural to Raymond de Chelles
to adore her and resist her as it had been to Ralph Marvell to
adore her and let her have her way.

At first, indeed, he appealed to her good sense, using
arguments evidently drawn from accumulations of hereditary
experience. But his economic plea was as unintelligible to her as
the silly problems about pen-knives and apples in the 'Mental
Arithmetic' of her infancy; and when he struck a tenderer note
and spoke of the duty of providing for the son he hoped for, she
put her arms about him to whisper: 'But then I oughtn't to be
worried . . .'

After that, she noticed, though he was as charming as ever, he behaved as if the case were closed. He had apparently decided that his arguments were unintelligible to her, and under all his ardour she felt the difference made by the discovery. It did not make him less kind, but it evidently made her less important; and she had the half-frightened sense that the day she ceased to please him she would cease to exist for him. That day was a long way off, of course, but the chill of it had brushed her face; and she was no longer heedless of such signs. She resolved to cultivate all the arts of patience and compliance, and habit might have helped them to take root if they had not been nipped by a new cataclysm.

It was barely a week ago that her husband had been called to Paris to straighten out a fresh tangle in the affairs of the troublesome brother whose difficulties were apparently a part of the family tradition. Raymond's letters had been hurried, his telegrams brief and contradictory, and now, as Undine stood watching for the brougham that was to bring him from the station, she had the sense that with his arrival all her vague fears would be confirmed. There would be more money to pay out, of course—since the funds that could not be found for her just needs were apparently always forthcoming to settle Hubert's scandalous prodigalities—and that meant a longer perspective of solitude at Saint Désert, and a fresh pretext for postponing the hospitalities that were to follow on their period of mourning.

The brougham—a vehicle as massive and lumbering as the pair that drew it—presently rolled into the court, and Raymond's sable figure (she had never before seen a man travel in such black clothes) sprang up the steps to the door. Whenever Undine saw him after an absence she had a curious sense of his coming back from unknown distances and not belonging to her or to any state of things she understood. Then habit reasserted itself, and she began to think of him again with a querulous familiarity. But she had learned to hide her feelings, and as he came in she put up her face for a kiss.

'Yes—everything's settled——' his embrace expressed the satisfaction of the man returning from an accomplished task to the joys of his fireside.

'Settled?' Her face kindled. 'Without your having to pay?'

He looked at her with a shrug. 'Of course I've had to pay. Did you suppose Hubert's creditors would be put off with vanilla éclairs?'

'Oh, if *that's* what you mean—if Hubert has only to wire you at any time to be sure of his affairs being settled——!'

She saw his lips narrow and a line come out between his eyes. 'Wouldn't it be a happy thought to tell them to bring tea?' he suggested.

'In the library, then. It's so cold here—and the tapestries smell so of rain.'

He paused a moment to scrutinize the long walls, on which the fabulous blues and pinks of the great Boucher series looked as livid as withered roses. 'I suppose they ought to be taken down and aired,' he said.

She thought: 'In *this* air—much good it would do them!' But she had already repented her outbreak about Hubert, and she followed her husband into the library with the resolve not to let him see her annoyance. Compared with the long grey gallery the library, with its brown walls of books, looked warm and homelike, and Raymond seemed to feel the influence of the softer atmosphere. He turned to his wife and put his arm about her.

'I know it's been a trial to you, dearest; but this is the last time I shall have to pull the poor boy out.'

In spite of herself she laughed incredulously: Hubert's 'last times' were a household word.

But when tea had been brought, and they were alone over the fire, Raymond unfolded the amazing sequel. Hubert had found an heiress. Hubert was to be married, and henceforth the business of paying his debts (which might be counted on to recur as inevitably as the changes of the seasons) would devolve on his American bride—the charming Miss Looty Arlington, whom Raymond had remained over in Paris to meet.

'An American? He's marrying an American?' Undine wavered between wrath and satisfaction. She felt a flash of resentment at any other intruder's venturing upon her territory—('Looty Arlington? Who is she? What a name!')—but it was quickly superseded by the relief of knowing that henceforth, as Raymond said, Hubert's debts would be some one else's business. Then a third consideration prevailed. 'But if he's engaged to a rich girl, why on earth do *we* have to pull him out?'

Her husband explained that no other course was possible. Though General Arlington was immensely wealthy, ('her father's a general—a General Manager, whatever that may be,') he had exacted what he called 'a clean slate' from his future son-in-law, and Hubert's creditors (the boy was such a donkey!) had in their possession certain papers that made it possible for them to press for immediate payment.

'Your compatriots' views on such matters are so rigid—and it's all to their credit—that the marriage would have fallen through at once if the least hint of Hubert's mess had got out—and then we should have had him on our hands for life.'

Yes—from that point of view it was doubtless best to pay up; but Undine obscurely wished that their doing so had not incidentally helped an unknown compatriot to what the American papers were no doubt already announcing as 'another brilliant foreign alliance.'

'Where on earth did your brother pick up anybody respectable? Do you know where her people come from? I suppose she's perfectly awful,' she broke out with a sudden escape of irritation.

'I believe Hubert made her acquaintance at a skating rink. They come from some new state—the general apologized for its not yet being on the map, but seemed surprised I hadn't heard of it. He said it was already known as one of "the divorce states," and the principal city had, in consequence, a very agreeable society. *La petite n'est vraiment pas trop mal.*'*

'I daresay not! We're all good-looking. But she must be horribly common.'

Raymond seemed sincerely unable to formulate a judgment. 'My dear, you have your own customs . . .'

'Oh, I know we're all alike to you!' It was one of her grievances that he never attempted to discriminate between Americans. 'You see no difference between me and a girl one gets engaged to at a skating rink!'

He evaded the challenge by rejoining: 'Miss Arlington's burning to know you. She says she's heard a great deal about you, and Hubert wants to bring her down next week. I think we'd better do what we can.'

'Of course.' But Undine was still absorbed in the economic aspect of the case. 'If they're as rich as you say, I suppose Hubert means to pay you back by and bye?'

'Naturally. It's all arranged. He's given me a paper.' He drew her hands into his. 'You see we've every reason to be kind to Miss Arlington.'

'Oh, I'll be as kind as you like!' She brightened at the prospect of repayment. Yes, they would ask the girl down . . . She leaned a little nearer to her husband. 'But then after a while we shall be a good deal better off—especially, as you say, with no more of Hubert's debts to worry us.' And leaning back far enough to give her upward smile, she renewed her plea for the *premier* in the Hôtel de Chelles: 'Because, really, you know, as the head of the house you ought to——'

'Ah, my dear, as the head of the house I've so many obligations; and one of them is not to miss a good stroke of business when it comes my way.'

Her hands slipped from his shoulders and she drew back. 'What do you mean by a good stroke of business?'

'Why, an incredible piece of luck—it's what kept me on so long in Paris. Miss Arlington's father was looking for an apartment for the young couple, and I've let him the *premier* for twelve years on the understanding that he puts electric light and heating into the whole hôtel. It's a wonderful chance, for of course we all benefit by it as much as Hubert.'

'A wonderful chance . . . benefit by it as much as Hubert!' He seemed to be speaking a strange language in which familiar-sounding syllables meant something totally unknown. Did he really think she was going to coop herself up again in their cramped quarters while Hubert and his skating-rink bride luxuriated overhead in the coveted *premier*? All the resentments that had been accumulating in her during the long baffled months since her marriage broke into speech. 'It's extraordinary of you to do such a thing without consulting me!'

'Without consulting you? But, my dear child, you've always professed the most complete indifference to business matters—you've frequently begged me not to bore you with them. You may be sure I've acted on the best advice; and my mother, whose head is as good as a man's, thinks I've made a remarkably good arrangement.'

'I daresay—but I'm not always thinking about money, as you are.'

As she spoke she had an ominous sense of impending peril; but she was too angry to avoid even the risks she saw. To her surprise Raymond put his arm about her with a smile. 'There are many reasons why I have to think about money. One is that *you* don't; and another is that I must look out for the future of our son.'

Undine flushed to the forehead. She had grown accustomed to such allusions and the thought of having a child no longer filled her with the resentful terror she had felt before Paul's birth. She had been insensibly influenced by a different point of view, perhaps also by a difference in her own feeling; and the vision of herself as the mother of the future Marquis de Chelles was softened to happiness by the thought of giving Raymond a son. But all these lightly-rooted sentiments went down in the rush of her resentment, and she freed herself with a petulant movement. 'Oh, my dear, you'd better leave it to your brother to perpetuate the race. There'll be more room for nurseries in their apartment!'

She waited a moment, quivering with the expectation of her husband's answer; then, as none came except the silent darkening of his face, she walked to the door and turned round to fling back: 'Of course you can do what you like with your own house, and make any arrangements that suit your family, without consulting me; but you needn't think I'm ever going back to live in that stuffy little hole, with Hubert and his wife splurging round on top of our heads!'

'Ah——' said Raymond de Chelles in a low voice.

XXXIX

UNDINE did not fulfil her threat. The month of May saw her back in the rooms she had declared she would never set foot in, and after her long sojourn among the echoing vistas of Saint Désert the exiguity of her Paris quarters seemed like cosiness.

In the interval many things had happened. Hubert, permitted by his anxious relatives to anticipate the term of the family mourning, had been showily and expensively united to his heiress; the Hôtel de Chelles had been piped, heated and illuminated in accordance with the bride's requirements; and the young couple, not content with these utilitarian changes had moved doors, opened windows, torn down partitions, and given over the great trophied and pilastered dining-room to a decorative painter with a new theory of the human anatomy. Undine had silently assisted at this spectacle, and at the sight of the old Marquise's abject acquiescence; she had seen the Duchesse de Dordogne and the Princesse Estradina go past her door to visit Hubert's *premier* and marvel at the American bath-tubs and the Annamite* bric-a-brac; and she had been present, with her husband, at the banquet at which Hubert had revealed to the astonished Faubourg the prehistoric episodes depicted on his dining-room walls. She had accepted all these necessities with the stoicism which the last months had developed in her; for more and more, as the days passed, she felt herself in the grasp of circumstances stronger than any effort she could oppose to them. The very absence of external pressure, of any tactless assertion of authority on her husband's part, intensified the sense of her helplessness. He simply left it to her to infer that, important as she might be to him in certain ways, there were others in which she did not weigh a feather.

Their outward relations had not changed since her outburst on the subject of Hubert's marriage. That incident had left her half-ashamed, half-frightened at her behaviour, and she had tried to atone for it by the indirect arts that were her nearest approach to acknowledging herself in the wrong. Raymond met her advances with a good grace, and they lived through the rest of the winter on terms of apparent understanding. When the spring approached it was he who suggested that, since his mother had consented to Hubert's marrying before the year of mourning was over, there was really no reason why they should not go up to Paris as usual; and she was surprised at the readiness with which he prepared to accompany her.

A year earlier she would have regarded this as another proof of her power; but she now drew her inferences less quickly. Raymond was as 'lovely' to her as ever; but more than once, during their months in the country, she had had a startled sense of not giving him all he expected of her. She had admired him, before their marriage, as a model of social distinction; during the honeymoon he had been the most ardent of lovers; and with their settling down at Saint Désert she had prepared to resign herself to the society of a country gentleman absorbed in sport and agriculture. But Raymond, to her surprise, had again developed a disturbing resemblance to his predecessor. During the long winter afternoons, after he had gone over his accounts with the bailiff, or written his business letters, he took to dabbling with a paint-box, or picking out new scores at the piano; after dinner, when they went to the library, he seemed to expect to read aloud to her from the reviews and papers he was always receiving; and when he had discovered her inability to fix her attention he fell into the way of absorbing himself in one of the old brown books with which the room was lined. At first he tried—as Ralph had done—to tell her about what he was reading or what was happening in the world; but her sense of inadequacy made her slip away to other subjects, and little by little their talk died down to monosyllables.

Was it possible that, in spite of his books, the evenings seemed as long to Raymond as to her, and that he had suggested going back to Paris because he was bored at Saint Désert? Bored as she was herself, she resented his not finding her company all-sufficient, and was mortified by the discovery that there were regions of his life she could not enter.

But once back in Paris she had less time for introspection, and Raymond less for books. They resumed their dispersed and busy life, and in spite of Hubert's ostentatious vicinity, of the perpetual lack of money, and of Paul's innocent encroachments on her freedom, Undine, once more in her element, ceased to brood upon her grievances. She enjoyed going about with her husband, whose presence at her side was distinctly ornamental. He seemed to have grown suddenly younger and more animated, and when she saw other women looking at him she remembered how distinguished he was. It amused her to have him in her train, and driving about with him to dinners and dances, waiting for him on flower-decked landings, or pushing at his side through blazing theatre-lobbies, answered to her inmost ideal of domestic intimacy.

He seemed disposed to allow her more liberty than before, and it was only now and then that he let drop a brief reminder of the conditions on which it was accorded. She was to keep certain people at a distance, she was not to cheapen herself by being seen at vulgar restaurants and tea-rooms, she was to join with him in fulfilling certain family obligations (going to a good many dull dinners among the number); but in other respects she was free to fill her days as she pleased.

'Not that it leaves me much time,' she admitted to Madame de Trézac; 'what with going to see his mother every day, and never missing one of his sisters' *jours*, and showing myself at the Hôtel de Dordogne whenever the Duchess gives a pay-up party to the stuffy people Lili Estradina won't be bothered with, there are days when I never lay eyes on Paul, and barely have time to be waved and manicured; but, apart from that, Raymond's really much nicer and less fussy than he was.'

Undine, as she grew older, had developed her mother's craving for a confidante, and Madame de Trézac had succeeded in that capacity to Mabel Lipscomb and Bertha Shallum.

'Less fussy?' Madame de Trézac's long nose lengthened thoughtfully. 'H'm—are you sure that's a good sign?'

Undine stared and laughed. 'Oh, my dear, you're so quaint! Why, nobody's jealous any more.'

'No; that's the worst of it.' Madame de Trézac pondered. 'It's a thousand pities you haven't got a son.'

'Yes; I wish we had.' Undine stood up, impatient to end the conversation. Since she had learned that her continued childlessness was regarded by every one about her as not only unfortunate but somehow vaguely derogatory to her, she had genuinely begun to regret it; and any allusion to the subject disturbed her.

'Especially,' Madame de Trézac continued, 'as Hubert's wife——'

'Oh, if *that's* all they want, it's a pity Raymond didn't marry Hubert's wife,' Undine flung back; and on the stairs she murmured to herself: 'Nettie has been talking to my mother-in-law.'

But this explanation did not quiet her, and that evening, as she and Raymond drove back together from a party, she felt a sudden impulse to speak. Sitting close to him in the darkness of the carriage, it ought to have been easy for her to find the needed word; but the barrier of his indifference hung between them, and street after street slipped by, and the spangled blackness of the river unrolled itself beneath their wheels, before she leaned over to touch his hand.

'What is it, my dear?'

She had not yet found the word, and already his tone told her she was too late. A year ago, if she had slipped her hand in his, she would not have had that answer.

'Your mother blames me for our not having a child. Everybody thinks it's my fault.'

He paused before answering, and she sat watching his shadowy profile against the passing lamps.

'My mother's ideas are old-fashioned; and I don't know that it's anybody's business but yours and mine.'

'Yes, but——'

'Here we are.' The brougham was turning under the archway of the hotel, and the light of Hubert's tall windows fell across the dusky court. Raymond helped her out, and they mounted to their door by the stairs which Hubert had recarpeted in velvet, with a marble nymph lurking in the azaleas on the landing.

In the antechamber Raymond paused to take her cloak from her shoulders, and his eyes rested on her with a faint smile of approval.

'You never looked better; your dress is extremely becoming. Good-night, my dear,' he said, kissing her hand as he turned away.

Undine kept this incident to herself: her wounded pride made her shrink from confessing it even to Madame de Trézac. She was sure Raymond would 'come back'; Ralph always had, to the last. During their remaining weeks in Paris she reassured herself with the thought that once they were back at Saint Désert she would easily regain her lost hold; and when

Raymond suggested their leaving Paris she acquiesced without a protest. But at Saint Désert she seemed no nearer to him than in Paris. He continued to treat her with unvarying amiability, but he seemed wholly absorbed in the management of the estate, in his books, his sketching and his music. He had begun to interest himself in politics and had been urged to stand for his department. This necessitated frequent displacements: trips to Beaune or Dijon and occasional absences in Paris. Undine, when he was away, was not left alone, for the dowager Marquise had established herself at Saint Désert for the summer, and relays of brothers and sisters-in-law, aunts, cousins and ecclesiastical friends and connections succeeded each other under its capacious roof. Only Hubert and his wife were absent. They had taken a villa at Deauville, and in the morning papers Undine followed the chronicle of Hubert's polo scores and of the Countess Hubert's racing toilets.

The days crawled on with a benumbing sameness. The old Marquise and the other ladies of the party sat on the terrace with their needle-work, the curé or one of the visiting uncles read aloud the *Journal des Débats* and prognosticated dark things of the Republic, Paul scoured the park and despoiled the kitchen-garden with the other children of the family, the inhabitants of the adjacent châteaux drove over to call, and occasionally the ponderous pair were harnessed to a landau as lumbering as the brougham, and the ladies of Saint Désert measured the dusty kilometres between themselves and their neighbours.

It was the first time that Undine had seriously paused to consider the conditions of her new life, and as the days passed she began to understand that so they would continue to succeed each other till the end. Every one about her took it for granted that as long as she lived she would spend ten months of every year at Saint Désert and the remaining two in Paris. Of course, if health required it, she might go to *les eaux* with her husband; but the old Marquise was very doubtful as to the benefit of a course of waters, and her uncle the Duke and her cousin the Canon shared her view. In the case of young married women, especially, the unwholesome excitement of the modern watering-place was more than likely to do away with the possible benefit of the treatment. As to travel—had not Raymond and his wife been to Egypt and Asia Minor on their wedding-journey? Such reckless enterprise was unheard of in the annals of the house! Had they not spent days and days in the saddle, and slept in tents among the Arabs? (Who could tell, indeed, whether these imprudences were not the cause of the disappointment which it had pleased heaven to inflict on the young couple?) No one in the family had ever taken so long a wedding-journey. One bride had gone to England (even that was considered extreme), and another—the artistic daughter—had spent a week in Venice; which certainly showed that they were not behind the times, and had no old-fashioned prejudices. Since wedding-journeys were the fashion, they had taken them; but who had ever heard of travelling afterward? What could be the possible object of leaving one's family, one's habits, one's friends? It was natural that the Americans, who had no homes, who were born and died in hotels, should have contracted nomadic habits; but the new Marquise de Chelles was no longer an American, and she had Saint Désert and the Hôtel de Chelles to live in, as generations of ladies of her name had done before her.

Thus Undine beheld her future laid out for her, not directly and in blunt words, but obliquely and affably, in the allusions, the assumptions, the insinuations of the amiable women among whom her days were spent. Their interminable conversations were carried on to the click of knitting-needles and the rise and fall of industrious fingers above embroidery-frames; and as Undine sat staring at the lustrous nails of her idle hands she felt that her inability to occupy them was regarded as one of the chief causes of her restlessness. The innumerable rooms of Saint Désert were furnished with the embroidered hangings and tapestry chairs produced by generations of diligent châtelaines,* and the untiring needles of the old Marquise, her daughters and dependents were still steadily increasing the provision.

It struck Undine as curious that they should be willing to go on making chair-coverings and bed-curtains for a house that didn't really belong to them, and that she had a right to pull about and rearrange as she chose; but then that was only a part of their whole incomprehensible way of regarding themselves (in spite of their acute personal and parochial absorptions) as minor members of a powerful and indivisible whole, the huge voracious fetish they called The Family.

Notwithstanding their very definite theories as to what Americans were and were not, they were evidently bewildered at finding no corresponding sense of solidarity in Undine; and little Paul's rootlessness, his lack of all local and linear ties, made them (for all the charm he exercised) regard him with something of the shyness of pious Christians toward an elfin child. But though mother and child gave them a sense of insuperable strangeness, it plainly never occurred to them that both would not be gradually subdued to the customs of Saint Désert. Dynasties had fallen, institutions changed, manners and morals, alas, deplorably declined; but as far back as memory went, the ladies of the line of Chelles had always sat at their needle-work on the terrace of Saint Désert, while the men of the house lamented the corruption of the government and the curé ascribed the unhappy state of the country to the decline of religious feeling and the rise in the cost of living. It was inevitable that, in the course of time, the new Marquise should come to understand the fundamental necessity of these things being as they were; and meanwhile the forbearance of her husband's family exercised itself, with the smiling discretion of their race, through the long succession of uneventful days.

Once, in September, this routine was broken in upon by the unannounced descent of a flock of motors bearing the Princess Estradina and a chosen band from one watering-place to another. Raymond was away at the time, but family loyalty constrained the old Marquise to welcome her kinswoman and the latter's friends; and Undine once more found herself immersed in the world from which her marriage had removed her.

The Princess, at first, seemed totally to have forgotten their former intimacy, and Undine was made to feel that in a life so variously agitated the episode could hardly have left a trace. But the night before her departure the incalculable Lili, with one of her sudden changes of humour, drew her former friend into her bedroom and plunged into an exchange of confidences. She naturally unfolded her own history first, and it was so packed with incident that the courtyard clock had struck two before she turned her attention to Undine.

'My dear, you're handsomer than ever; only perhaps a shade too stout. Domestic bliss, I suppose? Take care! You need an emotion, a drama . . . You Americans are really extraordinary. You appear to live on change and excitement; and then suddenly a man comes along and claps a ring on your finger, and you never look through it to see what's going on outside. Aren't you ever the least bit bored? Why do I never see anything of you any more? I suppose it's the fault of my venerable aunt—she's never forgiven me for having a better time than her daughters. How can I help it if I don't look like the curé's umbrella? I daresay she owes you the same grudge. But why do you let her coop you up here? It's a thousand pities you haven't had a child. They'd all treat you differently if you had.'

It was the same perpetually reiterated condolence; and Undine flushed with anger as she listened. Why indeed had she let herself be cooped up? She could not have answered the Princess's question: she merely felt the impossibility of breaking through the mysterious web of traditions, conventions, prohibitions that enclosed her in their impenetrable net-work. But her vanity suggested the obvious pretext, and she murmured with a laugh: 'I didn't know Raymond was going to be so jealous——'

The Princess stared. 'Is it Raymond who keeps you shut up here? And what about his trips to Dijon? And what do you suppose he does with himself when he runs up to Paris? Politics?' She shrugged ironically. 'Politics don't occupy a man after midnight. Raymond jealous of you? *Ah, merci!* My dear, it's what I always say when people talk to me about fast Americans: you're the only innocent women left in the world . . .'

XL

AFTER the Princess Estradina's departure, the days at Saint Désert succeeded each other indistinguishably; and more and more, as they passed, Undine felt herself drawn into the slow strong current already fed by so many tributary lives. Some spell she could not have named seemed to emanate from the old house which had so long been the custodian of an unbroken tradition: things had happened there in the same way for so many generations that to try to alter them seemed as vain as to contend with the elements.

Winter came and went, and once more the calendar marked the first days of spring; but though the horse-chestnuts of the Champs Elysées were budding snow still lingered in the grass drives of Saint Désert and along the ridges of the hills beyond the park. Sometimes, as Undine looked out of the windows of the Boucher gallery, she felt as if her eyes had never rested on any other scene. Even her occasional brief trips to Paris left no lasting trace: the life of the vivid streets faded to a shadow as soon as the black and white horizon of Saint Désert closed in on her again.

Though the afternoons were still cold she had lately taken to sitting in the gallery. The smiling scenes on its walls and the tall screens which broke its length made it more habitable than the drawing-rooms beyond; but her chief reason for preferring it was the satisfaction she found in having fires lit in both the monumental chimneys that faced each other down its long perspective. This satisfaction had its source in the old Marquise's disapproval. Never before in the history of Saint Désert had the consumption of fire-wood exceeded a certain carefully-calculated measure; but since Undine had been in authority this allowance had been doubled. If any one had told her, a year earlier, that one of the chief distractions of her new life would be to invent ways of annoying her mother-in-law, she would have laughed at the idea of wasting her time on such trifles. But she found herself with a great deal of time to waste, and with a fierce desire to spend it in upsetting the immemorial customs of Saint Désert. Her husband had mastered her in essentials, but she had discovered innumerable small ways of irritating and hurting him, and one—and not the least effectual—was to do anything that went counter to his mother's prejudices. It was not that he always shared her views, or was a particularly subservient son; but it seemed to be one of his fundamental principles that a man should respect his mother's wishes, and see to it that his house-hold respected them. All Frenchmen of his class appeared to share this view, and to regard it as beyond discussion: it was based on something so much more immutable than personal feeling that one might even hate one's mother and yet insist that her ideas as to the consumption of fire-wood should be regarded.

The old Marquise, during the cold weather, always sat in her bedroom; and there, between the tapestried four-poster and the fireplace, the family grouped itself around the ground-glass of her single carcel lamp.* In the evening, if there were visitors, a fire was lit in the library; otherwise the family again sat about the Marquise's lamp till the footman came in at ten with tisane* and *biscuits de Reims*; after which every one bade the dowager good night and scattered down the corridors to chill distances marked by tapers floating in cups of oil.

Since Undine's coming the library fire had never been allowed to go out; and of late, after experimenting with the two drawing-rooms and the so-called 'study' where Raymond kept his guns and saw the bailiff, she had selected the gallery as the most suitable place for the new and unfamiliar ceremony of afternoon tea. Afternoon refreshments had never before been served at Saint Désert except when company was expected; when they had invariably consisted in a decanter of sweet port and a plate of small dry cakes—the kind that kept. That the complicated rites of the tea-urn, with its offering-up of perishable delicacies, should be enacted for the sole enjoyment of the family, was a thing so unheard of that for a while Undine found sufficient amusement in elaborating the ceremonial, and in making the ancestral plate groan under more varied viands; and when this palled she devised the plan of performing the office in the gallery and lighting sacrificial fires in both chimneys.

She had said to Raymond, at first: 'It's ridiculous that your mother should sit in her bedroom all day. She says she does it to save fires; but if we have a fire downstairs why can't she let hers go out, and come down? I don't see why I should spend my life in your mother's bedroom.'

Raymond made no answer, and the Marquise did, in fact, let her fire go out. But she did not come down—she simply continued to sit upstairs without a fire.

At first this also amused Undine; then the tacit criticism implied began to irritate her. She hoped Raymond would speak

of his mother's attitude: she had her answer ready if he did! But
he made no comment, he took no notice; her impulses of
retaliation spent themselves against the blank surface of his
indifference. He was as amiable, as considerate as ever; as ready,
within reason, to accede to her wishes and gratify her whims.
Once or twice, when she suggested running up to Paris to take
Paul to the dentist, or to look for a servant, he agreed to the
necessity and went up with her. But instead of going to an hotel
they went to their apartment, where carpets were up and
curtains down, and a care-taker prepared primitive food
at uncertain hours; and Undine's first glimpse of Hubert's
illuminated windows deepened her rancour and her sense of
helplessness.

As Madame de Trézac had predicted, Raymond's vigilance
gradually relaxed, and during their excursions to the capital
Undine came and went as she pleased. But her visits were too
short to permit of her falling in with the social pace, and when
she showed herself among her friends she felt countrified
and out-of-place, as if even her clothes had come from Saint
Désert. Nevertheless her dresses were more than ever her chief
preoccupation: in Paris she spent hours at the dress-maker's, and
in the country the arrival of a box of new gowns was the chief
event of the vacant days. But there was more bitterness than
joy in the unpacking, and the dresses hung in her wardrobe like
so many unfulfilled promises of pleasure, reminding her of the
days at the Stentorian when she had reviewed other finery with
the same cheated eyes. In spite of this, she multiplied her orders,
writing up to the dress-makers for patterns, and to the milliners
for boxes of hats which she tried on, and kept for days, without
being able to make a choice. Now and then she even sent
her maid up to Paris to bring back great assortments of
veils, gloves, flowers and laces; and after periods of painful
indecision she ended by keeping the greater number, lest those
she sent back should turn out to be the ones that were worn in
Paris. She knew she was spending too much money, and she had
lost her youthful faith in providential solutions; but she had
always had the habit of going out to buy something when she
was bored, and never had she been in greater need of such
solace.

The dulness of her life seemed to have passed into her blood: her complexion was less animated, her hair less shining. The change in her looks alarmed her, and she scanned the fashion-papers for new scents and powders, and experimented in facial bandaging, electric massage and other processes of renovation. Odd atavisms woke in her, and she began to pore over patent medicine advertisements, to send stamped envelopes to beauty doctors and professors of physical development, and to brood on the advantage of consulting faith-healers, mind-readers and their kindred adepts. She even wrote to her mother for the receipts of some of her grandfather's forgotten nostrums, and modified her daily life, and her hours of sleeping, eating and exercise, in accordance with each new experiment.

Her constitutional restlessness lapsed into an apathy like Mrs Spragg's, and the least demand on her activity irritated her. But she was beset by endless annoyances: bickerings with discontented maids, the difficulty of finding a tutor for Paul, and the problem of keeping him amused and occupied without having him too much on her hands. A great liking had sprung up between Raymond and the little boy, and during the summer Paul was perpetually at his step-father's side in the stables and the park. But with the coming of winter Raymond was oftener away, and Paul developed a persistent cold that kept him frequently indoors. The confinement made him fretful and exacting, and the old Marquise ascribed the change in his behaviour to the deplorable influence of his tutor, a 'laic'* recommended by one of Raymond's old professors. Raymond himself would have preferred an abbé: it was in the tradition of the house, and though Paul was not of the house it seemed fitting that he should conform to its ways. Moreover, when the married sisters came to stay they objected to having their children exposed to the tutor's influence, and even implied that Paul's society might be contaminating. But Undine, though she had so readily embraced her husband's faith, stubbornly resisted the suggestion that she should hand over her son to the Church. The tutor therefore remained; but the friction caused by his presence was so irritating to Undine that she began to consider the alternative of sending Paul to school. He was still small and tender for the experiment; but she persuaded herself that what he needed was 'hardening,' and having heard of a school where fashionable infancy was subjected to this process, she entered into correspondence with the master. His first letter convinced her that his establishment was just the place for Paul; but the second contained the price-list, and after comparing it with the tutor's keep and salary she wrote to say that she feared her little boy was too young to be sent away from home.

Her husband, for some time past, had ceased to make any comment on her expenditure. She knew he thought her too extravagant, and felt sure he was minutely aware of what she spent; for Saint Désert projected on economic details a light as different as might be from the haze that veiled them in West End Avenue. She therefore concluded that Raymond's silence was intentional, and ascribed it to his having shortcomings of his own to conceal. The Princess Estradina's pleasantry had reached its mark. Undine did not believe that her husband was seriously in love with another woman—she could not conceive that any one could tire of her of whom she had not first tired—but she was humiliated by his indifference, and it was easier to ascribe it to the arts of a rival than to any deficiency in herself. It exasperated her to think that he might have consolations for the outward monotony of his life, and she resolved that when they returned to Paris he should see that she was not without similar opportunities.

March, meanwhile, was verging on April, and still he did not speak of leaving. Undine had learned that he expected to have such decisions left to him, and she hid her impatience lest her showing it should incline him to delay. But one day, as she sat at tea in the gallery, he came in in his riding-clothes and said: 'I've been over to the other side of the mountain. The February rains have weakened the dam of the Alette, and the vineyards will be in danger if we don't rebuild at once.'

She suppressed a yawn, thinking, as she did so, how dull he always looked when he talked of agriculture. It made him seem years older, and she reflected with a shiver that listening to him probably gave her the same look.

He went on, as she handed him his tea: 'I'm sorry it should happen just now. I'm afraid I shall have to ask you to give up your spring in Paris.'

'Oh, no—no!' she broke out. A throng of half-subdued grievances choked in her: she wanted to burst into sobs like a child.

'I know it's a disappointment. But our expenses have been unusually heavy this year.'

'It seems to me they always are. I don't see why we should give up Paris because you've got to make repairs to a dam. Isn't Hubert ever going to pay back that money?'

He looked at her with a mild surprise. 'But surely you understood at the time that it won't be possible till his wife inherits?'

'Till General Arlington dies, you mean? He doesn't look much older than you!'

'You may remember that I showed you Hubert's note. He has paid the interest quite regularly.'

'That's kind of him!' She stood up, flaming with rebellion. 'You can do as you please; but I mean to go to Paris.'

'My mother is not going. I didn't intend to open our apartment.'

'I understand. But I shall open it—that's all!'

He had risen too, and she saw his face whiten. 'I prefer that you shouldn't go without me.'

'Then I shall go and stay at the Nouveau Luxe with my American friends.'

'That never!'

'Why not?'

'I consider it unsuitable.'

'Your considering it so doesn't prove it.'

They stood facing each other, quivering with an equal anger; then he controlled himself and said in a more conciliatory tone: 'You never seem to see that there are necessities——'

'Oh, neither do you—that's the trouble. You can't keep me shut up here all my life, and interfere with everything I want to do, just by saying it's unsuitable.'

'I've never interfered with your spending your money as you please.'

It was her turn to stare, sincerely wondering. 'Mercy, I should hope not, when you've always grudged me every penny of yours!'

'You know it's not because I grudge it. I would gladly take you to Paris if I had the money.'

'You can always find the money to spend on this place. Why don't you sell it if it's so fearfully expensive?'

'Sell it? Sell Saint Désert?'

The suggestion seemed to strike him as something monstrously, almost fiendishly significant: as if her random word had at last thrust into his hand the clue to their whole unhappy difference. Without understanding this, she guessed it from the change in his face: it was as if a deadly solvent had suddenly decomposed its familiar lines.

'Well, why not?' His horror spurred her on. 'You might sell some of the things in it anyhow. In America we're not ashamed to sell what we can't afford to keep.' Her eyes fell on the storied hangings at his back. 'Why, there's a fortune in this one room: you could get anything you chose for those tapestries. And you stand here and tell me you're a pauper!'

His glance followed hers to the tapestries, and then returned to her face. 'Ah, you don't understand,' he said.

'I understand that you care for all this old stuff more than you do for me, and that you'd rather see me unhappy and miserable than touch one of your great-grandfather's arm-chairs.'

The colour came slowly back to his face, but it hardened into lines she had never seen. He looked at her as though the place where she stood were empty. 'You don't understand,' he said again.

XLI

THE incident left Undine with the baffled feeling of not being able to count on any of her old weapons of aggression. In all her struggles for authority her sense of the rightfulness of her cause had been measured by her power of making people do as she pleased. Raymond's firmness shook her faith in her own claims, and a blind desire to wound and destroy replaced her usual business-like intentness on gaining her end. But her ironies were as ineffectual as her arguments, and his imperviousness was the more exasperating because she divined that some of the things she said would have hurt him if any one else had said them: it was the fact of their coming from her that made them innocuous. Even when, at the close of their talk, she had burst out: 'If you grudge me everything I care about we'd better separate,' he had merely answered with a shrug: 'It's one of the things we don't do——' and the answer had been like the slamming of an iron door in her face.

An interval of silent brooding had resulted in a reaction of rebellion. She dared not carry out her threat of joining her compatriots at the Nouveau Luxe: she had too clear a memory of the results of her former revolt. But neither could she submit to her present fate without attempting to make Raymond understand his selfish folly. She had failed to prove it by argument, but she had an inherited faith in the value of practical demonstration. If he could be made to see how easily he could give her what she wanted perhaps he might come round to her view.

With this idea in mind, she had gone up to Paris for twenty-four hours, on the pretext of finding a new nurse for Paul; and the steps then taken had enabled her, on the first occasion, to set her plan in motion. The occasion was furnished by Raymond's next trip to Beaune. He went off early one morning, leaving word that he should not be back till night; and on the afternoon of the same day she stood at her usual post in the gallery, scanning the long perspective of the poplar avenue.

She had not stood there long before a black speck at the end of the avenue expanded into a motor that was presently throbbing at the entrance. Undine, at its approach, turned from the window, and as she moved down the gallery her glance rested on the great tapestries, with their ineffable minglings of blue and rose, as complacently as though they had been mirrors reflecting her own image.

She was still looking at them when the door opened and a servant ushered in a small swarthy man who, in spite of his conspicuously London-made clothes, had an odd exotic air, as if he had worn rings in his ears or left a bale of spices at the door.

He bowed to Undine, cast a rapid eye up and down the room, and then, with his back to the windows, stood intensely contemplating the wall that faced them.

Undine's heart was beating excitedly. She knew the old Marquise was taking her afternoon nap in her room, yet each sound in the silent house seemed to be that of her heels on the stairs.

'Ah——' said the visitor.

He had begun to pace slowly down the gallery, keeping his face to the tapestries, like an actor playing to the footlights.

'*Ah*——' he said again.

To ease the tension of her nerves Undine began: 'They were given by Louis the Fifteenth to the Marquis de Chelles who——'

'Their history has been published,' the visitor briefly interposed; and she coloured at her blunder.

The swarthy stranger, fitting a pair of eye-glasses to a nose that was like an instrument of precision, had begun a closer and more detailed inspection of the tapestries. He seemed totally unmindful of her presence, and his air of lofty indifference was beginning to make her wish she had not sent for him. His manner in Paris had been so different!

Suddenly he turned and took off the glasses, which sprang back into a fold of his clothing like retracted feelers.

'Yes.' He stood and looked at her without seeing her. 'Very well. I have brought down a gentleman.'

'A gentleman——?'

'The greatest American collector—he buys only the best. He will not be long in Paris, and it was his only chance of coming down.'

Undine drew herself up. 'I don't understand—I never said the tapestries were for sale.'

'Precisely. But this gentleman buys only things that are not for sale.'

It sounded dazzling and she wavered. 'I don't know—you were only to put a price on them——'

'Let me see him look at them first; then I'll put a price on them,' he chuckled; and without waiting for her answer he went to the door and opened it. The gesture revealed the fur-coated back of a gentleman who stood at the opposite end of the hall examining the bust of a seventeenth century field-marshal.

The dealer addressed the back respectfully. 'Mr Moffatt!'

Moffatt, who appeared to be interested in the bust, glanced over his shoulder without moving. 'See here——'

His glance took in Undine, widened to astonishment and passed into apostrophe. 'Well, if this ain't the darnedest——!' He came forward and took her by both hands. 'Why, what on earth are you doing down here?'

She laughed and blushed, in a tremor at the odd turn of the adventure. 'I live here. Didn't you know?'

'Not a word—never thought of asking the party's name.' He turned jovially to the bowing dealer. 'Say—I told you those tapestries 'd have to be out and outers to make up for the trip; but now I see I was mistaken.'

Undine looked at him curiously. His physical appearance was unchanged: he was as compact and ruddy as ever, with the same astute eyes under the same guileless brow; but his self-confidence had become less aggressive, and she had never seen him so gallantly at ease.

'I didn't know you'd become a great collector.'

'The greatest! Didn't he tell you so? I thought that was why I was allowed to come.'

She hesitated. 'Of course, you know, the tapestries are not for sale——'

'That so? I thought that was only his dodge to get me down. Well, I'm glad they ain't: it'll give us more time to talk.'

Watch in hand, the dealer intervened. 'If, nevertheless, you would first take a glance. Our train——'

'It ain't mine!' Moffatt interrupted; 'at least not if there's a later one.'

Undine's presence of mind had returned. 'Of course there is,' she said gaily. She led the way back into the gallery, half hoping the dealer would allege a pressing reason for departure. She was excited and amused at Moffatt's unexpected appearance, but humiliated that he should suspect her of being in financial straits. She never wanted to see Moffatt except when she was happy and triumphant.

The dealer had followed the other two into the gallery, and there was a moment's pause while they all stood silently before the tapestries. 'By George!' Moffatt finally brought out.

'They're historical, you know: the King gave them to Raymond's great-great-grandfather. The other day when I was in Paris,' Undine hurried on, 'I asked Mr Fleischhauer to come down some time and tell us what they're worth . . . and he seems to have misunderstood . . . to have thought we meant to sell them.' She addressed herself more pointedly to the dealer. 'I'm sorry you've had the trip for nothing.'

Mr Fleischhauer inclined himself eloquently. 'It is not nothing to have seen such beauty.'

Moffatt gave him a humorous look. 'I'd hate to see Mr Fleischhauer miss his train——'

'I shall not miss it: I miss nothing,' said Mr Fleischhauer. He bowed to Undine and backed toward the door.

'See here,' Moffatt called to him as he reached the threshold, 'you let the motor take you to the station, and charge up this trip to me.'

When the door closed he turned to Undine with a laugh. 'Well, this beats the band. I thought of course you were living up in Paris.'

Again she felt a twinge of embarrassment. 'Oh, French people—I mean my husband's kind—always spend a part of the year on their estates.'

'But not this part, do they? Why, everything's humming up there now. I was dining at the Nouveau Luxe last night with the Driscolls and Shallums and Mrs Rolliver, and all your old crowd were there whooping things up.'

The Driscolls and Shallums and Mrs Rolliver! How carelessly he reeled off their names! One could see from his tone that he was one of them and wanted her to know it. And nothing could have given her a completer sense of his achievement—of the number of millions he must be worth. It must have come about very recently, yet he was already at ease in his new honours—he had the metropolitan tone. While she examined him with these thoughts in her mind she was aware of his giving her as close a scrutiny. 'But I suppose you've got your own crowd now,' he continued; 'you always *were* a lap ahead of me.' He sent his glance down the lordly length of the room. 'It's sorter funny to see you in this kind of place; but you look it—you always *do* look it!'

She laughed. 'So do you—I was just thinking it!' Their eyes met. 'I suppose you must be awfully rich.'

He laughed too, holding her eyes. 'Oh, out of sight! The Consolidation set me on my feet. I own pretty near the whole of Apex. I came down to buy these tapestries for my private car.'

The familiar accent of hyperbole exhilarated her. 'I don't suppose I could stop you if you really wanted them!'

'Nobody can stop me now if I want anything.'

They were looking at each other with challenge and complicity in their eyes. His voice, his look, all the loud confident vigorous things he embodied and expressed, set her blood beating with curiosity. 'I didn't know you and Rolliver were friends,' she said.

'Oh *Jim*——' his accent verged on the protective. 'Old Jim's all right. He's in Congress now. I've got to have somebody up in Washington.' He had thrust his hands in his pockets, and with his head thrown back and his lips shaped to the familiar noiseless whistle, was looking slowly and discerningly about him.

Presently his eyes reverted to her face. 'So this is what I helped you to get,' he said. 'I've always meant to run over some day and take a look. What is it they call you—a Marquise?'

She paled a little, and then flushed again. 'What made you do it?' she broke out abruptly. 'I've often wondered.'

He laughed. 'What—lend you a hand? Why, my business instinct, I suppose. I saw you were in a tight place that time I ran across you in Paris—and I hadn't any grudge against you. Fact is, I've never had the time to nurse old scores, and if you neglect 'em they die off like gold-fish.' He was still composedly regarding her. 'It's funny to think of your having settled down to this kind of life; I hope you've got what you wanted. This is a great place you live in.'

'Yes; but I see a little too much of it. We live here most of the year.' She had meant to give him the illusion of success, but some underlying community of instinct drew the confession from her lips.

'That so? Why on earth don't you cut it and come up to Paris?'

'Oh, Raymond's absorbed in the estates—and we haven't got the money. This place eats it all up.'

'Well, that sounds aristocratic; but ain't it rather out of date? When the swells are hard-up nowadays they generally chip off an heirloom.' He wheeled round again to the tapestries. 'There are a good many Paris seasons hanging right here on this wall.'

'Yes—I know.' She tried to check herself, to summon up a glittering equivocation; but his face, his voice, the very words he used, were like so many hammer-strokes demolishing the unrealities that imprisoned her. Here was some one who spoke her language, who knew her meanings, who understood instinctively all the deep-seated wants for which her acquired vocabulary had no terms; and as she talked she once more seemed to herself intelligent, eloquent and interesting.

'Of course it's frightfully lonely down here,' she began; and through the opening made by the admission the whole flood of her grievances poured forth. She tried to let him see that she had not sacrificed herself for nothing; she touched on the superiorities of her situation, she gilded the circumstances of which she called herself the victim, and let titles, offices and attributes shed their utmost lustre on her tale; but what she had to boast of seemed small and tinkling compared with the evidences of his power.

'Well, it's a downright shame you don't go round more,' he kept saying; and she felt ashamed of her tame acceptance of her fate.

When she had told her story she asked for his; and for the first time she listened to it with interest. He had what he wanted at last. The Apex Consolidation scheme, after a long interval of suspense, had obtained its charter and shot out huge ramifications. Rolliver had 'stood in' with him at the critical moment, and between them they had 'chucked out' old Harmon B. Driscoll bag and baggage, and got the whole town in their control. Absorbed in his theme, and forgetting her inability to follow him, Moffatt launched out on an epic recital of plot and counterplot, and she hung, a new Desdemona, on his conflict with the new anthropophagi.* It was of no consequence that the details and the technicalities escaped her: she knew their meaningless syllables stood for success, and what that meant was as clear as day to her. Every Wall Street term had its equivalent in the language of Fifth Avenue, and while he talked of building up railways she was building up palaces, and picturing all the multiple lives he would lead in them. To have things had always seemed to her the first essential of existence, and as she listened to him the vision of the things he could have unrolled itself before her like the long triumph of an Asiatic conqueror.

'And what are you going to do next?' she asked, almost breathlessly, when he had ended.

'Oh, there's always a lot to do next. Business never goes to sleep.'

'Yes; but I mean besides business.'

'Why—everything I can, I guess.' He leaned back in his chair with an air of placid power, as if he were so sure of getting what he wanted that there was no longer any use in hurrying, huge as his vistas had become.

She continued to question him, and he began to talk of his growing passion for pictures and furniture, and of his desire to form a collection which should be a great representative assemblage of unmatched specimens. As he spoke she saw his expression change, and his eyes grow younger, almost boyish, with a concentrated look in them that reminded her of long-forgotten things.

'I mean to have the best, you know; not just to get ahead of the other fellows, but because I know it when I see it. I guess that's the only good reason,' he concluded; and he added, looking at her with a smile: 'It was what you were always after, wasn't it?'

XLII

UNDINE had gained her point, and the *entresol* of the Hôtel de Chelles reopened its doors for the season.

Hubert and his wife, in expectation of the birth of an heir, had withdrawn to the sumptuous château which General

Arlington had hired for them near Compiègne, and Undine was at least spared the sight of their bright windows and animated stairway. But she had to take her share of the felicitations which the whole far-reaching circle of friends and relations distributed to every member of Hubert's family on the approach of the happy event. Nor was this the hardest of her trials. Raymond had done what she asked—he had stood out against his mother's protests, set aside considerations of prudence, and consented to go up to Paris for two months; but he had done so on the understanding that during their stay they should exercise the most unremitting economy. As dinner-giving put the heaviest strain on their budget, all hospitality was suspended; and when Undine attempted to invite a few friends informally she was warned that she could not do so without causing the gravest offense to the many others genealogically entitled to the same attention.

Raymond's insistence on this rule was simply part of an elaborate and inveterate system of 'relations' (the whole of French social life seemed to depend on the exact interpretation of that word), and Undine felt the uselessness of struggling against such mysterious inhibitions. He reminded her, however, that their inability to receive would give them all the more opportunity for going out, and he showed himself more socially disposed than in the past. But his concession did not result as she had hoped. They were asked out as much as ever, but they were asked to big dinners, to impersonal crushes, to the kind of entertainment it is a slight to be omitted from but no compliment to be included in. Nothing could have been more galling to Undine, and she frankly bewailed the fact to Madame de Trézac.

'Of course it's what was sure to come of being mewed up for months and months in the country. We're out of everything, and the people who are having a good time are simply too busy to remember us. We're only asked to the things that are made up from visiting-lists.'

Madame de Trézac listened sympathetically, but did not suppress a candid answer.

'It's not altogether that, my dear; Raymond's not a man his friends forget. It's rather more, if you'll excuse my saying so, the fact of your being—you personally—in the wrong set.'

'The wrong set? Why, I'm in *his* set—the one that thinks itself too good for all the others. That's what you've always told me when I've said it bored me.'

'Well, that's what I mean——' Madame de Trézac took the plunge. 'It's not a question of *your* being bored.'

Undine coloured; but she could take the hardest thrusts where her personal interest was involved. 'You mean that *I'm* the bore, then?'

'Well, you don't work hard enough—you don't keep up. It's not that they don't admire you—your looks, I mean; they think you beautiful; they're delighted to bring you out at their big dinners, with the Sèvres and the plate. But a woman has got to be something more than good-looking to have a chance to be intimate with them: she's got to know what's being said about things. I watched you the other night at the Duchess's, and half the time you hadn't an idea what they were talking about. I haven't always, either; but then I have to put up with the big dinners.'

Undine winced under the criticism; but she had never lacked insight into the cause of her own failures, and she had already had premonitions of what Madame de Trézac so bluntly phrased. When Raymond ceased to be interested in her conversation she had concluded it was the way of husbands; but since then it had been slowly dawning on her that she produced the same effect on others. Her entrances were always triumphs; but they had no sequel. As soon as people began to talk they ceased to see her. Any sense of insufficiency exasperated her, and she had vague thoughts of cultivating herself, and went so far as to spend a morning in the Louvre and go to one or two lectures by a fashionable philosopher. But though she returned from these expeditions charged with opinions, their expression did not excite the interest she had hoped. Her views, if abundant, were confused, and the more she said the more nebulous they seemed to grow. She was disconcerted, moreover, by finding that everybody appeared to know about the things she thought she had discovered, and her comments clearly produced more bewilderment than interest.

Remembering the attention she had attracted on her first appearance in Raymond's world she concluded that she had 'gone off' or grown dowdy, and instead of wasting more time in museums and lecture-halls she prolonged her hours at the dress-maker's and gave up the rest of the day to the scientific culti-vation of her beauty.

'I suppose I've turned into a perfect frump down there in that wilderness,' she lamented to Madame de Trézac, who replied inexorably: 'Oh, no, you're as handsome as ever; but people here don't go on looking at each other forever as they do in London.'

Meanwhile financial cares became more pressing. A dunning letter from one of her tradesmen fell into Raymond's hands, and the talk it led to ended in his making it clear to her that she must settle her personal debts without his aid. All the 'scenes' about money which had disturbed her past had ended in some mysterious solution of her difficulty. Disagreeable as they were, she had always, vulgarly speaking, found they paid; but now it was she who was expected to pay. Raymond took his stand without ill-temper or apology: he simply argued from inveterate precedent. But it was impossible for Undine to understand a social organization which did not regard the indulging of woman as its first purpose, or to believe that any one taking another view was not moved by avarice or malice; and the discussion ended in mutual acrimony.

The morning afterward, Raymond came into her room with a letter in his hand.

'Is this your doing?' he asked. His look and voice expressed something she had never known before: the disciplined anger of a man trained to keep his emotions in fixed channels, but knowing how to fill them to the brim.

The letter was from Mr Fleischhauer, who begged to transmit to the Marquis de Chelles an offer for his Boucher tapestries from a client prepared to pay the large sum named on condition that it was accepted before his approaching departure for America.

'What does it mean?' Raymond continued, as she did not speak.

'How should I know? It's a lot of money,' she stammered, shaken out of her self-possession. She had not expected so prompt a sequel to the dealer's visit, and she was vexed with him for writing to Raymond without consulting her. But she recognized Moffatt's high-handed way, and her fears faded in the great blaze of the sum he offered.

Her husband was still looking at her. 'It was Fleischhauer who brought a man down to see the tapestries one day when I was away at Beaune?'

He had known, then—everything was known at Saint Désert!

She wavered a moment and then gave him back his look.

'Yes—it was Fleischhauer; and I sent for him.'

'You sent for him?'

He spoke in a voice so veiled and repressed that he seemed to be consciously saving it for some premeditated outbreak. Undine felt its menace, but the thought of Moffatt sent a flame through her, and the words he would have spoken seemed to fly to her lips.

'Why shouldn't I? Something had to be done. We can't go on as we are. I've tried my best to economize—I've scraped and scrimped, and gone without heaps of things I've always had. I've moped for months and months at Saint Désert, and given up sending Paul to school because it was too expensive, and asking my friends to dine because we couldn't afford it. And you expect me to go on living like this for the rest of my life, when all you've got to do is to hold out your hand and have two million francs drop into it!'

Her husband stood looking at her coldly and curiously, as though she were some alien apparition his eyes had never before beheld.

'Ah, that's your answer—that's all you feel when you lay hands on things that are sacred to us!' He stopped a moment, and then let his voice break out with the volume she had felt it to be gathering. 'And you're all alike,' he exclaimed, 'every one of you. You come among us from a country we don't know, and can't imagine, a country you care for so little that before you've been a day in ours you've forgotten the very house you were born in—if it wasn't torn down before you knew it! You come among us speaking our language and not knowing what we mean; wanting the things we want, and not knowing why we want them; aping our weaknesses, exaggerating our follies, ignoring or ridiculing all we care about—you come from hotels as big as towns, and from towns as flimsy as paper, where the streets haven't had time to be named, and the buildings are demolished before they're dry, and the people are as proud of changing as we are of holding to what we have—and we're fools enough to imagine that because you copy our ways and pick up our slang you understand anything about the things that make life decent and honourable for us!'

He stopped again, his white face and drawn nostrils giving him so much the look of an extremely distinguished actor in a fine part that, in spite of the vehemence of his emotion, his silence might have been the deliberate pause for a *réplique*. Undine kept him waiting long enough to give the effect of having lost her cue—then she brought out, with a little soft stare of incredulity: 'Do you mean to say you're going to refuse such an offer?'

'Ah——!' He turned back from the door, and picking up the letter that lay on the table between them, tore it in pieces and tossed the pieces on the floor. 'That's how I refuse it!'

The violence of his tone and gesture made her feel as though the fluttering strips were so many lashes laid across her face, and a rage that was half fear possessed her.

'How dare you speak to me like that? Nobody's ever dared to before. Is talking to a woman in that way one of the things you call decent and honourable? Now that I know what you feel about me I don't want to stay in your house another day. And I don't mean to—I mean to walk out of it this very hour!'

For a moment they stood face to face, the depths of their mutual incomprehension at last bared to each other's angry eyes; then Raymond, his glance travelling past her, pointed to the fragments of paper on the floor.

'If you're capable of that you're capable of anything!' he said as he went out of the room.

XLIII

SHE watched him go in a kind of stupor, knowing that when they next met he would be as courteous and self-possessed as if nothing had happened, but that everything would nevertheless go on in the same way—in *his* way—and that there was no more hope of shaking his resolve or altering his point of view than there would have been of transporting the deep-rooted masonry of Saint Désert by means of the wheeled supports on which Apex architecture performed its easy transits.

One of her childish rages possessed her, sweeping away every feeling save the primitive impulse to hurt and destroy; but search as she would she could not find a crack in the strong armour of her husband's habits and prejudices. For a long time she continued to sit where he had left her, staring at the portraits on the walls as though they had joined hands to imprison her. Hitherto she had almost always felt herself a match for circumstances, but now the very dead were leagued to defeat her: people she had never seen and whose names she couldn't even remember seemed to be plotting and contriving against her under the escutcheoned grave-stones of Saint Désert.

Her eyes turned to the old warm-toned furniture beneath the pictures, and to her own idle image in the mirror above the mantelpiece. Even in that one small room there were enough things of price to buy a release from her most pressing cares; and the great house, in which the room was a mere cell, and the other greater house in Burgundy, held treasures to deplete even such a purse as Moffatt's. She liked to see such things about her—without any real sense of their meaning she felt them to be the appropriate setting of a pretty woman, to embody something of the rareness and distinction she had always considered she possessed; and she reflected that if she had still been Moffatt's wife he would have given her just such a setting, and the power to live in it as became her.

The thought sent her memory flying back to things she had turned it from for years. For the first time since their far-off weeks together she let herself relive the brief adventure. She had been drawn to Elmer Moffatt from the first—from the day when Ben Frusk, Indiana's brother, had brought him to a church picnic at Mulvey's Grove, and he had taken instant possession of Undine, sitting in the big 'stage'* beside her on the 'ride' to the grove, supplanting Millard Binch (to whom she was still, though intermittently and incompletely, engaged), swinging her between the trees, rowing her on the lake, catching and kissing her in 'forfeits,'* awarding her the first prize in the Beauty Show he hilariously organized and gallantly carried out, and finally (no one knew how) contriving to borrow a buggy and a fast colt from old Mulvey, and driving off with her at a two-forty gait* while Millard and the others took their dust in the crawling stage.

No one in Apex knew where young Moffatt had come from, and he offered no information on the subject. He simply appeared one day behind the counter in Luckaback's Dollar Shoe-store, drifted thence to the office of Semple and Binch, the coal-merchants, reappeared as the stenographer of the Police Court, and finally edged his way into the power-house of the Apex Water-Works. He boarded with old Mrs Flynn, down in North Fifth Street, on the edge of the red-light slum, he never went to church or attended lectures, or showed any desire to improve or refine himself; but he managed to get himself invited to all the picnics and lodge sociables, and at a supper of the Phi Upsilon Society, to which he had contrived to affiliate himself, he made the best speech that had been heard there since young Jim Rolliver's first flights. The brothers of Undine's friends all pronounced him 'great,' though he had fits of uncouthness that made the young women slower in admitting him to favour. But at the Mulvey's Grove picnic he suddenly seemed to dominate them all, and Undine, as she drove away with him, tasted the public triumph which was necessary to her personal enjoyment.

After that he became a leading figure in the youthful world of Apex, and no one was surprised when the Sons of Jonadab, (the local Temperance Society) invited him to deliver their Fourth of July oration. The ceremony took place, as usual, in the Baptist church, and Undine, all in white, with a red rose in her breast, sat just beneath the platform, with Indiana jealously glaring at her from a less privileged seat, and poor Millard's long neck craning over the row of prominent citizens behind the orator.

Elmer Moffatt had been magnificent, rolling out his alternating effects of humour and pathos, stirring his audience by moving references to the Blue and the Gray,* convulsing them by a new version of Washington and the Cherry Tree* (in which the infant patriot was depicted as having cut down the tree to check the deleterious spread of cherry bounce),* dazzling them by his erudite allusions and apt quotations (he confessed to Undine that he had sat up half the night over Bartlett), and winding up with a peroration that drew tears from the Grand Army* pensioners in the front row and caused the minister's wife to say that many a sermon from that platform had been less uplifting.

An ice-cream supper always followed the 'exercises,' and as repairs were being made in the church basement, which was the usual scene of the festivity, the minister had offered the use of his house. The long table ran through the doorway between parlour and study, and another was set in the passage outside, with one end under the stairs. The stair-rail was wreathed in fire-weed and early golden-rod, and Temperance texts in smilax* decked the walls. When the first course had been despatched the young ladies, gallantly seconded by the younger of the 'Sons,' helped to ladle out and carry in the ice-cream, which stood in great pails on the larder floor, and to replenish the jugs of lemonade and coffee. Elmer Moffatt was indefatigable in performing these services, and when the minister's wife pressed him to sit down and take a mouthful himself he modestly declined the place reserved for him among the dignitaries of the evening, and withdrew with a few chosen spirits to the dim table-end beneath the stairs. Explosions of hilarity came from this corner with increasing frequency, and now and then tumultuous rappings and howls of 'Song! Song!' followed by adjurations to 'Cough it up' and 'Let her go,' drowned the conversational efforts at the other table.

At length the noise subsided, and the group was ceasing to attract attention when, toward the end of the evening, the upper table, drooping under the lengthy elucubrations of the minister and the President of the Temperance Society, called on the orator of the day for a few remarks. There was an interval of scuffling and laughter beneath the stairs, and then the minister's lifted hand enjoined silence and Elmer Moffatt got to his feet.

'Step out where the ladies can hear you better, Mr Moffatt!' the minister called. Moffatt did so, steadying himself against the table and twisting his head about as if his collar had grown too tight. But if his bearing was vacillating his smile was unabashed, and there was no lack of confidence in the glance he threw at Undine Spragg as he began: 'Ladies and Gentlemen, if there's one thing I like better than another about getting drunk—and I like most everything about it except the next morning—it's the opportunity you've given me of doing it right here, in the presence of this Society, which, as I gather from its literature, knows more about the subject than anybody else. Ladies and Gentlemen'—he straightened himself, and the table-cloth slid toward him—'ever since you honoured me with an invitation to address you from the temperance platform I've been assiduously studying that literature; and I've gathered from your own evidence—what I'd strongly suspected before—that all your converted drunkards had a hell of a good time before you got at 'em, and that . . . and that a good many of 'em have gone on having it since . . .'

At this point he broke off, swept the audience with his confident smile, and then, collapsing, tried to sit down on a chair that didn't happen to be there, and disappeared among his agitated supporters.

There was a night-mare moment during which Undine, through the doorway, saw Ben Frusk and the others close about the fallen orator to the crash of crockery and tumbling chairs; then some one jumped up and shut the parlour door, and a long-necked Sunday school teacher, who had been nervously waiting his chance, and had almost given it up, rose from his feet and recited High Tide at Gettysburg* amid hysterical applause.

The scandal was considerable, but Moffatt, though he vanished from the social horizon, managed to keep his place in the power-house till he went off for a week and turned up again without being able to give a satisfactory reason for his absence. After that he drifted from one job to another, now extolled for his 'smartness' and business capacity, now dismissed in disgrace as an irresponsible loafer. His head was always full of immense nebulous schemes for the enlargement and development of any business he happened to be employed in. Sometimes his suggestions interested his employers, but proved unpractical and inapplicable; sometimes he wore out their patience or was thought to be a dangerous dreamer. Whenever he found there was no hope of his ideas being adopted he lost interest in his

work, came late and left early, or disappeared for two or three
days at a time without troubling himself to account for his
absences. At last even those who had been cynical enough to
smile over his disgrace at the temperance supper began to speak
of him as a hopeless failure, and he lost the support of the
feminine community when one Sunday morning, just as the
Baptist and Methodist churches were releasing their congre-
gations, he walked up Eubaw Avenue with a young woman less
known to those sacred edifices than to the saloons of North Fifth
Street.

Undine's estimate of people had always been based on their
apparent power of getting what they wanted—provided it came
under the category of things she understood wanting. Success
was beauty and romance to her; yet it was at the moment when
Elmer Moffatt's failure was most complete and flagrant that she
suddenly felt the extent of his power. After the Eubaw Avenue
scandal he had been asked not to return to the surveyor's office
to which Ben Frusk had managed to get him admitted; and on
the day of his dismissal he met Undine in Main Street, at the
shopping hour, and, sauntering up cheerfully, invited her to take
a walk with him. She was about to refuse when she saw Millard
Binch's mother looking at her disapprovingly from the opposite
street-corner.

'Oh, well, I will——' she said; and they walked the length of
Main Street and out to the immature park in which it ended.
She was in a mood of aimless discontent and unrest, tired of
her engagement to Millard Binch, disappointed with Moffatt,
half-ashamed of being seen with him, and yet not sorry to have
it known that she was independent enough to choose her
companions without regard to the Apex verdict.

'Well, I suppose you know I'm down and out,' he began; and
she responded virtuously: 'You must have wanted to be, or you
wouldn't have behaved the way you did last Sunday.'

'Oh, shucks!' he sneered. 'What do I care, in a one-horse
place like this? If it hadn't been for you I'd have got a move on
long ago.'

She did not remember afterward what else he said: she
recalled only the expression of a great sweeping scorn of Apex,
into which her own disdain of it was absorbed like a drop in the

sea, and the affirmation of a soaring self-confidence that seemed to lift her on wings. All her own attempts to get what she wanted had come to nothing; but she had always attributed her lack of success to the fact that she had had no one to second her. It was strange that Elmer Moffatt, a shiftless outcast from even the small world she despised, should give her, in the very moment of his downfall, the sense of being able to succeed where she had failed. It was a feeling she never had in his absence, but that his nearness always instantly revived; and he seemed nearer to her now than he had ever been. They wandered on to the edge of the vague park, and sat down on a bench behind the empty band-stand.

'I went with that girl on purpose, and you know it,' he broke out abruptly. 'It makes me too damned sick to see Millard Binch going round looking as if he'd patented you.'

'You've got no right——' she interrupted; and suddenly she was in his arms, and feeling that no one had ever kissed her before . . .

The week that followed was a big bright blur—the wildest vividest moment of her life. And it was only eight days later that they were in the train together, Apex and all her plans and promises behind them, and a bigger and brighter blur ahead, into which they were plunging as the 'Limited' plunged into the sunset . . .

Undine stood up, looking about her with vague eyes, as if she had come back from a long distance. Elmer Moffatt was still in Paris —he was in reach, within telephone-call. She stood hesitating a moment; then she went into her dressing-room, and turning over the pages of the telephone book, looked out the number of the Nouveau Luxe . . .

XLIV

UNDINE had been right in supposing that her husband would expect their life to go on as before. There was no appreciable change in the situation save that he was more often absent—

finding abundant reasons, agricultural and political, for frequent trips to Saint Désert—and that, when in Paris, he no longer showed any curiosity concerning her occupations and engagements. They lived as much apart as if their cramped domicile had been a palace; and when Undine—as she now frequently did—joined the Shallums or Rollivers for a dinner at the Nouveau Luxe, or a party at a *petit théâtre*, she was not put to the trouble of prevaricating.

Her first impulse, after her scene with Raymond, had been to ring up Indiana Rolliver and invite herself to dine. It chanced that Indiana (who was now in full social progress, and had 'run over' for a few weeks to get her dresses for Newport) had organized for the same evening a showy cosmopolitan banquet in which she was enchanted to include the Marquise de Chelles; and Undine, as she had hoped, found Elmer Moffatt of the party. When she drove up to the Nouveau Luxe she had not fixed on any plan of action; but once she had crossed its magic threshold her energies revived like plants in water. At last she was in her native air again, among associations she shared and conventions she understood; and all her self-confidence returned as the familar accents uttered the accustomed things.

Save for an occasional perfunctory call, she had hitherto made no effort to see her compatriots, and she noticed that Mrs Jim Driscoll and Bertha Shallum received her with a touch of constraint; but it vanished when they remarked the cordiality of Moffatt's greeting. Her seat was at his side, and her old sense of triumph returned as she perceived the importance his notice conferred, not only in the eyes of her own party but of the other diners. Moffatt was evidently a notable figure in all the worlds represented about the crowded tables, and Undine saw that many people who seemed personally unacquainted with him were recognizing and pointing him out. She was conscious of receiving a large share of the attention he attracted, and, bathed again in the bright air of publicity, she remembered the evening when Raymond de Chelles' first admiring glance had given her the same sense of triumph.

This inopportune memory did not trouble her: she was almost grateful to Raymond for giving her the touch of superiority her compatriots clearly felt in her. It was not merely her title and her 'situation,' but the experiences she had gained through them, that gave her this advantage over the loud vague company. She had learned things they did not guess: shades of conduct, turns of speech, tricks of attitude—and easy and free and enviable as she thought them, she would not for the world have been back among them at the cost of knowing no more than they.

Moffatt made no allusion to his visit to Saint Désert; but when the party had re-grouped itself about coffee and liqueurs on the terrace, he bent over to ask confidentially: 'What about my tapestries?'

She replied in the same tone: 'You oughtn't to have let Fleischhauer write that letter. My husband's furious.'

He seemed honestly surprised. 'Why? Didn't I offer him enough?'

'He's furious that any one should offer anything. I thought when he found out what they were worth he might be tempted; but he'd rather see me starve than part with one of his grandfather's snuff-boxes.'

'Well, he knows now what the tapestries are worth. I offered more than Fleischhauer advised.'

'Yes; but you were in too much of a hurry.'

'I've got to be; I'm going back next week.'

She felt her eyes cloud with disappointment. 'Oh, why do you? I hoped you might stay on.'

They looked at each other uncertainly a moment; then he dropped his voice to say: 'Even if I did, I probably shouldn't see anything of you.'

'Why not? Why won't you come and see me? I've always wanted to be friends.'

He came the next day and found in her drawing-room two ladies whom she introduced as her sisters-in-law. The ladies lingered on for a long time, sipping their tea stiffly and exchanging low-voiced remarks while Undine talked with Moffatt; and when they left, with small sidelong bows in his direction, Undine exclaimed: 'Now you see how they all watch me!'

She began to go into the details of her married life, drawing on the experiences of the first months for instances that scarcely applied to her present liberated state. She could thus, without great exaggeration, picture herself as entrapped into a bondage hardly conceivable to Moffatt, and she saw him redden with excitement as he listened. 'I call it darned low—darned low——' he broke in at intervals.

'Of course I go round more now,' she concluded. 'I mean to see my friends—I don't care what he says.'

'What *can* he say?'

'Oh, he despises Americans—they all do.'

'Well, I guess we can still sit up and take nourishment.'

They laughed and slipped back to talking of earlier things. She urged him to put off his sailing—there were so many things they might do together: sight-seeing and excursions—and she could perhaps show him some of the private collections he hadn't seen, the ones it was hard to get admitted to. This instantly roused his attention, and after naming one or two collections he had already seen she hit on one he had found inaccessible and was particularly anxious to visit. 'There's an Ingres there that's one of the things I came over to have a look at; but I was told there was no use trying.'

'Oh, I can easily manage it: the Duke's Raymond's uncle.' It gave her a peculiar satisfaction to say it: she felt as though she were taking a surreptitious revenge on her husband. 'But he's down in the country this week,' she continued, 'and no one— not even the family—is allowed to see the pictures when he's away. Of course his Ingres are the finest in France.'

She ran it off glibly, though a year ago she had never heard of the painter, and did not, even now, remember whether he was an Old Master or one of the very new ones whose names one hadn't had time to learn.

Moffatt put off sailing, saw the Duke's Ingres under her guidance, and accompanied her to various other private galleries inaccessible to strangers. She had lived in almost total ignorance of such opportunities, but now that she could use them to advantage she showed a surprising quickness in picking up 'tips,' ferreting out rare things and getting a sight of hidden treasures. She even acquired as much of the jargon as a pretty woman needs to produce the impression of being well-informed; and Moffatt's sailing was more than once postponed.

They saw each other almost daily, for she continued to come and go as she pleased, and Raymond showed neither surprise nor disapproval. When they were asked to family dinners she usually excused herself at the last moment on the plea of a headache and, calling up Indiana or Bertha Shallum, improvised a little party at the Nouveau Luxe; and on other occasions she accepted such invitations as she chose, without mentioning to her husband where she was going.

In this world of lavish pleasures she lost what little prudence the discipline of Saint Désert had inculcated. She could never be with people who had all the things she envied without being hypnotized into the belief that she had only to put her hand out to obtain them, and all the unassuaged rancours and hungers of her early days in West End Avenue came back with increased acuity. She knew her wants so much better now, and was so much more worthy of the things she wanted!

She had given up hoping that her father might make another hit in Wall Street. Mrs Spragg's letters gave the impression that the days of big strokes were over for her husband, that he had gone down in the conflict with forces beyond his measure. If he had remained in Apex the tide of its new prosperity might have carried him to wealth; but New York's huge waves of success had submerged instead of floating him, and Rolliver's enmity was a hand perpetually stretched out to strike him lower. At most, Mr Spragg's tenacity would keep him at the level he now held, and though he and his wife had still further simplified their way of living Undine understood that their self-denial would not increase her opportunities. She felt no compunction in continuing to accept an undiminished allowance: it was the hereditary habit of the parent animal to despoil himself for his progeny. But this conviction did not seem incompatible with a sentimental pity for her parents. Aside from all interested motives, she wished for their own sakes that they were better off. Their personal requirements were pathetically limited, but renewed prosperity would at least have procured them the happiness of giving her what she wanted.

Moffatt lingered on; but he began to speak more definitely of sailing, and Undine foresaw the day when, strong as her attraction was, stronger influences would snap it like a thread. She knew she interested and amused him, and that it flattered his vanity to be seen with her, and to hear that rumour coupled their names; but he gave her, more than any one she had ever known, the sense of being detached from his life, in control of it, and able, without weakness or uncertainty, to choose which of its calls he should obey. If the call were that of business—of any of the great perilous affairs he handled like a snake-charmer spinning the deadly reptiles about his head—she knew she would drop from his life like a loosened leaf.

These anxieties sharpened the intensity of her enjoyment, and made the contrast keener between her crowded sparkling hours and the vacant months at Saint Désert. Little as she understood of the qualities that made Moffatt what he was, the results were of the kind most palpable to her. He used life exactly as she would have used it in his place. Some of his enjoyments were beyond her range, but even these appealed to her because of the money that was required to gratify them. When she took him to see some inaccessible picture, or went with him to inspect the treasures of a famous dealer, she saw that the things he looked at moved him in a way she could not understand, and that the actual touching of rare textures—bronze or marble, or velvets flushed with the bloom of age—gave him sensations like those her own beauty had once roused in him. But the next moment he was laughing over some commonplace joke, or absorbed in a long cipher cable handed to him as they re-entered the Nouveau Luxe for tea, and his æsthetic emotions had been thrust back into their own compartment of the great steel strong-box of his mind.

Her new life went on without comment or interference from her husband, and she saw that he had accepted their altered relation, and intended merely to keep up an external semblance of harmony. To that semblance she knew he attached intense importance: it was an article of his complicated social creed that a man of his class should appear to live on good terms with his wife. For different reasons it was scarcely less important to Undine: she had no wish to affront again the social reprobation that had so nearly wrecked her. But she could not keep up the life she was leading without more money, a great deal more money; and the thought of contracting her expenditure was no longer tolerable.

One afternoon, several weeks later, she came in to find a tradesman's representative waiting with a bill. There was a noisy scene in the anteroom before the man threateningly withdrew—a scene witnessed by the servants, and overheard by her mother-in-law, whom she found seated in the drawing-room when she entered.

The old Marquise's visits to her daughter-in-law were made at long intervals but with ritual regularity; she called every other Friday at five, and Undine had forgotten that she was due that day. This did not make for greater cordiality between them, and the altercation in the anteroom had been too loud for concealment. The Marquise was on her feet when her daughter-in-law came in, and instantly said with lowered eyes: 'It would perhaps be best for me to go.'

'Oh, I don't care. You're welcome to tell Raymond you've heard me insulted because I'm too poor to pay my bills—he knows it well enough already!' The words broke from Undine unguardedly, but once spoken they nourished her defiance.

'I'm sure my son has frequently recommended greater prudence——' the Marquise murmured.

'Yes! It's a pity he didn't recommend it to your other son instead! All the money I was entitled to has gone to pay Hubert's debts.'

'Raymond has told me that there are certain things you fail to understand—I have no wish whatever to discuss them.' The Marquise had gone toward the door; with her hand on it she paused to add: 'I shall say nothing whatever of what has happened.'

Her icy magnanimity added the last touch to Undine's wrath. They knew her extremity, one and all, and it did not move them. At most, they would join in concealing it like a blot on their honour. And the menace grew and mounted, and not a hand was stretched to help her . . .

Hardly a half-hour earlier Moffatt, with whom she had been visiting a 'private view,' had sent her home in his motor with the excuse that he must hurry back to the Nouveau Luxe to

meet his stenographer and sign a batch of letters for the New
York mail. It was therefore probable that he was still at home—
that she should find him if she hastened there at once. An
overwhelming desire to cry out her wrath and wretchedness
brought her to her feet and sent her down to hail a passing cab.
As it whirled her through the bright streets powdered with
amber sunlight her brain throbbed with confused intentions.
She did not think of Moffatt as a power she could use, but
simply as some one who knew her and understood her grievance. It was essential to her at that moment to be told that she
was right and that every one opposed to her was wrong.

At the hotel she asked his number and was carried up in the
lift. On the landing she paused a moment, disconcerted—it had
occurred to her that he might not be alone. But she walked on
quickly, found the number and knocked . . . Moffatt opened the
door, and she glanced beyond him and saw that the big bright
sitting-room was empty.

'Hullo!' he exclaimed, surprised; and as he stood aside to let
her enter she saw him draw out his watch and glance at it
surreptitiously. He was expecting some one, or he had an
engagement elsewhere—something claimed him from which
she was excluded. The thought flushed her with sudden resolution. She knew now what she had come for—to keep him
from every one else, to keep him for herself alone.

'Don't send me away!' she said, and laid her hand on his
beseechingly.

XLV

SHE advanced into the room and slowly looked about her.
The big vulgar writing-table wreathed in bronze was heaped
with letters and papers. Among them stood a lapis bowl in a
Renaissance mounting of enamel and a vase of Phenician glass
that was like a bit of rainbow caught in cobwebs. On a table
against the window a little Greek marble lifted its pure lines. On
every side some rare and sensitive object seemed to be shrinking
back from the false colours and crude contours of the hotel

furniture. There were no books in the room, but the florid console under the mirror was stacked with old numbers of *Town Talk* and the New York *Radiator*. Undine recalled the dingy hall-room that Moffatt had lodged in at Mrs Flynn's, over Hober's livery stable, and her heart beat at the signs of his altered state. When her eyes came back to him their lids were moist.

'Don't send me away,' she repeated. He looked at her and smiled. 'What is it? What's the matter?'

'I don't know—but I had to come. To-day, when you spoke again of sailing, I felt as if I couldn't stand it.' She lifted her eyes and looked in his profoundly.

He reddened a little under her gaze, but she could detect no softening or confusion in the shrewd steady glance he gave her back.

'Things going wrong again—is that the trouble?' he merely asked with a comforting inflexion.

'They always *are* wrong; it's all been an awful mistake. But I shouldn't care if you were here and I could see you sometimes. You're so *strong*: that's what I feel about you, Elmer. I was the only one to feel it that time they all turned against you out at Apex . . . Do you remember the afternoon I met you down on Main Street, and we walked out together to the Park? I knew then that you were stronger than any of them . . .'

She had never spoken more sincerely. For the moment all thought of self-interest was in abeyance, and she felt again, as she had felt that day, the instinctive yearning of her nature to be one with his. Something in her voice must have attested it, for she saw a change in his face.

'You're not the beauty you were,' he said irrelevantly; 'but you're a lot more fetching.'

The oddly qualified praise made her laugh with mingled pleasure and annoyance.

'I suppose I must be dreadfully changed——'

'You're all right!—But I've got to go back home,' he broke off abruptly. 'I've put it off too long.'

She paled and looked away, helpless in her sudden disappointment. 'I knew you'd say that . . . And I shall just be left here . . .' She sat down on the sofa near which they had been standing, and two tears formed on her lashes and fell.

Moffatt sat down beside her, and both were silent. She had never seen him at a loss before. She made no attempt to draw nearer, or to use any of the arts of cajolery; but presently she said, without rising: 'I saw you look at your watch when I came in. I suppose somebody else is waiting for you.'

'It don't matter.'

'Some other woman?'

'It don't matter.'

'I've wondered so often—but of course I've got no right to ask.' She stood up slowly, understanding that he meant to let her go.

'Just tell me one thing—did you never miss me?'

'Oh, damnably!' he brought out with sudden bitterness.

She came nearer, sinking her voice to a low whisper. 'It's the only time I ever really cared—all through!'

He had risen too, and they stood intensely gazing at each other. Moffatt's face was fixed and grave, as she had seen it in hours she now found herself rapidly reliving.

'I believe you *did*,' he said.

'Oh, Elmer—if I'd known—if I'd only known!'

He made no answer, and she turned away, touching with an unconscious hand the edge of the lapis bowl among his papers.

'Elmer, if you're going away it can't do any harm to tell me— is there any one else?'

He gave a laugh that seemed to shake him free. 'In that kind of way? Lord, no! Too busy!'

She came close again and laid a hand on his shoulder. 'Then why not—why shouldn't we——?' She leaned her head back so that her gaze slanted up through her wet lashes. 'I can do as I please—my husband does. They think so differently about marriage over here: it's just a business contract. As long as a woman doesn't make a show of herself no one cares.' She put her other hand up, so that she held him facing her. 'I've always felt, all through everything, that I belonged to you.'

Moffatt left her hands on his shoulders, but did not lift his own to clasp them. For a moment she thought she had mistaken him, and a leaden sense of shame descended on her. Then he asked: 'You say your husband goes with other women?'

Lili Estradina's taunt flashed through her and she seized on it. 'People have told me so—his own relations have. I've never stooped to spy on him . . .'

'And the women in your set—I suppose it's taken for granted they all do the same?'

She laughed.

'Everything fixed up for them, same as it is for the husbands, eh? Nobody meddles or makes trouble if you know the ropes?'

'No, nobody . . . it's all quite easy . . .' She stopped, her faint smile checked, as his backward movement made her hands drop from his shoulders.

'And that's what you're proposing to me? That you and I should do like the rest of 'em?' His face had lost its comic roundness and grown harsh and dark, as it had when her father had taken her away from him at Opake. He turned on his heel, walked the length of the room and halted with his back to her in the embrasure of the window. There he paused a full minute, his hands in his pockets, staring out at the perpetual interweaving of motors in the luminous setting of the square. Then he turned and spoke from where he stood.

'Look here, Undine, if I'm to have you again I don't want to have you that way. That time out in Apex, when everybody in the place was against me, and I was down and out, you stood up to them and stuck by me. Remember that walk down Main Street? Don't I!—and the way the people glared and hurried by; and how you kept on alongside of me, talking and laughing, and looking your Sunday best. When Abner Spragg came out to Opake after us and pulled you back I was pretty sore at your deserting; but I came to see it was natural enough. You were only a spoilt girl, used to having everything you wanted; and I couldn't give you a thing then, and the folks you'd been taught to believe in all told you I never would. Well, I did look like a back number, and no blame to you for thinking so. I used to say it to myself over and over again, laying awake nights and totting up my mistakes . . . and then there were days when the wind set another way, and I knew I'd pull it off yet, and I thought you might have held on . . .' He stopped, his head a little lowered, his concentrated gaze on her flushed face. 'Well, anyhow,' he broke out, 'you were my wife once, and you were my wife first—and if you want to come back you've got to come that way: not slink through the back way when there's no one watching, but walk in by the front door, with your head up, and your Main Street look.'

Since the days when he had poured out to her his great fortune-building projects she had never heard him make so long a speech; and her heart, as she listened, beat with a new joy and terror. It seemed to her that the great moment of her life had come at last—the moment all her minor failures and successes had been building up with blind indefatigable hands.

'Elmer—Elmer——' she sobbed out.

She expected to find herself in his arms, shut in and shielded from all her troubles; but he stood his ground across the room, immovable.

'Is it yes?'

She faltered the word after him: 'Yes——?'

'Are you going to marry me?'

She stared, bewildered. 'Why, Elmer—marry you? You forget!'

'Forget what? That you don't want to give up what you've got?'

'How can I? Such things are not done out here. Why, I'm a Catholic; and the Catholic Church——' She broke off, reading the end in his face. 'But later, perhaps . . . things might change. Oh, Elmer, if only you'd stay over here and let me see you sometimes!'

'Yes—the way your friends see each other. We're differently made out in Apex. When I want that sort of thing I go down to North Fifth Street for it.'

She paled under the retort, but her heart beat high with it. What he asked was impossible—and she gloried in his asking it. Feeling her power, she tried to temporize. 'At least if you stayed we could be friends—I shouldn't feel so terribly alone.'

He laughed impatiently. 'Don't talk magazine stuff to me, Undine Spragg. I guess we want each other the same way. Only our ideas are different. You've got all muddled, living out here among a lot of loafers who call it a career to run round after every petticoat. I've got my job out at home, and I belong where my job is.'

'Are you going to be tied to business all your life?' Her smile was faintly depreciatory.

'I guess business is tied to *me*: Wall Street acts as if it couldn't get along without me.' He gave his shoulders a shake and moved a few steps nearer. 'See here, Undine—you're the one that don't understand. If I was to sell out to-morrow, and spend the rest of my life reading art magazines in a pink villa, I wouldn't do what you're asking me. And I've about as much idea of dropping business as you have of taking to district nursing. There are things a man doesn't do. I understand why your husband won't sell those tapestries—till he's got to. His ancestors are *his* business: Wall Street's mine.'

He paused, and they silently faced each other. Undine made no attempt to approach him: she understood that if he yielded it would be only to recover his advantage and deepen her feeling of defeat. She put out her hand and took up the sunshade she had dropped on entering. 'I suppose it's good-bye then,' she said.

'You haven't got the nerve?'

'The nerve for what?'

'To come where you belong: with me.'

She laughed a little and then sighed. She wished he would come nearer, or look at her differently: she felt, under his cool eye, no more compelling than a woman of wax in a show-case.

'How could I get a divorce? With my religion——'

'Why, you were born a Baptist, weren't you? That's where you used to attend church when I waited round the corner, Sunday mornings, with one of old Hober's buggies.' They both laughed, and he went on: 'If you'll come along home with me I'll see you get your divorce all right. Who cares what they do over here? You're an American, ain't you? What you want is the home-made article.'

She listened, discouraged yet fascinated by his sturdy inaccessibility to all her arguments and objections. He knew what he wanted, saw his road before him, and acknowledged no obstacles. Her defense was drawn from reasons he did not understand, or based on difficulties that did not exist for him; and gradually she felt herself yielding to the steady pressure of his will. Yet the reasons he brushed away came back with redoubled tenacity whenever he paused long enough for her to picture the consequences of what he exacted.

'You don't know—you don't understand——' she kept repeating; but she knew that his ignorance was part of his terrible power, and that it was hopeless to try to make him feel the value of what he was asking her to give up.

'See here, Undine,' he said slowly, as if he measured her resistance though he couldn't fathom it, 'I guess it had better be yes or no right here. It ain't going to do either of us any good to drag this thing out. If you want to come back to me, come— if you don't, we'll shake hands on it now. I'm due in Apex for a directors' meeting on the twentieth, and as it is I'll have to cable for a special to get me out there. No, no, don't cry—it ain't that kind of a story . . . but I'll have a deck suite for you on the *Semantic* if you'll sail with me the day after to-morrow.'

XLVI

IN the great high-ceilinged library of a private *hôtel* overlooking one of the new quarters of Paris, Paul Marvell stood listlessly gazing out into the twilight.

The trees were budding symmetrically along the avenue below; and Paul, looking down, saw, between windows and tree-tops, a pair of tall iron gates with gilt ornaments, the marble curb of a semi-circular drive, and bands of spring flowers set in turf. He was now a big boy of nearly nine, who went to a fashionable private school, and he had come home that day for the Easter holidays. He had not been back since Christmas, and it was the first time he had seen the new *hôtel* which his step-father had bought, and in which Mr and Mrs Moffatt had hastily established themselves, a few weeks earlier, on their return from a flying trip to America. They were always coming and going; during the two years since their marriage they had been perpetually dashing over to New York and back, or rushing down to Rome or up to the Engadine: Paul never knew where they were except when a telegram announced that they were going somewhere else. He did not even know that there was any method of communication between mothers and sons less laconic than that of the electric wire; and once, when a boy at school asked him if his mother often wrote, he had answered in all sincerity: 'Oh yes—I got a telegram last week.'

He had been almost sure—as sure as he ever was of anything—that he should find her at home when he arrived; but a message (for she hadn't had time to telegraph) apprised him that she and Mr Moffatt had run down to Deauville to look at a house they thought of hiring for the summer; they were taking an early train back, and would be at home for dinner—were in fact having a lot of people to dine.

It was just what he ought to have expected, and had been used to ever since he could remember; and generally he didn't much mind, especially since his mother had become Mrs Moffatt, and the father he had been most used to, and liked best, had abruptly disappeared from his life. But the new *hôtel* was big and strange, and his own room, in which there was not a toy or a book, or one of his dear battered relics (none of the new servants—they were always new—could find his things, or think where they had been put), seemed the loneliest spot in the whole house. He had gone up there after his solitary luncheon, served in the immense marble dining-room by a footman on the same scale, and had tried to occupy himself with pasting post-cards into his album; but the newness and sumptuousness of the room embarrassed him—the white fur rugs and brocade chairs seemed maliciously on the watch for smears and ink-spots—and after a while he pushed the album aside and began to roam through the house.

He went to all the rooms in turn: his mother's first, the wonderful lacy bedroom, all pale silks and velvets, artful mirrors and veiled lamps, and the boudoir as big as a drawing-room, with pictures he would have liked to know about, and tables and cabinets holding things he was afraid to touch. Mr Moffatt's rooms came next. They were soberer and darker, but as big and splendid; and in the bedroom, on the brown wall, hung a single picture—the portrait of a boy in grey velvet—that interested Paul most of all. The boy's hand rested on the head of a big dog, and he looked infinitely noble and charming, and yet (in spite of the dog) so sad and lonely that he too might have come home that very day to a strange house in which none of his old things could be found.

From these rooms Paul wandered downstairs again. The library attracted him most: there were rows and rows of books, bound in dim browns and golds, and old faded reds as rich as velvet: they all looked as if they might have had stories in them as splendid as their bindings. But the bookcases were closed with gilt trellising, and when Paul reached up to open one, a servant told him that Mr Moffatt's secretary kept them locked because the books were too valuable to be taken down. This seemed to make the library as strange as the rest of the house, and he passed on to the ballroom at the back. Through its closed doors he heard a sound of hammering, and when he tried the door-handle a servant passing with a tray-full of glasses told him that 'they' hadn't finished, and wouldn't let anybody in.

The mysterious pronoun somehow increased Paul's sense of isolation, and he went on to the drawing-rooms, steering his way prudently between the gold arm-chairs and shining tables, and wondering whether the wigged and corseleted heroes on the walls represented Mr Moffatt's ancestors, and why, if they did, he looked so little like them. The dining-room beyond was more amusing, because busy servants were already laying the long table. It was too early for the florist, and the centre of the table was empty, but down the sides were gold baskets heaped with pulpy summer fruits—figs, strawberries and big blushing nectarines. Between them stood crystal decanters with red and yellow wine, and little dishes full of sweets; and against the walls were sideboards with great pieces of gold and silver, ewers and urns and branching candelabra, which sprinkled the green marble walls with starlike reflections.

After a while he grew tired of watching the coming and going of white-sleeved footmen, and of listening to the butler's vociferated orders, and strayed back into the library. The habit of solitude had given him a passion for the printed page, and if he could have found a book anywhere—any kind of a book— he would have forgotten the long hours and the empty house. But the tables in the library held only massive unused inkstands and immense immaculate blotters: not a single volume had slipped its golden prison.

His loneliness had grown overwhelming, and he suddenly thought of Mrs Heeny's clippings. His mother, alarmed by an insidious gain in weight, had brought the masseuse back from New York with her, and Mrs Heeny, with her old black bag and waterproof, was established in one of the grand bedrooms lined with mirrors. She had been loud in her joy at seeing her little friend that morning, but four years had passed since their last parting, and her personality had grown remote to him. He saw too many people, and they too often disappeared and were replaced by others: his scattered affections had ended by concentrating themselves on the charming image of the gentleman he called his French father; and since his French father had vanished no one else seemed to matter much to him.

'Oh, well,' Mrs Heeny had said, discerning the reluctance under his civil greeting, 'I guess you're as strange here as I am, and we're both pretty strange to each other. You just go and look round, and see what a lovely home your Ma's got to live in; and when you get tired of that, come up here to me and I'll give you a look at my clippings.'

The word woke a train of dormant associations, and Paul saw himself seated on a dingy carpet, between two familiar taciturn old presences, while he rummaged in the depths of a bag stuffed with strips of newspaper.

He found Mrs Heeny sitting in a pink arm-chair, her bonnet perched on a pink-shaded electric lamp and her numerous implements spread out on an immense pink toilet-table. Vague as his recollection of her was, she gave him at once a sense of reassurance that nothing else in the house conveyed, and after he had examined all her scissors and pastes and nail-polishers he turned to the bag, which stood on the carpet at her feet as if she were waiting for a train.

'My, my!' she said, 'do you want to get into that again? How you used to hunt in it for taffy, to be sure, when your Pa brought you up to Grandma Spragg's o' Saturdays! Well, I'm afraid there ain't any taffy in it now; but there's piles and piles of lovely new clippings you ain't seen.'

'My Papa?' He paused, his hand among the strips of newspaper. 'My Papa never saw my Grandma Spragg. He never went to America.'

'Never went to America? Your Pa never——? Why, land alive!' Mrs Heeny gasped, a blush empurpling her large warm face. 'Why, Paul Marvell, don't you remember your own father, you that bear his name?' she exclaimed.

The boy blushed also, conscious that it must have been wrong to forget, and yet not seeing how he was to blame.

'That one died a long long time ago, didn't he? I was thinking of my French father,' he explained.

'Oh, mercy,' ejaculated Mrs Heeny; and as if to cut the conversation short she stooped over, creaking like a ship, and thrust her plump strong hand into the bag.

'Here, now, just you look at these clippings—I guess you'll find a lot in them about your Ma.—Where do they come from? Why, out of the papers, of course,' she added, in response to Paul's enquiry. 'You'd oughter start a scrap-book yourself— you're plenty old enough. You could make a beauty just about your Ma, with her picture pasted in the front—and another about Mr Moffatt and his collections. There's one I cut out the other day that says he's the greatest collector in America.'

Paul listened, fascinated. He had the feeling that Mrs Heeny's clippings, aside from their great intrinsic interest, might furnish him the clue to many things he didn't understand, and that nobody had ever had time to explain to him. His mother's marriages, for instance: he was sure there was a great deal to find out about them. But she always said: 'I'll tell you all about it when I come back'—and when she came back it was invariably to rush off somewhere else. So he had remained without a key to her transitions, and had had to take for granted numberless things that seemed to have no parallel in the experience of the other boys he knew.

'Here—here it is,' said Mrs Heeny, adjusting the big tortoise-shell spectacles she had taken to wearing, and reading out in a slow chant that seemed to Paul to come out of some lost remoteness of his infancy.

'"It is reported in London that the price paid by Mr Elmer Moffatt for the celebrated Grey Boy is the largest sum ever given for a Vandyck. Since Mr Moffatt began to buy extensively it is estimated in art circles that values have gone up at least seventy-five per cent."'

But the price of the Grey Boy did not interest Paul, and he said a little impatiently: 'I'd rather hear about my mother.'

'To be sure you would! You wait now.' Mrs Heeny made another dive, and again began to spread her clippings on her lap like cards on a big black table.

'Here's one about her last portrait—no, here's a better one about her pearl necklace, the one Mr Moffatt gave her last Christmas. "The necklace, which was formerly the property of an Austrian Archduchess, is composed of five hundred perfectly matched pearls that took thirty years to collect. It is estimated among dealers in precious stones that since Mr Moffatt began to buy the price of pearls has gone up over fifty per cent."'

Even this did not fix Paul's attention. He wanted to hear about his mother and Mr Moffatt, and not about their things; and he didn't quite know how to frame his question. But Mrs Heeny looked kindly at him and he tried. 'Why is mother married to Mr Moffatt now?'

'Why, you must know that much, Paul.' Mrs Heeny again looked warm and worried. 'She's married to him because she got a divorce—that's why.' And suddenly she had another inspiration. 'Didn't she ever send you over any of those splendid clippings that came out the time they were married? Why, I declare, that's a shame; but I must have some of 'em right here.'

She dived again, shuffled, sorted, and pulled out a long discoloured strip. 'I've carried this round with me ever since, and so many's wanted to read it, it's all torn.' She smoothed out the paper and began:

'"Divorce and remarriage of Mrs Undine Spragg-de Chelles. American Marquise renounces ancient French title to wed Railroad King. Quick work untying and tying. Boy and girl romance renewed.

'"Reno, November 23d. The Marquise de Chelles, of Paris, France, formerly Mrs Undine Spragg Marvell, of Apex City and New York, got a decree of divorce at a special session of the Court last night, and was remarried fifteen minutes later to Mr Elmer Moffatt, the billionaire Railroad King, who was the Marquise's first husband.

'"No case has ever been railroaded through the divorce courts of this State at a higher rate of speed: as Mr Moffatt said last night, before he and his bride jumped onto their east-bound

special, every record has been broken. It was just six months ago
yesterday that the present Mrs Moffatt came to Reno to look for
her divorce. Owing to a delayed train, her counsel was late
yesterday in receiving some necessary papers, and it was feared
the decision would have to be held over; but Judge Toomey,
who is a personal friend of Mr Moffatt's, held a night session and
rushed it through so that the happy couple could have the knot
tied and board their special in time for Mrs Moffatt to spend
Thanksgiving in New York with her aged parents. The hearing
began at seven ten p.m. and at eight o'clock the bridal couple
were steaming out of the station.

'"At the trial Mrs Spragg-de Chelles, who wore copper
velvet and sables, gave evidence as to the brutality of her French
husband, but she had to talk fast as time pressed, and Judge
Toomey wrote the entry at top speed, and then jumped into a
motor with the happy couple and drove to the Justice of the
Peace, where he acted as best man to the bridegroom. The latter
is said to be one of the six wealthiest men east of the Rockies.
His gifts to the bride are a necklace and tiara of pigeon-blood
rubies belonging to Queen Marie Antoinette, a million dollar
cheque and a house in New York. The happy pair will pass the
honeymoon in Mrs Moffatt's new home, 5009 Fifth Avenue,
which is an exact copy of the Pitti Palace, Florence. They plan
to spend their springs in France."'

Mrs Heeny drew a long breath, folded the paper and took off
her spectacles. 'There,' she said, with a benignant smile and a tap
on Paul's cheek, 'now you see how it all happened . . .'

Paul was not sure he did; but he made no answer. His mind
was too full of troubled thoughts. In the dazzling description of
his mother's latest nuptials one fact alone stood out for him—
that she had said things that weren't true of his French father.
Something he had half-guessed in her, and averted his frightened thoughts from, took his little heart in an iron grasp. She
said things that weren't true . . . That was what he had always
feared to find out . . . She had got up and said before a lot of
people things that were awfully false about his dear French
father . . .'

The sound of a motor turning in at the gates made Mrs Heeny
exclaim 'Here they are!' and a moment later Paul heard his
mother calling to him. He got up reluctantly, and stood waver-

ing till he felt Mrs Heeny's astonished eye upon him. Then he heard Mr Moffatt's jovial shout of 'Paul Marvell, ahoy there!' and roused himself to run downstairs.

As he reached the landing he saw that the ballroom doors were open and all the lustres lit. His mother and Mr Moffatt stood in the middle of the shining floor, looking up at the walls; and Paul's heart gave a wondering bound, for there, set in great gilt panels, were the tapestries that had always hung in the gallery at Saint Désert.

'Well, Senator, it feels good to shake your fist again!' his step-father said, taking him in a friendly grasp; and his mother, who looked handsomer and taller and more splendidly dressed than ever, exclaimed: 'Mercy! how they've cut his hair!' before she bent to kiss him.

'Oh, mother, mother!' he burst out, feeling, between his mother's face and the others, hardly less familiar, on the walls, that he was really at home again, and not in a strange house.

'Gracious, how you squeeze!' she protested, loosening his arms. 'But you look splendidly—and how you've grown!' She turned away from him and began to inspect the tapestries critically. 'Somehow they look smaller here,' she said with a tinge of disappointment.

Mr Moffatt gave a slight laugh and walked slowly down the room, as if to study its effect. As he turned back his wife said: 'I didn't think you'd ever get them.'

He laughed again, more complacently. 'Well, I don't know as I ever should have, if General Arlington hadn't happened to bust up.'

They both smiled, and Paul, seeing his mother's softened face, stole his hand in hers and began: 'Mother, I took a prize in composition——'

'Did you? You must tell me about it to-morrow. No, I really must rush off now and dress—I haven't even placed the dinner-cards.' She freed her hand, and as she turned to go Paul heard Mr Moffatt say: 'Can't you ever give him a minute's time, Undine?'

She made no answer, but sailed through the door with her head high, as she did when anything annoyed her; and Paul and his step-father stood alone in the illuminated ball-room.

Mr Moffatt smiled good-naturedly at the little boy and then turned back to the contemplation of the hangings.

'I guess you know where those come from, don't you?' he asked in a tone of satisfaction.

'Oh, yes,' Paul answered eagerly, with a hope he dared not utter that, since the tapestries were there, his French father might be coming too.

'You're a smart boy to remember them. I don't suppose you ever thought you'd see them here?'

'I don't know,' said Paul, embarrassed.

'Well, I guess you wouldn't have if their owner hadn't been in a pretty tight place. It was like drawing teeth for him to let them go.'

Paul flushed up, and again the iron grasp was on his heart. He hadn't, hitherto, actually disliked Mr Moffatt, who was always in a good humour, and seemed less busy and absent-minded than his mother; but at that instant he felt a rage of hate for him. He turned away and burst into tears.

'Why, hullo, old chap—why, what's up?' Mr Moffatt was on his knees beside the boy, and the arms embracing him were firm and friendly. But Paul, for the life of him, couldn't answer: he could only sob and sob as the great surges of loneliness broke over him.

'Is it because your mother hadn't time for you? Well, she's like that, you know; and you and I have got to lump it,' Mr Moffatt continued, getting to his feet. He stood looking down at the boy with a queer smile. 'If we two chaps stick together it won't be so bad—we can keep each other warm, don't you see? I like you first rate, you know; when you're big enough I mean to put you in my business. And it looks as if one of these days you'd be the richest boy in America . . .'

The lamps were lit, the vases full of flowers, the footmen assembled on the landing and in the vestibule below, when Undine descended to the drawing-room. As she passed the ballroom door she glanced in approvingly at the tapestries. They really looked better than she had been willing to admit: they made her ballroom the handsomest in Paris. But something had put her out on the way up from Deauville, and the simplest way

of easing her nerves had been to affect indifference to the
tapestries. Now she had quite recovered her good humour, and
as she glanced down the list of guests she was awaiting she said
to herself, with a sigh of satisfaction, that she was glad she had
put on her rubies.

For the first time since her marriage to Moffatt she was about
to receive in her house the people she most wished to see there.
The beginnings had been a little difficult; their first attempt in
New York was so unpromising that she feared they might not
be able to live down the sensational details of their reunion, and
had insisted on her husband's taking her back to Paris. But her
apprehensions were unfounded. It was only necessary to give
people the time to pretend they had forgotten; and already they
were all pretending beautifully. The French world had of course
held out longest; it had strongholds she might never capture.
But already seceders were beginning to show themselves, and
her dinner-list that evening was graced with the names of an
authentic Duke and a not too-damaged Countess. In addition,
of course, she had the Shallums, the Chauncey Ellings, May
Beringer, Dicky Bowles, Walsingham Popple, and the rest of
the New York frequenters of the Nouveau Luxe; she had even,
at the last minute, had the amusement of adding Peter Van
Degen to their number. In the evening there were to be Spanish
dancing and Russian singing; and Dicky Bowles had promised
her a Grand Duke for her next dinner, if she could secure the
new tenor who always refused to sing in private houses.

Even now, however, she was not always happy. She had
everything she wanted, but she still felt, at times, that there were
other things she might want if she knew about them. And there
had been moments lately when she had had to confess to herself
that Moffatt did not fit into the picture. At first she had been
dazzled by his success and subdued by his authority. He had
given her all she had ever wished for, and more than she had
ever dreamed of having: he had made up to her for all her
failures and blunders, and there were hours when she still felt his
dominion and exulted in it. But there were others when she saw
his defects and was irritated by them: when his loudness and
redness, his misplaced joviality, his familiarity with the servants,
his alternating swagger and ceremony with her friends, jarred on

perceptions that had developed in her unawares. Now and then she caught herself thinking that his two predecessors—who were gradually becoming merged in her memory—would have said this or that differently, behaved otherwise in such and such a case. And the comparison was almost always to Moffatt's disadvantage.

This evening, however, she thought of him indulgently. She was pleased with his clever stroke in capturing the Saint Désert tapestries, which General Arlington's sudden bankruptcy, and a fresh gambling scandal of Hubert's, had compelled their owner to part with. She knew that Raymond de Chelles had told the dealers he would sell his tapestries to anyone but Mr Elmer Moffatt, or a buyer acting for him; and it amused her to think that, thanks to Elmer's astuteness, they were under her roof after all, and that Raymond and all his clan were by this time aware of it. These facts disposed her favourably toward her husband, and deepened the sense of well-being with which—according to her invariable habit—she walked up to the mirror above the mantelpiece and studied the image it reflected.

She was still lost in this pleasing contemplation when her husband entered, looking stouter and redder than ever, in evening clothes that were a little too tight. His shirt front was as glossy as his baldness, and in his buttonhole he wore the red ribbon bestowed on him for waiving his claim to a Velasquez that was wanted for the Louvre. He carried a newspaper in his hand, and stood looking about the room with a complacent eye.

'Well, I guess this is all right,' he said, and she answered briefly: 'Don't forget you're to take down Madame de Follerive; and for goodness' sake don't call her "Countess."'

'Why, she is one, ain't she?' he returned good-humouredly.

'I wish you'd put that newspaper away,' she continued; his habit of leaving old newspapers about the drawing-room annoyed her.

'Oh, that reminds me——' instead of obeying her he unfolded the paper. 'I brought it in to show you something. Jim Driscoll's been appointed Ambassador to England.'

'Jim Driscoll——!' She caught up the paper and stared at the paragraph he pointed to. Jim Driscoll—that pitiful nonentity, with his stout mistrustful commonplace wife! It seemed extraordinary that the government should have hunted up such insignificant people. And immediately she had a great vague vision of the splendours they were going to—all the banquets and ceremonies and precedences . . .

'I shouldn't say she'd want to, with so few jewels——' She dropped the paper and turned to her husband. 'If you had a spark of ambition, that's the kind of thing you'd try for. You could have got it just as easily as not!'

He laughed and thrust his thumbs in his waistcoat armholes with the gesture she disliked. 'As it happens, it's about the one thing I couldn't.'

'You couldn't? Why not?'

'Because you're divorced. They won't have divorced Ambassadresses.'

'They won't? Why not, I'd like to know?'

'Well, I guess the court ladies are afraid there'd be too many pretty women in the Embassies,' he answered jocularly.

She burst into an angry laugh, and the blood flamed up into her face. 'I never heard of anything so insulting!' she cried, as if the rule had been invented to humiliate her.

There was a noise of motors backing and advancing in the court, and she heard the first voices on the stairs. She turned to give herself a last look in the glass, saw the blaze of her rubies, the glitter of her hair, and remembered the brilliant names on her list.

But under all the dazzle a tiny black cloud remained. She had learned that there was something she could never get, something that neither beauty nor influence nor millions could ever buy for her. She could never be an Ambassador's wife; and as she advanced to welcome her first guests she said to herself that it was the one part she was really made for.

EXPLANATORY NOTES

3 *Princess de Lamballe*: companion and confidante of Marie Antoinette, and, like her, guillotined during the Revolution.

   'The Hound of the Baskervilles': Conan Doyle's novella was published in 1902.

5 *Washington Square*: the residential centre of old New York society, as portrayed in Henry James's eponymous novella. The Hotel Stentorian is on the *nouveau riche* upper West Side, at 72nd Street and Central Park West. The hotel on this corner was in fact the Hotel Majestic, opposite the famous Dakota apartment house, overlooking Central Park—the magnificent art deco apartment building now occupying the site, at 115 Central Park West, is still called the Majestic.

7 *down beyond Park Avenue*: Park Avenue, called Fourth Avenue before 1888, and renamed when the street became fashionable, runs north from Grand Central Station (between 42nd and 47th Streets), constructed by Cornelius Vanderbilt as the terminus of the New York Central Railroad in 1898. Its continuation south of the station, now called Park Avenue South, was not a fashionable area (hence 'the ladies' faces drooped').

8 *Central Park*: the park lies between Central Park West and Fifth Avenue from 59th to 110th Streets, dividing the upper West Side from the fashionable East Side.

15 *Atalanta*: an Arcadian princess, and a superlative runner. Her suitors had to race with her, and invariably lost. She was eventually defeated by Hippomenes, who was given three golden apples by Venus; whenever Atalanta passed him, he flung one of the apples to the side of the track, and Atalanta, unable to resist the gold, paused to retrieve it, and so lost her advantage. The story is in Ovid, *Metamorphoses*, viii.

18 *Dutch silver*: or German silver, an alloy of copper, nickel, and zinc used for cheap decorative objects.

   rainbow sandwiches: I have been unable to identify these, but James Beard, in *American Cookery* (Boston: Little, Brown (1972), 815), has a paragraph in praise of 'little sandwiches, sometimes called "reception sandwiches," popular from the turn of the century up to the end of the first World War. . . . The idea was to combine color, charm and daintiness.' Editions of Mrs Beeton from the early years of the century include mosaic, checkerboard, pyramid, and ribbon sandwiches.

25   *'When The Kissing Had to Stop'*: alluding to Browning's poem 'A Toccata of Galuppi's'; like 'Oolaloo' and 'The Soda-Water Fountain', not a real title.

Ned Norris: not a real comedian.

Berlin comedians who were performing Shakespeare at the German Theatre: in April 1902 Adolf von Sonnenthal brought his troupe to the Irving Place Theatre, the major German-language theatre in New York, for a season including *King Lear* ('comedians' is used in the old sense, as the generic term for actors).

American actress: Ada Rehan did classic drama in repertory at Augustin Daly's Theatre, Broadway and 30th Street. The novel is set near the end of her career; she retired in 1905.

Burnhard, 'Leg-Long', 'Fade': Bernhardt did Rostand's *L'Aiglon* in her New York appearances at Madison Square Garden in December 1900, and at the Metropolitan Opera House in April 1901, but there was no season when she performed both it and Racine's *Phèdre* in America, and she did not do *Phèdre* in New York at all after the 1880s. Undine could have seen *Phèdre* in Boston (or, ironically, in Kansas, and elsewhere in the West) only during Bernhardt's American tour in 1906.

a good deal older: Bernhardt was 56 in 1900.

27   *'Cavaleeria'*: Mascagni's *Cavalleria rusticana* was first performed in New York in 1891, and was instantly popular (then as now, regularly as part of a double bill with Leoncavallo's *I pagliacci*). Caruso made his Metropolitan début in 1903 in Verdi's *Rigoletto*, but he did not sing Turiddu there until November 1908; so—if it is really *Cavalleria rusticana* Undine means—he cannot be the new tenor in question. In the period of Undine's residence in New York before her marriage, the Met's regular Turiddu was Andreas Biddle, a tenor who generated little excitement. But for the season of 1902–3, Emilio de Marchi came from La Scala to sing the role; he was a major star, the original Cavaradossi in Puccini's *Tosca*, and he would be the new tenor whom Undine, along with all New York society, wants to hear. There is, however, an alternative possibility. To hear *Cavalleria* was also to hear *Pagliacci*, and Caruso made his Met début in the latter on 9 December 1903, to tremendous acclaim, and sang it frequently thereafter. Is it really the new tenor in *Pagliacci* whom Undine

means? And if so, how many of Edith Wharton's readers in 1913 recognized this particularly sly bit of New York condescension at another instance of the midwestern upstart's cultural illiteracy?

35 *Christmas-chromo*: Christmas card; chromos (for chromolithographs) were cheap colour prints.

43 *Café Martin*: at 9th Street and University Place, opened in 1883 and frequented by theatre and opera stars.

47 *the other end of Fifth Avenue*: Fifth Avenue runs north from Washington Square.

51 *divers et ondoyant*: as a characterization of Undine, the phrase in its original context is especially trenchant, and ominous: 'vain, diverse, and like waves of the sea', from Montaigne's description of the nature of mankind in the first essay of the first book of the *Essays*, 'By Diverse Means we Achieve the Same Ends'.

54 *Andromeda, Pegasus*: Andromeda, daughter of Cassiopeia, was condemned to be chained to a rock and devoured by a sea monster because her mother had declared herself happier than Juno. As Perseus was riding on the winged horse Pegasus, he saw the monster about to attack Andromeda, and rescued her, in recompense for which she was given to him in marriage. Ralph's literary imagination in this case projects an optimistic future; the couple, according to most commentators, lived happily, had many children, and after their deaths were both transformed into constellations.

Rosinante: Don Quixote's distinctly unheroic horse.

58 *Signers*: of the Declaration of Independence, 1776.

77 *ivory jack-straw*: a jackstraw is a stick in the game of pick-up-sticks, and must be retrieved from its pile without disturbing the others.

82 *a coals-of-fire call*: alluding to the biblical prescription for dealing with an enemy by returning good for evil, whereby 'thou shalt heap coals of fire on his head and the Lord shall reward thee.' See Proverbs 25: 21–2 and Romans 12: 20.

84 *'In the Gloaming'*: a mid-nineteenth-century popular song.

89 *Lecceto*: not a real town.

93 *lilies of the field*: 'they toil not, neither do they spin' (Matthew 6: 28).

95 *Ariel*: the airy spirit of Shakespeare's *Tempest*.

bird of Jove: the eagle.

95 *Prometheus*: the hero who stole fire from the gods to give to men, and thereby enabled them to develop industry and arts, and whom Jove punished by chaining him to a rock while an eagle endlessly devoured his liver.

114 *vendeuses*: saleswomen.

opopanax: cheap perfume.

119 *the Fifth Reader*: McGuffy's series of graded readers were standard school texts.

120 *'A Royal Sorceress', 'Passion in a Palace'*: not real titles.

ridden on the curb: a curb bit is designed to keep a difficult horse in check, as opposed to the looser snaffle bit.

125 *the High Bridge*: across the Harlem River at 175th Street and Tenth Avenue, part of the Croton Aqueduct.

126 *Boulevard*: Broadway above 59th Street, so called as part of the gentrification of the upper West Side.

137 *Morningside*: the heights above West 110th Street, where Columbia University now stands.

141 *noyade*: drowning.

144 *Tuxedo*: a town forty miles north of New York, centre of a fashionable resort area.

batrachian: frog-like.

152 *'A little farther . . .'*: the opening of Milton's *Samson Agonistes*— a peculiarly literary joke for Moffatt.

172 *Il n'y a pas à dire*: it goes without saying.

quant à cela: as for that.

173 *entresol*: a lower storey between the ground floor and the main floor (hence an apartment there would be very modest).

hôtel: mansion.

191 *Pegasus*: the winged horse of the muses.

195 *Battery, Bowling Green*: the oldest parts of New York, at the southern tip of Manhattan.

196 *lincrusta*: a type of thick wallpaper, the equivalent in wall covering of linoleum.

208 *The Twentieth Century*: the New York Central's crack train to Chicago began service in 1902.

Dakota: the Dakota Territory was divided into North and South

Dakota in 1887; the two states were admitted to the Union in 1889.

211 *Lovelace*: in Richardson's *Clarissa*, the heroine's seducer, and ultimately the cause of her death.

217 *Circumspice*: look around you, alluding to Wren's epitaph in St Paul's Cathedral: 'Si monumentum requieris, circumspice' (if you are seeking his monument, look around you).

219 *Semantic*: parodying the adjectival names of White Star transatlantic liners, such as the *Titanic* and *Olympic*.

226 *longanimity*: forbearance.

227 *Tauchnitz*: the popular paperback series, published in Germany and circulated throughout Europe.

234 *Hecuba*: wife of the doomed Priam, king of Troy.

240 *taffrail*: the rail around the stern of a ship.

243 *being cachottière*: concealing things.

244 *égarements*: missteps.

247 *Ah, si seulement . . .*: if only I could choose their lovers.

249 *aigrettes*: egret feathers.

256 *Adieu, ma bonne tante*: goodbye, dear aunt.

262 *reefer*: double-breasted jacket.

279 *tarpon-fishing*: the tarpon is a large Atlantic game fish; Van Degen could have been fishing for it in Florida, but not in California.

282 *'In youth you sheltered me'*: alluding to the famous sentimental poem 'Woodman Spare that Tree', by G. P. Morris (1802–64): 'Woodman, spare that tree! | Touch not a single bough! | In youth it sheltered me, | And I'll protect it now.'

293 *Voice that Breathed o'er Eden*: the hymn by John Keble.

299 *Il est bien beau*: he's very pretty.

302 *mal entourée*: in a bad set.

     Montmartre: Paris's *louche* district of night-clubs and prostitutes.

304 *Shatter-country*: for château country.

308 *légèreté*: flippancy.

309 *faire valoir*: make profitable.

310 *premier*: main floor.

313 *La petite . . .*: the girl in fact isn't bad looking.

316   *Annamite*: china.

321   *châtelaines*: mistresses of the château.

325   *carcel lamp*: 'a lamp in which the oil is pumped up to the wick by clockwork' (*OED*).

       tisane: herb tea.

327   *laic*: layman.

336   *Desdemona, anthropophagi*: from Othello's account of his wooing of Desdemona, which told 'of the cannibals that each other eat, | The anthropophagi, and men whose heads | Do grow beneath their shoulders'; it was these stories that she would 'with a greedy ear | Devour up', and that he says made her fall in love with him (*Othello*, I. iii. 143–50).

343   *stage*: carriage.

344   *forfeits*: a game in which the loser's forfeit is a kiss.

       two-forty gait: presumably covering a mile in 2 minutes 40 seconds, though this is not normal usage. Allowing for the weight of the carriage with two passengers, a horse at this speed would be going at an impressive clip: the record for a trotter in harness in 1905 was 1 minute $58\frac{1}{2}$ seconds.

       the Blue and the Gray: colours respectively of the Union (northern) and Confederate (southern) armies in the American Civil War.

       Washington and the Cherry Tree: in the famous anecdote first recorded in Parson Weems's hagiographic memoir, the child Washington cut down the tree and confessed his guilt to his father in preference to telling a lie.

345   *cherry bounce*: cherry brandy.

       Grand Army: the Union troops.

       smilax: greenbriar vines.

346   *High Tide at Gettysburg*: the poem, a favourite recitation piece, is by Will Henry Thompson.

	Oriental Tales
WILLIAM BECKFORD	Vathek
JAMES BOSWELL	Boswell's Life of Johnson
FRANCES BURNEY	Camilla
	Cecilia
	Evelina
	The Wanderer
LORD CHESTERFIELD	Lord Chesterfield's Letters
JOHN CLELAND	Memoirs of a Woman of Pleasure
DANIEL DEFOE	Captain Singleton
	A Journal of the Plague Year
	Memoirs of a Cavalier
	Moll Flanders
	Robinson Crusoe
	Roxana
HENRY FIELDING	Joseph Andrews and Shamela
	A Journey from This World to the Next and The Journal of a Voyage to Lisbon
	Tom Jones
	The Adventures of David Simple
WILLIAM GODWIN	Caleb Williams
	St Leon
OLIVER GOLDSMITH	The Vicar of Wakefield
MARY HAYS	Memoirs of Emma Courtney
ELIZABETH HAYWOOD	The History of Miss Betsy Thoughtless
ELIZABETH INCHBALD	A Simple Story
SAMUEL JOHNSON	The History of Rasselas
CHARLOTTE LENNOX	The Female Quixote
MATTHEW LEWIS	The Monk

A SELECTION OF **OXFORD WORLD'S CLASSICS**

ANN RADCLIFFE   **The Castles of Athlin and Dunbayne**
                    The Italian
                    The Mysteries of Udolpho
                    The Romance of the Forest
                    A Sicilian Romance

FRANCES SHERIDAN   **Memoirs of Miss Sidney Bidulph**

TOBIAS SMOLLETT   **The Adventures of Roderick Random**
                    The Expedition of Humphry Clinker
                    Travels through France and Italy

LAURENCE STERNE   **The Life and Opinions of Tristram**
                    Shandy, Gentleman
                    A Sentimental Journey

JONATHAN SWIFT   **Gulliver's Travels**
                    A Tale of a Tub and Other Works

HORACE WALPOLE   **The Castle of Otranto**

GILBERT WHITE   **The Natural History of Selborne**

MARY WOLLSTONECRAFT **Mary and The Wrongs of Woman**

JANE AUSTEN	Catharine and Other Writings
	Emma
	Mansfield Park
	Northanger Abbey, Lady Susan, The Watsons, and Sanditon
	Persuasion
	Pride and Prejudice
	Sense and Sensibility
ANNE BRONTË	Agnes Grey
	The Tenant of Wildfell Hall
CHARLOTTE BRONTË	Jane Eyre
	The Professor
	Shirley
	Villette
EMILY BRONTË	Wuthering Heights
WILKIE COLLINS	The Moonstone
	No Name
	The Woman in White
CHARLES DARWIN	The Origin of Species
CHARLES DICKENS	The Adventures of Oliver Twist
	Bleak House
	David Copperfield
	Great Expectations
	Hard Times
	Little Dorrit
	Martin Chuzzlewit
	Nicholas Nickleby
	The Old Curiosity Shop
	Our Mutual Friend
	The Pickwick Papers
	A Tale of Two Cities

A SELECTION OF   OXFORD WORLD'S CLASSICS

GEORGE ELIOT
Adam Bede
Daniel Deronda
Middlemarch
The Mill on the Floss
Silas Marner

ELIZABETH GASKELL
Cranford
The Life of Charlotte Brontë
Mary Barton
North and South
Wives and Daughters

THOMAS HARDY
Far from the Madding Crowd
Jude the Obscure
The Mayor of Casterbridge
A Pair of Blue Eyes
The Return of the Native
Tess of the d'Urbervilles
The Woodlanders

WALTER SCOTT
Ivanhoe
Rob Roy
Waverley

MARY SHELLEY
Frankenstein
The Last Man

ROBERT LOUIS STEVENSON
Kidnapped and Catriona
The Strange Case of Dr Jekyll and
    Mr Hyde and Weir of Hermiston
Treasure Island

BRAM STOKER
Dracula

WILLIAM MAKEPEACE THACKERAY
Barry Lyndon
Vanity Fair

OSCAR WILDE
Complete Shorter Fiction
The Picture of Dorian Gray

A SELECTION OF   **OXFORD WORLD'S CLASSICS**

	An Anthology of Elizabethan Prose Fiction
	An Anthology of Seventeenth-Century Fiction
APHRA BEHN	Oroonoko and Other Writings
JOHN BUNYAN	Grace Abounding The Pilgrim's Progress
SIR PHILIP SIDNEY	The Old Arcadia
IZAAK WALTON	The Compleat Angler

THOMAS AQUINAS	Selected Philosophical Writings
GEORGE BERKELEY	Principles of Human Knowledge and Three Dialogues
EDMUND BURKE	A Philosophical Enquiry into the Origin of Our Ideas of the Sublime and Beautiful Reflections on the Revolution in France
THOMAS CARLYLE	The French Revolution
CONFUCIUS	The Analects
FRIEDRICH ENGELS	The Condition of the Working Class in England
JAMES GEORGE FRAZER	The Golden Bough
THOMAS HOBBES	Human Nature and De Corpore Politico Leviathan
JOHN HUME	Dialogues Concerning Natural Religion and The Natural History of Religion Selected Essays
THOMAS MALTHUS	An Essay on the Principle of Population
KARL MARX	Capital The Communist Manifesto
J. S. MILL	On Liberty and Other Essays Principles of Economy and Chapters on Socialism
FRIEDRICH NIETZSCHE	On the Genealogy of Morals Twilight of the Idols
THOMAS PAINE	Rights of Man, Common Sense, and Other Political Writings
JEAN-JACQUES ROUSSEAU	Discourse on Political Economy and The Social Contract Discourse on the Origin of Inequality
SIMA QIAN	Historical Records
ADAM SMITH	An Inquiry into the Nature and Causes of the Wealth of Nations
MARY WOLLSTONECRAFT	Political Writings

APOLLINAIRE, Three Pre-Surrealist Plays
ALFRED JARRY, and
MAURICE MAETERLINCK

HONORÉ DE BALZAC Cousin Bette
Eugénie Grandet
Père Goriot

CHARLES BAUDELAIRE The Flowers of Evil
The Prose Poems and Fanfarlo

DENIS DIDEROT This is Not a Story and Other Stories

ALEXANDRE DUMAS (PÈRE) The Black Tulip
The Count of Monte Cristo
Louise de la Vallière
The Man in the Iron Mask
La Reine Margot
The Three Musketeers
Twenty Years After

ALEXANDRE DUMAS (FILS) La Dame aux Camélias

GUSTAVE FLAUBERT Madame Bovary
A Sentimental Education
Three Tales

VICTOR HUGO The Last Day of a Condemned Man and
Other Prison Writings
Notre-Dame de Paris

J.-K. HUYSMANS Against Nature

JEAN DE LA FONTAINE Selected Fables

PIERRE CHODERLOS Les Liaisons dangereuses
DE LACLOS

MME DE LAFAYETTE The Princesse de Clèves

GUY DE MAUPASSANT A Day in the Country and Other Stories
Mademoiselle Fifi

PROSPER MÉRIMÉE Carmen and Other Stories

A SELECTION OF   **OXFORD WORLD'S CLASSICS**

BLAISE PASCAL   Pensées and Other Writings

JEAN RACINE   Britannicus, Phaedra, and Athaliah

EDMOND ROSTAND   Cyrano de Bergerac

MARQUIS DE SADE   The Misfortunes of Virtue and Other Early
                        Tales

GEORGE SAND   Indiana
                     The Master Pipers
                     Mauprat
                     The Miller of Angibault

STENDHAL   The Red and the Black
                     The Charterhouse of Parma

JULES VERNE   Around the World in Eighty Days
                     Journey to the Centre of the Earth
                     Twenty Thousand Leagues under the Seas

VOLTAIRE   Candide and Other Stories
                     Letters concerning the English Nation

ÉMILE ZOLA   L'Assommoir
                     The Attack on the Mill
                     La Bête humaine
                     Germinal
                     The Ladies' Paradise
                     The Masterpiece
                     Nana
                     Thérèse Raquin

The Oxford World's Classics Website

www.worldsclassics.co.uk

- Information about new titles
- Explore the full range of Oxford World's Classics
- Links to other literary sites and the main OUP webpage
- Imaginative competitions, with bookish prizes
- Peruse *Compass*, the Oxford World's Classics magazine
- Articles by editors
- Extracts from Introductions
- A forum for discussion and feedback on the series
- Special information for teachers and lecturers

www.worldsclassics.co.uk

American Literature

British and Irish Literature

Children's Literature

Classics and Ancient Literature

Colonial Literature

Eastern Literature

European Literature

History

Medieval Literature

Oxford English Drama

Poetry

Philosophy

Politics

Religion

The Oxford Shakespeare

A complete list of Oxford Paperbacks, including Oxford World's Classics, Oxford Shakespeare, Oxford Drama, and Oxford Paperback Reference, is available in the UK from the Academic Division Publicity Department, Oxford University Press, Great Clarendon Street, Oxford OX2 6DP.

In the USA, complete lists are available from the Paperbacks Marketing Manager, Oxford University Press, 198 Madison Avenue, New York, NY 10016.

Oxford Paperbacks are available from all good bookshops. In case of difficulty, customers in the UK can order direct from Oxford University Press Bookshop, Freepost, 116 High Street, Oxford OX1 4BR, enclosing full payment. Please add 10 per cent of published price for postage and packing.